Book 4 of the aw

Historical N
Winner of *the Global Eb......* ... .
Finalist in t*he Wishing Shelf Awards, the Chaucer Awards* **and**
the Kindle Book Awards
Four Discovered Diamond Awards

'I absolutely loved this series. At the conclusion, I think I finally understood why I love Jean Gill's writing so much. She has taken real historical characters and events but added strong fictional characters whom I came to know and love.' Michelle Ryles, The Book Magnet blog

'For those who have read the previous Troubadours' *novels,* Song Hereafter *is a fitting and satisfying conclusion. For those who have not – you should! You will not find any better historical fiction, nor a more powerful evocation of a vivid past than in Gill's brilliantly written series.'* Paul Trembling, Local Poet

'Brava! Jean Gill's stories are so tightly woven into the tapestry of medieval France and England and their politics that I simply marvel as I read them. Her complex plot lines and immersion in the atmosphere of the regions and the time are wonderful; her use of Occitan lyrics throughout in her troubadors' songs enhances the authentic flavor.' Leslie Ficagglia, psychiatrist and artist

'The whole quartet is well written, well plotted and beautifully composed, and is brought to a rounded conclusion in this novel… highly recommended.' Cristoph Fischer, Ludwika

'Beautifully wraps up the tale. I highly recommend all four books. You will love this historic romance!' Autumn Birt, The Rise of The Fifth Order

'A thrilling page-turner and very hard to put down. For me, this book has it all; love, adventure and politics in the twelfth century make for another stunning read from the uber talented Jean Gill. I can see why the Troubadours Quartet has won many awards and highly recommend the whole series. You won't be disappointed.' Deb McEwan, Unlikely Soldiers

'Gill's skill at moving from culture to culture, savoring the distinctive colors of each, is breath taking. Through it all there is the music of the troubadours, Dragonetz and Estela. Their songs, which united them from the beginning, draw them always closer, sealing their bond of love and devotion. Even in the most harrowing moments of this story, there is no doubt of their commitment to one another, of a love that can withstand any trial.' Elizabeth Horton-Newton, Carved Wooden Heart

'I like a book that makes my heart race and The Troubadours did exactly that. It's a great story.' Molly Gambiza, A Woman's Weakness

'Fascinating history – the plot was terrific.' Brian Wilkerson, Trickster Eric Novels blogger

'Evocative and thoroughly riveting. A vividly-written, historical saga.' The Wishing Shelf

'A walk through time! That is what it was like to read this fine novel. It drew me into the pages and would not let go of me until done! Bravo for a wonderful read!' Arwin Blue, By Quill Ink and Parchment Historical Fiction blogger

'A remarkable achievement.' Deborah Swift, Pleasing Mr Pepys

JEAN GILL

SONG HEREAFTER

THE TROUBADOURS
BOOK 4

© Jean Gill 2017
The 13th Sign
ISBN 9791096459049
All rights reserved

Cover design by Jessica Bell

Jean Gill's Publications

Novels
The Midwinter Dragon - HISTORICAL FICTION
Book 1 The Ring Breaker *(The 13th Sign)* 2022

The Troubadours Quartet - HISTORICAL FICTION
Book 5 Nici's Christmas Tale: A Troubadours Short Story *(The 13th Sign)* 2018
Book 4 Song Hereafter *(The 13th Sign)* 2017
Book 3 Plaint for Provence *(The 13th Sign)* 2015
Book 2 Bladesong *(The 13th Sign)* 2015
Book 1 Song at Dawn *(The 13th Sign)* 2015

Natural Forces - FANTASY
Book 3 The World Beyond the Walls *(The 13th Sign)* 2021
Book 2 Arrows Tipped with Honey *(The 13th Sign)* 2020
Book 1 Queen of the Warrior Bees *(The 13th Sign)* 2019

Love Heals - SECOND CHANCE LOVE
Book 2 More Than One Kind *(The 13th Sign)* 2016
Book 1 No Bed of Roses *(The 13th Sign)* 2016

Looking for Normal - TEEN FICTION
Book 1 Left Out *(The 13th Sign)* 2017
Book 2 Fortune Kookie *(The 13th Sign)* 2017

Non-fiction
MEMOIR / TRAVEL
How White is My Valley *(The 13th Sign 2021)* ***EXCLUSIVE to Jean Gill's Special Readers Group***
How Blue is my Valley *(The 13th Sign)* 2016
A Small Cheese in Provence *(The 13th Sign)* 2016

WW2 MILITARY MEMOIR
Faithful through Hard Times *(The 13th Sign)* 2018
4.5 Years – war memoir by David Taylor *(The 13th Sign)* 2017

Short Stories and Poetry
One Sixth of a Gill *(The 13th Sign)* 2014
From Bedtime On *(The 13th Sign)* 2018 (2nd edition)
With Double Blade *(The 13th Sign)* 2018 (2nd edition)

Translation (from French)
The Last Love of Edith Piaf – Christie Laume *(Archipel)* 2014
A Pup in Your Life – Michel Hasbrouck 2008
Gentle Dog Training – Michel Hasbrouck *(Souvenir Press)* 2008

for John
who knows where the daggers are hidden
and how to disarm me.
With love, always.

CHAPTER ONE

Usually when El Rey Lobo bared his teeth, everyone in his line of sight wondered whether to do likewise and call it smiling, or to wait and pray for invisibility. Men had been killed for doing either. He had earned his nickname 'the Wolf King'. The men in front of the king today were not, however, his courtiers but his Christian neighbours of Barcelone: Ramon Berenguer and two of his commanders. They were not currying favour but seeking an alliance.

Ramon was sombre. 'Without the King of Murcia, we would have the Almohads in our gardens. I hear they make a virtue of killing.'

'And of dying, too. In order to *'purge'* this land.' the king replied. At the mention of the Almohads, El Rey Lobo's face darkened beneath his turban, and his mouth pursed as if accustomed to spit at the name. His swarthy features, oiled beard and flowing robes gave no sign of his Christian ancestry and it had been many generations since his family had converted to the Muslim faith of their overlords.

He continued, 'They will not rest until all our people are dead. All of our faith who have made this country our home for generations. We have 'sinned', we are 'unbelievers' and the penalty is death for me, for our wives, for our children, for men like your commander Malik. They will make slaves of Jews and Christians but us, they will kill.

They are superstitious barbarians from the hills of Africa! They shave their heads before battle. What pious man would do such a thing? And their black slaves thump on great drums the size of cartwheels. When you hear the beat of their war-drums, you hear your own death. This is what my men must face! Their own hearts beating in fear!'

Dragonetz listened intently to his Liege and the Wolf King, sifting courtesies from nuggets of information. They were all waiting for the king's terms.

El Rey Lobo dismissed the Almohads with a defiant gesture and began the bargaining. 'The Almohads are not causing me a problem today. If you want to solve the problems I have today, go and find me a mintmaster and an expert in siege warfare.' He paused for thought, then held up a third finger. '*And* somebody who will repair a paper mill. *These* are the problems that take up a king's time! When you take away these headaches, we can talk about protecting boundaries and Almohads!'

He laughed.

Each responded to the flashing teeth in his own manner, until the nervous echo died out.

Then, shocking in the silence, Dragonetz' laughter rang out, unforced, echoing against the stone walls of the Wolf King's antechamber.

'You find my problems entertaining, Dragonetz los Pros?' growled El Rey Lobo. He gave a sarcastic twist to Dragonetz' nickname *los Pros*, meaning 'the brave' in Occitan.

Dragonetz looked to his Liege, received a nod of consent, and responded directly to the king. 'Forgive me, Sire, but you said we would be hard put to respond to your needs unless we were mintmasters, paper producers and siege specialists. I expected your opening requests to be more difficult.'

'And I did not expect the Prince's man to be a braggart.'

'Show him, Dragonetz.' Ramon's voice carried without strain. 'We offer these skills freely to the kingdom of Murcia, our partner against the invaders, and are confident that we can agree the exact terms to our mutual satisfaction. If you continue to protect our southern boundaries against the Almohads, we can afford to show our gratitude.'

Dragonetz knew how vital this alliance with El Rey Lobo was to Barcelone. The king had taken the kingdom of Murcia as his own, and forged alliances with his Christian neighbours to hold the Spanish marches against the tide of Almohads. His own practice was supposedly tolerant of both Jews and Christians, meaning that he was equally likely to maim or execute Muslim citizens who defied his law. Such tolerance made him exactly the kind of leader the Almohads intended to eradicate, far more of a threat to 'the true faith' than were Christians.

His hatred of the Almohads made El Rey Lobo a natural ally for all who sought to maintain a Christian foothold in Hispania and his kingdom was already rich from negotiations with Castile and Genoa. Helping with Murcia's 'little problems' would not spare Ramon's purse but it was a good start to the bargaining.

'We will make ourselves comfortable first.' El Rey Lobo switched smoothly from Aragonese to Arabic as he gave orders to the servants hovering at the back of the ante-chamber. He gestured to the cushions arranged in front of the dais, where he was already comfortably seated. Malik and Dragonetz settled with practised ease, and Ramon folded himself more awkwardly into position.

The serving boys returned with goblets, a pitcher of wine and platters of mezze: savoury concoctions of aubergine, olives and rice; sugared almonds and honeyed cakes. Dragonetz took a tray from a bemused boy, set it in front of the King of Murcia and started arranging food.

'Let's begin with the weapons. Why do you need to know more about siege-towers? Nobody in his right mind would build one outside your wall, though they were camped outside for a year!' The king's fortress of Monteagudo was at the peak of a rocky outcrop, dominating the whole northern valley of the Huerta.

El Rey Lobo nodded. 'No. Food and water are the only potential weaknesses and we have grain reserves below the castle, enough to feed even the peasants for months, if not a year. And our water supplies run deep with hidden sources. I think we are safe from poison.'

'Nobody is safe from betrayal. We found that out in Damascus,' Dragonetz pointed out.

'Traitors.' El Rey Lobo shrugged. 'We have made enough examples. There won't be more.'

All present had heard of such examples. One more fortunate antagonist, El Rey Lobo's relative, Yusuf ibn Hilal, had merely been blinded and imprisoned. His wife had been given the option of surrender before the second eye was put out, but she refused. Such was the kindness of the Wolf King.

'Our castle's strength means that my men lack experience of modern weapons and they might need this knowledge to defend – or attack – elsewhere.'

Dragonetz nodded. 'Each siege is different, according to the terrain, the weaknesses of the stronghold, even the weather. You would only build a siege-tower if quicker methods have failed.'

He frowned in concentration and made a row of sugared almonds. 'Imagine this is the castle wall, the source of enemy fire. We want to get our men into the castle and one method is to breach the wall while protecting men from arrows.'

The king nodded. This was obvious. 'So we need a siege-tower. A wooden platform gives the men cover to fire, to put up ladders and swarm the walls.'

Dragonetz put an aubergine parcel in place. 'This is a traditional siege-tower, clumsy and static. Once it's in position, the defenders just concentrate their men at the point of attack.' He put some extra sugared almonds on the part of the wall by the aubergine parcel.

'But if it's on wheels, you can take advantage of any place in the wall where there's weakness.' He removed one almond further along 'the wall', and moved the siege-tower to take advantage of the breach. 'All siege-towers should be mobile. And with a platform, dropped by ropes.'

Dragonetz ate the rice filling from a second aubergine parcel. 'Cinnamon,' he observed appreciatively as he folded the aubergine and placed it on top of his siege-tower. 'Now, imagine this is the mobile platform.' He unfolded the aubergine to rest across the almond beside it.

El Rey Lobo's crumpled forehead cleared. 'A drawbridge across the wall. That might work.'

Dragonetz made a little pile of cake squares. 'This is another defence the castle inhabitants might use.' He tied a strip of aubergine round a date and, holding the other end of his makeshift 'rope', swung it along the almond wall, toppling the cakes. There was a polite silence while he ate the debris and licked his fingers.

Once finished, Dragonetz explained, 'Grappling irons, or any heavy weight can topple a tower. You can swing such a ready-made weapon along the castle wall but you need to beware deflections. You could make a hole in your own wall. The technique will only work on one siege-tower so if there are several, you have problems.' A piece of sticky cake had eluded him and he licked his little finger. 'You have to be inventive, respond to the situation with the material available. And that includes the men you have, not the men you'd like to have.'

'Ah, the men I'd like to have...' reflected El Rey Lobo. 'Talk to my engineer! Teach him what you know.'

Dragonetz glanced to Ramon for consent before giving his own, then spoke. 'From your words about the Almohads, it seems, my Lord, that *you* have much to teach *us*, and I would learn from your men so that we can prepare ours against this enemy.' Dragonetz' courtesy drew a grunt of approval from El Rey Lobo, so he continued. 'Is the same engineer responsible for the paper mill?'

'No.' This time the royal baring of teeth gave every impression of being a genuine smile. 'Unlike the Prince of Barcelone we have not found one man who does every job under the sun, so we employ several.'

Dragonetz flushed. 'It is not I who can advise for the paper mill but Malik.'

'Then Malik of the Banu Hud is also a skilled engineer. Why am I not surprised! And that must make Ramon Berenguer the Mintmaster if you divide these tasks equally?'

Ramon had a glint in his eyes as he denied such talents. 'Fortunately, I think Dragonetz has someone else in mind.'

Dragonetz did indeed have someone else in mind, and neither he nor Malik hesitated when asked to withdraw, 'to let your Prince and me agree the details of our alliance', as El Rey Lobo put it. No doubt Ramon's coffers would be short of several thousand morabetins when all was agreed.

Dragonetz would have loved to discuss the workings of the paper mill for in truth he did know rather more on the subject than he'd owned up to, but he could not be in two places at once – three if you counted the commission to find a Mintmaster. And, as Malik pointed out, Murcia's paper mills were the most advanced on the peninsula, so Dragonetz' contributions would be less useful than with the King's Engineer.

With a sigh, Dragonetz watched Malik saddle up for the ride towards the river, then turned his attention to the camp on the plain, where Ramon's troops were still setting up their tents and cookfires. A few astute guesses from the right men found the Englishman John Halfpenny, curled up in the back of a wagon, asleep on a sack of grain, and grumpy at being roused to work. Once he discovered that he was needed on a question of coinage, not to hump more sacks from one place to another, he cheered up considerably. When Dragonetz left him, he was muttering to himself, 'What can they expect if they work with gold...'

That left only a lesson in siege tactics to deliver. Starting with a raid in the guard room, Dragonetz replaced almonds with new recruits, and aubergines with freshly washed turbans, rashly left within his reach. Once he was satisfied with rehearsals, he sent a man to invite the King's Commander and his Engineer to an entertainment in which each was allowed to swing a giggling 'grappling iron' along a somewhat vociferous 'wall' while the pyramid of five men tottered dangerously.

The Engineer prodded one of the men's buttocks. 'You'd make wooden stairs here,' he pondered.

'Exactly,' Dragonetz confirmed.

The Commander instructed, 'Morge, stretch your arms out to the wall.' The fourth man teetered as he gripped the man below with his knees only, touching one somewhat wobbly stone in the wall with his finger-tips.

'Oi! Stop that!' was Morge's response to whatever the wall did to the finger-tips.

The Commander, the Engineer and Dragonetz ignored the somewhat flippant behaviour of their raw material.

'Top man!' called the Commander. 'Pretend to shoot! You're defending the men, who are crossing on Morge's arms – that's the drawbridge.'

Top Man formed a circle with one hand, stuck his finger through it and made a noise that could charitably have been thought of as the whoosh of an arrow, but which induced lethal giggles in Morge. He pulled in the drawbridge and clung on with both hands.

Then, part of the wall muttered, 'That sounded more like old Becky at the whorehouse than any arrow.' The resulting structural damage was beyond repair and the siege tower collapsed.

The Commander back-handed the nearest man across the head and giggling rippled into suppressed snorts, then the contented silence of men who have had a good training session.

Dragonetz fired questions at them, praised most of the responses, corrected mistakes and then answered questions. By this time, the Commander and Engineer *had* questions and no qualms about appearing ignorant. An afternoon swinging recruits by a living wall has that effect.

Despite all the activity, the January chill was noticeable, so Dragonetz happily joined in a drinking song and the drink that went with it. This gave an opportunity for him to further brief El Rey Lobo's military leaders regarding their own men: those who'd shown intelligence and ingenuity; those who'd worked well together; those who'd protected others; the brave and also the bullies.

'The weakness in a wall is where it will be breached,' Dragonetz told them, and they understood that he wasn't speaking only of stones.

Well satisfied with his day's work, Dragonetz met up with Malik on the battlements and watched the sun-set flushing rose the grey mountains and arid plains; limning with gold the spiked succulents that dotted the route up to the fortress. In daytime, the winter landscape was leached of all colour, except for a dusting of occasional snow on the highest peaks. This moment of grace before evening was a promise of better days. Dragonetz hoped so. He was more than ready to go home.

'Luxury!' he declared. 'Two nights on straw pallets instead of a cloak on the ground with the wind hurling through the tent flaps.'

Beside him, Malik sighed. 'I am ready to go home,' he admitted, speaking Dragonetz' thoughts aloud, as happened so often when they rode together. 'I am getting older, my friend. These campaigns test my luck more every time.'

Dragonetz bit back the instinctive reassurance. Was it true? Was Malik getting too old for this?

'At least we can relax now,' he told his friend.

How wrong he was, he didn't find out until after the evening meal. Until Ramon came to tell them both about the non-negotiable demand in El Rey Lobo's terms.

'It shall be as my Lord wishes,' Malik bowed his head in submission but could not hide the tightening of his jaw, knuckles whitening in his clasped hands.

'Your Lord very much does *not* wish!'

Dragonetz stated the obvious. 'We must agree terms with El Rey Lobo. He holds our boundaries safe against the Almohads and he can't do that without warriors – experienced fighters. It is a fair demand.'

'Indeed, I take it as a great compliment to Malik,' Ramon stated bleakly. 'If I thought there was another way... I have bartered Aragon and Barcelone to bare bones all afternoon and he has not wavered. He will take the money – *and* Malik to command one of his armies.' Ramon's face offered no hope.

'Did you suggest me instead?' asked Dragonetz.

Malik's, 'No!' was instinctive.

Ramon at least smiled, however wearily. 'You were mentioned at the start. El Rey Lobo made it clear that I was welcome to such a... creative general. I believe his words were, 'How do you control this man without removing one of his hands?'

Dragonetz laughed. 'I take *that* as a great compliment! Believe me, his men now have a better notion of how siege engines work than do most armies! But there is always another way. He shall not have Malik.'

'We have no choice in all courtesy. As you say, it is a reasonable demand. I could ask that he return to us in a year.' Ramon's tone betrayed his doubts that such a request would be considered.

Dragonetz had some idea how much 'just one year' riding with El Lobo would cost Malik's health, if he survived. El Rey Lobo was young enough to believe he was immortal; Malik knew he wasn't.

'Have you signed?' asked Dragonetz, and the walls held their breath. Ramon Berenguer would never go back on his word.

'Of course not!' The Prince's eyes flashed at the insult. 'I would not sign without Malik's consent.'

'And I give it, my Lord.' Malik bent to kiss Ramon's ring, and his Liege laid a hand on the turbaned head.

'I knew you would.' Ramon turned to Dragonetz. 'Unless my most creative commander can think of something?'

The silence spread from the foundations of the stone walls into each man's core. Dragonetz followed each line of thought to a dead end, blocked by honour, time or resources. Each line of thought but one.

Finally, no laughter in his voice, he said, 'I have a proposition. El Rey Lobo must want something more than he wants Malik, enough to ask for that instead. He couldn't *see* what you offered, didn't feel the burn of desire. We must make him feel that.'

Ramon frowned. 'We have no women with us that would make such an impact and no time to send for some. El Rey Lobo has no shortage of beauties already. We'd need somebody of unusual talent to make him lose his senses in such a way.' Ramon was not a man who understood the losing of senses but Malik did and he looked in horror at Dragonetz.

'No, my friend.' Dragonetz put a hand on his friend's shoulder. 'No woman will suffer because of you. I love you dearly but we can't be sure a woman would work magic, even if we found one who might. Only one woman would touch me so, and if El Lobo thinks I am too difficult to control, I suspect Estela would not be his choice of woman! No, jesting aside, what else would make El Rey Lobo fall in love at first sight?'

'No!' Malik guessed his intent.

'Yes,' replied Dragonetz, and he outlined his plan. The other two men made objections, found flaws, were rebuffed, and eventually all agreed that the plan might just work. Ramon's shoulders lifted, Malik's drooped, and Dragonetz went to the stables.

Nobody else was in earshot of Sadeek's stall and the destrier snorted as his master spoke soft words of love to him in Arabic. This princely gift of friendship from Malik had been his partner through hell and Holy Land. Their teamwork had won praise from the Saracen leader Nur-ad-Din and brought the skills of Moorish horsemen in Damascus to Provençal warriors in Les Baux.

Tethered on arid winter plains by his master's tent or ruminating in a stall, Sadeek had been Dragonetz' only confidante in affairs of the heart since he'd left Estela and baby Musca in Barcelona. You could lean against a horse's flank, feel the quiver of life, without fear of drawing harm to your companion. Yet here he was, contemplating exactly that.

For months, he and Sadeek had followed Ramon's route, seeking oaths of allegiance; securing the borders against the Saracen invaders; securing Aragon and Barcelone against the enemy within, back-stabbers and wranglers. A knight and his steed. Could a man even be called a knight without his horse? Unhorsed was another word for dishonoured.

There had been many days' travel between vassals, between the demonstrations of force, and oaths of allegiance. Waking at dawn to the bleached browns of endless Iberian plains, Dragonetz would seek the unholy trinity that freed his restless mind and gave him respite from black thoughts; man, horse and hawk. The rapid ki-ki-ki of his goshawk, Vertat, hunting. Classical Persian poetry ran through his mind.

'Bestow on me a hawk with sweeping wings,
plumes stroked clean by icy winds.

No man prouder than I
on our dawn rides
when my hand outflies the wind,
unleashes my dominion on the untamed.'

Death-dealing by hawk was a calming ritual, cleaner by far than his day's work sometimes proved to be and flying Vertat had been a daily release for man, horse and hawk.

When Ramon's army left Barcelone, there had been sideways glances at his new commander, envy of the black destrier and puzzlement at the orange-eyed goshawk, perched on Dragonetz' shoulder. But no man placed under Dragonetz' command objected to rabbits grilled on camp-fires or the Christmas treat of lamb. Especially as the latter came from lands less welcoming to Barcelone than the season warranted.

When his Liege or his Liege's vassals dictated otherwise, the young falconer Bran carried out his duties with love but he was not Dragonetz and his mount was no Sadeek. After a few days apart, Vertat would complain, chitter in pique, play hard to recall, like a jealous lover, and Dragonetz would have to woo her back. He sought her favourite terrain and Sadeek carried the double burden as fast

11

and smooth as flight itself. Dragonetz swore that Sadeek favoured one side when riding without the hawk and that Vertat crooned appreciation of the stallion's gait.

The stable kept its secrets as Dragonetz whispered his apologies to Sadeek, explained what must be done and why, then he went to wake Bran, the young falconer. Bran also needed to know what was to be done and, as man not beast, he could – and must – make his own choice.

CHAPTER TWO

There being nothing more to say in private, the Wolf King treated his guests to the full spectacle of his court. Ramon Berenguer was granted the privilege of a carved wooden chair on the king's right hand. The two rulers faced the ceaseless tide of supplicants, messengers and merchants. *Like an ill-matched queen and consort* thought Dragonetz from his stance behind Barcelone, hand resting lightly on his pommel. Equally impassive, Malik stood guard beside Dragonetz, scimitar gleaming through his robes.

Permission for Barcelone's commanders to keep their swords was a measure of El Rey Lobo's confidence that they *would* reach an agreement; confidence backed up by two dozen men-at-arms, forming a semi-circle around their king with a polite gap for the Christian visitors. Dragonetz and Ramon were the only people in the hall not wearing robes and the only men with hair loose and on show.

Barcelone wore a simple gold circlet and the velvet doublet, trimmed with civet fur, that he'd brought on the journey to show respect to the more prestigious of his hosts. Nobody would have guessed from the Comte's appearance that he'd been living as rough as his men during most of their months travelling and camping. When lodging in abbeys and strongholds, he'd caught up on sleep as well as oaths of loyalty. His only concession to practicality was the beard he'd allowed to grow – neatly trimmed but black and oiled as any Saracen's.

Dragonetz resisted the urge to check his own chin for stubble, reflecting that the only other people beardless in the Hall would be women, boys or eunuchs. He had no idea whether El Rey Lobo maintained this eastern court custom or not, and he thought it wiser not to ask. The less Malik heard about El Rey Lobo's social customs, the easier it would be for him to play his role. After all, if Dragonetz was wrong, Malik would be part of this court into which he fitted so easily by appearance; dark-skinned and turbaned.

Not all the men wore turbans. Perhaps as many as one in ten wore the cone-shaped caps that declared them Jewish. Apart from the headgear, the petitioners dressed alike in the wide, flowing Arab robes called jubbas; green, orange and rose butterflies.

The same old disputes that Dragonetz had heard in Christian courts were brought before the ruler; land disputes and claims of theft; forgery and murder. Though different gods were called to bear witness, the human offences were the same. There was a long silence during a particularly difficult case of what Ramon would have called 'beard-pulling', the petty injuries between noblemen.

El Rey Lobo was once more lost in thought, weighing judgement, considering his verdict. Having listened for months to Barcelone's passionate views on the law, Dragonetz was not surprised when Ramon Berenguer leaned closer to El Rey Lobo and murmured, 'This is why I have drawn up the Usatges. To make judgments quick and consistent, across our kingdoms, so that all men know that justice will be done.'

El Rey Lobo frowned at this slight on his efficiency in judgement. 'I doubt your Usatges show the same consideration of non-Christians as our laws do of a Dhimmi.'

Ramon side-stepped neatly. 'In your Kingdom, your faith leads your rule as mine does in my realm, but my laws in themselves apply reason and consistency in judgement and sentence. They have saved me much time as I no longer deliberate each case as though there had never been another like it.'

El Rey Lobo was still frowning but then his brow cleared, as if he'd reached some decision. Dragonetz felt Malik responding too, suddenly alert, sensing danger. But all that happened was another petitioner stepping forward and the two men relaxed a little. Too soon.

'We have heard much of the justice shown in Aragon and Barcelona,' announced El Rey Lobo, the boom of his voice echoing around the stone walls. No irony showed in his tone but if some were intended, Dragonetz could sympathise. The hospitality of Ramon's tent had often included long discussions of fit punishments for common crimes.

'We are honoured to have their Prince with us today,' continued the Wolf King, 'and he will be your judge. Let all men hear the justice he offers to share with his subjects and allies so that his judgment can be judged.' A subtler man would have left this unsaid. El Rey Lobo was not a subtle man. He laughed at his own joke, as did most in the Hall, whether they'd heard it or not, whether they'd understood it or not. The petitioners did not laugh.

One man at the back of the Hall laughed too long and changed the noise to a snorting cough that died away in the silence. El Rey Lobo and everyone else in the Hall looked at the Comte de Barcelone and waited. Dragonetz relaxed. Meting out justice was Ramon Berenguer's second nature.

'The test of my Usatges is not whether I can deliver judgement by their guidance but whether *all* those with authority can do likewise.' Calm, strong, the voice carried to the back of the Hall, where nobody laughed.

This was unexpected. Dragonetz' stomach clenched when his own name was mentioned but there was nothing he could do to prevent what must follow. His mind raced ahead as Barcelone declared, 'Lord Commander Dragonetz los Pros, will state the Usatges that fit the situation presented.'

Ramon nodded at the petitioners and rested an elbow casually on the arm of his chair, head propped on hand as if entertained by a jongleur's display of coloured balls. 'Then we will use them and any other laws relevant, to explain our judgement.'

El Rey Lobo laughed and Dragonetz would have at least smiled, if he had not been mentally revising thirty instances of crime and punishment. It would take a much wilier man than the Wolf King to dictate terms to Berenguer. Especially when Ramon could call on Dragonetz, that 'too troublesome knight' who was being asked to display why he might be worth his keep.

Ramon flexed his gloved hand. Soft kid leather, Dragonetz noted. Purely for fashion. Rather larger than was fashionable though, as if something tougher was worn underneath. Ramon raised his hand in a gesture that was noticed only by his commanders and a servant in leather jerkin, who disappeared from the Hall. Ramon glanced at Dragonetz and raised an eyebrow. They understood each other.

The Wolf King ordered the next petitioner to approach and state his case so the judgement of the Comte de Barcelone could be given. A bound woman was pushed to her knees in front of the dais and her turbaned companion began to speak. Dragonetz gave what could have been a silent prayer or a silent curse, depending on interpretation. Had fate or El Rey Lobo chosen that particular case?

'My wife's a whore,' stated the man. 'I want her stoned for adultery.'

'On what grounds do you believe this to be so?' Dragonetz asked.

'Do I have to answer this foreigner?' The man's belligerent tone drew a quick response, not from El Rey Lobo but from a guard. The flat of a blade dropped the man to his knees beside his unhappy wife. Her hair was shorn and uncovered, her face was bruised down one side and the rope binding her had drawn blood.

'Do I have to answer this foreigner, *my king*?' encouraged the guard, his scimitar hovering sharp side above the man's neck.

Not completely suicidal, the man took the hint. 'Beg pardon, my king. This woman is with child and I...' his voice dropped to a whisper, 'I have never made children on any woman.'

The guards shushed as mocking laughter rippled around the Hall.

Defiantly, the man added, 'And everybody knows she is faithless. Everybody.'

This just evoked more laughter. Which Dragonetz used, however lightly. Knowing that what he did was unfair. 'And you have brought 'everybody' with you to bear witness?' he jibed.

'No,' was mumbled.

'If not everybody, perhaps one witness?' Dragonetz' mocking tone brought a ripple of laughter.

More quietly again. 'No.'

Dragonetz' conscience was rubbed raw by the doe-eyed plea in the woman's eyes before she dropped her gaze to the floor, where a few spots of blood gleamed on the stone flags. Another drip fell.

'Untie her while she is tried,' Dragonetz ordered. A guard looked to El Rey Lobo, received a curt nod, then did as bid. The husband opened his mouth and closed it again.

So, the crimes for which Dragonetz should deliver punishment were disobedience, adultery and creating an illegitimate child. How ironic. Guilty as charged, admitted Dragonetz grimly to his inner judge. Even though Estela had only seen her husband for the brief ceremony of their wedding day, his mistress was nevertheless a married woman. However, he must distance himself from his sins if he were to judge others. So Ramon had taught him.

He did not so much as glance at his Liege as he racked his memory for Usatges which could be applied without loss of body part as a sentence. Ramon would never duck his duty in sentencing but if Dragonetz could cite a kind judgment, the Prince might take that option.

Whatever was said and done here must convince El Rey Lobo that the justice of Barcelone and Aragon was indeed justice. And the Wolf King's measures would not be tempered with mercy.

'Are you this man's wife?' Dragonetz began the interrogation.

She raised her eyes to his, risked holding his gaze long enough to say, 'Since I was twelve.' Though her eyes were lowered again quickly, in proper submission, they spoke still. Of a body used and abused, of beatings, of a spirit not yet broken.

'And what say you to the charge?' he asked.

'I am with child,' she said. 'I am this man's wife so it must perforce be his child.'

'See how she speaks!' interrupted the man. 'Impudent! Unchaste. Twisting words!'

'And have you lain with another man?'

'I have given my body only as Allah willed.' When she looked at him as she spoke, Dragonetz knew beyond all doubt that she spoke truth *and* that she was an adulteress.

His blood ran cold as he heard Estela in his head. *As have I, my love. And this woman never gave her body to the brute beside her – she was taken.* But laws were not devised to protect criminals, nor assuage the consciences of those who had no right to throw stones.

'She twists words,' protested the husband. 'Whatever she swears, she lay with another man and carries proof in her belly!'

His words earned him another kick and command from the guards. 'Silence!'

Dragonetz quoted from the Usatges. 'Adultery *which could not be overlooked* has always been judged, settled or punished according to law.' He spoke directly to the petitioner. 'You have the right to settle in private, whatever you believe, whether you are right or wrong.' He didn't point out how much 'settling' had already been carried out on the wife's body. It was the husband's right.

'She should be stoned,' muttered the man. 'I want the full law.'

'Then the full law it shall be. As is meet, men are judged by their degree. As a knight bears more responsibility for others so does his oath bear more weight and, if he commits a crime, he must be judged as a knight. What manner of man are you?'

The answer was obvious from the man's weathered looks and rough garb. 'A peasant, my Lord.'

'Then oaths have no currency whatever either of you may swear. You accuse this woman of cuccugia. The Usatges of Barcelone pronounce that the wife of a peasant must answer to such an accusation from her husband through the ordeal of boiling water. Let her place her arm up to the elbow in a vat of boiling water, and if she is innocent God will heal her. Within three days there will be signs of healing or ailing, showing her innocence or her guilt. Let the ordeal occur in a sanctified place so that God's judgement will be in his own house.

Should she be innocent, you must honourably keep her and make compensation to her. If she is guilty, she is returned to your custody in dishonour, with all she has, for your disposal.'

'The whore's guilty,' muttered the man. He sneered, 'But boiling water and a festering arm will be a start.'

The wife showed no gratitude. Dragonetz had expected none, although ordeal by water was preferable to the removal of noses, lips, ears and breasts by blade and 'burning at the stake if necessary' recommended as justice for women. With God on her side, the woman might hope for a scalded arm, a verdict of innocence and a future with the man beside her. And a baby, who might or might not look like his father. Which might or might not be a good thing.

'I have cited the Usatges,' continued Dragonetz, 'but what is writ can only be a guide.' He bowed to Ramon Berenguer. 'The authority in this matter is my Lord Comte de Barcelone, Prince of Aragon, whose judgement is known throughout Christendom and beyond.' *And let's hope to God he is in more of a boiling water mood than one for cutting off body parts.* 'There are times one must make an example,' Ramon had told his men, when commenting on the Usatges.

'Well summed up, my Lord Dragonetz. We would not usually spend as long on such a common affair, but sharing our knowledge of the law is important, so that our citizens may dwell in peace and security.

God knows which of these two tells truth, so God's judgement is truly needed; the ordeal by water fits the lack of clear evidence. Most men would be overjoyed at the gift from God of a son and heir, and there has been many a Zechariah surprised by this treasure late in life. They do not cast aspersions on their wives' chastity.'

An interesting slant, thought Dragonetz. *Almost implying a man could look the other way and be grateful for the issue he could not otherwise produce. Never underestimate Ramon's knowledge of people.* It seemed Ramon had not reacted favourably to the plaintiff.

'My Lord Dragonetz has made clear what the trial shall be and what its outcomes mean but he overlooked one fine point of the law.' All eyes were now fixed on Ramon Berenguer. 'Should this woman be found guilty, all her possessions shall be divided equally between her husband and his Liege Lord, for any criminal act is an affront to the law itself, as represented by the Authority in any realm, as well as an affront to the wronged individual.'

Ramon addressed the husband directly. 'If you win your case, your marriage is without honour and you lose half of all goods this woman brought with her as dowry or has as personal possession. As you disown the child she carries, he will belong to your Liege, and to protect this property I decree that the adulteress and her child be placed in your Lord's service until the child is seven years of age and no longer needs his mother. Then she must return to your custody.'

'But that's not right!' The husband earned another swift kick.

'The law is not your lapdog,' declared Ramon, letting his voice ring out round the Hall. 'When you choose to go to process, you put your affairs in the hands of a greater authority and must abide by the judgment given. If you would decide your own affairs, you err in coming here.' Several people shuffled out the Hall, avoiding eye contact.

'If this woman is found innocent,' continued Ramon, 'you may return home with your wife, and cherish her in all honour, and enjoy the babe growing up at your hearth, learning your trade and calling you father. You have three days to prepare yourself for the justice you have called down on your wife.'

He turned to El Rey Lobo. 'This is my judgement, my Lord.'

The Wolf King nodded. 'It is well said. Take the woman to the entry to the mosque and let her ordeal be in the sight of Allah and all our citizens.'

Cowed, hunched over, the man slunk away to hide among the waiting petitioners, irrelevant, as his wife was led by guards out of the Hall. After a moment's hesitation, the husband followed her, tied to his wife's fate by more than Ramon's words. Dragonetz wondered what the man hoped for now, knowing that he would be so much worse off if he gained the guilty verdict he had asked for. *Never underestimate Ramon*, he told himself again as there was a commotion at the back of the Hall.

Guards responded instantly to the kafuffle, which also drew the Wolf King's attention. A space was cleared around an odd-shaped creature silhouetted in the doorway, a creature that screeched in high dudgeon and flapped giant wings; that dwindled from mythical beast to a falconer carrying an unhooded goshawk on his glove. A very irate goshawk.

'What is the meaning of this?' roared El Rey Lobo, jumping to his feet at the perceived threat. Dragonetz winced as the hawk bated and its handler struggled to soothe the orange-eyed madness of the bird as it flapped and fought its tether. All present knew enough of hawks and wolves to keep a respectful distance from both and hold their tongues.

The calm, carrying tones of Ramon Berenguer surprised the silence. 'My apologies, my Lord. I had no opportunity to apprise you of my intentions. I wanted to give a lesson in obedience and I was sure you'd approve. May I?'

It was unwise for any ruler to allow chaos in his Hall, amid throngs of petitioners, many unhappy with the judgements (for in most judgements only one person *can* be happy); amidst men who might be rivals, guards who might be bribed; amidst new allies who had not yet agreed terms.

El Rey Lobo bared his teeth. He had always admired courage above wisdom.

The Comte de Barcelone remained seated, gaze fixed on the young falconer, who seemed to have the hawk under control again. Once more, Ramon's judgement was key, and he didn't know Vertat. He hadn't manned the hawk, walking cobbled streets with a goshawk riding one shoulder. He hadn't flown the hawk, seeing the hare behind the hedge with twilight eyes and accepting the death-shriek. Crucially, he had never felt Vertat fly to the glove. But he was skilled in hawking, and he knew full well what the consequence of his words would be. A lesson in obedience.

'Dragonetz.' No courtesy, no 'My Lord' or 'If you please'. The command must be clearly seen as such. 'Call your hawk to you. I wish El Rey Lobo to see the quality of our training.'

Standing behind Ramon, Dragonetz obeyed without hesitation. He held out his arm and spoke, without emotion, as loud and clear as his Liege. 'As you wish, my Lord.'

Without checking what their king thought, everyone in the Hall gasped, looking from that naked wrist and hand – his right hand, his sword arm – to the talons of an enraged goshawk. No protection, no lure, no reward. If there had been time to place bets, the highest pile of coins would have been on Dragonetz losing an eye as well as a hand.

There was no time for such bets.

'Vertat,' his master called as Bran flung the bird into the air. The many people who ducked and doubled-over missed the seconds of confusion, of hesitation perched on a rafter – an anti-climax after all? But no, the orange eyes saw the one who'd named her, who'd called her, and who always made it worth her while to land on that thin branch he stretched in front of him. She didn't need the encouraging whistle from Dragonetz; she was already in flight, talons outstretched, beak dagger-sharp to take the flesh offered...

...when Ramon laid his arm on top of Dragonetz', his gloved right hand bouncing with the weight as Vertat landed, his left hand feeding the expected strips of dried rabbit. The hawk chittered a complaint, looked El Rey Lobo unblinking in the eyes. She shifted her feet anxiously before making her usual run to settle on a shoulder.

My beauty Dragonetz told Vertat, savouring the glorious sweep of her flight, the finely judged landing on another man's hand.

Two fine judgements. Although you left it a little late, my Liege. But there had never been any doubt. Ramon and he had ridden together long enough to trust. He did not move his arm till Vertat was gone. He needed to feel her weight, even through another man, one last time. His shoulder ached with absence, already.

Bran had pushed through the bemused onlookers, was claiming the bird. He offered more dried meat to calm her, then slipped on her hood and moved her to his well-padded shoulder. Let the hawk think herself safe as night. After all, Vertat was in his care now.

'I would like to buy that hawk,' said El Rey Lobo. Another one taking the bait.

'She belongs to Lord Dragonetz,' replied Ramon. 'Such training is priceless. Is that not so, my Lord?'

So, I am a Lord again, after the lesson in obedience, Dragonetz noted, saying nothing. Ramon played his part perfectly, too perfectly. Perhaps it gave him pleasure to play high-handed with his most creative knight.

'Yes, Sire.'

They had not misjudged El Rey Lobo. 'We have not yet signed,' he pointed out, his desire to own the hawk darkening his eyes. 'You were unhappy with one of the terms. I could be generous in return for such a gift.'

Ramon appeared to consider the matter. Dragonetz had no need to act his own apprehension at the prospect of losing Vertat. *A hawk with sweeping wing.* Neither of them looked at Malik.

Chewing his lip, Ramon came to a hard decision. Bargaining must never be easy if both parties were to be satisfied. 'Barcelone and Aragon would like to present this hawk as a gift to the king, as she has so pleased him. What do you say, my Lord Dragonetz? Is it not fitting?'

'It is an honour, my Lord, for my goshawk to be chosen.' The word *my* could be salt on a wound. He addressed El Rey Lobo. 'Her name is Vertat, *Truth* in my language, and she has flown straight as truth for me since the day I made her mine. I commend to you her keeper, Bran, who is as loyal to the bird as I to my Liege. He knows her ways, and will prove as true as Vertat should you accept him into your service.'

Bran made some sort of awkward motion with his hands gesturing obeisance, as any hint of a bow would be taken by the goshawk on his shoulder for an insult.

'We are agreed!' El Rey Lobo's smile sent a wave of relief around the Hall. 'Enough for today.' He dismissed the court and petitioners in one gesture.

Those who'd spent a day or more hoping for justice risked the question, 'When?' and were told with cuffs and kicks to wait until their waiting was over – and to think themselves lucky.

Ignoring lesser mortals, the king ordered that his new acquisitions be taken to the mews. 'Let us adjourn to somewhere quiet and sign our agreement.'

'Let's,' agreed Ramon Berenguer. He turned to his commanders. 'Please inspect the men. We'll raise camp tomorrow and return home.'

Dismissed, Dragonetz and Malik went by silent accord to the stables. In private, the friends allowed themselves a moment's weakness; a hug, a tear, a hand that shook.

'The price was too high,' murmured Malik. 'I could have served here a year or two. She was the hawk of your life.'

'Dearest friend of my mind, I thought he would hold out for Sadeek!'

'Then both our hearts would have broken.'

'I will not have another hawk.' The pause grieved. Friends do not place such weight on each other for too long. 'You'll have to find me a hound instead,' teased Dragonetz.

Malik was not ready to smile, not yet believing he would be allowed to ride home. But he tried to answer lightness with lightness. 'Nici would not allow it.'

Dragonetz imagined Estela's great white guard dog welcoming some upstart wolfhound or long-eared scent dog into the family. 'If he did, I suspect he would take charge of the training, not me!'

They went to the camp and ensured that the men would be ready to ride out the next day. The word 'home' worked its own miracles of efficiency.

John Halfpenny was outside one of the tents and Dragonetz stopped to thank him for his work. 'El Rey Lobo says his Mintmaster was well pleased with the help you gave.'

Halfpenny shrugged. 'I just told them to make two trussles for every pile because there's more wear and tear on the lower die. Saved them some waste.'

Dragonetz wasn't sure whether his expression showed polite interest or complete ignorance but Halfpenny took the lack of response as an invitation. He explained, 'You need a pair of dies, one long one with the coin image on the top and one stubby one with the coin's other image. You nail the long one, the trussle, to a block, put the coin on it and hammer the top die down, making the two sides.' His arms were making their accustomed movements as he spoke and Dragonetz was surprised by the bulging muscles. Not such a useless man in a fight after all, he noted, as he continued making his rounds.

Dragonetz did not ride at twilight, when a king would be flying his new hawk, exalting in her. Instead he sought his Liege.

'He signed?'

'He signed,' confirmed Ramon Berenguer, new grey in his beard. 'That was bravely done, Dragonetz. I owe you a boon. Do not hesitate to ask.'

Dragonetz already knew what boon he sought. His need had come to him while riding the plains at dawn and dusk, knowing that the secrets he carried were too heavy for him and that he must seek help.

The word 'home' filled him with equal dread and joy. Estela was his life but while he kept from her all that he knew, there was a barrier between them. Yet it was his duty to protect her and he could not speak, especially now, after months of pretending. How could he tell her that Geoffroi de Rançon, the man she thought to be their friend, had murdered the youth they'd rescued in the Holy Land?

He should have told her straight away, when he found out, but de Rançon's death had upset Estela so much that Dragonetz didn't have the heart to speak ill of the dead. He'd been shocked himself, unable to speak of the evil he'd uncovered. His deepest fear was that if he did try to find the words, Estela would not believe him, would think jealousy spoke.

No, it was all too difficult to untangle now. Better to let sleeping dogs lie. There came a time in every man's life where he eased his troubled soul in walking and this was his time. He would share his burden with the Lord, do penance for his own sins and seek the strength to endure these secrets between him and his lady. She would be over her grief and he could forget de Rançon. Then they could be happy together.

As Dragonetz expected, Ramon Berenguer did not question his knight's desire to be a pilgrim. But Lord knew what Estela would make of it.

However long you were away from home, it was always the nights just before you returned that tormented you most, anticipating your lover warm in your arms. He ought to be enjoying his last night in El Rey Lobo's castle and a comfortable bed, but he might as well have lain on cactus prickles. Dragonetz shifted position yet again, conscious of the empty cot beside his, and of Ramon sleeping peacefully on his other side.

The door swung open slowly and Malik slipped back in, cautious in the dark. Soft clunks as he removed his boots. A rustle as he settled back under the blanket.

'You reached her?' Dragonetz whispered.

'I reached one who will ensure the poultice is applied. There will be no infection, just some scarring.'

'Is that the better choice?' *Reconciliation with such a man? Was it possible?*

'The alternative could be death if infection took hold. Perhaps the child will heal other wounds.'

'She...' Dragonetz stumbled over the words and tried again. 'It could have been...'

'No,' said Malik. 'No, it couldn't have been. There is no likeness in their situations. Nor in their characters.'

Dragonetz hid his tears in darkness and silence.

'You are outgrowing my service, Dragonetz.' Ramon Berenguer was not asleep and his disembodied voice had the authority of God himself. 'Today you gave judgement on my behalf and none could improve on your manner or your decision. The time is coming when you will rule on your own behalf. A man can be a king in his own domain if he rules well, be it Aragon or a fief in Aquitaine.'

'My Lord,' Dragonetz murmured, not willing to point out that Ramon's nickname *El Sant* indicated, among other things, that his domestic circumstances were rather more acceptable to the church than were his own. Nor that the fief in Aquitaine to which he should be heir was currently willed to the devil by Dragonetz' own words to his father. No doubt Ramon could quote an appropriate Usatge to cover Dragonetz' circumstances – or if not, he would set about formulating one.

When finally sleep took Dragonetz, it brought the leap and crackle of flames. Even asleep, he knew that he should stay away from the fire but the flames held such fascination. They drew him closer until he could hold back no longer and he leapt into the white-hot heart of fire till his sword Talharcant was edged in silver flame and he himself had melted, ready for the forge, a hammer poised over his head.

CHAPTER THREE

Estela hiccupped. She self-diagnosed another measure of honeyed wine, which was perhaps not watered as much as usual. No, probably not, she reflected happily, drinking a little more of the hiccup cure and settling even more comfortably into the soft depth of damask cushions. A little bowl of sweetmeats was conveniently placed, and the sticky confection of honey and nuts was no doubt desirable as a way of preserving her from cold humours.

After a day working in Malik's library, making notes on medical complaints and treatments, Estela felt entitled to relax, and she felt more at home here than in the cold castle in Barcelone where she passed her days as the celebrated troubadour. Celebrated, hah! Estela took another sip of wine. If she'd realised how uncivilised this court was, she'd have been less enthusiastic in accepting Queen Petronilla's invitation. The local musicians barely knew the names of the great troubadours! If they knew of Dragonetz, it was as Barcelone's new commander, not as the man who'd composed the most famous aubade of all. And sung it with her, his rich baritone blending with her soprano to make the lyric come alive. Her insides dipped with longing, not just for her homeland.

'How do you bear Malik's absence?' she asked Layla. Mutual respect had grown to something warmer between the two women while their menfolk were travelling. 'I can't imagine years apart, such as you knew.'

Layla was also lounging on cushions, elegant despite the signs of more years than Estela carried. Her hair showed grey at the roots but was blackened, and shiny with henna, and she'd left it long and loose – another sign of their intimacy. Night-black eyes outlined with kohl added to her glamour. Estela imagined Layla's younger days as a harem education in silken sensuality, but she would never have been so intrusive as to ask about such matters. Except in the interest of medical science. She suddenly remembered a term from the afternoon's reading that had been beyond her Arabic and made a mental note to ask what it meant. Later.

'I do everything he disapproves of,' Layla replied lightly. 'Drink wine and gossip.' Estela raised her goblet in toast to wine and gossip. And waited. Sure enough, Layla cared enough for the younger woman to give a more serious answer.

'We had six children and Malik chose exile for their sake, and for mine.' She shrugged, fatalistic. 'It was exile or death. Just because his family lost Zaragoza did not mean they lost their right to be kings. Our people would have fought to put Malik on his throne if he had just raised one finger.'

'Why didn't he?'

'Because they would have lost. Again. He knew our time was over and the Christians' time was come.' Her face dragged down into the lines of old sorrows. 'I know he was tempted to raise that one finger and see who came to his call. To leave this world shouting aloud that he was the King of Zaragoza, son of kings.'

Estela added this detail to her knowledge of the man who had taught her so much, and who shared her love of medicine, music and Dragonetz. Had her serene mentor really been a young firebrand, ready to win back his Moorish kingdom with a thousand corpses? His wife's dark eyes said it was so.

'Then Ramon Berenguer offered him another way. If Malik left his country, there would be peace here. Promises were made.'

'Were they kept?'

Another gesture of resignation. 'Berenguer did his best. But you know how it is.'

Estela did indeed. It was complicated. Although daily life in the city mixed Christians and their infidel neighbours, there were rules, both written and unwritten, about socialising. Even that most strict of abbots, Bernard of Clairvaux, preached tolerance of Jews, pointing out that Jesus was a Jew. But the letter of the law demanded segregation. She should not even be dining with one of Malik's faith and yet they all blessed their bread before they broke it – Muslims, Christians *and* Jews!

Layla continued. 'And Malik ended up an anonymous servant in Douzens.'

'With the Knights Templar.' Layla nodded. 'He was given to them as if he were a cart or table for their use! Imagine! But he told me his real work was to learn, to know his enemy. He was to keep Berenguer informed of all the politics he heard while serving food or digging their gardens.

And Berenguer passed on the messages Malik sent to me. Angry at first, and he took no pains to hide this. Then he found pleasure in the herbs and simples of a monk there. Malik said the brother was a true man of faith, though not of ours. He cited scripture to Malik and brought him back to a different book. Malik read the Surahs,' Estela looked puzzled so Layla explained, 'the chapters in the Koran. He quoted this one to me often, *And Indeed, Allah is with those who are of service to others.* He found his own true beliefs while dwelling in the house of a God that was not his.'

To serve others. Estela thought of Malik's skills as a doctor, of all he'd taught her, of her own vocation.

'When he came home, I did not recognise him. But my heart did. Because I had been changed too and we were a match for each other.'

'How did you change? How did you stay true?' Estela never doubted for a second that Layla *had* stayed true. As had she. But for that one moment of weakness with Dragonetz' friend, Geoffroi de Rançon, God rest his soul. Just one kiss, when she'd been alone so long. It had meant nothing, and yet, she wondered whether that kiss prevented Dragonetz grieving for his friend. He behaved oddly at any mention of Geoffroi and she kept her own tears private, when she could. Another friend lost too young. Such a tragic death. She shook off the morbid thoughts and concentrated on what her friend was saying.

'Six children,' Layla repeated and laughed. 'My two eldest boys would never have let a man near me who wasn't old, ugly or a close relative! And they're still the same. As to how I changed... like Malik, I was angry. I should have been Queen of Zaragoza, living in the Aljaferia, the Palace of Joy – you haven't been there?'

Estela shook her head. 'The Queen–' she broke off and flushed.

Layla patted her hand. 'I'm used to it. If I cried every time someone said 'the Queen' and didn't mean me, I'd have drowned years ago.'

'Petronilla wanted me with her for the birth,' continued Estela, 'and she's not left Barcelone this winter. She is reluctant to leave home.' Strange for Barcelone to be home for the Queen of Aragon but Petronilla had lived there under her betrothed's roof since babyhood. Everything about Petronilla's upbringing had been strange. 'I think she might go to Zaragoza after Whitsun...'

'Whitsun?'

Sometimes you forgot that your friend lived different festivals, a different calendar. 'May,' clarified Estela.

'They also call the Aljaferia *the Summer Palace*. You should have seen it then, with oranges fruiting in the garden and the sparrows drinking from the fountain. Where Malik should have walked in the path of his ancestors, and I beside him. But the waters ran through a different channel. At first, I hardened my children to hatred. Each day a list of wrongs. And it was so easy to stir up rebellion, to connect with those on dark streets with revenge in their hearts.

One day, my daughter Janni came home from her studies of the Koran and said she'd seen a dog skewered like a sausage because he was in the way – those were her words. I held her, hoping to heal the hurt she must be feeling and she wriggled out of my arms, said, 'It's all right, Mama. It was a Christian dog. I wish it was his owner and his head hung from the battlements of the Aljaferia along with all his fellows.' Her eyes were stones and they fell into the pool of my shame, stirring up the wrong I had done.

I found Malik's messages, read them all, from his first outpouring of bile to the Surahs in the recent ones. I followed in his footsteps to regain the true path and I held my children close by my side. You have seen Janni?'

'She makes sweetmeats fit for the gods, and her children's laughter brings joy to her eyes.' Speaking Arabic made the formal phrases natural even to Estela's clumsy command of the language.

Layla nodded. 'Just so. And her children's laughter brings joy to my eyes too. I am a queen to my family. And to my husband. I have learned to say *Inshallah* with my heart not just with my lips.'

Estela thought of the queens for whom she'd sung. Petronilla, forever compensating for original sin and convinced that her baby son's sickly disposition was God's punishment. Mélisende of Jerusalem, whose very healthy adult son had taken her to war in order to win by force the inheritance his mother was unwilling to cede. And Aliénor of Aquitaine, ex-Queen of France and would-be Queen of England, hoping that Henri of Anjou's seed would be stronger than Louis' and bring the sons her ambition craved.

Queens bled, birthed and were judged by the number and quality of their sons even more than other women. Was that what it meant, to be a woman? Was she, Estela, merely Musca's mother and a poor example of fertility?

As if reading her thoughts, Layla asked, 'What sort of woman do you want to be, Estela?'

No doubt due to the wine, Estela brimmed with tears, envying Janni. Her own mother would never know Musca. Her thoughts shied away from her father and brother, who would prefer her dead. Dragonetz' family would probably be ashamed of his son, their only child despite three years together. Founding dynasties did not seem to be her forte.

And yet she did have a dream. 'I want to be like my mother,' she confessed. 'She died when I was eight.' Like Layla and the word *queen*

Estela had practised speaking of her mother's death so as not to feel the words. 'But I watched her in her duties on the domain. She knew every villager, every animal, every plot of land and how to tend them. She knew herbal medicine and was not afraid to visit where there was sickness.' She whispered the truth that had made her brave as a little girl. 'And she loved me just as much as my brother. She said I should never ever bury my talents and she gave me the oud.'

Only as she spoke, did Estela realise fully the answer to Layla's question. 'I want to be a loving wife and mother, I really do, and to place my husband and children's needs above my own. But there is something in me, that my mother encouraged, and if I keep singing and keep learning, then I will make her happy, where she is now. I would love her to see me as Lady of Dragonetz' domain, with Musca and however many children God wills, with plentiful harvests, honey and cheese. I want us to sing our songs. And I want to write up my studies of Malik's books.'

'That is a lot of wanting,' said Layla, gently.

'I know,' sighed Estela. 'If I were Petronilla I would be at confession all day.'

'The poets have written of this feeling.

'Watch the river flow and wonder whether
you travel with or against its force
and why.'

Listening to the music of Arabic, Estela suddenly remembered the word from her day's reading that she needed to be translated. 'What does *mwsabiaqa* mean?'

Layla choked on a sip of wine. 'Estela! I hope you are not suffering from Dragonetz' absence to that degree!'

'I thought it was a medical term,' clarified Estela, without adding that she'd found it in a book entitled *The Sultan's Love Potions*, found between *The Sipping of Saliva and the Fruit of Lovers* and *A Treatise on Whether Engaging in Coitus with Low Frequency Increases Lifespan*. All very educative, and requiring copious notes.

Layla still looked suspicious. 'It is a word for what the Greeks call *gynaikerastria*.' Estela must have looked as blank as she felt.

'Love of women,' explained Layla, 'as was common on Lesbos where the Greek poet Sappho wrote of the art of loving women.'

'Ah.' She feigned complete understanding. She obviously had a lot of further reading to do, and wondered how much of these scientific minutiae Dragonetz knew. After all, he and Malik spent long nights round a campfire when on campaigns. What did they talk about?

'That makes sense. Thank you.' *What was the reference in 'The Sultan's Love Potions'? Ah, yes. 'If a man can't lead a woman to her satisfaction, then she might turn to another woman.'*

Estela considered the implications with suitable detachment. *There is never any shame in science*, she reminded herself of the Arabic quotation, dismissing a fleeting thought of her father confessor's probable reactions to her studies, should she mention them. She was *not* Petronilla. She resolved to write up the note with her conclusions in the morning.

'My Lady?' A girl approached Layla and prostrated herself.

'Gizlane,' Layla gently reminded her. 'A bow of the head suffices.'

The girl coloured, stood up and bowed her head, in one graceful movement that matched her name. 'My Lady's other guest has arrived.'

Layla clapped her hands and her ear-rings jangled in excitement. 'This falls well. Please bring her in.'

'A new servant?' Estela asked, knowing full well that one of Layla's manservants bought slaves at private sales so she could liberate at least some of her own faith. Unless you could do likewise and offer employment, it was better to avoid Plaça Nova in the morning and Plaça Sant Jaume at any time.

Before she'd known what was traded in these markets, Estela had stumbled on the horrors of people chained and whipped, displayed like meat. If her man Gilles had not taken her arm and rushed her past the haggling buyers, Estela's healing instincts would have drawn her into endless work. Nici was treated better than these poor heathens! How could this beautiful girl have come from such foul treatment?

'What a lovely name,' Estela said gently, earning a tentative glance from the girl.

'It means *Gazelle*,' Layla explained. 'I thought it suited her. Yes, I think she will learn her duties quickly.' Gizlane flushed at the praise.

'And my steward always chooses well. He knows the merchant.'

He would do, thought Estela, *having been a slave himself. At least he now had power over the merchant, not the reverse.*

'You are lucky,' Estela told Gizlane, who bowed her head in acknowledgement. The long, graceful line of her young neck. Gazelle indeed. Was she lucky? What if Estela had been captured by southern Saracens, sold in Granada? She shuddered, took another sip of wine, repeated Gilles' words to her. *You cannot right the world. You will just lose yourself in sorrow. What would happen to Dragonetz and Musca – and me – then?* She'd laughed, replied, *'And Nici!'* but truly, something about this urban life sapped her spirits.

'Ella!' Layla greeted her new guest. The woman who joined them was younger than Layla, also beautified in the Eastern style. Petronilla frowned on make-up, but, in Aliénor's company, Estela had become familiar with rouged cheeks and lips, lead-whitened skin, and eyes brightened with belladonna – although Estela had heeded her mother's warnings of such substances.

From her accent, the newcomer was clearly Jewish. On hearing her name, Estela gasped and jumped to her feet. Not even the mellow effect of the wine could dull the awe inspired by a singer who had brought even the prosaic court of Barcelone to tears. A singer who came from Cordoba, that sophisticated city in the mythical south still known as al-Andalus, and who was here in friendship to give a private recital.

After appropriate courtesies, with appropriate quantities of wine, Layla spoke the words Estela had been waiting for. 'Will you sing for us?'

'If you will play?' was Ella's reply. Layla reached for the flute she called a nay and tested a few husky notes. Estela's fingers itched to find the notes on her oud but she clasped her hands in her lap and bade herself listen. From the first pure notes, she didn't have to try to sit still as the song caught at her soul, even if she missed the meaning of some words. Ella recited the lyric, translating the Judo-Spanish words into Catalan and then sang it again.

'Arvoliko de yasimín,
Yo lo ensembrí en mi guerta.
Yo lo kresí, lo 'ngrandesí,
Otros s'están gozando.'

'I grew this jasmine tree from seed
in the garden that was mine alone.
I tended it and so it bloomed
but for others' pleasure, never mine.'

The lament reached its heart-wrenching close, the plaintive flute fading to echo.

'No ay ken sepa mi dolor,
Ni ajenos ni parientes.'

'No one knows my pain,
not my kin, not anyone.'

'Beautiful!' Estela wiped her eyes, feeling no shame.
'It is an old Sephardic love song,' Ella told her.
'You must write the words down for me! Can you teach me the oud accompaniment?'
'I can.' Layla stretched out her hand for Estela's oud. 'I will show you, then you can repeat it.'
And so the evening blossomed in the violet dusk. Three black-haired, olive-skinned women spoke of poetry and song, as the night grew velvet dark with the promise of spring. What was the difference

between a Moor, a Jew and a Christian in the privacy of a stone mansion in the wealthy suburbs of Barcelone?

Only my eyes, thought Estela. *But for my Christian-coloured eyes we could be a family. Three generations of women.* The thought warmed her.

Estela paused at the narrow slit of window, breathing in the first scents of spring; jonquils and, of course, jasmine perfumed the night air. She should blow out the candle, seek sleep, but the same force that woke Layla's garden made her restless. She didn't hear him enter the room, so soft-footed he could be when he chose.

'Stand still.' An order.

She closed her eyes to imagine better who and what were behind her. And she stood very still. This was not a moment for questions.

She heard steel drawn from scabbard, ragged breathing. So, he was not unmoved. Good.

The blade swished like a hawk's wing and the candle flickered in the arc of air. Estela shivered as the tip of a sword touched the nape of her neck like a damascene kiss.

'Still,' he warned her, 'very still.'

The point swept down but she felt nothing as her gown split neatly in two, cascading to the tiles around her, leaving her naked in a billow of rose silk, tipped gold in the candle-light. She bent towards her abandoned clothes. The sword pierced the pile that had been her cotton underskirt. She paused.

'Minx,' he told her. 'I heard it clank and you can leave it where it is.'

She could pick up the dagger later. She turned to face a sword she knew by name, stepped lightly over the folds of fabric and berated her visitor.

'That was my best gown!' she told Dragonetz. 'And I'll have to stitch my dagger into another underskirt. You know I hate sewing!'

He sheathed Talharcant and smiled, unfastening his swordbelt. 'No, it wasn't. You wore that one to work in the dispensary at Les

Baux. The green silk is your best gown. Brings out the colour of your eyes better than the pink. You told me so. And a lady doesn't keep a dagger in her underskirt.' Though his mouth smiled, his eyes were dark and his breathing betrayed him.

'What weapons does a lady keep?' She asked him, allowing the candlelight to play over her curves.

'I've missed you,' she told him simply, moving into his arms, unfastening his outer garments, unbuttoning those underneath, while his mouth made free of her body.

'Show me how much,' he whispered and Estela realized with pounding heart that the night had just begun.

CHAPTER FOUR

Sometimes, there is only here and now. Joy and jouissance; love and fusion, days or weeks without distinction. And in between times alone together, there was a toddler's laughter and a dog earnestly washing his master's ear.

'Enough, Nici!' Dragonetz pushed away the big white dog, who dug in his heels and did not budge, determined to clean away all trace of absentee insubordination. Musca climbed onto his father's lap to catch his share of the tickling tongue and Nici redoubled his work. Swinging his wriggling armful of son high above the dog's reach, Dragonetz wondered whether he needed to go on pilgrimage at all. The past could be left there and his salvation be here and now, with his family. Estela smiled at him and came into the circle of his arms. Nici's joy was complete and his tail formed another circle, a plume of white pleasure.

'So,' Dragonetz kissed the top of his lady's head and asked her, 'how fares the best troubadour in the court of Barcelone.'

Estela freed herself and pulled up a stool, smoothing Nici absent-mindedly as she entertained Dragonetz with court gossip. Musca started sucking his thumb, then fell asleep in his father's arms while his parents talked.

As they relaxed, Estela left amusing anecdotes for more honest and personal reflections. 'I miss the quality of musicians we knew in Les Baux,' Estela admitted.

'Of course.' His smugness made her laugh.

'Not just you! Troubadour music is still new here and the musicians at court struggle with anything but cansos in their own language. They can play the lute well, in their fashion, but they sneer at my oud because it has no fret. They sneer at anything that is not their own tradition and they know nothing of Arabic and Jewish instrumentation. They pluck at their strings with their over-sharpened quills as if contact with their fingers would sully their Christian hands! When we came here I expected to learn from the richness of a city. To know more friendships like Malik's. Instead we all live in different quarters, different worlds.'

Her words chilled their hearth with heresy. 'Estela! I hope you don't speak like this to anybody else! You mustn't confuse respect for others with acceptance of their beliefs!'

She shook her head fiercely. 'Don't worry. I know exactly what is expected of me. Petronilla makes sure of that and, as one of her *ladies*, I never miss confession!'

This bitterness was new and worrying. Dragonetz put the thought aside, for later consideration. 'You know that many troubadours use only quills. And, even if they appreciate our techniques, you know how hard it is to learn new ways, to admit that you *have* something new to learn.'

'I know.' Estela bit her lip. 'But it's in the way they look at me. As if I'm a remarkable trained monkey. As if my technique is some kind of magic spell you cast on me. I'm sure they think you wrote my songs. And, if only they let me, I could *show* them how to cut their quills so there's no click on the down-stroke.'

'It's my fault. You've been alone too long with so much that's new and different. I can understand you feeling sensitive. Nobody will look askance at you when I'm there and I'll make them think twice about what they do when I'm not!' His resolve strengthened. He would do all in his power to protect her.

Far from looking reassured, Estela was frowning at the stone floor.

'Do you remember Peire Rogier from the Auvergne?' she asked.

'Who sang in Narbonne, at the court of love? I wasn't there but you told me about him.'

'He passed through on his way south.' Her face lightened. 'We played together and I think that performance was truly appreciated. He brought new songs with him. There is one by Bernart de Ventadorn that everyone is singing.'

Her face glowed when she spoke of music.

'Sing it for me,' he ordered, and she didn't have to be asked twice. Even without oud accompaniment the song was haunting from the start. He could see the lark as the melody rose, feel the lover's fall from grace, his disenchantment with all women.

'Teach me!' he told her and they sang together. He lost himself in her eyes, faltering over the words, earning a fiery rebuke, forced to repeat the lines till he had them.

'Miralhs, pus me mirei en te,
m'an mort li sospir de preon,
c'aissi.m perdei com perdet se
lo bels Narcisus en la fon.'

'Since I looked in you, Mirror, and saw myself,
such sights have slain me.
I am my own destruction like
Narcissus, too beautiful in springtime.'

'That will do,' Estela told him.

'Peire Rogier is a hard taskmaster!' Dragonetz complained. 'But it is a lovely song.'

'Peire has such talent and it was good for me to feel that rapport again.'

'Rapport?' Dragonetz allowed his lip to curl, an eyebrow raised. 'Should I run him through?'

'No indeed!' Estela chose to take the threat seriously. Perhaps she was right to do so. 'That's the first time I've enjoyed singing with a friend since...' her eyes filled and she couldn't speak.

De Rançon. Dragonetz could not speak either.

Her golden eyes, misty with tears, were raised to his, pleading. 'I know you miss him too but why won't you talk to me? When Arnaut died, we cried in each other's arms but since Geoffroi died, you've held it all inside. I don't understand why, what I'm doing wrong.' Her voice broke again. 'Is it because I kissed him once? I told you what happened.'

Musca stirred but didn't wake. Dragonetz adjusted the cradle his arms made round the sleeping boy and murmured, 'You've done nothing wrong, Estela. Of course, de Rançon's death is a painful memory, for us both, and I just want to leave the past behind.'

Bile rose in Dragonetz' throat. *So I never have to tell you that your friend was a liar and a murderer.* He said, 'Tell me about Petronilla.'

Estela dashed the tears from her eyes. Obeyed. 'She is eaten with worry over Pedro and she has reason. The boy is sickly. Luckily, he's too young to know he is the hope of Aragon and Barcelone, but Petronilla has carried that hope since *she* was a baby, and her own health is suffering. Only another baby will ease her mind. More than one, to make the kingdom safe. I am glad on several counts to see Ramon Berenguer back home! Babies do not beget themselves!'

She coloured, glancing at their only child on Dragonetz' lap, and rushed on, making light. 'If prayers and donations could make babies, Petronilla would have a bevy! She keeps showing me jewels that she has purchased and, at first, I was pleased with these signs of vanity. If a woman takes no care of her personal appearance it is but a short step to imbalance of humours and chronic melancholy.

But no! The coronet with pearls, the emerald pendant and the gilded Book of Hours are all destined for the Madonna of Zaragoza. Petronilla's votive offerings include whole outfits for the Madonna – even an ermine-trimmed cloak – that will be presented to the Bishop when we change quarters for the summer and ride to the Palace of Joy. Petronilla is convinced that her prayers and gifts to the Madonna will bring her what she desires. I hope that it does! Meanwhile, we suffer in the gloom of a queen who has not fulfilled her duty, and of a mother who has an ailing child.'

'Is he in your care?' asked Dragonetz.

'No, the Lord be thanked! Petronilla wanted one of the old court physicians to attend the boy and I have no wish to fail in healing the prince.'

There was some feeling here between Petronilla and Estela that Dragonetz misliked, very different from the respect in which the young queen had held her midwife when he had last seen them together. How had he ever thought that home was a less complicated place than a campaign seeking allegiance from vassals?!

Estela told him of her research, her notes, her ideas for a book. 'Travellers need all kinds of information and nowhere is it compiled as a companion for the road.'

Dragonetz told Estela of El Rey Lobo and the hawk. Her eyes understood his loss. He did not tell her of the woman taken in adultery.

He made her laugh; she made him laugh. Yet the low beat of a tabor played beneath their duet, thumping ever louder in Dragonetz' head. *All is not well, this cannot go on; all is not well, this cannot go on!*

Estela knelt in the chapel of Santa Maria del Mar, in the fishermen's church She felt more comfortable opening her heart before the blue-robed figure of Maria than in front of the crucified Christ. Her confessor would never hear anything but what he expected from the sinful woman that the church continually told her she was. But she felt the Mother of God might understand.

'How can it be wrong?' she asked, as the votive candles flickered around her, pin-points of light and heat. 'I feel that we are married, in the eyes of God and man. Our son is beautiful, healthy and happy. Is that really why Petronilla has turned against me? Not because I live in sin with my lover but because she has been punished and we have not? And yet I feel nothing but pity for her. Perhaps that pity is too hard for her to bear from a 'fallen woman', a 'whore', 'mother of a bastard.' She tried out all the names that had been used about her at Petronilla's court. There was a certain pleasure in the taste of forbidden words on the tongue. How could she be a troubadour and not sing all the songs? The bawdy and the sacred, all of them.

'It's not just about me and Dragonetz,' she told the serene plaster statue. 'If there is never any shame in science, why am I supposed to hide my studies? Do *you* want me to count beads and say Novena each morning for twenty days for every time I sing, or read an article on problems with coitus? Petronilla would not have had her baby and lived, if I didn't have the knowledge to help her. And the forbidden words to understand it! It is unjust!

And now Musca, 'the bastard fruit of adultery', has been banned from court as if he's contagious. I don't know what I should do. I can't tell Dragonetz what people say or there will be blood spilt. The only people who might understand are outside your grace and the Queen has warned me that I am becoming corrupted by frequenting heathens. Am I?

Yet I'm supposed to confess to a man who sees holy office as a way to hear the detail of joys he has foregone. I hear the sounds he makes as he suggests the sins he wants to hear about. I'm sure I'm not the only woman who plays along with his little game to avoid worse but who would believe any of us? 'The fevered imaginings of sinful women' would be the judgement on us if we spoke up. He makes me feel dirty but Petronilla is too innocent to see the truth and I dare not earn even more of her displeasure. There are worse things in life for women so I suppose I should be thankful I have no more than a lustful priest's noises to endure.'

She paused. 'And then there's Dragonetz. Something is on his mind and he won't tell me. Any mention of Geoffroi and his face sets hard. He says it's not my fault but I don't believe him. I know I should not have kissed Geoffroi but you know why I did. If you can forgive me perhaps Dragonetz can. I am willing to do penance for my *real* sins.'

She paused again. But there was no point in confession if you hid the worst. 'I thank you for Musca. He is a joy and I understand Petronilla's pain. If Musca were as ill as Pedro, I would never sleep. And even if I had seventeen other children, I would feel the same. I know that it is my duty to provide as many children as I can for my Lord but the truth is... I don't want to die bearing children. I have seen it enough times and I know it's a woman's lot if she's not a nun – or lucky – or,' she whispered the word, 'careful.' There, she'd said it.

'I do want more children, but not too many, and not too quickly. Is this wrong? I want to be a good...' she stumbled over the next word but it was the best fit, 'wife *and* mother, and also to sing, to heal, to be Dragonetz' true companion in everything. Is that wrong? What must I do? Please give me a sign!'

A candle flickered. It was not a sign, not an answer. Estela sighed and rubbed her knees as she stood and crossed herself. Maybe the Virgin's silence *was* the message. She should make her own decisions, choose her own path.

When she joined the Queen and her Ladies, they went quiet then all spoke at once.

One kinder than the others said, 'Tell Lady de Matin the story and see what judgement she makes.'

Reluctantly, one unfolded the moral tale for Estela's consideration and she obliged with a verdict that would have disappointed her father confessor in its lack of sin. The insipid day continued on its course and, as it was Sunday, not even the prospect of song lay ahead. Like the goodwife in the tale, Estela wrapped a girdle of goodness around herself and pulled it tight. If she squeezed her goodness girdle any tighter she would surely burst into a million perfect pieces.

Late spring greened the new foliage and Barcelone stank. Dragonetz strode through the Mercada towards the city walls. He tried not to breathe as he passed the fish stalls but rotting fruit was almost as bad. No doubt thrifty housewives could make conserves from the stewed mess but it turned his stomach to see flies hatching from the discarded produce. Affluent stewards for the noble houses came early in the morning, chose their stalls with care and picked out the freshest goods. They also bought their fish straight from the nets, down at the harbour, not here.

Suffering another breath of fish-scented air, Dragonetz missed Vertat and the open plains, the knife-cold wind and rush of a galloping horse.

'Buy my oranges! Blood-red and juicy!' 'Buy my sardines! Caught this morning!' The sellers' cries assaulted his ears and if those sardines were fresh, he was the king of Cordoba.

Someone bumped into him, murmuring automatically, 'Beg pardon, my Lord.' Just as automatically, Dragonetz used his misericorde dagger to stab the hand feeling for a pouch. A satisfying screech followed and the would-be cutpurse ran for his life. Dragonetz returned the knife to its usual place in his belt. It had seen more use than had his sword since he'd returned to the city. Of course, the man should be tried and sentenced to the appropriate maiming but if you followed up on every thief in the Mercada, you'd never do anything else.

The day had already seen enough time wasted. Dragonetz kicked a cabbage out of his way. He'd hoped that the brothers in Santa Eulalie would have understood what he wanted. But he'd not been optimistic after visiting the Abbey of San Pau the previous day.

Their choir was known throughout the realm and their voices blended perfectly in their chant. When Dragonetz told the Abbot of the heavenly music haunting him, the priest had nodded, encouraged Dragonetz to describe his vision in more detail. The moment he explained that he wanted the monks to take different melodies, the Abbot's face showed his confusion.

'It can't be done, my son,' had been the gentle rebuttal. 'And if it is, it will sound like cats on spring nights. A bestial sound, not fit for God's ears.'

Dragonetz *knew* how wonderful it would sound but he could not make others hear the music that played in his head. Telling the Abbot that his vision had come to him during a poppy dream would not help his case so, frustrated once again, he left the abbey and its singers to their chants.

The route back into the city from the Abbey followed La Rambla, the winter stream that returned to sewage each summer. His search for the heavenly music brought him only the stench of humanity. It was a moot point whether the Mercada smelled worse than the Rambla but at least both were outside the city walls and away from where he lived.

Surely there was somewhere on God's earth that people sang in– he didn't even know what to call it! Un-unison? Even Estela and Malik had difficulty understanding what he meant.

He passed ragged children jumping on a straw heap with goat kids, all vying energetically for the peak. The young would always find a way to amuse themselves. He thought of Musca and his heart clenched into a fist. Surely, he could stay with his family and forget the past.

Vertat, he thought. *The bird named Truth. How ironic that he was missing Vertat.*

He had walked off most of his ill humour by the time he returned to the Carrer de Montcada, Ramon's gift to the city, named for one of Barcelone's foremost families. On this street stood Ramon's gift to his Commander, a town-house kept sweet and clean by Estela's care and direction. Dragonetz had no idea how she managed it, but, even when she was at court duties, the household never missed a beat. He had no idea how many servants they employed, but he saw the same ones in the same places each day, as in some dance measure where each trod the path that made up a pleasing pattern.

No doubt there were many daily chores which he would notice only if they were not carried out, as with military campaigns. He *did* know that no comfort was lacking: clothes and household linen smelled of dried rose petals; salt was whitened; candles down to the wick made a miraculous recovery from one night to the next. All due to Estela's household management.

He rushed upstairs to the living rooms and paused in the doorway to appreciate the vision of domesticity. Estela was sitting with her back to him, bent in thought over her escritoire. Her slender neck was bare, asking to be kissed. In all chivalry how could he refuse such a demand? He pressed his lips to the warm skin, enjoyed the scent of roses.

She turned her face towards him and he saw the tears streaming down her cheeks. *Grieving for de Rançon again.* He said what was expected but his heart withdrew. 'You are sad, my Lady?'

'I don't want to count to four,' she said, still controlling a sob.

Was this better or worse than grieving for de Rançon? He didn't know yet! 'Is there any reason why you should?'

'Yes,' she told him. 'If you should ask it of me.'

'Then you need not cry for I shan't ask it of you.' He was completely at a loss.

'You don't understand,' she said.

'No, I don't. Explain it to me.'

'Petronilla and her ladies... we hear and discuss Goodness and how we should behave. We hear stories that help us to be better women. There was the tale of the wife who tittle-tattled about her husband's business and he lost everything because of her loose words.' She ticked off the stories on her fingers. 'Then the one about the wife who tested her husband's love by killing his dog and apologising, to see whether she would get away with having a lover. That did not end well.'

The third finger was held up. 'And then there was the wife who jumped over the stick when her husband told her to, three times, and each time she said but one word, 'Willingly'... so his friend wished to prove that *his* wife was equally loyal only *that* wife grew angry and of course her husband lost both the wager and his honour – you would not want to hear that one!'

'I don't want to hear any of them,' Dragonetz laughed, snatching at her hand and curling it up under his kisses. 'But how has this sermonising made you cry and what has it to do with counting to four?'

'Obedience.' Estela regarded him earnestly, her golden eyes, still wet with tears. 'A good wife is obedient without question. And all the men trusted their wives to show their goodness.'

'Estela, what men? What did the wives have to do?'

'The men were sure that their wives were good and they were provoked by an unmarried friend who said, 'Let each man ask his wife to count to four, slowly and without mockery, and should all the wives do so, I will acknowledge you the happiest of men and pay for our weekly meal together; should any wife not do so or show her displeasure, then that man shall pay for all.' The men were so confident in their wives that they accepted the bet. Three of the wives were full of pride and on the second or third time of counting, they said instead, 'One, two, thirteen' or 'What nonsense is this' and their husbands lost the bet and were ridiculed. The story finished with the words that all those with well brought-up wives were contented, won the wager, and were happy ever after.

I don't want to let you down.' She frowned, her eyes on his, guileless. 'But I don't want to be made to do stupid things.'

'Sweetheart! These tales have nothing to do with us. I won't ask you to count to four! Or make bets on your obedience – I'd lose.'

She took a moment to realise he was teasing her and then she smiled weakly.

He took her hand. 'You're a troubadour. A physician. A special woman. And mine. We'll make our own rules.'

'You don't know what it's like, being told all the time what a woman should do,' she murmured, held against his chest.

The citron tree (bontziderbaum), on which the great citron grows, is more hot than cold. It signifies chastity. A person who has daily fevers should cook the leaves of this tree in wine, strain the wine through a cloth, and drink it often, and he will be cured. The fruits of this tree, when eaten, also check fever in a person.

Estela paused in copying from the *Physica*, then dipped her quill again in the inkwell. She had a few observations of her own to add.

When pruning the tree or harvesting leaves or fruit, a wise man wears gloves or risks pustules of the skin. The leaves of this tree transfer their heat when touched and the unfortunate recipient will manifest skin burns when the greater heat of the sun in the sky draws the stored heat to the surface.

She could think of somebody who would benefit from a reminder that chastity was a virtue and a lemon tree would be the perfect gift for such a man. An anonymous gift. Left by the confessional box with his name on it. Estela dotted the point with satisfaction and jumped when Dragonetz kissed the top of her head. She had not heard him come in, so engrossed in her work had she been.

Musca was clearly used to his mother's abstraction and was talking to himself with one shoe on each hand. On closer inspection, the shoes were talking to each other, via Musca.

Dragonetz ignored his son. 'Is that von Bingen?' he asked, reading over Estela's shoulder.

'And my own work,' she told him, 'learned the hard way.'

The shoes paused in their conversation as Musca realised that his father was in the room. A grin split his face and he scrambled to his feet, dropped the shoes and picked up one of his toys.

'Teefs!' shouted Musca as he charged at his father, spiking him with a wooden sword.

'Teefs?' queried Dragonetz, holding his offspring at a safe distance while the toddler swung his blade wildly.

Estela shrugged, equally at a loss.

Dragonetz turned his little boy, so they faced the world together. He placed his own hand over the tiny one so that they could control the sword together, thrust and parry.

'Teefs!' yelled Musca.

'Teefs!' agreed Dragonetz.

The game was progressing well until another player joined them. Attracted by the noise, their great white guardian bounded into the room and stopped, confused as to who was in danger from whom. Another whoop and thrust decided him. He took a stance between Estela and the wooden sword and growled a warning.

'Teefs!' observed Musca gleefully, pointing his sword at two sharp white rows of them.

Estela soothed Nici. 'Enough teefs,' she told them, reaching for the sword. Musca's bottom lip trembled but he knew his mother well enough to hand over his precious weapon.

He'd grown up with his nurse's child and knew what was fair, so he turned to his father and held out his hand. 'Acan', he demanded and pointed at Dragonetz' swordbelt. There was no mistaking his meaning.

'Once again you disarm me, my Lady.' His eyes held hers as he unbuckled 'Acan' and passed her the sword, to his son's approval. 'You always will.' He kissed the hand that took the sword, under Nici's watchful eye.

'He's named his sword.' Estela pointed out with pride.

'Of course. And it bites!'

'He needs a little tuition, I think.'

'And one day he will surpass us both. Our son,' Dragonetz said softly.

'Our son.' Some words expressed fulfilment.

In the end, it was not tears and grieving but their closeness that made the difference. As Estela lay half-asleep in his arms, the desire to share his burden breached every wall of Dragonetz' spirit. He flung himself out of bed, dressed as if each item of clothing was an armed foe.

Estela lay half-raised on one elbow, her hair a cascade of black covering her nakedness. The scar on her shoulder was visible through the silken strands. Her lover didn't need to see her body to know it, eyes shut, every dune and dimple.

There was no easy way to say this. Dragonetz stood, statue-still, on guard. 'I have been putting off telling you, Estela. I didn't want to spoil this precious time together, and nobody could love you more than I do.'

'But?' She pulled the blanket round her, clasped hands around the huddle of her knees and waited, watchful.

'Ramon Berenguer has given me permission to go on pilgrimage and now I seek yours.'

Her eyes, golden and wary, measured him. 'You're not suffering the cravings again without telling me?'

It would have been easy to say 'Yes,' to give her a reason for his pilgrimage that she could understand. What was one more lie, in order to protect her from the knowledge he withheld?

'No,' he said, drawing a line. 'I have put the poppy behind me.'

'Then why?' No emotion.

Why indeed? 'I have things on my conscience. I need to earn forgiveness.'

'Things you don't want to talk to me about.' The same colourless tones.

'I'm a knight. There are always matters of conscience.' The evasion lay heavy between them.

'I would not stand in my Lord's way in matters of conscience. Rome? Jerusalem?' To one who knew her as he did, her voice betrayed a slight quiver at the mention of a place where she'd rescued him from the poppy. And had brought Geoffroi de Rançon with her. His resolve hardened.

'The Camino de Santiago.'

'A year then.' There was no need to answer. They both knew that the pilgrim's way across northern Hispania would take a year's walking. And pilgrims walked.

'In sackcloth and ashes?'

He couldn't help the gesture of impatience. 'Of course not!'

'There is no 'of course' to me about this – this plan of yours!' Her mask slipped a little but he had taught her well. She could control her breathing and her voice for the most complex of tensos, taking both voices in such a song if she chose. Show anger or flirt, to order. She'd had months in Petronilla's court to perfect her self-control.

Dragonetz took a deep breath. 'I have your blessing?'

'I shall pray for you, my Lord.' Her eyes never left his but she had wiped all accusation from them and her tone was meek. Horrible beyond all his worst fears.

'God's breath, Estela! I don't want you to be a goodwife!'

They both ignored his curse.

'If you must be a pilgrim then you make a goodwife of me,' she returned, preternaturally calm. 'Your household will accompany the Queen to Zaragoza for the summer and stay there to await your return. If it please my Lord, would you leave now so I may dress in private?' She looked away, dismissing him, withdrawing as completely as if she herself were in Santiago de Compostela.

Dragonetz left, silently condemning Geoffroi de Rançon to all the tortures of hell, but he *knew* he was doing the right thing. There was no need for her to be tortured by the truth, as he was. He just needed to gain the strength to hide it better from her. He would find that strength as a pilgrim.

When he'd gone, Estela dressed mechanically. She had to tie her sash three times to get it right. Then she floated through their palace, immune to all noise but the scream gathering in her head.

She could not understand why he'd gone and she chased every possible motive. What if he'd tired of her? Maybe all she'd felt when they made love had been one-sided.

What if he'd come to believe their love was wrong, as so many around them thought: he'd spent more time with Ramon than she had with Petronilla, no doubt hearing the same sanctimonious condemnation. What if he was preparing to leave her, for his soul's sake. Should she be glad for him?

What if the Templars had finally won Dragonetz and this pilgrimage was his first step towards chastity and joining the Order? She knew they'd invited her lover often enough, with bribes and promises that would make any man tempted. Any unmarried man.

Somewhere in the corridors, Nici found her and loped along beside her. She had no idea where she was going so she followed the mocking cry of the seagulls, walking until she and her dog were alone.

The sea stretched to the edge of the world, sparkles dancing on the waves, a reminder of how unimportant she was. Three empty rowboats were hauled up on the beach, the very image of the industrious fishermen who owned them. She took in the harmony of the scene, the music of sea and sky, the texture of the wood. Then she picked up a large rock and started smashing the nearest boat to splinters, shredding her hands without noticing. Nici whined anxiously but she ignored him. He lay down, watched over her.

Eventually she stopped. Shivering, wet and drained, she looked at the rock in her hand, wondered what it was doing there, and carefully put it down on the sand. She fished her pouch from beneath her skirts and left coin on the planks that remained of the boat, to pay for the damage. Then she returned to her magnificent, empty home. Dragonetz had gone.

Estela treated her abused hand with salve and frowned at the thought of being unable to write, for a couple of days at least. If this was the sign from above that she'd prayed for, she was doomed. She sat down on the floor of her lonely chamber, hugged Nici and cried.

CHAPTER FIVE

From the moment Dragonetz' men received his parting orders, Estela was guarded so closely that she complained of being treated as a prisoner.

'What do you think will happen?' she rounded on Gilles, the unfortunate on duty. 'Someone will be so inflamed at the sight of me buying ribbons that he'll rape me on the stall? Or knife me to steal them?'

Gilles had known his mistress since her childhood and was neither shocked nor diverted by her crudeness. 'My Lord's orders,' he repeated. 'He said he knows the city and you were taking too many risks.' He shook his one hand at her. 'And he was right!'

'If my Lord cared he would be here, not walking hundreds of miles with only his conscience for protection! He's more at risk than I am! If not a proper escort, at least you or Raoulf should have gone with him!'

Gilles said nothing. He had indeed known her a long time. And she knew he would no more leave her side than would Nici if danger threatened. But there *was* no danger!

During one such dispute, a messenger interrupted.

'Gizlane!' Estela recognized the girl at once.

'Mistress,' Layla's servant curtseyed, with an ease that suggested her practice had been diligent. Despite the courtesy, her words tripped over each other. 'Please come. It's the master. He's had a fever for days and the Mistress sent me to get you. To tell you to bring your medicines and that you can use the Master's. She said you will know what to.'

Estela's stomach lurched. 'Malik,' she murmured but Gilles had already nodded, gone to get the horses saddled. She tried to get more information from Gizlane but all she could work out was that the master had a fever, after some domestic accident. He had not been attacked. It sounded trivial but Layla would not have sent for her if this was not serious.

'How did you get here?'

'I walked. Ran sometimes. I can go back on the wagon that came to market.'

'You did well coming so quickly.' Estela recovered her manners and rewarded the girl with some coin. The anxious expression did not change. Whenever a master or mistress was ill, the whole household felt the chill. 'Don't worry. Your master will get better.' *He had to.*

Estela calmed herself by reciting a litany of herbs and procedures. She changed into boots and a riding gown, picked up her medicine box, then headed for the stables. Gilles was holding two placid mares, already saddled. He boosted her up, mounted, and they set off to ride the four miles out of the city to Malik's villa. Whatever Estela had not brought with her could be found in situ, whether books or needles. This was not how she had hoped to win some freedom.

Estela barely paused to unpack her medicine box from the saddlebag and throw the reins to a servant before she rushed into the house, sought directions and entered the chamber where Malik lay. There were so many people in the room that she could hardly see her patient and the air was stale with sweat, sickness and fear. Too late to worry that Malik had something infectious!

Barging past the huddle at the doorway, Estela used elbows and medicine box without mercy to carve a way to the bedside, muttering a dulcet-toned, 'Excuse me,' as she did so.

She recognized Malik's children and grandchildren, sobbing quietly. The others were probably neighbours, and at the front were Layla, weeping over the figure in the bed, and a man with turban and long beard, arms raised, intoning what was unmistakably a prayer. An Imam, no doubt.

Estela fought her way to the man lying in the bed, and, more gently, reached past Layla to make a physician's judgement. Malik grimaced as a spasm shook him, tried to speak through gritted teeth but whatever he wanted to say was unintelligible.

Estela nodded, getting all the confirmation she needed. Only one thing spoiled the colourful emotion of this death-bed scene. The patient was still alive and, if Estela had her way, he was going to remain so. She reached for Malik's wrist, lying limp on the bed, and felt the pulse to see how strong his heart was. Its beat was faster than it should be, but strong.

The Imam ignored her, except for perhaps increasing the volume of his incantation. Layla wiped her face, whispered, 'It is too late. We must let Allah's will be done.'

Biting back the angry words that came to mind, Estela looked instead at her mentor, hearing his words in her mind. *Observe, as you and I know how to do. Tell me what you see.*

As if there were only the two of them in that room preparing for death, she touched Malik's forehead, regardless of the gasps and disapproval in the room. 'Clammy,' she murmured, confirming what she'd been told, that he had a fever. But she hadn't been told that his jaw was clenched or that his body jerked into spasm, throwing off the covers, then returned to a shuddering norm.

Shutting out the noise, she took the chance to observe any parts of his body revealed by the thrashing movements, and she saw the minor wound on his arm. She kept the arm above the sheets as she gently protected his modesty again. 'No sign of putrefaction,' she murmured, frowning. 'Healing well.'

Layla was watching her actions, accepting them as she accepted

Allah's will, without hope. The others in the room watched Layla and made no move to interfere.

'He tended the wound himself,' said Layla. 'He thought it had healed well.'

'He was right,' said Estela, puzzled. She had to examine Malik further but for that she needed to get all these people out of the chamber. They would all sicken and die in this foul air!

'Layla, I need to examine Malik if I am to find out what ails him and what healing is required.'

'It is too late,' Layla repeated, her eyes dull with despair. 'He cannot speak the Shahada, the last prayer, but the Imam will say the Talqeen for him instead, and accompany his soul to paradise.'

The Imam broke off his ululation. 'If the great physician could not heal himself then Allah has already spoken.' He looked at Layla. 'It is time for the widow's white veil.' Malik stirred restlessly, made incoherent noises. His wife took his twitching hand and held it against her cheek as she knelt by the bed.

Physician heal thyself thought Estela bitterly. But of course, the Imam would not know the bible verse. And she had to convince a Muslim leader that she could heal Malik. And that everybody really had to leave the room before she lost her temper!

What would Malik have done? What would he have said? *Our profession dates back to Galen, to Hippocrates*, she remembered him saying. And she had quoted the words of Bernardus Carnotensis back to him, *'We are dwarves on the shoulders of giants.'* Dwarf that she was, she must use those ancient giants.

Heart racing, Estela put her medicine box on the bed and opened it. The precious herbs would impress nobody so she undid the ribbon and opened the roll of cloth to reveal a gleaming array of surgical instruments. That drew a gasp. She held Malik's wrist, pursed her lips and studied the collection, a gift from her patient. Sighing, she let the wrist drop, picked up the biggest knife in one hand and tweezers in the other.

The Imam had stopped his keening, the Lord be thanked, and the throng was silent as Estela spoke, waving her weapons aloft, carefully. The knife was *very* sharp.

'Your Lord, Malik, walked in the footsteps of the great healers, Galen, Hippocrates, Pythagoras, Plato, Aristotle,' she drew breath then extended the list. *The more, the better.* 'Al-Razi, Inb al-Haytham, Ahmad ibn Abi al-Ash'ath, Yahja Ibn Adi...'

Maybe she was pushing her luck to name the author of *The Benefits and Disadvantages of Coitus, and ways of practicing it* but a physician's mind was an eclectic bookshelf.

She rushed on, 'Trota and Hildegard von Bingen, Christian women whose work your Lord respected.' *Should she say 'your king' or some other title? So much she did not know about these people.* 'As he followed in the footsteps of these great healers, so your Lord named me his disciple, worthy of carrying on his work, applying his principles. I am his instrument.' She let the light catch the scalpel blade. 'And I say to you that my Lord Malik would have me use my skills, use what he taught me.'

They were still listening. She had to find some way to clinch that belief in her as a physician. What had her mother taught her? When they were working in poor cottages with women whose superstitions made no sense. *Work with their beliefs.*

'My Lord Malik said Allah was all-powerful and that if we did our best work as healers, Allah would still decide whether a man's time had come or not. But if we did nothing, Allah would judge us for having stepped aside from the task given. This is a sick man and I must follow the calling Lord Malik showed me but I need your prayers too.'

The silence was broken only by the sick man's involuntary sounds. Estela looked at him. She would win this fight! The cloth in the medicine box caught her attention. Maybe...

She put the shining tools down carefully beside the potions and pulled out the silk brocade. She held it up, showing the three circles, symmetrical designs; the signature in Arabic. Arabesques and interlaced points, a mystery that had never been solved but that would serve her now. 'This is the mantle given me by my Lord Malik when he declared me worthy as a physician. See the mystic symbols of our profession, the signature?' She gave a flourish and folded it neatly on top of the box, like a jongleur making the coloured balls disappear.

She had her audience now, she could feel it. 'I need a concoction of galingale and fennel in equal weights, with twice the amount of both nutmeg and feverfew, to diminish his fever and banish the bad humours. And I need your prayers, which should be offered in a holy place, without the distraction of human frailty present in this chamber. Layla?' She asked gently.

Layla looked at her husband, at the Imam, at Estela. She nodded, without hope. 'Please do what you can. It is what he would have done for me.' The man in the bed stirred and made a supreme effort to speak.

It sounded like 'Teborny,' which Estela thought had something to do with his burial.

Layla started weeping again, kissed him, said, 'Nene, no, no,' and stood up.

'Myrrh is the only potion that will be needed,' was the Imam's parting shot but he stalked out from the chamber and the others followed.

Layla gave one last look, said 'I will send servants with water and soap. They will do your bidding.' To everyone else, she said, 'We will let Malik's chosen physician do her work. And, meantime, we will let only prayers and positive thoughts enter our minds, as the Prophet said was meet in the presence of a sick or dying person: 'for verily the Angels say Amen to whatever you say'. We will call on the angels.'

Then Estela was left alone with her patient. What in God's name was wrong with him and could she save him? Anything else was unthinkable and she set to work, washing her hands and freshening the room. Under her instructions, a manservant sponged Malik with a compress soaked in feverfew, while Estela paced the room, murmuring, *'Cut, not deep, healed. Maybe no connection. Nine days later, fever, spasms. Difficulty talking. Not tertial or quartial fever but quotidian.'* If only he could talk to her. She had always relied on his hints and encouragement when she was making a diagnosis. And now he might as well be mute.

Then it hit her. 'Difficulty talking! Ask your mistress to send me Hippocrates from the library!' she told the servant. 'Quickly!' And if she was right? Was there anything she could do about it?

The servant who brought the man a flagon of wine looked at his travel cloak, at his swordbelt, anywhere but his face. The man was used to it, even enjoyed the effect he had on strangers. Truth to tell, he preferred those who knew him to be scared too. He deliberately adjusted the leather mask covering half his face, drawing the lad's eyes to follow the gesture. The boy gulped and turned to leave. Where was the fun in that?

'Your coin.' The boy knew an order when he heard one and turned back to collect payment.

'You want to look, don't you? To see what's behind the mask.'

Wide-eyed like a rabbit before the kill. 'No sir, I didn't mean to be rude sir, I'm sorry sir.'

The man suddenly lost interest. 'Go,' he told the boy, who didn't wait for a change of mind.

The wine was good. Rich and red, like blood. He swirled the liquid. The torchlight flamed in the reflections and he flinched, shut his eyes and took a deep draught. It was very good, worth coming all this way for. Unlike the annual duty of paying dues to the noble Comte de Barcelone and his royal wife. Each year there was some new name for taxes: rents, questas, toltas, forcias all meant more money lost from Montbrun to their Liege of Carcassonne, and from Raymond of Carcassonne to *his* Liege of Barcelona.

Unlike the wine, duty never made travel a pleasure, but it left the domain of Montbrun in peace for another year. His domain now.

The day had been frustrating. Finding Estela's house had been easy enough. The famous commander Dragonetz los Pros and his harlot had been known throughout the city and the splendid new house on the Carrer de Montcada reeked of their ill-gotten wealth and status. Sometimes it was hard to believe that God was just. But with a little help, God could indeed deliver justice. The man had helped in such matters before.

He'd been disappointed to find Estela away from home but he'd left a message for her. If he hadn't heard barking somewhere in the house – that infernal dog! – he could have got to the child and left a stronger message.

'Who shall I say called?' asked the sweet-faced girl at the door. She hadn't minded when he chucked her under the chin. Had gazed impudently into both his eyes, regardless of what was hidden. Or attracted by it. There were girls like that.

'Family,' he said. 'Tell your mistress family is looking for her. Has found her,' he corrected with a smile. 'And will be back.'

The girl had curtseyed, with a pert smile that looked forward to his return. To be encouraged. He gave her a coin and a wink. He could still wink. The rage washed over him again and he turned on his heel, so the girl could not see what no mask could hide, burning, burning inside him.

'Family,' he repeated. And, of course, it was true.

Estela placed a warm poultice on Malik's jaw and was rewarded by him shutting his eyes in relief. 'Tetanos,' she said to him. He tried to nod but grimaced. 'Your neck hurts,' she observed, without needing a reply.

She sat on a stool by the bed with the relevant passage from Hippocrates open on her lap. With any other patient, she would have kept her thoughts to herself but this was no ordinary patient and if ever she'd needed a second opinion, this was the moment.

'The patient cannot open his mouth, his eyes are wet with tears...' Malik's dark eyes were brimming but whether with relief or from sickness, who could say. Estela placed one hand on his arm. 'We will conquer this,' she told him. 'We have to. Dragonetz' damned conscience would require a pilgrimage of twenty years if we lost you and I have not enough years in my life to make amends.' Did she imagine a smile in Malik's eyes?

'Concentrate,' she said, more to herself than to him. 'lower limbs jerk... quotidian fever... If there are spasms...' her voice faltered but his eyes were hard on her. He knew. '...If there are spasms, the prognosis is fatal. All patients with tetanos die in four days.'

She asked Layla. The spasms had started the previous day, and it was now nine days since the wound had let in contaminated air. The wound itself was clean and healed.

Estela could not believe that a gash from rose thorns could lead to such an illness. 'Gardening!' she said aloud. 'After all those years in battle!'

Malik's eyes clouded and she berated him. 'No. You are not going to die from a bush attacking you! Not if I have anything to do with it! Not to mention the prayers of your very large family and opinionated Imam!'

She chewed her lip. The floor was strewn with dried lavender and lady's bedstraw, and now smelled like a place of healing. She'd managed to slip an infusion of the galingale medicine through his lips, and some fish broth to sustain him. She'd used the heat to relax his jaw. But she could feel the heat in his body. How to balance the humours... ice, she thought.

Layla had promised her crushed ice in sherbet for the summer months, fetched from the ice-house. She would have her ice now and use it for more than a cooling drink.

By the time the servant returned with a jar of ice, Estela had told Malik her proposed regimen. It was better than nothing. *Prognosis fatal* said the voice in her head and when Malik sipped the draught of poppy through his clenched teeth, she wasn't sure whether he was hoping to live or to slip easy into death. She had three days to make his muscles relax. As well as the poppy internally, she would apply hot and cold treatments alternately to his jaw and legs, where the spasm occurred; and she would pray. With all her heart. If Malik survived she would do anything God wanted of her, anything.

Time passed in a sleepless haze of medicine and broth. The servants took care of Malik's base needs but Estela trusted nobody else with his treatment. If she nodded off by her patient's bedside, she woke with a start to the gut-wrenching certainty that she'd lost him. Then she'd see the painful breathing and know the fight continued. She remembered that other fight, with poppy as the enemy, when she and Malik had saved Dragonetz from himself.

Layla sat with her, watching with her. While Malik lay between life and death, Estela risked asking, 'What does *Teborny* mean?'

'May my grave precede yours,' was the answer, 'it is an Arab way of saying *I love you, I cannot live without you.*' She rested her hand on that of her husband, as he lay in the poppy stupor. 'But you see my dear, we have an impasse. Te'borny,' she whispered. 'Te'borny.'

On the fourth day, Estela wondered whether Hippocrates was wrong. Not about the disease being fatal but about how long it took to die. What if she reduced the poppy dose and Malik died? She reduced the poppy dose.

Malik did not die. His jaw unclenched and his eyes opened. But he was weak and unwell. Now he could perhaps talk, he was reluctant to do so. He had walked too far down the road to death for the return to be easy. And the poppy demanded a price, as they both knew.

Estela talked to him as he lay there and learned how to carry on living.

'I do not understand Dragonetz,' she told him and went into detail.

'I do not know how to be a good woman,' she told him and went into detail.

'I am glad you are alive,' she told him and burst into tears.

After what could have been years but was probably days or even hours, Malik said, 'I am well enough now. It is good to lie here, to let go.'

'To let go?' she queried sharply.

'Only of my responsibilities, dear friend, not to let go of this world, not yet. Not after all you have done to bring me back. Go home now. Dragonetz must find his own path. Inshallah.'

Of course Malik would think a pilgrimage normal, Estela muttered to herself as she headed home. *He spent years in an abbey!* But all the same she stopped at a shrine on the way home. She placed a posy of wildflowers in the stone niche and knelt before the Madonna, who raised her hand in blessing. Maybe there had been a sign after all but Estela had yet to interpret what it meant.

She did not seek words but let gratitude and humility flood her. Before she stood up, she asked Maria to watch over a wayfarer on the pilgrim's route and to let him know how much he was loved. No conditions, no bargaining, just love.

Musca and Nici were not surprised at being hugged. That was normal when Estela returned from wherever she went. This tendency towards salty damp face was new though. It tasted nice but was not to be encouraged; it was somehow upsetting.

At first, Estela berated herself for imagining demons. She had not needed Dragonetz' warning about Barcelone's cut-throats and pickpockets to be alert as she walked the city streets, kicking up dust as the weather dried towards summer. She always had Gilles as bodyguard, even for the short distance between home and the Palace. Sometimes Nici loped alongside her. She saw no demons when Nici was at her side.

Having accepted that her imagination was playing crazy tricks, Estela fought the impulse to run when a voice she knew spoke behind her as she hesitated between a roll of gold-shot green silk and the crimson. Gilles had grown bored and was gossiping with some he knew, within sight but not within earshot.

'Take the gold and green, Roxie. It will bring out the colour in your eyes.' The words were friendly enough, intimate even: too intimate and there was a sneer in the voice. Gilles was the only person in Barcelone who used her childhood name and this was not Gilles.

She whirled around to face whoever it was and was thrown off balance for a moment by the leather mask, covering the right side of a man's face. But then she knew for sure. His eyes, so like her own: their mother's eyes.

'Miquel,' she said, striving for calm. Surely the whole marketplace could hear her heart thumping! Her hand was on the hilt of her dagger, prepared to draw and to do whatever she must.

There was no point pretending amity, so she told him. 'I have given up any claim on Montbrun so I am no threat to you.' *You don't need to follow me, endanger my child... Musca, where was Musca?* Panic flooded her. Maybe her brother had taken Musca, was here to tell her the worst. *Be still, idiot. Musca is at home, with Prima, with Raoulf and with Nici.*

'Nici,' she said aloud, remembering Miquel's attack on her baby, and what it had cost him. She realised what lay behind the leather mask. 'The burns left scars,' she stated the obvious, adding automatically, 'if there is any pain, you could still use a honey poultice, though it should have been done straight away for most effect...' She tailed off, looked away from a gaze hard and dull as sling-shot. Her mother's eyes had never carried such an expression, nor her own, she hoped.

'The burns left scars,' he mimicked, the open side of his face twisting, uglier than any burn scars Estela could imagine. 'Spare me the false sympathy and the quackery. Your face might be prettier than mine but we are the same beneath the skin.'

Gilles had rushed over, sword in his one hand, sensing the tension though he had not yet identified the stranger. Estela stopped him with a gesture.

'The trusty henchman, Gilles Lack-Hand!' They all knew that Miquel could easily best Gilles in a sword-fight if it came to that.

But a dagger in the back would top two swords thought Estela. *If it comes to that.*

Miquel raised his hands, empty of weapons. 'We are both half-men. You have but one hand and I but half a face, so we are even.

And my business with my lovely sister is just that: business. I am come to visit the Comte de Barcelone on behalf of my Liege of Carcassonne, to pay *his* dues to *his* Liege and I thought to bring news of our family to its disgraced daughter. Was that not kind of me?'

Estela waited and he made her wait longer. *Family news?*

Miquel continued, 'I doubt you are au fait with news, here in exile. Our Lord, Raimon Trencavel of Carcassonne, has become fearful, torn between the Lords of Toulouse and of Barcelone. He owes allegiance to both because of his holdings and he hates Toulouse with a passion – God knows why – but is too weak to antagonize him. Barcelone he respects but,' Miquel gestured to the bustling streets, 'all this enterprise is good only for trade. I hear the Comte has armies that control the world, and the best commanders.' More sarcasm.

'But, you see, *the world* is a long way from Carcassonne and Toulouse would reduce the city's new walls to powder before *El Sant of Barcelone* even heard of it. Our Liege's solution is to sit quivering inside those city walls and to send others on his behalf, whether to Toulouse or to Barcelone. And here I am.' He bowed with a flourish.

Estela was impatient. 'I know all this! What about our family?'

Content at forcing her response, Miquel told her, 'They're dead. Your father died of dysentery, your beloved stepmother died from the consequences of a difficult childbirth. There is only me, now.'

Nothing. Estela felt nothing. You were supposed to grieve when a father died but how could she? He had not been her father since her mother died. And her stepmother? She crossed herself, murmured 'Peace be with them,' so as not to think about how glad she was that Costansa had left the world, so as to hide from her own thought, *I hope it hurt!* Perhaps she and her brother *were* alike.

He was saying something else. She tried to concentrate.

'...the child.'

'The child lives?'

'Disappointed? Costansa's child is a beautiful boy and, of course, my heir.' *If rumours were true, the baby was closer than a mere heir to Miquel.* 'You may console me for my losses or congratulate me on becoming the Lord of Montbrun, or both.'

'It matters not,' Estela tried to marshal her thoughts, if not her feelings. 'I have revoked all claim, formally, with witnesses.'

'I'm so glad you still feel that way. Otherwise my visit might have taken a less friendly turn.'

'Not while I live!' Gilles could no longer hold his tongue but Estela put his arm on his.

'It is not our business, Gilles. I'm sure Miquel is keen to go home, to exercise his new duties. Our paths need not cross again. In fact, you could come to our house, share a drink for old times' sake,' her anger grew into folly, 'perhaps stroke my dog? He always remembers old friends.'

His half-face greened and crumpled, then wiped blank, but too late. She'd seen his fear, and that he knew she'd seen it. He would never forgive her. But then, had he forgiven her for what Nici had done to his face? She doubted it. *Let it be over,* was all she asked.

'That was tactless of me, wasn't it,' she said sweetly. 'I'm sure you want nothing more than to put the past behind you. As do I. Montbrun is yours and... your heir's.' The hesitation made him glare at her sharply and she was starting to enjoy herself, beyond fear.

She even relaxed enough to ask the one question she wanted to ask her dead father. 'As Lord of Montbrun, you should be aware that I possess two heirlooms; our mother's oud and a scarf, both bearing the same Moorish symbol. Do you know anything of their provenance?'

He looked irritated. 'No. And you can keep them.'

She didn't waste time protesting his right to decide. 'If you do find their history at... in Montbrun,' she could not call it *home* and her stomach knotted with a sharp pain, to be diagnosed later, 'perhaps among our mother's things,' another pang, 'then I would appreciate being informed. And I would be suitably grateful.'

'I don't want money from the Commander's whore,' he threw at her.

'Enough, Roxie,' said Gilles, taking her arm.

Tight-lipped, she nodded and turned her back on her brother, feeling his stare skewer her back, twisting in her entrails, gutting her. She had not congratulated him on becoming Lord of Montbrun. Or on fatherhood.

CHAPTER SIX

'You can't trust him, Roxie. You have to forget the boy you grew up with – he doesn't exist anymore.'

'I know,' Estela told Gilles, as she struggled to keep up. They didn't have to explain the urgency with which they headed home. She did know, better even than Gilles. *A stable-boy's corpse swinging in the dark, just because he'd known her. A sword-blade swinging near a baby's head, her baby's head. Foiled by fire and Nici. Neither weapon would ever be forgiven and if fire was immortal, Nici was not.* Words that slashed were the least of it if Miquel reached any of her family.

The moment Estela crossed the threshold, she sent curt orders in every direction. 'We leave for Zaragoza today.' If eyebrows were raised at this sudden haste, no comments were made, and Estela's household was nothing if not efficient. Servants had already packed chests in preparation for the Court's imminent removal to the Summer Palace, and the stable master had horses and wagons reserved. Nobody would query the Queen's troubadour leaving in advance of the royal party. The Queen certainly wouldn't care, Estela thought. Messengers scurried in every direction and, much to his loud annoyance, Nici was shut in a room so he could be found when they were ready to leave.

Estela's household was almost too efficient. Prima could organise the little boys' belongings and travel needs without any input from her so Estela found herself supervising the boys themselves. They were playing with each other and there was a lull in questions and orders, so Estela sat on a stool like Cassandra watching Troy burn. A woman alone.

'Estela!' Gilles had entered without her even noticing, so deep she was in black thoughts.

'I wish Dragonetz was here,' she told him simply.

'And he *should* be! If it wasn't for his mad notions of honour, he'd have told you about de Rançon. He wouldn't be wearing a hair-shirt and walking miles in the dust!' Gilles stopped dead, white-faced but it couldn't be unsaid.

'He's not wearing a hair shirt,' Estela replied automatically. Then, with the inevitability of Troy's fall, 'What about de Rançon?'

'He'll kill me,' Gilles stated.

'Then he'll kill you. Are you his man or mine?' Estela stood up, attracting the toddlers' interest briefly. They glanced at the adults but Uncle Gilles talking to Musca's mother was ordinary, however serious they both looked. The boys returned to pat-a-cake, with the variation of some cold ashes from beside the fire.

Gilles was gruff. 'He was wrong not to tell you. I told him so in the Holy Land and I told him so in Les Baux but he thought he could keep it to himself and not hurt you.'

'Keep what to himself?' Estela wanted to wring the truth out of him now, with both hands, and a lot of screaming, but she could feel that he would speak if she just waited.

And what if she regretted asking? Then this would be the moment before she knew the truth. She remained very still, contemplating the moment, the boys playing, the shaft of sunlight piercing the window-slit, the raised green nap on a square cushion, and her unshakeable love for Dragonetz. Unshakeable.

Then Gilles shook it. He told of treachery, double-dealing, lies. And of a boy's murder.

'How do you know?' she asked, not believing.

'I was there at the dye-yard in Jerusalem, when de Rançon tried to kill Dragonetz. Until then I thought as you did, nay, more. I thought that de Rançon was a noble knight, generous in forgiving all grudges against his 'friend' Dragonetz. By then, you and I trusted de Rançon, and had good reason to doubt Dragonetz. If he'd spoken against De Rançon, would we have believed him? We were both played by an expert!'

Estela dropped back to the stool, clasped shaking hands. 'He was my friend,' she repeated.

'You were a means to hurt Dragonetz.'

'I don't believe you.' *But that's what Dragonetz had thought she'd say. That's why he hadn't told her the truth.* 'Why would he hate Dragonetz so much?'

'Some business of fathers and fairness. Don't expect me to understand! What makes Miquel so full of hate? You're the doctor – you tell me.'

'Bile,' she said. 'Imbalance in the humours so bile dominates. But de Rançon showed no bile.' She'd talked into the night with him. He'd saved her from seasickness. They'd ridden camels together. She'd kissed him.

'Muganni,' she said, a name that cut her tongue. An Arab boy with an angel's voice.

'De Rançon had Muganni's diamond. Dragonetz made him confess. Would have killed him if God hadn't taken the lying bastard first.'

'Why didn't he tell me?' Estela didn't mean Geoffroi.

'That's why.' Gilles nodded at her. 'How you are now. He wanted to spare you.' White-knuckled, stomach cramping worse than any sea-sickness, Estela could only imagine the picture she presented.

'I made it worse,' she whispered. 'I grieved for a man who didn't exist.'

'You couldn't know if you weren't told!'

'I know now.' Estela stood up again. 'And *you* should have told me before! You will make amends by guarding my family en route to Zaragoza and God help you if anything happens to so much as a hair of Nici's head, never mind Musca's! Tell Raoulf and Dragonetz' men, you're moving out and I will join you in a few days.'

'You can't–'

She silenced him with a glance. 'I most certainly can! This whole mess is because Dragonetz and you have treated me like spun sugar. You have your orders. You may go.'

He stood, with the stubbornness of a man who'd known her as a little girl.

She relented enough to say, 'I'm going after Dragonetz and this I *will* do alone!'

His mouth was thin in disapproval but he merely nodded.

Stomach churning, Estela gathered her usual accoutrements for healing, and changed into riding skirt and travelling boots. By the time she reached the stables, she'd already decided what was due to a lady who'd been treated badly and her request brooked no refusal. Saddled up, stirrups shortened, her mount was readied. She accepted the proffered help mounting and took a deep breath before she tugged on the left rein lightly and looked to the left. That was all the direction needed.

When Estela left the stable, and Barcelone, she was riding Sadeek. As it turned out, she wasn't alone. Outside the city wall there was no camouflage for the white shape dogging them.

Already, Dragonetz had lost interest in what day it might be or how long he must walk before he even reached the pilgrims' path, the Camino de Santiago. Once he'd filled his leather skin with fresh water from well or stream, and bartered for bread and cheese, he had only to set one foot in front of the other, let his thoughts gallop, unbridled. He'd chopped wood for a peasant family the day before, slept in the barn and been paid with roast chicken, so today promised fair.

Sleeping on the open road was no hardship in early summer but he took the chance of a straw bed when it was offered. His labour could always buy shelter for a night and the generosity of his hosts humbled him. As a commander, he had requisitioned food and lodging for an army, as needed, and although he'd taken with restraint, he'd still taken. Now, as a simple pilgrim, he was offered sustenance, even by those who had little enough to give.

When travelling to the Holy Land, as a young man, he'd seen the countryside ravaged by the Crusading armies – the friendly countryside, where their own people had been forced to give up their harvests for the good cause. Where the people had starved to death after the German armies had passed through, leaving nothing. Dragonetz had learned hard lessons about the cost of war and Ramon had shown other ways of fighting for peace, but never before had he been invited into a family's rough cottage, to sup pottage with them, in the additional company of a goat, a dog and some hens. Precious beasts.

His feet had purpose but his thoughts meandered far from the route he'd planned. The pilgrim life was seductive in its simplicity. He'd been invited to join the Templars, or the Hospitallers, more than once. He could have relinquished the world, as a knight or in cloisters. He wouldn't be the first troubadour who'd ended his days in the quiet discipline of an abbey. How peaceful it must be to let go of all responsibilities, to obey. To sing the set hours, rise before dawn, sleep peacefully with a clear conscience. Such peace. A guilty thought for a man like him.

Although others would say he was not yet on the pilgrim route, Dragonetz knew he was. The name of the road did not determine the pilgrim's state of grace, or lack of, and he had been praying, openhearted, from the moment he'd left Barcelone. His prayers shaped no spoken words but only music, always music. He heard the blended voices of his opium dreams and although the melody was the same, the lyric was changing. He listened as he walked and felt the music playing through him.

Sometimes he'd sit, take out his lute and sing, not the heavenly music but the songs that bound him to his other life, to Estela. When he sang, men stopped instead of passing by. They smiled, tears in their eyes, and old loves softening their hearts and opening their purses. They threw him a coin or a crust, gave him a sip of wine. A sour party of black-clad pilgrims cried shame on him for licentious frivolity. He bowed his head, wished them Godspeed when he'd finished singing. Men might walk the same road but see it differently.

The more he tried to think of de Rançon, the more his thoughts turned slippery as eels. Nobody was asking him to read a sentence from the Usatges that fitted such a twisted man. Nobody was asking him to judge whether he *could* have been that man himself. All he needed to know was that he was not. All that was asked of him was to watch Estela grieve for the man who'd been her friend. To spare her the pain of grieving for a boy and his murder, by the friend who was no friend.

If he'd been stronger, she'd have healed more quickly, but it was so hard to hide his true feelings from her. His music played, took him to the times when they shared everything.

How far could a man walk in a week? Estela asked herself. *Too damned far* was always the answer! She hadn't ridden as far in a long time but at least she was prepared for her knees giving way at the end of the day. She'd been scouting a suitable company as daylight faded and she stopped with relief the moment she saw the encampment of what seemed to be a party of travelling merchants, to judge by their pack-horses. Sleeping would be safer beside a larger group, probably; possibly; hopefully.

Although Estela's travelling attire was simplest dun linen and her valuables well hidden, she could not hide the biggest attraction to thieves: Sadeek. Neither could she hide the biggest deterrent. Nici had loped in and out of sight as she rode, but, the moment she set up camp, he slumped to the ground by her saddle-bags and blanket.

'Bite anybody who comes near you,' she whispered softly in his ear, then shared her bread and water with him. His eyes followed her as she checked that Sadeek was comfortable and secure.

'Thank you,' she murmured, stroking the aristocratic nose, up to the tuft of mane on his forehead. He whickered. No wonder Dragonetz loved this horse so much, more than he loved her she had teased him, and the question had never been answered. Malik's gift moved with compressed energy, a smooth trot from powerful quarters. She'd concentrated so hard on his every move through the city that her forehead was probably pleated for life. If she felt his attention wander, she nudged for a change of direction and she spoke to him in Arabic.

Whether he was accustomed to lines of love poetry or not, the stallion responded to her touch, his mouth so soft she felt she only had to think what she wanted from him and it was done. The river of pedestrians divided in two around the rider and continued as one after the horse's passage.

When a boy stumbled into their path, Sadeek danced gracefully sideways. Dragonetz had always said Sadeek could turn on a denarius and Estela remembered the stories of their display in the Holy Land. She had no such ambitions and prayed to all the saints that they could avoid any amorous mares or competitive peers.

Once out of the city, she'd relaxed. The white shadow was all the protection she needed and could track them at his own pace. Sadeek had lengthened his gait to something magical that was like a trot but felt like floating. Estela had no idea what she should do in response so just sat, kept her balance, and felt the horse's joy in movement become her own joy.

Arabic sang itself into Occitan phrases and snippets of melody, that she would write down later in the day. A float of black mane, ears flicked forward to the road ahead then back to listen to her very thoughts, Sadeek was not the means but the meaning.

By the time Estela broke for food, she had lost all fear in her love of riding with Sadeek. Though it was she who gave him his head or brought him to a stop, shifting her weight back in the saddle, she no longer felt she was riding *on* a horse. If she felt like this in one day, what must Dragonetz feel?

One of the merchants in the night camp passed her, leading two pack-mares towards the stream and carefully giving Nici a wide berth. *Good* thought Estela as she bade him a polite 'Good evening.'

Maybe Dragonetz had joined such a company and maybe these men had passed him on the road. It didn't hurt to ask but as she searched for words to describe him, she suddenly realised how anonymous he would be. It was a pity Nici wasn't travelling with Dragonetz instead. Then she'd find them easily enough. As it was, she had little hope of any useful response but she approached a group seated on tussocks, preparing their bedrolls.

Her description of a tall black-haired knight, on pilgrimage, bearing a fine sword, brought curious glances but no hint of recognition. What a fool she was! He would hardly be waving his sword and he would be in ordinary attire. She had no way of identifying him. Dragonetz could be anywhere along the road and if he took shelter she could ride past him without knowing. Then all she could do would be to ride the Camino herself, wait for perhaps a year until Dragonetz showed up at Sant Iago's shrine. Could she guarantee she wouldn't miss him there? Heavy-hearted she knew there was only one sensible thing to do: go home.

Dragonetz. If only she could show the image in her mind to these travellers, eyes black as Sadeek's coat, shining with passion; hands long-fingered and delicate. She knew every callus made by plucking his lute and every pore on her body knew his touch.

His lute. Perhaps he had his lute with him.

Without hope, she said, 'He's a troubadour. He might have a lute on his back.'

A bearded man laughed. 'Not on his back, sweet maid, for he was playing it.'

'And not the sort of songs to win grace for a pilgrim's soul!' said another. 'He caused a right to-do among some who wished for more godly entertainment!'

'Where? When? How many days back?' The questions fell over each other but all Estela really knew from the answers was that she was not going back home. Desperate to press on, she forced herself to spend the night beneath a tree, near enough to the travellers for her comfort and far enough for Sadeek's. At daybreak, she was up, and now she knew the question to ask every living being she passed.

'Have you seen or heard a troubadour with his lute, perhaps singing?' Estela had a good idea what sort of songs would have caused offence, and she smiled. He was still hers.

She heard him before she saw him, singing the song she had taught him. Sadeek heard his master too and his ears flicked forwards. Trained for battle, he picked his way with disdain through the small crowd who'd gathered round the troubadour. As usual, men moved aside for the princely stallion and Dragonetz broke off in mid song.

He repeated a line, found his place again in the lyric but then Nici reached him, brushing a cacophony of false notes with each swipe of his tail. Dragonetz put his lute down as he stood to greet his dog, his horse, then his mistress, meeting her eyes as he sang for her.

D'aisso.s fa be femna parer
ma domna, per qu'e.lh' o retrai,
car no vol so c'om deu voler,
e so c'om li deveda, fai.

And so my Lady shows herself to be
a woman, and deserves to be chidden,
for she does not want what she *should* want,
and does just *that* which is forbidden.

He broke off, his words completing the song's accusation. 'You shouldn't be here!'

'A sweet voice but empty,' she teased him. 'It lacks the maturity the song needs.' He bowed, acknowledged the hit, his own words from their first meeting thrown back in his face. Only this time, Estela was the lady and Dragonetz the dusty-footed traveller seeking redemption.

She slipped off the great horse, handed the reins to Dragonetz and picked up the lute. There was an audience waiting, rapt, so she delivered the next verse, as intent on her lover as he on her.

'Chazutz sui en mala merce,
et ai be faih co.l fols en pon;
e no sai per que m'esdeve,
mas car trop puyei contra mon.'

'Deep into disaster I have dropped
and acted like the fool upon the bridge;
I know not why I should fall so low,
unless I strove to climb too high.'

She stopped playing to point at Sadeek, her high horse, and to mime sighs, drawing laughter from the crowd, but Dragonetz no longer wanted to play. She could see his eyes darkening but whether in anger, desire or something else, she didn't know. She curtseyed demurely, passed him the lute so that both his hands were occupied. She should have known better.

Dragonetz passed the lute to a lad who'd been mouthing the words and nodding his head. 'Please, sing for these good people while I attend to my Lady, whose unexpected visit leaves me temporarily without voice.'

He took Estela's arm in a grip that looked to be the height of courtesy and was in fact pure steel. She doubted that Sadeek's reins were held as tightly on Dragonetz' other side but she let herself be steered away from the crowd, who soon lost interest in the drama as they listened to the pleasant voice of the young man. Nici's tail was a white plume of happiness.

'They need water,' Estela pointed out.

'What possessed you to take such risks? You're lucky to be here in one piece! When did you leave Barcelone? Where's Gilles? Or Raoulf. You're not on your own, I hope.' She knew he could read the answers in her face. 'Estela! Sadeek's no palfrey!'

'And I'm no palfrey either!' she fired back, freeing her arm and facing him. He took the chance to inspect his beloved horse's mouth and she stroked the satiny coat. 'He's beautiful,' she murmured. 'I know why you love him and I took care. We floated,' she declared, unable to conceal her pride.

Dragonetz was still checking that his horse showed no sign of damage or distress. 'He did that for you?' Finally, he turned to face her and opened his arms. 'Of course he did,' he murmured, and his kiss was a promise she had to break. She had to say the words.

'I know,' she said, 'about de Rançon. Gilles told me.'

Dragonetz flinched as if he'd been hit then swore, at length, reducing Gilles' ancestry to four-footed farmyard inhabitants.

Estela withstood the blast. 'You had no right to silence *my* man!'

'It was to protect you,' he said, carefully, studying her. Quiet now, he asked, 'How do you feel?'

The words came out in an unstoppered stream. 'Dirty, stupid, gullible, insulted, demeaned, horrified, heart-broken... Muganni... I can't believe it.' Her voice broke. 'And I kissed such a man. I thought him my friend.'

Dragonetz took her hand, spread his bedcloth on the ground, invited her to sit. She did so. 'What exactly did Gilles tell you?' he asked.

Falsehood. Treachery. The murder of a boy with an angel's voice. She stumbled over the tissue of lies that Gilles had exposed, and her own role in them. The way de Rançon had pretended to her that he was Dragonetz' friend and yet managed to disparage the character of his 'friend' with subtle references to the past and 'all being forgiven'. The way Geoffroi had been charming, pretending to love Estela but holding back, from chivalry.

'It wasn't that we kissed,' she whispered. 'It's that *I* kissed *him* and he nobly sent me below decks. How he must have crowed that his revenge was working! And Muganni.' Her voice shook. 'Then he came to Les Baux to complete his devilish work. He taunted you with cowardice and tempted you with the poppy and I just watched! Thought him your friend! It's my fault.' She glared at him. 'And it's your fault for not telling me! You've treated me like a child!'

Tears in his eyes, Dragonetz laughed, raw and humourless. 'Now you know what I've been telling myself since I found out the worst. But when you arrived in Jerusalem, what you saw... me as I was then...' Estela remembered only too well the poppy's deadly work.

'De Rançon's poison was deep in you too, Estela. Not the poppy but words. I could see how he'd won you over, and I didn't know what he'd said about me but I knew that he was no friend! I didn't even know what he was up to until he tried to kill me in the dye-yard and Gilles heard all.

If I'd spoken against him, I might have played into his hands. I thought we could just leave the past behind.'

'In Jerusalem, maybe,' Estela conceded, 'but later, when we'd found each other again, when you were yourself, you should have told me!'

'Why would I hurt you?'

'Because you've hurt me more by not sharing the pain sooner. How do you think I feel now? I've been grieving for months for a murderous bastard! While you – you've been glad he's dead and wishing I'd stop wailing!'

'No.' Dragonetz was hesitant. 'I read his papers in Les Baux when I was called to his rooms after he died. He blamed me for his father's dismissal and disgrace but Geoffroi's parents believed that *he* was a curse upon them, that he was responsible for all their woes. What they wrote to him would have driven any man mad. I think the man you thought him *was* also inside his tortured soul. When we fought together, as brothers, that was the man he could have been, and his evil self was also the way *we* could have been.'

'I don't understand. Von Bingen speaks of gicht taking a man, the need for cooling the humours. Perhaps blood-letting would have rid him of the poisonous thoughts.' Estela remembered all too well the use to which her leeches had been put, on Geoffroi's behalf. 'Perhaps he suffered a head wound. Galen writes of a procedure called trepanning, where the skull is drilled to remove pressure. Such injuries can result in mad behaviour.' Estela babbled, seeking relief from her roiling stomach in the wisdom of the ancients, distancing herself.

'Maybe,' Dragonetz aired the terrible thought quietly, 'maybe we *were* as brothers. Maybe I would have become as he did if I'd borne the same burdens.'

'No!' Estela was adamant. 'Our natures are not malleable in such a way. When you speak to me of brothers, I *know* that the same childhood does not lead to the same wickedness in two children!' Then she told him about Miquel and her soul-sickness eased as she shared her own burdens. She told him about Malik's illness, and Dragonetz held her when she started to shiver, reliving her responsibility for life and death. Her body knew how many shocks she'd suffered even though her mind denied them.

When they had talked out the daylight, they shared their rations and made camp as best they could, rolled in a bedcloth under the stars. Estela did not say how she'd camped in such a way, but alone in her bedcloth, when riding with Geoffroi de Rançon to join his friend Dragonetz in the Holy Land. But she remembered. Camaraderie and reminiscences, woodsmoke and exhausted legs.

'He did love you,' Dragonetz murmured sleepily, reading her mind. 'How can I not understand that.' She curved her body into his, comforted.

Later, much later, as she turned in the night, half-waking, Estela thought she heard her lover say, 'If I understand them, I cannot kill them,' but she probably dreamed it.

In the morning, Estela searched Dragonetz' face for signs that the world had changed. Instead she saw a lop-sided smile.

Carefully, she asked, 'Do you still wish to complete your pilgrimage, my Lord?'

He read her eyes. 'You'll come with me if I do, won't you!' He laughed.

The pause and flicker of eyelids had been miniscule but Estela noticed. She doused her involuntary spark of anger, spoke without accusation. 'There is peace in pilgrimage, in letting go of the burdens, responsibility to Ramon, to me, for men, for your family. In a simple life.' She thought of Malik, his relief at not dying and his peace at being confined to bed. 'Maybe you need this for your own soul.'

'No.' He was firmer. 'There is much to think about but I can do that at home now.' A thought struck him. 'Where is home?'

'Zaragoza,' she told him. 'Our household is on its way to the court, in the Aljaferia. I think we had best meet them there.'

'Malik's Palace of Joy. And Malik?'

'Recovering in Barcelone. I don't think he's well enough to join Ramon. He wouldn't be of any use.'

Dragonetz looked at Sadeek, grazing peacefully. 'How exactly did you intend getting me to Zaragoza once you'd rescued me?' he enquired politely.

'I didn't think about it,' she admitted. 'I should have brought another horse along.'

'Thank God you didn't! You would have found out quickly enough the difference between a stallion and a gelding! Sadeek would not have tolerated you leading another horse!'

'I could commandeer a wagon,' she mused, 'and drive you there, with Sadeek attached to the wagon. 'Or you could drive the wagon while I ride Sadeek? Nici can run alongside.'

'I think not,' he told her, smiling. 'Sadeek will take us both if we take it in easy stages. But for your impudence you can sit behind me and I warn you he has a short back compared with the hacks you're accustomed to, so if he takes a sudden fancy to speed up, you'll land on your behind. And if you provoke me, my Lady, Sadeek will be the first to know about it.'

Estela decided to save her protests for a time when her pride was less likely to take a fall. Sitting on the magnificent stallion, behind Dragonetz, with her arms tight around him, was not such a bad position for a woman after all. Nici made full circles around them in his enthusiasm, until he settled to the pace of a dog escorting a lost sheep home.

CHAPTER SEVEN

The stone bridge stretched ahead of them across the broad race of the River Ebro to Zaragoza itself but it was not the treacherous currents that made Estela gasp. Like the desert mirages she remembered from the Holy Land, fairy-tale spires glittered on the opposite bank. The morning sun turned the river into golden waves, from which foundation rose the massive building like some heraldic beast. The great bell in its cage flashed, a miniature sun in captivity.

As Estela's eyes adjusted to the glare, she could see builders climbing the walls, erecting ropes and pulleys, and the magic diminished to a large building with structural work taking place.

Dragonetz dismounted, grinned up at her. 'Unless my Lady wishes to test the behaviour of the fool on the bridge?'

'Not I, my Lord. I know when to come off my high horse!' she retorted and slipped off Sadeek into her lover's sure arms.

Partly to confirm that she was not dreaming the vision ahead of them, Estela wondered aloud, 'The Aljaferia?'

'I think not. It is not the style of a Moorish fortress. No, I think we have reached a pilgrim shrine, made holy by Sant Iago, though not the one I sought.' He drew Talharcant, knelt on the dusty bridge and kissed the cross of the hilt. 'Hail Mary.'

Another sign. Mary. The first and most famous shrine to Mary in all Christendom, the Cathedral of Our Lady of the Pillar, and Estela was here, re-united with Dragonetz. She put her hand on his shoulder and promised an offering to the Madonna, though not new clothes and jewels. She would leave the wardrobe provision to Queen Petronilla.

'My Lady?' Dragonetz, rose, took her arm and they crossed the Ebro. A group of mallards fought their way against the current, caught in eddies. Like us, thought Estela, as the ducks escaped the fierce rush of the centre, to the lesser pull of the sides and then the calm of the bank, under some trees. Battered by winds, and mud at their roots, the trees leaned drunkenly but held their ground. No doubt they were half-submerged in winter floods but now, in summer drought, they merely bowed their heads to the scorching sun.

May the Palace of Joy live up to its name. Prayer or hope, the thought walked with Estela over the bridge to the plaza of the cathedral. Dragonetz' Aragonese was better than hers and she tried to tune in as he asked for and received directions. It was similar to the Catalan she was used to in Barcelone, or to her own native Occitan, but there were 'b' sounds added to familiar words and the pronunciation was strange to her ears.

They walked on through the plaza, away from the cathedral and the river, heading west along a wide, paved road that told of an older city, before even the Moors and Goths. So much paving! And how could all these people go about their business without stopping to gaze, open-mouthed, at the beauty carved in wood and stone, in every façade. Not even in Barcelone had Estela seen such grandeur. If, as men said, Byzantium was the most dazzling of cities, then surely Zaragoza must be its sister.

They rounded a corner, still on flat ground, and this time there was no mistaking the Moorish fortress; solid semi-circular towers jutted out from golden walls made of stone blocks big as barrels.

'Malik's Palace of Joy.' Estela spoke the thought aloud, earning a warning squeeze from Dragonetz.

'The thought we do not speak,' he told her.

'But you feel it too? How things might have been? And the knowledge of who walked here before us?'

The silence stretched, full of turbaned rulers and their silken-robed wives, of a little prince playing in the home of his ancestors. 'Yes,' he acknowledged, his curtness another warning, spoken by the King of Aragon's Commander.

Atop the towers, the pointed crenellations on brick bands made it seem that each tower was wearing a coronet, the arrow-slit windows like eyes. One square tower loomed at the back of the palace.

'The strongest part, defensively, if it has access to drinking water,' pointed out Dragonetz as he too assessed the Aljaferia but with different priorities. He had been muttering to himself about the flat environment, the parched moat, the feeble protection for archers afforded by the fancy crenellations.

Interlaced arches made stone borders in the massive walls and the entrance was a keyhole arch in the style of Muslim shrines. Stones curved outwards from the keyhole shape, a miracle of architecture.

'How does it not fall on us?' Estela looked up at the curving fan of stone wedges.

'I don't know,' admitted Dragonetz, while they waited for the guards to obtain permission to let them into the palace, 'but I trust it will not!'

Permission received, Dragonetz ascertained that Ramon and a party of his men had arrived, and that the Queen was expected within the week. After Sadeek had been stabled, Dragonetz sought an audience with Ramon and found their allocated chambers. At which time, he and Estela took to their bed and slept soundly, while they could.

Once a big white dog had confirmed the family's safety and enthusiasm at seeing her again, Estela busied herself in organising the new household. She wasn't sure whether to be proud or sorry that they managed so well without her but she found fault with the storage of linen just to keep her staff on their toes.

'Do I need to keep out of his way?' asked Gilles, on hearing that the master had returned with the mistress. His gaze was steady and no regret in his eyes, as loyal as Nici. 'And I bought this for you, in the market.'

Estela nodded thanks, running her fingers over the tooled leather belt, with its dagger sheath. It was very practical and would fit neatly under any of her skirts.

'Beautiful,' she told him. 'The leatherwork in Iberia is second to none.' She remembered the lessons he'd taught her when she was growing up and inspected the stitching. 'Beautiful *and* well-made, I think.'

His smile of approval showed that he remembered too but faded quickly.

'Best get it over with sooner rather than later,' she told him frankly.

'If he hits me, he hits me.' Gilles shrugged. 'But I won't be dismissed. I won't leave you.'

The thought had never occurred to Estela. 'Tell him to hit you if he wants,' she advised her man, 'but that you'll always put me first. Then he won't hit you. And you're not his to dismiss. He knows that.'

Gilles' furrowed forehead suggested his confusion but he left, presumably to find Dragonetz and test Estela's theory. She dismissed the thought. She had been challenged to a duel with wooden swords, to end when the first combatant demanded cuddles and honeyed sweetmeats. A less pleasurable appointment was to follow.

For the fifth time, Estela bade the page-boy wait. It was just as well that she was not required in a hurry to attend the Queen in the palace gardens, as she could not walk through the Aljaferia without stopping to stare at some new architectural marvel.

Her family and entourage had been allocated the third and top floor of the square tower that had gained Dragonetz' military approval. Even this older, more basic accommodation was decorated with strange plants and birds morphing into the inscription, 'Allah's is the kingdom'. Whatever she was not supposed to say, the ghosts of Malik's ancestors were all around her.

She had a stiff neck from gazing at the painted ceilings, which were not as fancy or colourful as in the newer parts of the palace but still boasted brightly patterned stars and symmetries. As did the broad undersides of arches in the horseshoe doorways. She was surrounded by curves when she was accustomed to rectangles; the illusion of ethereal light when she was used to dark solidity.

As she followed the boy down the steps from the peaceful top storey, the brick walls grew thicker and the echoes louder from soldiers and servants. The alabaster walls of the first storey showed signs of fire damage, scorched and fractured in who-knows-what attack or siege. Also on the first floor was access to the baths and, through a narrow passage, to a deep circular well. Dragonetz had been disproportionately excited on discovering the well, especially when he found that it drew from the River Ebro itself.

She walked along the passageway bordering the garden, past the Throne Room and between the marble columns, past the Oratory of the Moorish kings. The Christians in the Palace mostly pretended it didn't exist, closed their eyes to the sweep of the vault, the exquisite stonework of the prayer niche. A Muslim guard was kneeling there now, murmuring prayers in liquid Arabic.

A heathen, condemned to hell, Estela reminded herself. Dragonetz was right. It was important to use the right names in Zaragoza, the capital of Christian Aragon. But how, Estela wondered, did the Queen see only her own religion in the Palace of Joy? Was there some magic, which made invisible all that Estela could see and touch?

Her hands reached out of their own accord to lace made of alabaster; flowers that looped into Arabic script; dazzling in bright red, blue, green and gold. Her dress and slippers made rose petals and shadows on white marble flooring.

'Porphyry, mother-of-pearl, ivory, ebony and coral,' she

murmured, naming the precious materials as if a line of poetry. She could hear the song of wood and stone, of magical craftsmanship. Her fingers traced the plasterwork, feeling for the artist's thoughts. If the craftsmen had turned stone to lace, they had made of plasterwork their embroidery. The fine details of fruit, flowers, curling leaves and Arabic script teased Estela's fingers, asking to be read by touch.

She closed her eyes, the better to trace a line of Kufic script, opened them again, smiled. She had not been wrong. One craftsman had sneaked his own words onto the stone, not those of the Surahs. 'Should you find any mistake in my work, I shall be surprised!'

Conscious that she must not keep the Queen waiting, she quickened her footsteps but her eyes were drawn to a pattern on the wall. Just one more stop, she told the boy, and herself, as she inspected a familiar symbol. There could be no mistake. She'd seen the same interlaced arabesques a thousand times, on her lute and on the fabric she'd recovered from the caves in les Baux.

The Gyptian's words were slippery as serpents, and yet they'd proved true before, in retrospect, if you knew how to interpret them. The first time they'd met, in Narbonne, the fortune-teller had chilled Estela with her predictions and she'd been wary when their paths crossed again.

The Gyptian had sent her down a tunnel, told her *'The girl should know what she came for. Even though she doesn't know yet what she came for. Family. You should know where you're from.'* Estela shivered, remembering the dark closing in, the sensation that something was watching her, the legends of Moorish treasure and a demon guardian in the place known as le Val d'Enfer, the Valley of Hell. Remembering a heap of antique metal and pottery goods, and the instruction, *'Touch only what is yours.'* And she had left with a piece of silk brocade, embroidered with the same design as her oud.

Estela had defied the Gyptian, told her she sought nothing and would pay nothing, but the response had been, *'Payment is always taken.'* And Estela *had* gone into the tunnel.

She shivered again, looking with disbelief at *her* motif engraved on a palace wall. A man who'd learned to form such swirls by carving bones had carved the motif of her oud, of her brocade, in alabaster that must be a hundred years old, perhaps more.

The symbol looked at first glance to be the same as its fellows, joining in an endless repeated pattern. Except that it was not endless. Estela's symbol stopped in a corner, tailing into a signature, the same signature as on the fabric but carved in stone. It was as cheeky an insertion as the one she'd found by an engraver who claimed he made no mistakes.

What this meant she had no idea, but she was certain that she'd found a clue to her history in the Moorish Palace of Joy. To be considered later. She had an oud, passed down through her mother's family and then to her. She had a swathe of cloth, found in a cave in Provence, with the same pattern and strange signature, looking Arabic, and yet nothing Malik knew. And she had the words of a dead woman, who claimed the gift of prophesy.

She skirted the pebbled beds, the red-flowered pomegranate and the orange trees, whose tiny fruit had just set, and she reached a figure seated by the rectangular pool, in the shade of a vine-covered trellis.

'My Lady.' Estela curtseyed deeply to the Queen, whose face looked sallow and tired. Never a beauty, Petronilla had glowed with the bloom of pregnancy when Estela had first known her. Was that but a year ago? The ill health of her child showed in the Queen's mien, and Estela knew what she could never say. The only cure was to have more children, to provide for the kingdom and herself against the loss that was only too likely. As a mother, Estela screamed without words; as a healer, she knew how many children died, how many babies were not born and how many women died giving birth. No, it was not easy to be a woman. She must make more allowances for the Queen's sharpness and extremes of piety. What was it Dragonetz had said? *Maybe, that could have been me.*

'Can I bring you some relief, my Lady?' she asked gently, rising from her curtsey to stand before the ruler of Aragon.

Brown eyes, red-rimmed and dull, met hers. 'Not unless you can tell me what ails my son.'

'I would have to study him as a patient before I could treat him.' Estela stayed soft, wondering whether the Queen would finally turn to her for help, wondering whether she could in fact diagnose the condition which left such a precious child so sickly.

Petronilla waved her hand in a gesture that dismissed the offer and all hope. 'I hardly think you could succeed where our finest doctors fail. It is not a woman's work to practice medicine.'

Estela bit her lip, hard.

'But the court needs entertainment. I wish you and Dragonetz to sing for us tonight.'

'Of course, my Lady.' Estela lowered her eyes, hoping to express demureness rather than seething resentment. She could still feel the Queen's gaze.

'And I hope there's been no misunderstanding about your quarters.'

Estela waited, her head bowed.

'Ramon was very generous and tolerant in Barcelone but you are under my roof now and we must set an example. My Lord Dragonetz has his own accommodation, as befits Ramon's Commander. You and your entourage have yours. I don't expect there to be immodest contact between the two. Your reputation has suffered enough and it is my duty to lead you back to the paths of righteousness.'

Estela kept her eyes on the paths of multi-coloured pebbles, apparently random in placement and yet forming strictly mathematical patterns, weaving and interweaving, like the arabesques on her oud. She and Dragonetz would have to sneak around again to lie together, perhaps even to see each other. And how did Dragonetz' son fit into Petronilla's view of a righteous life?

The Queen was still speaking. 'You must of course look after the child, whatever his origin. We were all born in sin.' Her tone said clearly enough how much more sinful bastardy was. Or whatever she considered to be Musca's condition. 'Nobody is above criticism.'

Certainly not someone whose father renounced his monk's vows to sire her, then returned to the monastery, Estela realized. There must have been some church doubts on the legality of such a renunciation and of its issue. Estela's rush of compassion was stemmed at the Queen's next words.

'But Pedro needs peace and protection from the rough behaviour I have seen from your offspring and his rather inappropriate companion.' *How it must hurt to see Musca's rude health and the games played by the two little boys.* Estela tried to maintain a level of understanding. If she did not, she would commit treason.

With magnanimity, Petronilla added, 'You must keep them out of sight and hearing but you may exercise them outside the Palace. I trust we understand each other and that you have no complaint regarding our hospitality in such magnificent surroundings.'

'I have never seen anywhere that shows man's works and God's glory to such effect,' was the safest response Estela could find. It was not safe enough.

'God's glory is indeed around us and, in time, we will knock down the heathen mosques and domes, replace them with works of faith.'

Nothing was all the response required or given. *May Malik and Layla never see such times.*

The Queen continued, 'But even infidels can be very skilled and the architecture does deserve our admiration. There are even some good Moors at our court. I can only hope they see the error of their ways and find salvation in our Christian kingdom.

My dream is to see Pedro crowned in Zaragoza, to achieve that for which I was born and to unite Barcelone and Aragon forever!' For a few seconds, Estela recognized the innocent child-bride she'd helped give birth, then the veil of misery descended again. If only that first child had been healthy, how different everyone's life would have been!

'I wish you to come to prayer with me. I need all my ladies to accompany me and we shall walk, in penance and humility. We will go to the cathedral this very afternoon and make offerings so you need to change into your outdoor shoes and clothing suitable for church. Wait in the entrance courtyard when you are ready.'

'At once, my Lady.' *More garments and jewels for the statue of the*

Virgin, thought Estela, as she returned to her chambers, kicking the stairs as she climbed and scuffing the toes of a rather pretty pair of silk slippers.

She could no longer avoid telling Dragonetz exactly how she was perceived in court and his reaction would *not* be conciliatory. She would soften the comments about them sharing chambers and he would accept the need to be discreet, for her sake. After all, they'd observed the same charade in Les Baux.

However, there was no way of softening Musca's banishment or the slight on his lineage. Nor any way Dragonetz would accept either. She would wait until after they performed together, then suggest they found a place of their own, away from court, as they had in Barcelone. The further away, the better, as far as she was concerned! *Exercising* Musca indeed! Their dog was more welcome than their son at this court!

Nici had already discovered the joys of the fields and ditches surrounding the palace on three sides and was undoubtedly a better companion for Musca and his foster brother than any of its other residents. *More intelligent too!* Estela fumed. The only good thing to come out of the interview was the prospect of singing with Dragonetz in public. They would have fun drawing up a programme, practising together, singing always for each other, however big their audience was. They would bring joy to this palace, as it deserved!

And she did owe Mary a debt of gratitude so the visit was well-timed. She knew what she should give as an ex-voto, to say thank you. When she thought of Malik, between life and death, only one precious possession could express how she truly felt. After all, it was less of a sacrifice than a goshawk. And she had an unfinished conversation with Mary to continue. She had just learned what kind of woman she was *not*.

Wearing the drabbest costumes they could find, with the highest necklines, Petronilla's ladies progressed solemnly along the paved streets between the Aljaferia and the cathedral. The sun was past its mid-day burn but still glaring. Estela could feel the sweat trickling in furrows underneath the dun linen gown. She'd pulled the clean white wimple as far across her forehead as it would reach without blinding her and she was glad of having had it well starched.

Some of her companions were suffering floppy headgear that was already damp and offered little protection from the sun. One white-skinned redhead had even worn a lightweight cloak, the hood concealing even her eyes, earning a disapproving look from the Queen. Those with the palest skin would toast first, thought Estela with a certain unchristian satisfaction. She'd been criticized often enough for her olive skin, however she'd tried to lighten it with lemon juice and whatever care she'd taken with gloves and gowns that covered every pore of skin.

Sweat attracted the flies and Estela was not the only one surreptitiously jutting out her bottom lip to blow an insect off her face. The instinct to flail her arms around, each time she felt the prick of landing or – worst – crawling, was difficult to master but Petronilla's beady eye was surveilling her troubadour closely.

Already the wonder of Zaragoza's architecture was reduced by familiarity to merely beautiful surroundings and Estela could resist the urge to stop and stare at marquetry doorways, which combined eight different woods into three-dimensional patters of stars and suns; or friezes that brought to life the gardens of paradise.

The cathedral itself was less impressive close-up than in the first impression across the shimmering Ebro. Building work was in full swing and Petronilla gave a nod of satisfaction at the progress. Watching the lines of men and donkeys hauling on ropes, shifting stone blocks into place, Estela reflected that she was not the only one sweating. Then she was blinded as she stepped into the dark of the cathedral.

Blinking as she grew used to the light, Estela's attention was drawn by the queue of supplicants to the jasper pillar and the wooden figure of Madonna and child on its flat top. Petronilla's guards would have moved the queue aside to let the Queen through but she stopped them.

'In the eyes of God, we are equals,' she said and took her place behind a man in peasant-brown breeches and jerkin. Her ladies followed suit, not without some sighs. Petronilla's piety might be admirable but emulating it was not always popular. At least it was cool in the stone interior, and untroubled by flies.

The Lady's Chapel was the heart of the cathedral, hundreds of years old, like the pillar and statue. In turn, each person knelt on the marble floor to kiss the pillar and pray. There was no need to guess at the Queen's prayers but Estela closed her eyes as she waited and felt the other stories in that place of worship. What songs were there. Songs beyond romance, of a mother's love, of a man's fear of death, of repentance and hope, of desperation and projects planned. As a healer, Estela had heard many such stories and, opening her eyes, she read the people around her. Shabby shoes, a terminal cough, a woman clutching her empty belly.

What would somebody read in her own appearance, she wondered, as she stepped in her turn to the place before the pillar. As she knelt, she slipped a little on the marble, worn uneven by so many feet and prayers. Cold even through her gown, dispassionate, the floor had absorbed a million stories without comment.

Estela kissed the pillar. *Jasper* she thought, remembering von Bingen's description of the stone, *'When a woman brings forth an infant, from the time she gives birth through all the days of its infancy, she should keep a jasper on her hand. Malign spirits of the air will be much less able to harm her or her child.'* Estela's little jasper stone was in her scrip with her money, tied around her waist under her skirts. Hers was reddish in colour whereas the pillar was green veined, as far as she could tell in the dim candle-light.

Above her, at about the height of a tall man, Mary looked serene, with her own child tucked under her arm, a carved dove on his hand. Her mantle was fine white lace with gold braid borders. Her coronet sparkled with green gems. If the outfit was one of Petronilla's offerings, the gems would be real emeralds; if not, they could be glass, but offered honestly. Nobody offered counterfeit in prayers to the Virgin.

Estela offered her heartfelt thanks, for Malik, for Musca, for Dragonetz. She took the piece of old fabric out of her scrip and looked at the symbols one last time. 'The Gyptian said it was a piece of my life,' she murmured, 'that would show me who I am, where I'm from. I don't understand what the pattern on my oud was doing in a cave in Les Baux. And now in the Palace of Joy.

But she always spoke in puzzles that I'd probably be better off not solving. I don't know what she meant by payment but it sounded like a threat to me, to my true family. Dragonetz and I have suffered enough from my relatives and I won't let them hurt Musca. I'm giving this to you, part of who I am. If you mean me to find out more, then you will lead me to that understanding. If not, then be with me and my family as we travel through life.'

There was an impatient cough from the queue, waiting at a discreet distance behind Estela, and she finished quickly with an *Amen* and crossed herself. She laid the cloth in front of the altar, with the flowers and trinkets of the other votive offerings, and moved away quickly before she could change her mind. Petronilla's precious gifts, a cloth of gold mantle and coronet with diamonds for the Virgin, would be given directly to the new bishop, just in case a lifetime's wealth left in the open could tempt a poor man to sacrilege.

Estela walked into the daylight, blinked again and felt eased. She had shared the burden of whatever these family mysteries meant, and she felt stronger to deal with whatever threats conventional piety posed to the people who mattered now. Dragonetz, Musca and Nici were *her* family and her duty was to them and all who depended on them. That did not include the relatives she'd left behind in Montbrun. May they stay away from her forever. Dead or living, they were no longer part of her life.

With no deliberate intent to rebel, her feet took her away from the plaza where the Queen was organizing her ladies into a return procession. Estela went around the corner, over the bridge to the far bank, where she and Dragonetz had first seen Zaragoza. The sun was going down and the front of the building was now in shadow. Instead of the river dazzling with sunshine, it gleamed a twilit blue reflection of the cathedral, Mary's blue. Another sign for the fool on the bridge. As she leaned on her elbows, hanging over the side of the bridge to drink in the view, something butted the back of her knees, hard.

Pickpocket! Estela automatically reached for her dagger as she whirled round, then laughed and stroked the deep, white fur. She'd wondered whether she'd glimpsed him as the ladies made their progress. Nici was in the habit of keeping a watchful eye from a distance and bounding along on any outing where he spotted his family. Outside the palace, he mixed cheerfully with the street curs, although he could hardly be said to blend in.

'Come on, you,' Estela told him. 'We have a performance to prepare.' Her return to the Palace was more leisurely, her affection for this timeless city growing daily. Accompanied by Nici and a thousand turbaned ghosts, she regained the Aljaferia and, deliberately rebelling, found joy in the Palace with Dragonetz that night.

CHAPTER EIGHT

Even though he knew the Palace of Joy was poor defensively, Dragonetz did his best. His own man Raoulf was training the guards, once more practising a retreat to the tower in case of siege. The last practice had been executed to perfection, apart from the fact that the royal party would have been left sleeping in their chamber, over-run by barbarians. On the positive side, while Ramon and Petronilla were being murdered in their beds, all those in the tower would have been safe in a solid keep of almost Christian design. The keyhole doorways and decoration showed otherwise but these did not affect Dragonetz' military plans.

He gazed at the vaulted cellar, and at the spiral staircase up from the lowest level with a satisfaction as deep as the circular well. He was dispatching a hundred Almohads when his imaginary fights were interrupted by the English Mintmaster, John Halfpenny.

'My Lord? May I speak with you.'

Dragonetz realized with surprise that he'd not found time to speak with the man since the brief thank you for his work at Monteagudo. Normally, he'd *make* time to learn from a master craftsman and he'd enjoy debating metals and making.

He'd intended to visit the notary today and write his will but doing so in another day or two would make little difference. He ignored his conscience reminding him that he'd been postponing the unpleasant task 'one more day' for as long as he could remember, ever since realizing that his mortality affected a woman and child.

'Of course,' he said, quickly reviewing the man's current role, and possible suit.

Although in Ramon's employ, Halfpenny owed his life to Dragonetz and his allegiance showed in his eyes and actions. Given his wiry physique and lack of skill at arms, taking him on campaign should have been merely food wasted, and yet, the man's skills had helped gain the vital alliance with El Rey Lobo. An alliance that should prevent the tower's defence being tested at all.

John Halfpenny had cleaned up from his prison filth to be red-haired and red-bearded, with a silvered skin like his own coins. His eyes were still mud-coloured, no longer hopeless, but sharp, like a ferret's.

'You did good work with Murcia's Mintmaster,' Dragonetz told him again.

Halfpenny's eyes darted sideward and he licked his lips. It seemed he wasn't seeking praise, and he wasn't sure of himself. Dragonetz waited.

When the Mintmaster did speak, he gabbled in bursts, in that strange northern accent of his. 'Gold is all they think about in Murcia, in Zaragoza, with their new dirhams and morabetins, and their old bezants from Byzantium. Gold be difficult to get and difficult to work so a man can't sleep for worrying about the relief –,' Dragonetz' face must have shown his puzzlement for Halfpenny barely paused for breath while explaining, 'that is the surface on the coin – and it distresses just by looking at it – that is it rubs off, so fragile the gold is, and I've told them the coins should be smaller and fatter but they can't get the gold and they won't change the dies – that is, the molds. Half the workers be heathens and the rest – well, if they're not competing with Byzantine coinage, they're keeping up with the Saracens who lived here before, and some of them live here still, and it's driving me mad! I can't remember half the names of all these coins and I can't do my job with metal that don't behave right and is worth more than a year's bread for each coin. Don't bear to think about what mistakes cost.'

With the air of one about to make a huge confession, he took a deep breath and, enunciating each word separately, said, 'I don't like working with gold.' Then, head bowed, he waited for the sword to descend.

Totally at a loss for how to respond, Dragonetz hedged as he tried to understand what, apparently, had been made clear to him. 'You're making gold dirhams – morabetins,' he corrected, 'in the Zaragoza mint.'

Halfpenny looked at him as if he were an idiot, which Dragonetz took as assent. 'You can't get the gold?' he hazarded.

'Gold comes from Oltra mar, over the sea,' Halfpenny explained as if to a dull-witted schoolboy. 'Like silk, so it's very expensive. But you can't heat silk up and use it again so you don't get some stupid idiots wanting to melt down silk as you do with bezants – beautiful coins! – and then they use the gold for the thin rubbish we're turning out here. They'll be lucky if there's a raised pattern after a year, never mind the king with his orb and sceptre like they want. Ridiculous! Breaks my heart to do such shoddy work! If they'd been in England in the days of old King Henry they'd have learned to give exact measure, or they'd have lost their privates!'

Dragonetz refrained from pointing out that Halfpenny had been accused of forgery when they first met. He was starting to understand what Halfpenny didn't want but not what he did. 'And when you're not working with gold...' he prompted.

'Base metal will last,' Halfpenny conceded. 'But there is nothing like hammered silver and best of all is hammered *English* sterling silver.'

The man was home-sick! 'I thought you had to leave England because you were in danger there?'

'King Stephen will not live forever.'

Of course. Dragonetz remembered now. The man had sided with Queen Matilda, then made coins for various barons displaying their images, not an act popular with the King's Mint he supposedly worked for.

'If you wish to return to England, you must put your request to your Liege. It is not in my hands.' Dragonetz frowned. 'Even if it were, I confess I'd rather a skilled man like you were working for me. There are few with your talents.'

'That's what I was hoping, my Lord,' was the odd reply, made even more puzzling by Halfpenny's next words. 'Should you be travelling north, my Lord, I'd be glad to go with you.'

Dragonetz laughed aloud. 'I'm sorry to disappoint you, Halfpenny, but I have no plans to travel north and as for voyaging to England, I'd rather see the tusked monsters of India than risk the flux in such barbaric wetlands.'

'Yes, my Lord,' said the Mintmaster but he did not sound disappointed and, although he bowed his head respectfully, his demeanor suggested he knew something his Lord didn't.

Dragonetz frowned after the man for a while, wondering what gossip had entertained a roomful of coin-makers. Estela too had implied that 'what people said' was upsetting. *Pff, rumour-mongers. A man had more serious worries. And pleasures.* He dismissed the conversation from his mind, and mused on the far more entertaining topic of which songs he and Estela were to sing before the court.

The throne room of the Aljaferia was the jewel in the palace crown, from the white marble flags with black veins, to the wooden ceiling panels and painted friezes. Dragonetz and Estela had sung in palaces from Narbonne to Jerusalem but never in one as opulent. Not content with mere arches, the Moorish architects had embellished curves with inner arches and curlicues, drawing the eye to outer passageways and more columns, in an illusion of infinite space.

The columns supporting their confection of plasterwork were as symmetrical, and as individual, as people, each one topped by exquisite carvings – a flower, a fish, a pine cone. Everywhere in the palace were pine cones, their overlapping scales repeating the pattern of the interlaced archways. Everywhere the poetry of mathematics, the harmony, until Dragonetz felt his head spin with looking.

'My Lord?' A boy filled his goblet with wine and drew Dragonetz' attention back to the pleasures of the table. He and Estela had seats at the top table with Ramon, Petronilla and other privileged guests. The marbled Hall was set out in the same way as any ordinary castellan's would be, with trestle tables running the length of the room.

From the top table, Dragonetz could see the boys entering through the keyhole doorway with trays of food, and his stomach growled in response. As any experienced performer knew, it was a jongling act to be polite to his noble hosts but also restrained in what he ate and drank, if his performance was not to suffer. He saw Estela cover her goblet with her hand and the boy pass on to the next guest. She had long since mastered all the social skills required for her role.

The civet of singed veal claimed his attention, in a cameline sauce that mixed sweetness with a tang he could not identify. Estela could no doubt tell him not only the name of each spice, but in what quantities and how they were prepared. He glanced at her again.

Watching his lover in animated conversation with her neighbour, Dragonetz tried to see her as others did. Words like accomplished, beautiful, vivacious no more portrayed her true nature than did black-haired. They were all true but empty. When he'd looked up on that dusty road and seen her on Sadeek, his universe had breathed one word, *Estela,* and in that one word was every moment they'd lived together. He could remember the moment he'd first seen her golden eyes and grubby-clothed passion, how dazzled he'd been. She darted a sudden smile his way, as conscious of him as he of her, however many people sat between them. He was still dazzled.

It was time for them to take to the floor. Excusing himself to his neighbours, Dragonetz stood. Estela took her cue from him and accepted the hand he offered to escort her to the place they'd left his mandora, her oud and two chairs.

Always the flutter of nerves beforehand, hidden in a cough, the tuning of instruments. Always the two of them, facing the world together, and breathing when the song dictated they could.

At first, Estela accompanied Dragonetz as he sang two of her compositions. The audience knew them well, but the male interpretation in rich baritone brought out different qualities from Estela's soprano performance. Dragonetz brought the timbre of war and weapons to *the Song of Arnaut*. His voice carried his love for his brothers-in-arms, past and present. He sang for Malik and for Ramon, who raised a goblet from the top table.

Then Estela lay down her lute, turned her back on her lover and the Hall waited, whispered their guess at what song might follow, recognized the opening straight away, the lark beating its wings. *Ventadorn* murmured the listeners.

Dragonetz pointed at the wilful woman as he sang *car no vol so c'om deu vole, for she wants what she should not,* and the audience sang the second line with him, quietening to listen and enjoy the lover's anguish and haughty response as the troubadours threw the lines to each other with their own personal touch. Estela mocked him as he sang of her wickedness and his despair. The audience loved their act.

Then Dragonetz slipped into his own best-known songs, or versions of them. As he relaxed, he extemporized, drawing laughter from around the Hall as he slipped in current events and well-known characters, emphasised by his comic acting and rich baritone. He switched moods, drew his audience into a sensual longing that made couples glance at each other, hands touch surreptitiously under the table.

When the mood was right, he glanced at Estela and she strummed the opening notes of his aubade. A murmur of appreciation swelled round the Hall as everyone recognized the song before it had even started. Dragonetz sang a verse then turned to his lady and she sang the next, while he joined her in playing his lute. They embellished the melody with their nimble fingers as well as their voices and wove the last verse into a duet of passion and loss. *Their* duet of passion and loss, of their meeting and parting, of the time when they had known they should be together and thought it impossible.

*'If only day would never come
If only night could spare the pain
Of each new parting, little Death
That leaves enough to die again.'*

As the last notes died, there was silence, then an uproar as the audience reacted, shouting for more. Dragonetz looked at Estela and she nodded. Her face was well-schooled but he could detect both strain and determination. They had discussed this and both felt the need, however hard it might be.

The Hall hushed as people strained to hear Dragonetz' words.

'...in memory of a singer who died too young. We're going to sing the dawn song again but as it was sung in the court of Jerusalem by a boy we loved. I will sing the song in Occitan, as my Lady Estela de Matin did on that day, and Estela will take Muganni's part. May he sing forever with the angels.'

Dragonetz sat down and took up his lute. Estela moved to stand behind Dragonetz and put her hand on his shoulder, a gesture of affection in the audience's eyes, no doubt. He could feel her hand clenching the velvet of his tunic and knew she was steadying herself. Then his shoulder was light and he played the first notes, sang one line, as had Estela in Jerusalem, when she and Muganni had gifted Dragonetz with their duet, prepared in secret, with love.

Echoing every line in the Arabic of Muganni's translation, Estela faltered at first, missed a note and then found her way. Willing strength to her, Dragonetz embroidered her lines with minor chords, adding to the oriental effect, and she responded with a mournful vocal technique she'd learned from Ella.

*'My sweet, my own, what shall we do?
Day is nigh and night is over.
We must be parted, my self missing
All the day away from you.'*

As Estela sang the closing words, Dragonetz let his fingers play a last goodbye to the boy he'd rescued from a brute's tent, and who'd sung for a queen before whatever death he'd suffered. Then the hand stilled, the echo died and the lute was silent. Dragonetz felt Estela's grip on his shoulder once more and he guessed she was spent. They'd intended to lift the mood with one of Estela's popular compositions but he knew it was not possible.

He took Estela's hand in his own, held it tight as he stood beside her. He bowed, she curtseyed in the silence that lingered, let the audience wipe their eyes, come back in their own time from the magical otherworld they'd visited through song. A communal sigh ran like a wave through the Hall, responded to another bow with applause and weak shouts for more. Everyone understood that the performance was over, and everyone understood the tear-tracks on the singers' faces. Everyone knew grief and loss.

'*I brau*, well done,' Petronilla told them as they returned to their places at table. Her eyes were shining and Dragonetz remembered what Estela had told him. His heart looped. Did the Queen have another boy's loss in mind?

Ramon, too, was generous with praise, said 'Would that Malik had been here to credit the finer points of the music!' He chewed his lip, came to a decision, said, 'I would talk to you tomorrow, in the cool of evening.'

'My Lord,' Dragonetz acknowledged the appointment without question. Outwardly. Inwardly, he wondered. It was going to be a busy day as he had a notary to visit in the morning and this time he *would* go. One day death would come, will he or nill he, and he must make provision for his lady and child.

'My Lord Dragonetz!' Estela toasted him from further along the table, her eyes dancing as she realized how much they had moved their audience, how they had shone, together.

'My Lady Estela,' he returned, raising his goblet and kissing its rim, his eyes never leaving hers. Death could wait. Tonight was theirs and they would continue in private what they had started in public.

Estela blushed but her gaze never wavered. Her imagination could match his, in all things. He smiled.

CHAPTER NINE

Dragonetz drummed his fingers on his knee, wondering how notaries were all imbued with the same mind-numbing nit-picking capacity to spend hours 'clarifying' what was clear to any sensible man in minutes. He concentrated on the lawyer's hat to keep from walking from the shop while the lawyer studied his bookshelves and muttered.

It was in the style that some Jews chose to affect, soft, round-brimmed with a hemisphere as the centre and a strange spike on top. *Like a breast with a stiff tassel*, thought Dragonetz, remembering some of the more esoteric entertainments in Damascus. It was unlikely that Master ben Aaron would appreciate the comparison. Below the hat, he wore the customary jubba, in green silk, the sweat stains under the wide sleeves refreshed with recent damp.

It was worth it to have the notary's mark on a legal document, Dragonetz reminded himself. Examples of such were strewn on the table and if complexity of design were an indication of professional status, Master ben Aaron was a paragon among lawyers. His mark included five criss-crossing strands like a cat's cradle and what could have been a crow's beak or an instrument of torture scrawled across the ensemble. Not easily forged, which presumably was the point.

Once more seated, Master ben Aaron clasped his hands and

cracked the knuckles. His quill remained unemployed in its stand. There was more clarification required. Dragonetz sighed.

'You wish to make provision for your concubine, who is of noble birth and in an adulterous relationship with you. You also wish to acknowledge her issue, specifically one male, named Txamusca, as your son and heir.'

There was no judgement intended by the notary's words but Dragonetz had to force himself to spit out the word, 'Yes.' His instinct was rather to draw Talharcant and slash things. What did lawyers know of love and complications? He looked at the books Master ben Aaron had laid on the table, *Liber Iudicorum*, *Lex Antiqua*. Maybe the lawyer did know something of complications.

'There is a presumption of fatherhood in the husband's favour, you know? You could find a way to dissolve the marriage, make your situation regular through wedlock but leave the child's status as the legitimate son of his married parents.'

'The husband never consummated the marriage and I want to acknowledge my son.' How Dragonetz hated speaking of such private matters but, whatever he said, the lawyer maintained the same matter-of-fact tone. It was all codas and clauses to him. And, of course, gold, when he was paid for his work. A lot of gold.

'Aha!' Ben Aaron's tone was more enthusiastic. 'If the husband is impotent, that makes an annulment easy.'

'He has four children from a previous marriage.'

Pause. A new line of attack. 'Adultery gives the husband the right to a divorce under Visigothic law... you could come to an arrangement with him?'

'No,' said Dragonetz shortly.

'Hmm... under Roman law, the lady herself can end the marriage if she wishes?'

'No.' The husband had been a gift from Queen Aliénor and Viscomtesse Ermengarda of Narbonne, a gift suggested by Dragonetz himself (for which he cursed himself daily) and extricating herself would not endear Estela to those two powerful women.

'Even if she did,' pursued the notary, 'and the two of you married, the adultery remains a legal problem, as does the bastardy.' Dragonetz winced but the notary didn't seem to notice. 'You should be aware that canon law proposes some constraints on the advancement of an illegitimate child, of whichever category. If, in the future, canon law is applied in a more systematic way, and if you acknowledge the child as spurius, then your issue will face more restrictions on his future activity than if he were the presumed child of your concubine's husband.'

'For God's sake, stop calling my Lady that! And what in the name of hell's demons is a spurius?'

Ben Aaron brushed a non-existent speck off his jubba and looked down his nose. 'Legal terms avoid ambiguity,' he declared, without apology, 'and I use them as you, my Lord Dragonetz would refer to a weapon by its name. You came to me for my expertise. My point is that annulment of the woman's marriage should in no way affect the legitimacy of issue from that marriage. Only think of modern France; Queen Aliénor and King Louis' children are legitimate even though the marriage was deemed incestuous.'

Chastened, Dragonetz accepted the implied rebuke, while thinking that he had not been so humiliated since childhood, when his tutor had made him stand on the table to recite a bible passage that he had bungled earlier.

'The law recognises different categories of bastard.' Ben Aaron fixed him with a stern gaze and ticked them off on his fingers. 'One, a child born before its parents marry; two, *mamzer*, the child of a whore; three, *nothus*, the issue of a low-born woman; and four,' he ticked off the fourth finger, '*spurius*, the child of illicit sexual relations, such as your own, or indeed the issue of those who have sworn vows of chastity.'

'And what difference does it make?' Dragonetz spoke through gritted teeth.

'I cannot foresee what difference it will make in the future.' How like a lawyer to protect himself from future plaint! 'Precedent allows for many born of concubine mothers,' he stressed the word 'concubine', with a frown at Dragonetz, 'to reach greatness. William, King of

England; Sancho of Leon-Castile, whose concubine mother was Muslim – except he died in battle, of course, but he was heir – and then the half-sister, who was also of concubine mother, but a Christian one – what was her name now? The half-sister, not the mother... But in none of these cases was the child born of an adulterous relationship.'

Dragonetz could feel his anger mounting and was about to say something he'd regret when ben Aaron's next question caught him off-balance.

'What is the estate you leave to the child? Of what are you yourself heir?'

What, indeed? Dragonetz' personal wealth was considerable, both from the paper mill and from the mission to the Holy Land, but what of his inheritance? His right to Ruffec had been relinquished when he told his father to go to hell. What if his father knew of Musca?

Enough of these weasel words! 'I leave my estate to the child. Surely to God that's clear enough! Pick up your quill and I will tell you what to write. You may put it in your unambiguous terms but I shall have my will!'

Ben Aaron took his quill from the stand, dipped it in the inkwell and held it poised over the blank parchment. His mouth formed a thin line of disapproval but he held his tongue.

'In her lifetime, I leave all my worldly goods–'

'That would be *dominium,* not *possession,* and include *largissime, communiter* and *proprie,*' muttered the lawyer as his nib scratched away.

'That would include everything,' Dragonetz stated baldly, without a clue as to what any of the terms meant.

'To the Lady Roxane de Montbrun, known as Estela de Matin...' He paused to let the quill catch up with him. Reading the Latin upside down, he saw that Ben Aaron had started with the date, the place, the nature of the document, some formal opening, and then used ten words for every one Dragonetz had dictated, but it was close enough.

'Her married name?' queried ben Aaron blithely.

'Not needed,' Dragonetz said, thinking it a miracle the man was still alive.

Ben Aaron opened his mouth to object, then changed his mind, shaking his head.

Dragonetz continued, '...in trust for my son and heir Txamusca.' He glared at the notary, daring him to ask for another name.

Meekly, ben Aaron asked him, 'Do you wish to make provision for more issue my Lord?'

Dragonetz barked a harsh laugh. 'More bastards, you mean? Not to my knowledge. I have but one.'

'And if my Lord should be blessed with more, you will need to add a coda to this will or make a new will to ensure provision.'

Dragonetz just grunted. It was enough to put a man off having children, the very thought of another such ordeal by clause and precedent. 'That will do well enough,' he said, ready to leave. 'How much do I owe you?'

Appalled, ben Aaron said, 'You must sign the document, with witnesses. Please, my Lord, wait here an instant.' He rushed out the room as if worried his client would disappear in his absence.

Dragonetz took the opportunity to read the document but, irritating as it was, he could do no better by his family.

The notary returned with his two witnesses, who barely murmured good-day, so accustomed were they to doing their duty and departing. Dragonetz signed his name, the witnesses wrote theirs and left, while ben Aaron carefully scribed his mark, made a final flourish and blotted the whole.

'There are many accommodations possible within the law,' ben Aaron informed Dragonetz. 'Indeed, our illustrious Queen's father not only left the sanctity of the cloisters to do his duty by Aragon but also arranged matrimonio en casa for her and the Prince – that is, betrothal at any age, however young, to preserve the patrimony. Ipso facto, we now have the continuing line of Aragon. It therefore behoves you to consult again with a lawyer who is well-informed in such matters, such as myself, when you have given them proper consideration.

I will have a copy made for you and the original will rest with me unless you take up residence elsewhere and wish to transfer it to another notary.'

'That will do.' Coin changed hands and Dragonetz left, wiping his boots on the doorstep as he left. As he returned to the palace by the riverside instead of the city streets, he still felt unclean, as if he'd betrayed Estela rather than provided for her. And his thoughts turned to his family home in Ruffec. His ex-inheritance.

He didn't need the letters in his hand to see the formal words by which his father had disinherited him or the tear-stained note from his mother. His sire's readiness to believe he was an oath-breaker was just one more blow in a stormy relationship but his mother's affirmation that she loved him 'despite everything', her pain at his disgrace, still unmanned him worse than poppy withdrawal had done.

He had banished all thought of Ruffec since he'd sent the message telling his father to go to hell but how could he think of Musca's future without thinking of where his son came from, where *he* came from? Did they know they were grandparents? Had they named Dragonetz' eldest sister in his place as heir? Or preferred a male cousin? If he'd had a brother no doubt his father would have passed him over as the chosen one long since! But his rogue imagination insisted on a picture of Musca hand-in-hand with his grandmother, picking herbs in the knot garden that was her pride and joy. As he had done.

Musca with his wooden sword, and pride in Lord Dragon's eyes as he played with his grandson. Saying, 'Well done, son,' to Dragonetz. Didn't every child want to hear those words? Especially from a father who found them impossible to say.

He did without a mid-day meal, sitting on a tree stump, watching the current carry driftwood where it willed, swirling and rushing, going underwater, then popping up somewhere quite different.

Hours passed.

It was with a heavy sense of foreboding that he left the river bank to keep his appointment with Ramon Berenguer IV, Comte de Barcelone, Prince of Aragon.

'I have letters from Malik addressed to you and Estela,' announced Ramon, without ceremony, inviting Dragonetz to sit and take the letters.

'Estela told me he'd been ill.' Dragonetz' worst fears pounded all sense to dust, so loud in his head that he barely heard Ramon's quick reply.

Ramon repeated, 'He's recovering, Dragonetz, but still weak.'

The pounding diminished, slowly. Dragonetz noticed the seals had been broken. If Ramon wanted to read letters surreptitiously, his ministers could open seals and steam them shut invisibly, so this flaunted intrusion was deliberate. Dragonetz swallowed the insult, told himself it saved time in the discussion that was inevitably to follow. Ramon was prepared and he was not, but his Liege had done him the courtesy of letting him know this.

Should he read the message to Estela at all? He hesitated, looked at Ramon, who nodded. So be it. *'Dearest colleague and daughter of my heart, greetings...'* Dragonetz scanned the words that could only be from Malik to Estela, that were written in recognition of a life nearly lost, a life saved.

He looked up from his reading. 'Malik speaks of a gift?'

Without words, Ramon handed him a wooden box with marquetry lid. Dragonetz opened it, saw the neatly ranged surgical instruments, each in its velvet bed. Malik's own instruments.

Dragonetz frowned and opened his own missive. *'Dearest friend of my mind...'* Had it been only four years since Dragonetz read those words and discovered his friend's true identity? Four years since he'd been given Sadeek, a gift as precious as was Estela's now? A gift that had also been a farewell and an explanation. Dragonetz took his time, considering not only the words but their implications for the conversation that was to follow, in this room. There had been another gift from Malik, in the letter to Dragonetz.

There was too much he did not know so he merely stated what he did. 'Malik is no longer able to serve as your commander. He is giving up his work as physician too. He is staying in Barcelone and offers his country home here, near Zaragoza, to my family for indefinite use.'

Ramon just nodded.

'I should have gone back to Barcelone instead of coming here! I should have gone to see how he was!' *What if he'd died? While Estela and I were singing for one loss, what if there had been another?*

Ramon shook his head. 'No. Malik sent word to me too, that he was out of danger and that you must not change your plans for his sake.' Similar words had been in the letter to Estela but Dragonetz still doubted. The urge to see his friend, in case it should be a last time, flooded him.

Ramon smiled. 'His words were, *'as far as any man can say he is out of danger. Who shall say what God wills'*. But he asked my permission to leave our service. He said, *'Tell Dragonetz I shall not be a weak stone in his wall.'* This means something to you?'

A nod. 'Nobody can replace him,' he told Ramon and realised at the same moment that somebody already had. 'De Montcada,' he said.

'Yes. Nobody starts off with experience but he has the skills and background.'

'And you want me to train him.' Inevitably. The idea of riding beside Malik's replacement already fretted at Dragonetz like a saddle sore.

'I would have liked that.' Ramon's level gaze read Dragonetz easily. 'But it will not be possible. There is another letter for you.'

This time the seal was unbroken. A seal Dragonetz recognised and had last seen on the letter accusing him of oath-breaking, of ignoring a summons from his ancestral Liege Lord, of disgracing his country, his family and himself. Aliénor did not usually spare words when her temper was roused.

Dragonetz read the opening, his lip curling. *'Aliénor, by the grace of God Queen of England to her vassal Lord Dragonetz of Ruffec...* He was torn between fury – how *dare* she assume rights after such treatment of him! – and a hope that had never been extinguished – this was his chance to clear his name completely. How like the fiery

Aliénor to appeal to his loyalty, offer a reward and then threaten him!

'When I sent for your help in my hour of need, you came not. Now, there is a mission I can trust to nobody but you, which could decide the fate of our kingdom. You may, by this act, make up for past wrongs and be well rewarded for the service. By your oath of fealty, I command you to attend my pleasure in Angers, with all speed. And you do not, may God be my witness, you shall be held as an example of a faithless knight, throughout Aquitaine and England!'

'You know the letter's contents?' Dragonetz asked.

'Queen Aliénor wrote me a polite request that I should release my commander to pursue matters of state. She did point out that you are her vassal and owe her allegiance before me.' Ramon's tone was neutral but Dragonetz was not misled. Neither did he overstep his rank and congratulate Ramon on receiving a polite letter from Aliénor.

'You are willing to release me?'

'I fear I must. The misunderstanding is partly my doing. If I'd let you know that the Duchesse was at war, you would have left Les Baux to lead her armies and Barcelone would have been the poorer this last year. And, as I recall, I gave you permission to go for a pilgrim. I was not expecting you back this year so I had already made preparation.'

'Even without Malik? You would let me go?'

'There is no question. You must go.' Long afterwards, too late to ask him, Dragonetz would wonder about Ramon's ready acquiescence. He should have known that Barcelone and Aragon came first for El Sant, always. At the time, he was grateful to have a clear path in his duty. A pilgrimage of a different kind, perhaps, however unexpected.

Perhaps not so unexpected to others. He frowned, then considered the potential use of a wiry, muscular Mintmaster as his squire on such a journey. Especially when said squire would be beside himself with gratitude at gaining an interview with she who called herself Queen of England. John Halfpenny had supported Queen Matilda and would no doubt wager his future on this new queen without hesitation.

'My Lord? Could you also replace the English moneyer? His knowledge of those barbarian lands could be useful to the Duchesse.' *Should he call her Queen? Where did Ramon stand with regard to northern politics?* 'I would take him with me as squire.'

The Prince nodded. 'He's a troublesome little man anyway. I get complaints every day regarding weights and standards. He has served his purpose and the mint will function more smoothly without him. Take him with my blessing!'

'Thank you, my Lord.' Dragonetz knelt, kissed Ramon's ring and wondered whether that was true of him too. Troublesome, as El Rey Lobo had observed, and too keen on standards.

'Dragonetz.' Ramon's expression was severe, almost pained. 'You have my thanks for all you have done. I know your worth and nobody could value you more highly; you and Malik together have been my right hand. I will miss you, beyond words. You have kept your oath and I will always keep mine.'

This most reserved of rulers clasped Dragonetz in his arms, man to man.

'Some training is priceless,' Dragonetz replied. 'The three of us my Liege: you, me and Malik; we made a whole. When my service for Aliénor is done, I shall return,'

Ramon released his grip, said nothing about the future, so Dragonetz bowed and walked away. When he glanced back, his lord's gaze still followed him, unwavering, until the door closed between them.

Pausing in the passageway, Dragonetz sighed, realising that the path of his duty would perhaps not seem as clear to Estela.

Things had been going well. Dragonetz had shared Malik's letters, given Estela the little wooden box. While she was distracted, removing each blade and muttering what might have been 'piercing' and 'fine excision', Dragonetz mentioned the summons from Aliénor.

Estela's fury made Aliénor's threats seem like froth. Dragonetz had *not* expected the direction it took.

'No,' he told her.

'Yes,' she replied, and she would not be shaken. For every argument he came up with as to why she should not go with him, she found a counter-argument that made good sense.

'I was hoping for the patience and understanding that you showed when I told you I was going on pilgrimage.' He hoped his expression was a cross between puppy-dog and righteous disappointment.

'You forfeited any rights to such wifely forbearance when you showed yourself capable of jumping off a bridge because you'd seen your own reflection!'

'That's harsh,' he protested. 'The rivers were so dried up there was hardly any water and I felt no urge whatsoever to jump off bridges. I just wanted to walk, and not watch you crying.'

'Then you should be happy. There will be no crying this time because I'm going with you.'

He tried another tack. 'You said you ought to go back to Barcelone and check on Malik. You could take Musca back and wait for me there.' He knew it was low to use their friend's illness in such a way and so did she.

'Shame on you!" She rounded on him. 'Malik tells you not to come to him so you think I should stand in for you and ease your conscience while you go adventuring with Aliénor?

'For Aliénor,' he corrected meekly, earning another glare. Undaunted, he tried, 'Musca needs his mother.'

'Musca needs his father to come back alive! If *your* Aliénor can leave a child to go on crusade then I can leave mine for a few months. He has his nurse, a playmate, Gilles, Nici and they can live in the house Malik has so kindly offered. They'll be in heaven and much safer there than in that foetid city!'

Dragonetz hadn't realised how much Estela hated Barcelone and made a mental note to find out why. His conscience twinged. He'd been pre-occupied, not sensitive to his lover's needs.

Unfortunately, a twingeing conscience did not help him come up with good arguments for leaving Estela behind.

'And another thing,' she pressed home her advantage, 'what exactly is this mission that you are the only man in the world capable of carrying out? And how long will it take you?'

'I don't know.' The admission was the final capitulation and she jumped on it with enthusiasm.

'Then we'll go and find out!' She rightly took his silence for her victory. 'Can I ride Sadeek?'

'We won't even take Sadeek.' He struggled to re-assert some authority. 'We'll hire horses and change them. It's a long way.'

Then, at last, she looked doubtful. *Damn. He should have talked of the hardships of the trip, right from the start. Too late. She'd never give up the idea now.*

Chin jutting, she said, '*How* long a way? And where is Angers anyway?'

Then he laughed. 'Three weeks,' he told her, watching her jaw clench. 'And I would rather start from anywhere other than here to get to the Frankish north. Angers is in her husband's duchy of Anjou.'

Inspired, he added, 'Or we could take a sea route?'

Her face took on a greenish tint but he was right. Not even the prospect of her usual sea-sickness could change her mind. 'We can discuss the finer details of northern politics on the journey,' she told him airily. 'I have to pack and instruct our household. I'll need Gilles to employ a trustworthy steward – I was never happy with the one we left in Barcelone – and more servants, to supervise the move to Malik's house.'

She continued thinking aloud, planning. 'I need to make lists for the steward, provisions to buy in... he must not pay more than three solidi for a quarter of mutton or a side of beef, and he should check the hearth in the new kitchen. If the pot so much as touches even the burning embers, vegetables will stick to the bottom. And he should only buy wild duck, with black or red feet, not the domestic ones with yellow feet. The cook will leave if she has inferior produce and we are so lucky to have her. Gilles, I need to speak to Gilles.'

The domestic details washed over Dragonetz as he imagined Estela's forthcoming conversation with Gilles. She would have as much difficulty persuading Gilles that he must stay here as he'd had with her – but more success. One mention of Musca, and Gilles would accept the need to protect the little boy. He would however berate Estela soundly for leaving them. There was some satisfaction in that thought.

Later that day, as he headed off to find John Halfpenny, Dragonetz noticed Estela carefully packing the box of surgical instruments, still talking to herself. He only hoped she hadn't packed her leeches but if she hadn't, and he asked, she might well do so. He kept very quiet and left.

CHAPTER TEN

The horses were watered and tethered, the southern evening was balmy, and a night in the open was no hardship. John Halfpenny had withdrawn to a discreet distance and was flat out with his eyes closed. Dragonetz rested his back against a tree and watched Estela, as she sat in the dwindling light from their cookfire, writing.

When she'd pulled the wooden board, paper, quill and ink out of her saddle-bag he'd teased her about wasting precious space on such luxuries. Then she'd told him, 'I'm writing a guide to travelling, for Musca, so he will benefit from our experience, and so he will know I thought about him every day. When I rode after you, I thought how useful it would have been to read guidance on such matters as food, greetings, local customs, dangers, precautions and medical treatment for emergencies. So, I am writing such a book. After all, we have travelled widely.'

'That's a good thought,' he told her. When he looked over her shoulder and realized the level of her guidance, his respect increased. 'Truly, I think this would be useful to more than Musca. We shall have it copied when we return.'

He was rewarded with a glowing smile but she quickly returned to her work, making the most of the dying light. He must wait until the embers turned to ash before he could hold her under their blanket and watch the stars together. He 'accidentally' kicked a little earth over the fire as he walked past, earning a reproachful gaze.

He sat down and waited, watching the quill scratch its route across paper from his mill. Words. Travel. Time in between the start and the destination. Perhaps he should say this to Estela and she could add his thoughts to her journal. Perhaps there would be a song from their journey.

The next thing he knew, Estela was shaking him awake so they could lay out the blanket and snuggle under it. He had not known he was so tired but sleep claimed him again straight away. The stars danced in all their brilliance, without his appreciation.

As they journeyed, their destination seemed ever less important and the road itself lulled them into a daily routine of provisions, care for themselves and the horses, breaks, food, water and sleep. Sometimes they camped outside, sometimes they found lodgings and a change of horses. Silences were as comfortable as speech, which came without the niceties or tact of social convention.

While crossing the Pyrenees, he told her he'd seen a notary, made a will leaving everything to her and acknowledging Musca. She wondered what that meant and also what it *would* mean, one day in an unimaginable future without him. She didn't want to think about it, so she didn't.

Somewhere after Bordeaux, he said, 'You travelled like this with him.'

'We travelled together,' Estela said carefully, 'and the road makes comrades of those who travel together, but it was not like this. With him,' she too found it easier not to say Geoffroi's name, 'I could talk about you, hear stories of your childhood and youth.' Bitterly, she added, 'Some of them may have been true.'

'And some of them damned me as a bully who'd been forgiven by the saintly knight.'

Estela said nothing.

They passed Poitiers, neither of them saying that this was the closest they'd been to Dragonetz' family home since they'd been together. Only two days' ride away.

Instead, Estela said, 'I think about him. My brother.'

'I think about Ruffec,' he admitted. 'Maybe we never forget where we're from but we *can* choose what hold it has on us.'

'Maybe,' she said and wrote more of her book.

'Can I read it?' Dragonetz asked one evening.

From then on, Estela passed him her notes from the day before, during their mid-day break and Dragonetz read them aloud. John Halfpenny sat with them, his face intent as he listened to extracts from *The Wise Traveller*.

Wine
Shun the company of any person who is in a state of inebriation and banish any such from your service. Be moderate in your own consumption.

'Inebriation,' began Dragonetz. 'Do you remember that night...'

Estela's lips tightened. 'This is a book of guidance, Dragonetz, not a journal of our wilder moments.'

'A pity.'

Drunken behaviour is a danger, especially when travelling. You might forget to place your candle far from your bed, or to check that it is properly snuffed, and regrets will be too late after the inn has burned to the ground. Drunken travellers fall easy prey to wolves of all kinds, which might wear beast's fur or fancy velvets but which are alike in their desire to fleece you.

'I like 'wolves of all kinds' and 'fleece'. That is well found.'

'Thank you,' said Estela.

When boarding at an inn, look well at the casks from which your wine is served, that they are oak, clean and free of insects. If you see any specks in your wine, drink it not. Breathe in the wine smell and if there is a hint of vinegar, drink it not. Add sweet water to the wine to maintain a clear head and if you require heat, crushed savory and a spoonful of honey will balance the humours, which suffer from the fatigue and unaccustomed food caused by a journey.

'You should write about Master Taverner, as an example of drink's evil consequences, with his wine-red face and nose like a knobbled oak trunk,' observed Dragonetz. 'Not to mention his habit of drinking half of each jug he served. Never have I seen such short measures!'

Unable to stay quiet any longer, John Halfpenny added, 'Short measure be a good topic to make a traveller wise. I can tell you of the different coins and how men are cheated by them while travelling! Not one false penny reached my scrip in all the journey between London and Marselha! But you must know what you're looking for.' He tapped his nose knowingly, then his eyes darted from Dragonetz to Estela, worried he'd overstepped the mark.

On the road, all companions were equal and all knowledge shared. 'I would gladly hear your stories,' Estela told the moneyer, 'and learn all you can tell, whether of people, place or goods.'

And so, useful information on the different monies of Christendom, and how to tell false from true, was added to *The Wise Traveller*.

Just as no false coin could be slipped past John Halfpenny, so innkeepers had no chance of gulling Dragonetz with a spavined nag. He read this particular section with great interest.

Horses
Changing horses will enable you to make a long journey more quickly but beware! Innkeepers are untrustworthy and if you are not to lose time because of an unsound mount, you must check its quality, even more carefully than if you were buying the horse.

A horse has sixteen attributes. Three like a fox: short, straight ears; clean, healthy skin and a stiff brush tail. Four like a hare: a fine head, alertness, suppleness and a rapid gait. Four like cattle: wide haunches, a big belly, protruding eyes and low-set legs. Three like a donkey: good feet, strong spine and a good character. And four like a young girl; a beautiful mane, a well-formed chest, defined waist and large buttocks.

'Did I say that?' asked Dragonetz. '*the qualities of a young girl, large buttocks?*'

'Yes, you did.'

'If I'd known you were going to quote me, I would have chosen my words more carefully.'

'You know more about horses than I do. I try to quote experts when I can. Even if their language can be a little too colourful.'

'This is a bit general. You'll have to write an extra section about Arabian horses like Sadeek. They're very different from those beasts.' He gestured at the large-buttocked hired mares, grazing peacefully.

'The book is not all about horses. It's a travel guide.'

He read on.

You can tell a horse's age up until he is seven years old by the formation of his teeth. If he is past seven and without defect, then none will appear.

''Tis well I'm not a horse,' John Halfpenny cackled, displaying his blackened smile.

Between inns, they asked basic provisions from homesteads and farms and sometimes offered small services in return. John Halfpenny repaired a cart; Estela brewed rosemary tea for a farmer's pregnant wife to encourage labour; Dragonetz chopped wood for an old man who had but daughters.

Essential Purchases when Voyaging
Avoid paying an innkeeper for anything other than essential wine, horses and lodging as he will surely charge you double what you would pay a peasant for foodstuffs or emergency replacement of provisions.

'You could have mentioned his nose,' commented Dragonetz, disappointed.

'The wise traveller might go nowhere near that particular tavern,' Estela pointed out.

'Wouldn't be wise if he did,' was John Halfpenny's contribution.

Should your boot be worn through, you should seek a peasant of your size, with sturdy boots, and give him coin or barter to have the cobbler repair your boot. You should then take his boots thereby avoiding time lost waiting for the mending of boots. He will appreciate the quality of boots you leave for him and he will welcome future travellers.

A wise traveller will have packed goods likely to be of use to those he will meet on the journey, in case services or goods are needed in return. Suitable goods which take up little space are buttons, nails, ribbons, dried fruit, and spices. Coins, gold and jewels enable you to carry much wealth, but are easy to steal, and too valuable for daily transactions.

If you can do a man service by your labour or your skill, this is the best form of payment and can be carried wherever you go, without adding weight to your pack. However, doing such service will take time so the wise traveller will consider the journey to be as important as the destination in his life's path. No opportunity to do service can be a wrong choice.

'I sound like Malik!' Estela looked startled at her own words.

'That is no bad thing,' said Dragonetz. 'And they are good words. A good thought.'

'Maybe, there is more than one way to be a good woman.' Estela's eyebrows were knitted in a frown.

'Maybe,' said Dragonetz, gently.

The longer the journey, the stranger it feels to reach its end. It was as if they were blown by a magical wind, transported in their own rhythm, while groups of people came into their ken and went beyond or behind them. Sometimes they travelled with company, and sometimes they went faster, leaving others behind. Sometimes inns came to them, occasionally a town but nothing changed the essence of their day, riding, the three of them.

When they rested among trees, with no onlookers, Estela practised throwing her dagger, appraised by the two men. She would name her target or mark a spot on the tree, measure a distance by paces, and throw.

'She be good,' observed John Halfpenny, as the knife flew in an arc from twenty paces, to land straight and true in the red circle on the willow trunk. While travelling, Estela's make-up was worn more frequently by trees than by its mistress.

'Learnt as a child,' explained Dragonetz. 'She could aim within two inches of my head every time and never hit me.'

'I don't believe you!' said Halfpenny at the same time as Estela said, 'Dragonetz!' Too late. Dragonetz had made himself comfortable, lounging against the tree.

'Here,' he suggested pointing to a spot above his head.

'Move your hand then!' she told him, assessing the throw. Then she shook her head. 'I'd kill you,' she told him. 'You're too tall for me to be sure. An upward trajectory is more difficult to control.' She thought a moment and instructed him, 'On your knees!'

'My cruel Lady,' he hammed, dropping to his knees and waving his arms like a lovesick swain.

'Arms by your sides and stop singing! Your head moves!'

'You don't have to–' objected Halfpenny feebly. 'I do believe you.' But the game had taken on a life of its own and the risk was part of the fun.

Dragonetz watched Estela count her paces away from the tree, away from him. She balanced the dagger, holding it in the light grip of an expert, forefinger stretched along the hilt, ready to slide as she let loose. Her arm swung in the hinged movement that powered the blade. Timing of release was everything. He felt rather than saw the moment the dagger flew and shut his eyes. There was barely time to realise how completely he trusted her before the vibration above his head told Dragonetz that Estela's strike was true.

'Now your turn,' Dragonetz challenged Halfpenny, with a gleam in his eyes.

'What be in it for me?' the little man asked.

'Your manhood!' Dragonetz clapped him cheerfully on the back.

'It's more likely I shall keep that if I don't stand before a thrown knife,' Halfpenny replied, adding, 'Not questioning your expertise my Lady.'

'Of course not!' Dragonetz said. 'But you are a man who requires motivation – I understand that.' He ignored the pleading looks coming his way from Estela. 'One denarius for playing target this time. And a diamond for you if you agree to target practice any time my Lady requires.' He saw the greed flare in Halfpenny's eyes. 'To be given to you when you leave our service to go to your family. Do we have an agreement?'

'If I survive, my Lord.' The moneyer went to kneel by the tree.

'You can stand,' Estela told him.

'Joy upon joy,' he said, but his misery was that of a comedian and his eyes danced with mischief, as fired up with the dangerous game as Dragonetz himself. In truth, it was an easy way to win the riches of a lifetime. Or die.

'If she kills you, your family shall have two diamonds. You have my word.'

'Just as well they don't know that then,' quipped Halfpenny, through the side of his mouth, watching Estela judge both distance and aim.

'Shut your eyes,' advised Dragonetz. 'The instinct to duck a weapon aimed at you is more likely to kill you than the weapon in this instance.'

Halfpenny didn't have to be asked twice.

Once more the dagger flew true, crumbling bark into the hair of its human target as it quivered in the trunk, inches above him.

'I do think I've pissed myself,' observed Halfpenny but his companions ignored him.

Estela was flushed with pride as she reclaimed her dagger and checked the blade.

'I need a wet stone,' she said.

'We'll look for one at the next river we cross,' agreed Dragonetz, 'and sharpen all the blades.'

'That will make me feel much better,' said Halfpenny. 'I will feel better still if there are no trees from here on.'

He did not get his wish. However, he *did* gain several denarii and provide much amusement for Dragonetz, who pointed out several times that Estela's skills could be useful on the road. And unexpected. She would be their secret weapon.

John Halfpenny took every opportunity to glean information from people heading south. He explained to one and all that he was heading home to England and wanted to know how the land lay. His working man's clothes and foreign accent testified to the truth of his story, and he relayed the gossip he acquired to Dragonetz and Estela. Thus, they learned that while Aliénor was in Angers, her husband Henri was once more fighting on English soil to claim his crown.

Increasing numbers of folk warned that another town approached or rather, as Dragonetz forced himself to realise, *they* were about to enter a town. Not just any town. They had reached Angers. Where a fiery Queen awaited their arrival, and where they must throw off the simplicity of travel for the sophistication of court.

Estela was adamant. 'Before you announce our arrival to anyone, I want new clothes and a bath! I am not attending court like this and you are not going without me.'

Lodgings

The advantage of lodging on the ground floor of an inn is that a bath can easily be brought to your room and the hot water required will not have lost its heat during a journey upstairs. Servants will more readily replenish the water should you wish to restore your aching body after a long journey. The wise traveller will have packed a small bottle of lavender oil and will add three drops of this healing medicament to the water, to soothe muscles, prevent infection should there be any minor cuts acquired on the road, and to perfume the body.

A change of clothing is desirable as it is quite likely that you have spent weeks, nay months, in the same riding attire. If you have two days' grace in one lodging, the soiled garments can be now be given to the washerwoman.

Instruct that no starch should be used as little is more uncomfortable on horseback than stiff clothing. When these garments are returned, clean and dry, fold them neatly, pressing out all air to make them as small as possible and pack them carefully in your saddlebag. There is no knowing how soon you will be travelling again, or with how little notice.

CHAPTER ELEVEN

'What is she doing here?' Aliénor demanded, two hectic spots of colour in her white cheeks.

Not make-up, decided Estela, risking a glance upwards, assessing the full belly and breasts that could not be hidden by the Duchesse's voluminous gown. *Not just Duchesse but Queen again*, Estela reminded herself, and like all queens, she wanted an heir. This time for England, not for France. The reason for Aliénor's seclusion in Angers was reaching full term, if Estela was any judge. But that was not the reason for her anger. Estela and Dragonetz remained on their knees, eyes on the stone flags.

The question had been flung at Dragonetz but, if she did nothing, Estela could see herself being banished from the ante-chamber and that was *not* going to happen if she could help it. Heaven knew what decisions would be taken without her in a private exchange between Dragonetz and Aliénor.

'My Lady,' she said softly, 'I bear witness to my Lord Dragonetz' loyalty in your service. He is not, and never was, an oath-breaker.' She peeked up at Aliénor but the Queen's gaze was fixed on Dragonetz, burning holes in him.

He said nothing.

'I needed you and you didn't come!' Aliénor's voice cracked, as if she were an ordinary woman. But she wasn't.

Regal, she continued, 'The messenger who never found you has received the payment he merits.' Estela shivered. 'But you should have made it your business to know what was happening in Aquitaine! Instead, you were seduced by Provence and forgot about us.'

Dragonetz opened his mouth to speak but was silenced with one gesture. 'No, there is nothing you can say. But you can act. I have summoned you here because I have a use for you.'

Not *because I need you*. Estela's knees could feel the stone's cold through the linen of her new gown. What must it be like if you were old and had audience with Aliénor? Would she show pity for aching knees? Estela sneaked another look at the Queen's face. The lines had hardened in the last three years. Strands of unruly red hair rebelled against the demure coif but the late stages of pregnancy added to an impression of goodwife. No sign of the passionate crusader or of 'the whore of Antioch'. But no sign of pity either. *A woman can be many things in one life-time.*

As if sensing Estela's thoughts, or perhaps the babe's movements, Aliénor put her hand on her belly in that protective gesture common to all pregnant women, and said, 'You may stand.'

She herself was seated in a carved wooden chair with arms, a chair for a queen. Estela pictured another Aliénor on a different throne. *The birthing chair makes all women queens and all queens women.* Her knees thanked her as she flexed them, standing, but carefully thinking herself invisible so there was no further suggestion that she leave the audience.

Aliénor spoke only to Dragonetz. 'The King my husband is in England to claim his crown. This he will do. And we will make our kingdom great so that my son's fame will be trumpeted throughout Christendom.'

If it's a boy this time, thought Estela, remembering the disappointment of Aliénor's two previous babies, both daughters. At least Petronilla had never been considered a disappointment.

'Do you remember Bledri coming to our court?'

Dragonetz nodded. 'The bard from Gwalia? With tales of knights and monsters?'

'Yes. He told me much about his country and its people.' She hesitated, which was unusual enough to make Estela concentrate hard and keep very still. 'I believe that the King underestimates the importance of Gwalia. He has many concerns, and he sees the Welsh as weak barbarians easily kept in place by the Marcher Lords. This is not the picture Bledri painted.

Barbarians or not, the Welsh leaders could be important allies – or enemies – once we take our place on the throne of England. I want you to go to the leader in the south of Gwalia, and win him to Henri's cause. The north is already predisposed to support us but the south could become a thorn in Henri's side. Make yourself useful so that your counsel is trusted by them, win them to our cause. Find out all you can and report back to me.'

There was stunned silence.

Estela bit her tongue. She must not speak when Dragonetz was being asked – no, ordered – to give service to his Liege. She knew how much it would mean to him to clear his name of that accusation, oath-breaker, which clung to him even though it was untrue. Only Aliénor's favour could restore his honour in his own country. But a voyage to the Isles of Albion? Where griffins and dragons lurked? He would need an army of three hundred men at least. Whatever the practicalities, he could not say no, and her heart sank.

'I am yours to command,' Dragonetz said, as he must, without hesitation. He knelt and kissed Aliénor's hand. 'I will return to Zaragoza and organize an army. I'm sure the Comte de Barcelone will allow me a hundred mercenaries, in addition to my men.' He was calculating the total. 'How many do you give me?'

'None,' replied the Queen. 'My husband would never condone such a venture nor such expenditure.' Was there bit*terness? Already?* 'You go as a troubadour to visit a people famed for their music. As such, you will be made welcome. You were taken by a longing to visit the land of Bledri's legends or some such romantic sentiment.' Aliénor waved an airy hand as she condemned Dragonetz to a solitary quest more dangerous than any pilgrimage.

'As a spy, then,' stated Dragonetz, without any inflexion. 'So be it. I shall 'make myself useful' and try to win these men to your – our – cause.'

'Don't try, Dragonetz. Succeed or stay there.'

Estela tasted blood from biting her lip but she kept her peace.

Dragonetz merely replied, 'I shall escort my Lady back to Zaragoza and then embark by sea for wherever takes me closest to your destination. I will need some more details from you.'

'No,' said Aliénor. 'You must go now. And I will arrange for your Lady's return home. She must be eager to see her child once more.'

Musca. Estela looked at her lover's set jaw, imagined him riding away, leaving her again. Imagined going home, to Musca's dimpled grin, Nici chasing his tail, her dispensary, proper bathing. *Musca.* Dragonetz was his own man, a warrior who always came home. She'd accepted that before. Why should this time be any different?

'You may leave us to prepare for your journey, while Dragonetz and I talk politics,' said the Queen, the woman who'd left her own toddler to lead Aquitaine's armies to the Holy Land.

It hurt more than her knees, but Estela knelt once more. 'My Lady, I owe you a debt that can only be paid by offering you the same service you ask of Dragonetz. I beg you to hear me out!'

Estela could only imagine the oaths that her lover was swearing, none of them fit for his Liege's ears and she was grateful he couldn't speak his mind. While he was working out what he *could* say politely, Aliénor nodded for her to continue.

'You rescued me, you saved my life and you gave me a noble position, outside the control of those who wished me harm, and now I have the chance to repay you. Surely you will honour me by accepting my service?' She rushed on, wanting to make her points before either of the others cut her off. 'I am the troubadour you allowed me to become, not without reputation, and if I travel with

Dragonetz it will be obvious even to suspicious minds that our journey is not military in objective. I also have healing skills, which could be useful.

And,' she finished, 'my child is but young, the same age as when you put duty before your little one's need of you, and you took the cross. My son is well cared for, and if I can serve the realm, then a few months' absence will be as nothing.' *There!* Dragonetz could hardly argue that she should be with Musca or he'd be insulting Aliénor. His drawn brows suggested he knew that and was not happy.

'So be it.' Aliénor wasted no more words on such a trivial matter, accepted Estela's kiss of fealty and motioned her to stand. 'Go you both. You leave tomorrow and ride to Barfleur, where a boat is waiting. The captain or his men can no doubt tell you how to continue the journey but you should seek the rulers of Cantref Mawr, the son of Gruffudd ap Rhys, in south Gwalia. Avoid the Marcher Lords or you will have no welcome from the Welsh. My husband knows well enough the bellicose disposition of the barons – they are not your affair.'

'The more we know, the better, if we are travelling in this land,' Dragonetz pointed out and Aliénor told them what she knew, or what she chose to tell, of relationships in her new kingdom. She was old in statecraft, heiress to Aquitaine from birth and Queen of France by her first marriage, and her depiction of Albion was an eye-opener to Estela. No innocent in politics herself, Estela knew nothing of the north, and if half of what she heard were true, dragons and griffins would be the least of their problems.

When they were finally dismissed, Dragonetz asked, 'Would you like your troubadour to sing for you tonight?' He indicated Estela. 'Or both your troubadours?'

Aliénor stood and, from the dais, was tall enough to look the knight in the eyes as she told him, 'I have a new troubadour. I replaced you with somebody better.'

Dragonetz took the hit without any change in demeanor, bowed, took Estela's arm and they left.

As soon as the door swung to behind them, they looked at each other and said, 'Ventadorn!'

'So, you shall get the chance to hear your favourite troubadour,' Dragonetz teased.

'It has been a long time since I languished for a minstrel of quality,' she responded in kind.

He drew her into a dark recess, kissed her fiercely on the mouth. 'Are you languishing yet?' he asked her, low, urgent.

She took his face between her hands, saw the shadows of his eyes, his cheekbones. She traced the tilt of his mouth but it was no longer smiling. 'I know you're angry,' she whispered. 'But in a few years Musca will need a father more than a mother. You are more likely to come back from this alive if I am there, to make you seem harmless, to tend to you if you are ill or wounded. And I can't bear you going off again without me. Not so soon after...'

He trapped her hands in his own, pulled her to him. 'You think I'm harmless when you're with me?' he said. 'Well, my Lady, you have a lot to learn.'

A coughing fit alerted them to people coming their way and they separated, to walk sedately across the rooftop. If Estela was a little flushed as she passed a gaggle of Aliénor's ladies inside the castle, the dark passageways left nobody the wiser.

Dragonetz led her up one flight of spiral stairs to a doorway. She gasped as the door swung open onto the castle gardens, a green refuge above the hurly-burly below.

An audience with a queen and a garden: but where the gardens in the Palace of Joy had pebbled patterns and channeled water, Angers had squares hedged by rosemary, filled by roses in bare earth, flouncing their scarlet and vermilion.

She breathed in the heady sweetness. 'The roses of Provence are the best for placing amongst clothes,' she murmured, 'when dried in August and sieved so that the worms fall through the holes.'

Dragonetz took her hands. 'This is no rose harvest, Estela, and the worms can kill. I shall worry about you all the time.'

'We had this conversation in Zaragoza. If I don't go, *I* shall worry about *you* all the time. And we are safer together. I meant what I said to Aliénor.'

He shook his head but more in exasperation than in denial. He was not going to naysay her. Her complaint that she had been treated as a child must have made an impression. 'It is another ten days on horseback.' He paused. 'And a sea crossing from Barfleur. I've heard the English Sea is beset with storms, choppy seas...'

Estela's stomach roiled just at the thought. 'Then I will get used to rough seas,' she said, remembering more of the Gyptian's forked words. *A straight path until you cross the sea.* Maybe the sea voyage from Marselha to Barcelone had not been what the cards foretold. *Not into calmer waters but into more troubles. Seas or troubles... real water. Then you will use Pathfinder to help make your choice. I see gold... no, not for you directly. Your lord should beware gold.*

Estela reached instinctively for the Runic brooch she wore as a buckle. Pathfinder, a gift from a Viking Prince, its runes suggesting the crossroads of life and its powers helping the bearer choose well. Nonsense, of course. All nonsense. But she wondered about the embroidered brocade she had left in Mary's Sanctuary in Zaragoza. And she thought about gold.

'Has Aliénor offered you gold for this mission?' she asked.

His puzzled look answered her. 'No. She is my Liege and has the right to demand service. Besides, we have gold enough.' He frowned. 'Do you feel we need more?'

'No, indeed,' she reassured him hastily. *You expect him to share his thoughts with you and yet you hide so much?* her conscience chid her. 'In truth,' she said, 'you remember the fortune-teller? The Gyptian I saw again in a cave in les Baux? Who told Hugues des Baux of his grand lineage and made him a happy man? I did not want to worry you with all that she said, about me, about us...'

And so she told him all: the prediction that he would be named Oath-breaker, how she'd dismissed it as impossible and yet, it had come true, in a fashion. She told him all the Gyptian's words and described her own find in the dark tunnel, the symbol that linked the fabric with her oud and a Moorish palace wall, her offering.

His face was dark, brooding. 'Why didn't you tell me?'

'You were busy with more important things. And I wanted to protect you from any worries.' *And deal with things myself* she thought. Having opened up, she couldn't stop without speaking her worst fear. 'What if there is something terrible, something I don't know about my parents? About my blood? Something awful that I have given to Musca without knowing? Something that would make it impossible for you and me?'

He laughed.

'It's not funny!' she told him.

'It is. There is *nothing* you could discover that would change who we are. What did you fear?'

'I don't know,' she admitted. 'That's the problem. I have no idea. What if...' she searched for horrible possibilities, 'what if we were brother and sister?'

'Now you mention it, we do think much alike on some matters...' His eyes danced and she glared at him for teasing her.

'If you'd met my father and mother, you would *know* how impossible that is,' he told her, 'but I agree that the Montbruns are capable of anything. Forget them! And forget the foolish sayings of a fortune-teller. Such people do but prey on our fears.'

'You're right.' She felt better for hearing her fears spoken aloud. They sounded foolish. Yet her fingers still traced the Pathfinder runes.

'John Halfpenny will be delighted,' Dragonetz observed. 'It seems we are going to England!'

'Gwalia,' Estela corrected.

'By way of England. No doubt the man will abandon us on his home shores.'

'I'm not sure what use a moneyer would be. We can hire a man.' Estela dismissed the comical foreigner as irrelevant, then winced as her finger caught an edge on the engraved gold of her brooch. 'Packing will be short work and then I can prepare myself for the evening's entertainment.'

'Make yourself beautiful to meet Ventadorn? Shall I need Talharcant?' Dragonetz enquired casually.

'You *will* need to be on your mettle,' Estela punned.

'Then I shall need practice with sword and sheath, my Lady.'

'Perhaps we can find an hour or two between packing and beautifying...'

CHAPTER TWELVE

Estela's table companion, a wine-merchant, was loud and irritating, much to Dragonetz' amusement. Not invited to the top table, they had found places as far from it as possible, the better to gossip freely. This was their chance to catch up on news and glut on good food before suffering shortage of both.

Sucking the meat from frog legs, the merchant showed gobbets of spittle as he told her, 'The best way to catch frogs is with a rod and line. Bait the hook with a little meat and hop! You'll get a basketful! You need to cut them down the middle, near the thighs. Gut them, of course.'

He paused to wipe his shining mouth on the back of his hand and helped himself to more legs. 'Cut off the feet, rinse them in cold water – and this is the real secret – soak them for a whole night in cold water. That's how these are so tender.' He smacked his lips. 'Then rinse them in tepid water, dry them with a cloth and roll them in flour. Fry them in goose fat and serve them in a bowl, sprinkled with spices.' He pointed at the bowl on the table in front of them, which was emptying rapidly, and then he helped himself to another pair of legs.

'Thank you,' said Estela, aware of the tilt to Dragonetz' mouth. 'A sophisticated man like you must meet many travellers from the north? Hear wondrous tales of the Isles of Albion?'

The merchant's face darkened. 'You can barely do business with them, so thick is their speech.'

'That must be very difficult for you,' Estela sympathised. 'But you manage to trade with them?'

He preened, nodded. 'Wool,' he told her, 'and salt. That's what they bring me so they can have my wines.'

'And,' she lowered her voice, 'is trade difficult while King Henri is not yet on the throne? I'm sure you know so much about what's really going on.'

'Our King,' he said loudly, then dropped his voice, 'between you and me, he could take ten years to reach the throne if he doesn't die of the bloody flux in the bogs where he keeps his armies, waiting. A wise man sends good cases of wine to Eustace as well as,' he raised his voice again, 'supporting King Henri and his armies.'

Estela frowned. 'I'm from the south. Who is Eustace?'

'The Usurper's nephew, his heir.' He must have seen that Estela was lost. 'The Usurper – King Stephen,' he whispered. Estela could well imagine that Stephen was not to be named 'King' in this Hall, despite the fact he'd ruled England as such for decades.

'A man must be careful which port he sends to, with which instructions, but there is money to be made from conflict.'

This was all very interesting to Estela but unfortunately the next course proved too strong a diversion for the merchant. The venison was mouth-watering; bloody and tender.

'You know the best time to hunt stag?' he asked her, chewing with relish. '*Mid-May, mid-head,* as they say, because the antlers are only half out. But the best time to hunt *is* from the fête de la Croix in May to the day of St Madeleine – the deer just get fatter and fatter. You *can* hunt right up to the fête de la Croix in September but then the season's over.'

Estela then suffered a detailed account of how to dismember a deer and serve its different parts and was grateful when the flagon of wine started her neighbour on a different track.

He took a slurp and then confided, 'This isn't red wine.'

Estela looked at the rose-coloured wine in her goblet and wondered if he was crazed.

He laughed. 'I know what you're thinking – but it *looks* red.'

'Well, yes,' Estela admitted.

'And it does!' he reassured her. 'But it is a white wine, *turned* red by powdered flowers.' Triumphant, he said, 'I know by the taste.'

'Which flowers,' asked Estela, genuinely interested now. She could write this up in her travel guide. Perhaps he wouldn't want to share his secrets? She need not have worried. Discretion had no chance against pride.

'Red flowers of the field,' he told her. 'Corncockle, nigella, hollyhock. Dry them, crush 'em to powder and slip 'em into white wine. Easy to do with one glass.' He shook his head in admiration at the work which had turned the contents of a hundred flagons from white to red.

Rose-coloured indeed, thought Estela, sipping, tasting different flavours now she knew what made the drink so light and floral. She managed to glean some more titbits about England and its ways but paid for the knowledge with much unwanted detail about jellying calves' trotters and setting blancmange.

She'd accepted that she could wring no more out of him that was useful when one of the top table rose to his feet, bowed to the Queen and took up a pose in a clear space under a sconce, where stool and lute awaited him. He wore a long, drab tunic, like that of a university student, brightened by a drape of green cloak, pinned on one side and edged in gold. His hair fell just below his shoulders in golden waves, a halo in the flickering torchlight.

'That's Bernart de Ventadorn,' her neighbour informed her, needlessly. No other musician would have such assurance at Aliénor's court. Except of course... She looked at her lover but he seemed merely curious about this troubadour who was 'better' than him. Maybe Aliénor no longer meant to him what she once did. Estela felt the little stab of jealousy and dismissed it.

Ventadorn had picked up his lute, all his attention on its notes as he tuned the strings, as if he were alone in the Great Hall. Estela judged him with a professional eye, noting his deft handling of the instrument and his audience. Rumour said he was a baker's son, allowed to learn a different trade in the chateau of Ventadorn, in the Limousin. There was no trace of his lowly origins in his clothes or demeanour. His talent and Aliénor had seen to that.

Rumour also said that he'd had to leave the chateau speedily, when the Lady of the household showed too much appreciation of the troubadour. Estela considered this aspect of his reputation with a more than professional interest. Ventadorn was of middling height but very slim and looked tall in his long tunic. He still had a boyish fineness of face, at odds with the severe scholar's cap he wore.

Estela judged that he was young enough to still assume garb that would make him appear older, and talented enough that he could forget such posturing when he performed. She hoped so. And yes, he was a pretty enough boy to justify the rumours about him and an equally young, pretty castellan's wife. Especially when his themes were beautiful women and lovesick men.

Her neighbour was whispering again and she had to lean close to him, her ear against his mouth, to catch the words. 'They say he's *her* lover, you know. That he wrote the songs for her.'

Her mouth a perfect O of shock, Estela whispered back, 'Do you think it's true?'

'Not while she's pudding-shaped!'

'One reason she's here is because her mother-in-law won't have her in the same house, not when she's bedded father *and* son.' A coarse laugh spluttered into a cough and a swig of wine. Estela instinctively glanced at Dragonetz. How would he feel about such a slur on Aliénor's character? He was studiously looking the other way, involved in some deep conversation about roses with the lady beside him. Which probably meant that he'd heard every word. As Aliénor's vassal, he could not take part in such a conversation without taking his sword to the speaker, but she could, and it was all useful information.

If such confidences were his usual style when his tongue was loosened with wine, she wagered he'd not keep that tongue much longer. Aliénor didn't hesitate when an example was needed. Estela shivered. She'd come close to being one of Aliénor's examples, on their first encounter.

The merchant took her shudder as the horror natural at such lewd behaviour and he clarified, 'Not at the same time, of course, but you can understand a wife wouldn't take too kindly to her son marrying his father's whore!' The merchant gave another coarse laugh and was shushed by those around, as Ventadorn finished tuning his lute, and prepared himself to begin.

Undeterred, Estela's neighbour continued, sotto voce, 'Mark my words, she bet on the wrong horse if she thinks she can keep her pet when Henri returns. *If* her husband comes home, the troubadour will be playing his instrument somewhere far away! If he doesn't, well then!' was the cryptic prediction.

Ventadorn struck a pose, one green, leather-clad slipper pointed forward, ready to tap the rhythm. Then he opened his mouth and Estela was swept into the magic of song. His voice was sweeter and higher than she'd imagined, very different from Dragonetz' baritone.

Songs new to Estela overwhelmed her senses. Disconnected phrases lingered, *disinherited by love* or *madder than he who sows in sand*, imprinting themselves on her memory. Double meanings made her smile; a clever rhyme pleased her. She would seek copies of the songs she liked and practise them until she made them part of her own repertoire.

When Ventadorn sang the lyrics familiar to her, she mouthed every word, appreciating where the stress or the mood fell differently from her own interpretation.

'Genius,' she murmured, when the troubadour bowed several times to his audience and waited for those who wished to speak to him and show their appreciation personally. Estela wished. She was out of her seat and hovering as close to Ventadorn as she could get, as she had years earlier with Marcabru.

Her height gave her the advantage, she told herself, when –

wonderful! – Ventadorn noticed her and summoned her to his side with a wave of his hand.

'That was a magistral performance of such beautiful songs!' she told him, from the heart, earning a dazzling smile.

'I'm glad I pleased such a beautiful woman,' he told her, taking her hand and holding it to his lips. 'When I least expect inspiration, there you are, standing before me. Miracle!'

Estela flushed, not unhappy with such attention, but she would have little time with such a master, and no intention of wasting it on flirtation. 'The echo of *no sai on* is so clever, fits with the allusions to Narcissus and placed as a *cobla* then the *tornada*, itself an echo – genius!'

Again, that winning smile. He released her hand with a sigh. 'Ah, I am doomed to sigh in vain and give my heart where there can be no hope. Beautiful stranger, your words tell me that you already have a lover, a troubadour of some renown, is that not so?'

'Well, yes,' said Estela, 'but–'

'But he asked you to praise me on his behalf. I guessed as much!'

Estela flushed and this time not from being paid compliments. She tried again to find out some of the technical detail she wanted. Perhaps if she showed understanding of the themes first? Then approached the meter indirectly? 'The fool on the bridge,' she began, 'another marvellous image. The way he holds the high ground, is not willing to get down from his high horse – you imply so much for those who know the old story, without spelling it out.'

Those wishing to speak to Ventadorn were growing impatient with Estela for hogging his attention and she received at least one 'accidental' elbow in the ribs as people, mostly women, jostled to get past her.

The troubadour was no longer smiling. Indeed, his brows were knit in a petulant frown as he looked past Estela. 'You must tell your gallant that he is quite wrong. He has quite missed the point. Sometimes I wonder why I write at all when people have not the wit to understand my lines! Excuse me, I have others seeking a word.' He cast his smile wider, bestowing the vision of even, white teeth equally on his admirers.

He focused briefly on Estela again, or rather on her cleavage, his golden voice a caress again. 'It seems we are both unlucky in love, my Lady. Should you wish instruction in the art of song, from a real expert, I would be happy to deploy my instrument in your service.'

Luckily, some neat footwork, by one of the most determined admirers, caught Estela off-balance even more than had the troubadour's remarks. Before she could recover and speak her mind (which might involve destroying tableware) she had been forced to the back of the crowd around Ventadorn. Still flushed, she returned to her place at table, where Dragonetz had not moved, unless it was to stretch out his long legs and cross them at the ankles.

Real boots, Estela noted with approval, *not cross-laced slippers but black boots. Dusty, serviceable, made for adventures and made to last.*

'How,' she asked him, 'can such a gifted troubadour be such a donkey's arse of a man?'

Dragonetz' smile was not only one to melt gaggles of admiring geese; it was genuine. And it was for her. 'I don't need Talharcant?' he enquired gently.

'I would dearly like to see you take that boy across your lap and use the flat of your blade on him,' she admitted.

'But?' he enquired.

'But there are some battles I must either fight myself or walk away from.'

'Women's battles?'

So, he *had* been watching and understood quite enough of what was going on! 'You didn't come and rescue me?'

'I had a better view from here.' His gaze raked her from top to toe and returned to meet her eyes. 'He's good. I liked three of the songs very well so I allowed him three times.'

'Three times?'

'He could kiss your hand three times before I considered my honour slighted. Then you would have had your wish regarding the flat of my blade and the donkey's arse.' He shrugged.

'Which three?' Estela asked. Dragonetz' response led to a deep discussion of *canzos, coblas* and *tensos* that made Estela quite forget that Ventadorn was even in the Hall.

'He's good. But he's not better,' she told her lover, much later that night.

'Because?'

'Because he cares only about how good he is. He could never partner somebody. Nor teach somebody.'

'Perhaps he merely lacks maturity, and an experienced tutor,' suggested Dragonetz, wickedly.

'Let me show you just how mature I have become, under your tuition!' replied Estela, matching actions to words.

CHAPTER THIRTEEN

Somewhere between Angers and Reims, when John Halfpenny was out of hearing, Estela asked Dragonetz, 'Do you believe it of Aliénor?'

'It's possible,' he replied, without needing time to think.

'Do you care?' she risked.

'No.' Then he paused and thought. 'Not for myself,' he amended, smiling. 'I've been replaced by the donkey's arse. But such allegations are not good for Aquitaine – or England. I wonder what they will make of their new queen – if Henri wins.'

What indeed, Estela wondered. And what did Henri think of his wife's reputation? Would he find it less entertaining after they were married than before he gained Aquitaine? Aliénor's belly would decide much about her status. A son would bring her the respect she'd never had as Queen of France and mother of two daughters.

Musca. The pangs of separation clawed at Estela again and once more she assuaged her guilt by writing her journal.

The Ideal Traveller

Travel is of its nature arduous, trying, and wondrous, by turns. You will meet men of all persuasions and humours, and travelling companions who will test your patience and your goodwill. Should you hold to opinions that you wish to enforce without contradiction throughout your travels, travel will bring on an excess of choler, which should be combatted by carrying the stone chalcedony, which is strong against wrath. A person prone to such imbalance is not best suited to travel and will be healthier for remaining in a familiar land.

Hardships are likely to include foul weather, lameness in a pack-donkey or toll-brutes with stout sticks, who try to extort coin from unwary pilgrims and travellers. A companion who can impose on such criminals by his fighting strength, skill and an even stouter stick or other weapon, is to be recommended. Travelling in a large party has advantages for those who have the patience required to endure, or even enjoy, the variety of human faiths and frailties.

Wonders there will be aplenty for those open in spirit, in all aspects of man's work and of nature's. I have crossed mountains where wolves howled and bears shambled into the forests with their young.

In the Frankish north, I have seen artisans' and shopkeepers' houses exquisite as paintings, with exteriors of black beams across white walls bearing wrought iron signs for carpenter or cobbler.

At table, I have been served fish big as Jonah's whale and peacock that was surely stolen from Juno, so heavenly its taste.

Such adventures leave a trace on your soul so that all travel is a pilgrimage, if you treat it as such.

John Halfpenny was in high spirits at the prospect of going home at last and Estela pumped him for information about the Isles of Albion. He confessed he had never been into the wilds of Gwalia, which was a disappointment, but he could talk for England about small beer, wool and coins.

Estela grew bored listening to the superior quality of English sheep and wool but noted the importance for trade. She was more interested in coins, because of what they showed about politics, and the subject allowed her to follow her own agenda.

'Gold,' she began. 'The gold coins of England. I'd love to hear all about them.'

The Mintmaster looked at her, open-eyed with shock at her ignorance. 'There be none,' he told her. 'English mintmasters do have more sense! Gold's a terrible metal to work with and far too valuable for trading use. You put in all that work to make coins and all they be good for – *if* they turn out all right – be for stashing in some lord's treasure hoard. I want my work in the marketplace, changing hands every day and lasting forever! No, silver be the metal for coins, every time. And weighed true!'

'Oh,' was all Estela could say, disappointed. Whatever the Gyptian's prophecy meant would be no clearer from listening to John Halfpenny. Not that the prophecy meant anything.

There was no polite way to ask the other question of interest. 'What did you do?' she asked. 'Why did you have to leave the country?'

'Stephen's men caught up with me.' Estela noted that King Stephen had no title in the moneyer's eyes, so he'd been for Matilda in the wars – which meant he would support her son, Henri.

'The barons all grabbed what they could while Stephen and the Queen fought their wars and each of them did want his own head on his own coins. I had a family... I made coins for whoever forced me. Until Stephen's men found out. I had warning and ran.'

'If they didn't catch you making them, how did they know you were the moneyer.'

'Because I was stupid. I rushed the work and did not blunder my name enough.'

'Blunder?'

'Beat out the shape.'

'What will you do when you go back?'

'Find my family.' There was a silence. Both knew the darker possibilities. 'When Henri's king, I'll go back to Winchester – the King's Mint – and offer him my services. I'll recall every one of those damned irregular coins and hammer my name out of them all! And I'll deface all those which depict Stephen!'

For the first time, Estela saw beyond the funny little foreigner to a proud artisan, whose work had pleased kings. Before disgrace, forgery and dungeons.

His eyes guarded shadows. When Estela had touched him to wake him or call him for food, he flinched instinctively. She'd become more careful, spoke to him first.

'What if he loses? What if Stephen wins?' The open road was as good a place to talk treason as any.

A shrug. 'He's weak. Henri will win.'

'What about Stephen's sons?'

'They are their father's sons. They won't withstand Henri. I'd bet all my money on Henri for king.' He gave a weak smile at the bad joke.

What if he loses? Like his mother had. She and Dragonetz would be far from home, at the mercy of some barbaric Welsh prince, surrounded by hostile Marcher Lords, in a land at war with itself.

She kicked herself, mentally. They would be in exactly the same situation if Henri won.

Money

As you travel north, you will observe different types of coin in use, designated by a local personage on one side and a symbolic design, such as a cross, on the reverse, sometimes with the name of the moneyer and mint. The further coins travel, the more they are regarded with suspicion, so you would be wise to exchange goods or coin as you travel, to ensure that you always have money from a location that can be recognized by those you trade with.

Forgery is a common scourge and if you do not know the coinage, you will not realise that a coin is lightweight, until it breaks or is rejected by men who know their coins better.

In England, silver pennies are customary and a part coin is not to be shunned. Halfpennies and quarters are cut deliberately to make smaller denominations, and are good currency, or 'sterling' as English money is named. Englishmen are proud of their coinage and the wise traveller will hide any surprise over the lack of gold dirhams or their like.

John Halfpenny approved Estela's latest entry and she thought about his name, now she knew more about English coins. A small man, a moneyer: of course.

Ten days' riding took them to their destination: Barfleur. Dragonetz enthused about the fleecy clouds scudding across blue skies, not for their poetry but for their practicality. A fair wind and fine weather would let them leave as soon as captain and ship were ready. Estela followed Dragonetz' enthusiasm to the harbour: watched the boats bobbing; the glitter of wakes and waves, breaking against wooden hulls; ropes tugging taut, longing to free themselves. Old timbers creaked and the seagulls screamed their greed.

Estela brushed strands of hair from her eyes, smelled brine, waited with John Halfpenny. Dragonetz returned from his errand, energized by action, and accompanied by a man who could only be the captain. Weather-beaten as old oak, any age between twenty and fifty, the captain was in animated conversation with Dragonetz, when they reached Estela.

'My Lady,' the man bowed. Estela had grown used to the northern Frankish but this accent was new to her.

'Captain Robert is an Englishman.' Dragonetz introduced him. 'And that is our vessel.'

Just when Estela thought she'd steeled herself for the voyage, her stomach took off with the seagulls. Their vessel was not a ship; it was a boat. As far as Estela was concerned, they might as well cross the seas in a bathtub, for all the protection these few bits of wood offered.

Unable to speak, Estela nodded regally to the captain and allowed herself to be helped aboard the floating prison. She chewed doggedly on the cloves she'd brought, and thought only of the last entry in her journal. It was to be the last she'd write for two very long days.

Travelling by Sea
Those unfortunate enough to be affected by motion sickness should take

preventative measures. You must fast before your voyage, consuming only bitter fruits such as quince, orange and pomegranate. Sweetmeats or seeds which encourage belching are also desirable.

Chewing on cloves or nutmeg helps reduce the smell of the sea and its effect.

During the voyage, the wise traveller will sit upright, only moving his head with the motion of the ship, and holding tightly to the supports.

Should vomiting occur, the person so affected should refrain from eating, other than the afore-mentioned bitter fruits, until the nausea has left him.

Dragonetz sat on a bench at the stern of the small cog, watching the white froth of the wake that trailed behind them in the murky water like a hairy star in a dark sky. Such a hairy star had presaged the doom of Harold of England. No doubt Estela's Gyptian would read such an omen and predict a new King of England.

Dragonetz needed no skills in divination to predict a new King of England. His mission would become not just suicidal but pointless otherwise. Risking death was part of a warrior's life but he preferred to do so for a cause that at least made sense to him. He had risked his life for a chimera too often in the crusade and he had grown used to sharing Ramon Berenguer's vision. Now he was fighting blind. And he was not just risking his own life.

He glanced at Estela, who had spent hours clutching the side, chewing as if her life depended upon it, and was now asleep in a blanket on the decks, overcome by exhaustion. This was no life for a lady, crouching to relieve herself in the pot she'd found, with only a blanket held in front of her for privacy. And yet she never complained. She just wrote her traveller's guide, for Musca. And she gained men's respect.

On first sight, the shipmen's gaze had lingered on her face and assessed her body, but their attitude changed to respect once Estela gave them directions about fruit and spices from the side of her mouth, while still chewing. Before the sea's motion had taken all her attention, she even marched to the trapdoor, insisted on looking into the hold, screwed her face up in horror and instructed them on how better to stack and secure the cargo of wine.

She pointed out that if all the barrels were stacked sideways, the next layer placed in the hollows of the one before, not only would they take less room and be more stable, but the wine would travel better for being laid sideways. Estela had indeed gleaned all she could from her dinner companion at Angers. There was much laughter at the idea of wine travelling well but the captain made his sailors do as Estela bid.

There was now room in the hold for twelve more butts of wine and the captain promised each of the ten shipmen his share of one such barrel, once they reached harbour, for having done the extra work. This made Estela extremely popular and, after ascertaining that the return cargo was indeed wool, she took the opportunity to lecture them on the importance of waterproof storage and how oiled sailcloth would do nicely. Then, her face took on a greenish hue and she took her place on a bench where she could lean over the side whenever nature required.

The oarsmen took the boat into open sea, the sail caught the wind and their departure was without hitch. Except from the viewpoint of a traveller for whom the sea itself *was* the hitch. Such was the respect that Estela had gained that when one sailor commented, 'Looks like the wine travels better than the lady,' he was frowned down by his shipmates.

Yes, Estela handled herself well, and Dragonetz knew he must draw deep on his self-control to be the match she deserved. He had not gained the scallop badge of the pilgrim who reached Santiago but by God, he walked an even harder path! He was accustomed to risking his own life but risking Estela's was unthinkable.

Every day he asked himself why he had not forced her or tricked her into staying in Zaragoza, where she was safe. Every day he remembered her accusation that he treated her like a child, not a partner. And, in truth, he was starting to enjoy the adventure more for sharing it with his lover. In addition to the connection between them, she had skills that complemented his. As had Malik and Ramon. To find such a partnership with a woman was not what he'd been brought up to expect, but how could the future be shaped, if it was built on the past? Their mission was to shape the future and, if they defied convention, then so be it.

Which brought his thoughts, choppy as the sea, to the mission itself. Estela had asked him how he was going to persuade the Welsh lords to support Henri. 'Make myself indispensable,' he'd told her, 'then plant the seeds that grow into decisions'. How exactly he was going to do this, he had no idea whatsoever.

Meanwhile, he turned around to watch the large steering oar on the starboard side and the billowing sail. *God grant us a kind wind,* he prayed, and he wasn't just thinking of the journey to Gwalia. Once they reached the shore, there would be no steering oar.

CHAPTER FOURTEEN

The winds were too kind. The captain crossed himself as protection against the caprices of the weather gods. The shipmen rested and cracked lewd jokes, quietly if they were near the sleeping woman, while their oars lay at peace. Like all sailors, they spent time at sea planning what they would do on land, and how often. On land, they would feel the restless call of the waves.

John Halfpenny blended in, presumably lost in his own thoughts of land and homecoming. When he'd realised that they were heading directly for Gwalian soil, he'd been silent.

When Dragonetz asked what he meant to do, the moneyer replied, 'Travel inland with you, if I may, until I cross the road east. If the news be as I hope, I will head eastwards to Winchester.'

Dragonetz nodded. 'Your company will be useful.' Then the little man had curled up by a coil of rope, just a head in a brown blanket, and there he stayed. Whether asleep or awake, who could tell?

'Wyn.' The Captain called one of the men over to where he and Dragonetz dunked hardtack in small beer and chewed the softened biscuit. He was experienced enough in sea travel not to crack his teeth on the food which lived up to its many nicknames, *jaw breaker* and *dog's delight* among them.

He winced at the bitterness of the beer, however much weakened, and thought wistfully of the good Frankish wine below deck. Maybe he should ask for some of Estela's fruit, but that, too, was bitter. He sighed. He must get used to the beer, and much besides, but at least the biscuit was but for two days. He supposed it was easier to carry and store than fresh food for otherwise such a short voyage could have been well provisioned.

Agile as a pet monkey, the sailor clambered along the planks to join them, instinctively shifting his weight and balance so as to cause no lurching.

'Wyn is a Welshman,' the captain told Dragonetz. 'He can tell you what you want to know.'

And so Dragonetz passed his waking hours aboard by learning the names of the Welsh lords, their holdings and their enmities; a smattering of Welsh words; the popular songs and stories. It seemed the Welsh were even fonder of tales than song, and of poetry most of all. Praise-singers were highly esteemed, and no praise could be too extravagant for the lord who was its subject.

That was one notion which crossed the sea easily, thought Dragonetz. Perhaps if he composed verses about the local lords and Welsh heroes, he might find acceptance. He searched his memory for the songs that had reached him, of Arthur, and of the seer, Merlin, Myrddyn in Wyn's tongue.

Dragonetz would have to sing them in his own Occitan and it became clear to him that he would need a translator. The noble sons of Gwalia were civilised enough to speak Latin and Frankish, but not Arabic or Occitan. Amongst themselves they spoke this strange tongue that sounded like coughing, then a river flowing, then more coughing. The peasants spoke nothing else.

It would be useful if he and Estela could add local references to their songs, as they were accustomed to doing in more civilised courts, so Dragonetz asked what songs were popular in south Gwalia. Would the Captain let him have Wyn, Dragonetz wondered, as the Welshman span his favourite stories: tales of trickery, marriage and a magic bag that could never be filled. All the Welsh names were confusing but the image of the poor victim tricked into the bag was as vivid as Wyn smacking his lips with pleasure at the violence.

'A man should ask, *What is in the bag?* and the Lord will reply, *A badger!* Then the man may take a cudgel to the badger. And the only way to escape the bag is to say, *Lord, I merit not this treatment.*'

'They beat a man in a bag?' asked Dragonetz, trying to make sense of the moral in the tale.

'Only until he proved himself worthy of release. A man has to show his character and to know the right words,' Wyn told him with a sly look.

Trickery seemed to be regarded as a racial virtue, Dragonetz noted, and violence was an entertainment, whatever a man's rank.

'You should also know the prophecies of Myrddin, known as Merlin in the Latin tongue,' continued Wyn, in his storytelling voice. He spoke of dragons battling, red against white; of feast and famine; of the boar of Cornwall and the she-lynx of Normandie. How easy it was to read your own fate into these prophecies, thought Dragonetz, wondering at the origins of his own Occitan title. Would he one day be Lord Dragon and Musca be Dragonetz, Little Dragon? Could Dragonetz himself be the man who would come with a drum and a lute to calm the savagery of the lion?

If the prophecies set him dreaming and interpreting, what must their effect be on the Welsh Lords when they heard that the land would be returned to its former peoples.

Dragonetz was musing on the Ass born in an owl's nest, who became king and terrified the people with his braying, when land was spied.

Too soon for Dragonetz, and too slowly for Estela, the boat gained the shores of Gwalia and was run up onto a long, flat beach. among sand dunes and grassy tufts. They startled a skylark and Estela murmured the opening lines of the song she'd taught Dragonetz.

'Can vei la lauzeta mover
de joi sas alas contra.l rai.'

'When I see the lark beat its wings
with such joy against the sunbeam.'

She's recovering! thought Dragonetz, saying, 'I see little sign of sunbeams, my Lady.'

She smiled, as weakly as the pale rays fighting thick cloud in the skies above. But it was still a smile, just as the pale rays were all they would see of what should be mid-day sun. They sat on a tussock of grass, with their saddlebags beside them, while horses were fetched from wherever the nearest habitation lay. There was no sign of a settlement but the mounts duly appeared.

'Ponies,' observed Dragonetz.

'Sturdy Welsh stock,' Wyn told him, reacting to what he took as a criticism. Robert had acquired another shipman in the same place he'd hired the ponies and Wyn was indeed to accompany Dragonetz as guide and interpreter.

The boat was not staying in such a barren waste, but continuing westwards to a lively trading haven, and as soon as Dragonetz' party had been organised, the shipmen ran the vessel back to sea and it became a black dot on the horizon.

Wyn laid out their journey. They would ride a short distance to the mouth of the Tywi River, pay the toll and cross by ferry, then ride upriver to the town and castle of Caerfyrddin, known to the Franks as Maridunum. This stronghold was in the hands of the Lords of Deheubarth, Maredudd and Rhys, 'for the moment' Wyn added.

Estela gave Dragonetz an anxious look but all he could do was shrug. 'For the moment' was to become their way of life while they were in this realm.

The plan was sound and Wyn's knowledge of the geography and politics of south Gwalia was that of a native. So he could not be blamed when the party was ambushed after crossing the river and quickly overcome by a band of more than two score bandits. Trussed, hooded and tied to a pony whose sturdiness was likely to be sorely tried, Dragonetz suffered every rut in a poor road and was conscious of only one recurring thought. Whatever the wise traveller might have to say on the matter, he should *never* have allowed Estela to come with him.

When the jolting finally stopped, Dragonetz was unloaded like a bale of cloth and dumped on hard soil. Amid the jangling of bridles and steel, as men dismounted, he could also hear chickens, and women's voices. A community then, not just a robbers' den. The men jabbered in their tongue and he wished he knew what they were saying.

Authority had its own sound in any language, and he recognised an order, guessing its meaning when the sack over his head was ripped off. He rolled to a sitting position, legs and arms still roped. Estela was also tied and sitting, but looked unharmed – *thank God!* Her chin had a defiance he recognised but she glanced at him and held her peace. They understood one another. First, find out what they were up against.

The earthen floor was rustic but the high stone walls surrounding them were not. They were in the courtyard of a castle built in the Frankish style, the solid oak doors of the gatehouse closed and barred. This was no robbers' lair. Had they been brought to Caerfyrddin?

The man in command pointed at Dragonetz, barked another order and there was uproar, men laughing and holding their sides at the joke. The commander smiled too, his grin promising entertainment that Dragonetz did not expect to enjoy. He tested the bonds, felt for stones on the grass beneath him, any friction that he could use.

Before he could so much as rub a strand loose, a large sack was thrown over him, he was tumbled between two men and the sack tied. He regained a sitting position inside the sack. Probably used for flour, he observed, coughing from a flurry of white dust. At least they had not gagged him.

'Bore da,' he shouted, 'Good-day', recalling his brief Welsh lesson from Wyn. Where was Wyn, anyway? And Halfpenny?

The laughter was even more raucous, from which Dragonetz gathered that saying 'Good day' in their language was not enough to break the ice.

He desperately tried to remember words that *might* help. 'Thank you' did not seem appropriate but he could try, 'Adolwyn? Please?'

The only response to him shouting, 'Adolwyn,' was what seemed to be a question from one of the men. Then an answer from the commander.

Perhaps he had made an impression? If so, it was not the one he wanted. The sacking crashed into his ribs, wrapped around a cudgel. He curled up into a ball, protecting his head as best he could, reminded of something, but not able to bring it to mind.

Again, what sounded like the same question – from a different man this time – then the commander's set answer, and then the stick, hitting his back this time. Estela was shouting herself hoarse, telling them to stop, offering them money. They mocked her, copying her voice, enjoying themselves.

Dragonetz lifted his head enough to call again. He'd remembered the names of their lords. 'Lord Maredudd, Lord Rhys,' he yelled, and repeated the names like a prayer. The question, answer and stick came again, catching the side of his head. He curled up again.

And then, despite the pain, he remembered. Wyn had told him a tale of a magical bag and the man who was put in a bag for punishment, to be beaten with a stick. These men were playing the game of badger in the bag.

'What is in the bag?' asks a man.

'A badger!' replies the Lord.

Then the man takes a cudgel to the offending badger.

And the only way out is for the man to say...

'Lord, I merit not this treatment,' yelled Dragonetz in Latin and then in Frankish. 'Lord Maredudd! Lord Rhys!' He screamed in Latin, 'I merit not this treatment!'

There was silence. A different voice spoke in their tongue but no cudgel followed.

The commander spoke, argued, capitulated.

Somebody opened the bag, pulled it down around Dragonetz, who blinked in the daylight.

'I am Lord Rhys,' said the newcomer, speaking Frankish as good as Dragonetz' own, 'and this – he indicated the man Dragonetz thought of as 'the commander', 'is my brother, Lord Maredudd.'

The family likeness showed in their eyes, round and guileless blue, but where Maredudd was brown-haired, Rhys was honey-blonde, his beard shorter to hide its wispy fineness.

Maredudd spoke sharply to Rhys, in Welsh again, but Rhys shook his head, spoke Frankish so Dragonetz could understand.

'This is not a badger. This is a man who does not merit such treatment.' The disappointment among the men as one of their lords ended the game was palpable, but they put down their cudgels.

'A foreigner who knows the story of Rhiannon's cunning is rare indeed.' Rhys looked down at Dragonetz, who could feel the ropes chafing, see blood trickling from his wounds, but the danger was not over and he said nothing.

Estela was outraged. 'My Lord Rhys, and my Lord Maredudd, if you have any nobility at all, untie me and let me tend to my own Lord's wounds. We are troubadours from Provence and have travelled far to hear the music for which your court is famed. *This* is the welcome you offer!'

Rhys looked to his men. One of them brought Dragonetz' sword to his Lord.

'This is not a troubadour's sword,' Rhys pointed out.

'It is *this* troubadour's sword,' Dragonetz retorted. 'And if you bring my lute I will show you how I can handle both instruments. I heard that the lords of Deheubarth were also gifted in both poetry and battle.' He knew how smug she would be afterwards, if they had an afterwards, but he had to use any argument he could, so he added, 'Would I have brought my wife with me if I meant harm? She too is a noted troubadour who wished to learn from you and I now regret bringing her to such an uncouth people.' That much was true.

Rhys did not stop a man punching Dragonetz for his rash words and he heard Estela sob.

'My brother is right,' Rhys said. 'You must be tested.' Dragonetz weighed up his chances in a duel against either of the brothers. In his present condition the outcome was unpredictable, but he would take his chances. Before he could say so, Estela spoke again, controlling her voice.

'In the name of your mother and the women you hold dear, please untie me. I need a salve from the medicine box in my bags, to tend to my Lord's wounds. I am a healer, and maybe you could profit from my knowledge *if* you treat me well!'

The sudden silence warned of danger. Dragonetz had no idea what Estela had said to draw such anger, as Maredudd shouted something and even Rhys was heated in reply. When he addressed Estela, his clipped tones shook with suppressed rage.

'My mother was beheaded on a battlefield, by a Frankish coward, when I was five years old. What *she* would do with you would be whatever is best for our people. You know nothing of the courage and endurance of Welsh women, so hold your Frankish tongue.'

Estela held her tongue – thank God! – and Rhys turned his attention back to Dragonetz.

'Kill him and be done with it!' Maredudd's eyes blazed and he wanted Dragonetz to know what was said.

'A dead man is of no use,' replied Rhys, and then said something in Welsh. Maredudd nodded.

'The test is simple,' Rhys continued. 'I want a simple answer to a simple question and if your answer is wrong, you die. Do you support Henri Courtmantel or Stephen as King of England?'

'Henri.' Dragonetz spoke without pause. For all he knew, a pause could bring death and he knew nothing that would help him give the answer Rhys wanted. There was no change in the tense atmosphere but he was still alive, for the moment. Maredudd's glare had not wavered and Rhys' stare was equally fixed, unnerving.

'Then I have much news for you,' Rhys told him. 'but not good in your eyes. Henri is dead in a great battle for Wallingford Castle.' There was a ripple of surprise around the courtyard. Rhys had clearly brought back news fresh to the men gathered there.

The end to Aliénor's hopes of sitting on the English throne. The end to their mission and his own hope of redemption. Aliénor would have greater things on her mind. They could go home, return to Musca, thought Dragonetz, his eyes on the ground. If Rhys did let him live, which seemed unlikely now. If not, he might be executed here or handed over to Stephen's men.

'Spare my Lady,' Dragonetz asked. He heard Estela gasp as she had not done at the news of Henri's death.

Rhys ignored the plea and continued his scrutiny of Dragonetz. 'There's more,' he said. 'Henri's wife has produced a son.'

'A bitter joy!' Estela could not hold back her reaction. 'My poor Lady, to know the son she longed for just when his future is ripped to tatters.'

Dragonetz spoke, only for Estela. If these were his last moments, he would not dissemble. 'She will not let go. She has fought before – you should have seen her in the Holy Land – and she will fight to the death for her son's rights. When you leave here...' he paused. *When I'm dead.* 'Go to her, offer her service. Aquitaine will never desert her, and she is strong enough to hold Anjou while the baby grows. Musca,' his voice faltered, 'I'd like Musca to be knighted by his Liege of Aquitaine.'

'Then you'd better see to it,' Estela told him.

Maredudd was impatient at the exchange but Rhys calmed him with a gesture, frowned, seemed to come to a decision.

'Henri's death in battle *was* one rumour flying in the winds of war but it was not the truth,' Rhys told them. 'A crossroads was indeed reached in Wallingford, but it was Henri that won a truce. Stephen has named him heir, to end the wars.' The collective gasp at such news grew to a rumble. 'Quite a spectacle I believe. An army on either side of the Thames, with rival kings shouting terms to each other.'

'Why should I believe you, when you lie so easily?' Dragonetz demanded.

Rhys shrugged. 'Whether you believe or not, this is the truth.'

'And more news again,' Rhys continued, not taking his eyes off Dragonetz. 'Stephen's son Eustace is dead, in mysterious circumstances, just after Henri was named heir. He was not too happy with the truce by all accounts. It seems food can be more dangerous than fasting. How fortunate for Henri – to gain a son and lose a rival on the very same day.'

So much to take in and consider! But all better than the first 'news'. 'Stephen's other son?' asked Dragonetz. 'He must feel he has rights? And has lost them?'

'He is happy that there will be peace and that provision will be made for him. He is no warrior. Perhaps he'd also like to eat his dinner without fear.'

Dragonetz ignored the implied accusation against Henri and waited. He commended his soul to heaven, in case.

Rhys looked to his brother in unspoken query and it was Maredudd who gave the command. 'Free them.' They might differ in their views but the brothers worked together. Something else to consider, now that he had, apparently, survived his test.

Dragonetz rubbed the circulation back into his wrists, stood on shaky knees. He was taller than the Welshmen.

'Would you really have killed me if I'd declared for Stephen?' he asked.

'No,' replied Rhys, evenly, with splendid indifference to the irony of his response. 'I'd have killed you if you lied.'

Trickery is a virtue. Dragonetz wondered what had shown on his face of his reactions to Rhys' news, wondered whether he'd shown too much or not enough. Perhaps Estela's outburst, or the words between them, had made the difference. Such small things a man's life turned upon. Whatever the case, he was alive.

'A dead man is of no use,' he quoted Rhys' words to his brother. 'What did you say to my Lord Maredudd, in Welsh?'

'It is one of our sayings since our mother was betrayed by one she trusted. *A dead man is of no use; but a liar is only safe when dead.* If you lied, I'd have killed you.'

Estela had been freed and was already checking Dragonetz' wounds, tutting. 'Get me my medicine box from my saddlebags!' she demanded. 'And I want Wyn and John Halfpenny here, now – the men who were with us – so I can speak Welsh through Wyn and make sure our party are treated as they should be!' She glared at Maredudd.

'It's all right, wife,' Dragonetz told her, and saw her eyes fill with tears: delayed shock triggered by an endearment never used before. 'There has been a misunderstanding and all is well now.'

She turned on him, dashing the tears away with one hand. 'This is the last adventure you drag me on. You might not be a badger or a liar but you merit punishment!'

He smiled as best he could manage through a split lip. 'Willingly, good wife. Willingly.'

The men watching the spectacle might not have understood the words, but they got the gist of the situation well enough to guffaw and elbow each other. The mood changed again. *From the prospect of my being battlement décor, to a puppet-show of Noah and his wife*, thought Dragonetz, but he was glad to keep his head on his shoulders for another day. And he was sore. He was also wondering about the coincidence of Wyn telling him a tale of a badger in a bag. There had been many tales so perhaps it *was* a coincidence. But what if the Welshman had wanted him to show his character and his worth? Trickery is a virtue in Wales, he reminded himself, and Wyn was useful. But he could not be trusted.

Sharing a rush mattress in the Great Hall seemed like heaven to Estela, especially after a stomach-full of mutton stew, rustic but tasty, and flavoured by hunger. The stone walls echoed with snores and farts but Estela cared nothing for the crudity of her company if Dragonetz was beside her. His breath in sleep was even, helped by the tisane of hops and valerian she had given him. She laid her hand gently on his back, just to feel the warmth, be sure he was there, and she moved as far as she could manage to put some space between herself and her neighbour on the other side. She liked John Halfpenny well enough but unless the cold grew worse, she preferred to avoid the physical contact.

She was already recovering from the heart-stopping fear, and, unlike Dragonetz, physically she had suffered mere discomfort, so there was no point dwelling on how bad it could have been. What mattered was that they had done it! They were here, in one of the Welsh castles. Now all they had to do was to make themselves indispensable, give their political advice and go home. With such comforting thoughts, Estela let herself drift into sleep. The wise traveller slept whenever he – or she – could.

The Land of the Welsh

To the west and north of Gwalia, the Welshmen have strongholds from which they dispute the lands occupied by Frankish lords. They claim that all Gwalia was theirs before the Franks conquered some parts and belongs to them by right. All owe allegiance to King Henri, to whom the west of England is already loyal, even though Stephen still sits on the throne, but there is much fighting over how these lands are held and by whom.

Although the Welsh lords converse well in Latin and Frankish, common Welshmen speak no civilised tongue and a native guide is recommended.

Provisions are basic because the frequent battles require nomadic habits. However, the terroir is green and fertile, and the livestock tasty from good grazing. This land is richer than its natives wish the Saes (their word for foreigners) to discover.

The wise traveller will note that Welshmen are prone to deceit and do not like badgers.

CHAPTER FIFTEEN

While Dragonetz was recovering, Estela gleaned as much information as she could, flitting from kitchen to battlements: carrying messages; unloading and storing provisions; fetching firewood. She made herself useful, if not indispensable, and she ensured that John Halfpenny did likewise.

Wyn was a law unto himself, disappearing among his countrymen and re-appearing with a genial apology. Telling him she needed him for translation was like catching water in a sieve, so she sent him to Dragonetz instead. That would make it harder for the Welshman to absent himself and at least one of them would be able to learn more of this difficult language. She was picking up the words she heard most often but 'Come here, wench!' and 'Take this to the kitchen' were unlikely to help Dragonetz much in his political aims.

She had been mistaken in thinking there were no women in the castle. There weren't many and they worked hard by day, and just as hard at night, finding their way onto privileged, shared mattresses in the Hall. Farts and snores were not the only noises that disrupted others' sleep and only the Lords of Deheubarth bothered with a curtain for some privacy. Estela wondered where they found the energy. She was exhausted by the end of each day and sleep was the only pleasure she needed.

It was the women she could identify first, putting names to weather-beaten faces. Aliénor's ladies would have swooned at the very thought of putting down their embroidery to labour as these women did. As Estela drew another bucket of water from the well, she spared a wistful thought for the last time she'd enjoyed a bath, with other women filling the tub, squandering the precious liquid. Such luxury was unimaginable here.

Luckily, her hands had toughened on the journey or the blisters would have crippled her. Coarse they might be, but the women were tough and practical as Welsh ponies. Which was how the men treated them. Some of the women were lucky enough to service one man only, others were shared. The former guarded their man fiercely and fights were common but brief and apparently without rancour. Survival took priority and that required working together.

When the men returned from wherever they'd raided during the day, Estela watched which woman greeted which man, memorised the links, thought about the rank of the men, and of the women. She had been called 'whore' more than once in her life and now here she was, with whores for companions. She should despise them but how could she, when she worked alongside them every day? Sinful they might be, but, by God, they laboured as hard as any man.

Listen to her! She was blaspheming as easily as any soldier! Her next confession would be long, and would have pleased the vile priest she'd suffered in Zaragoza, and who would have lectured her on all women being sinful. The Welsh priest who rode with Rhys and Maredudd might be more practical, but Estela was in no hurry to speak to him. She would leave confession until she had more of their language, and no doubt even more to confess. For now, she would keep her thoughts and prayers private.

When the horn announced the men's return, followed by hooves, jangles and a clamour of voices, the women's work stopped. Or rather changed, as they tended to their men, then to the ponies. Bright-faced with success, the Deheubarth men nevertheless brought back injuries and gaps in their ranks. Joy at a man's return, wailing at his absence, were the daily prospects for the women, who gathered the news of battles like wildflowers, for contemplation.

Foremost among the party were always Rhys and Maredudd, riding together, first to dismount into their women's embrace. Maredudd favoured Enid, a bouncy girl whose curves were barely hidden by her badly-laced dun gown. When the men were not around, most of the women behaved differently, seeking more efficient ways to work rather than to swing their hips with greater allure. Enid, however, was the same bright spirit, hiding nothing and changing nothing, whoever she was with. Estela found her easy company and perhaps Maredudd did too.

Rhys' choice was a darker character, in looks and personality. Mair's hair was black as Estela's but curled wildly and cropped short, as was the Welsh habit with both sexes. Estela found it strange to see the blunt cut fringes hiding their foreheads. Back home, this would have been considered both ugly and lowborn but here, lords and peasants alike all wore this chopped style.

Mair was forever tossing her head like a pony, to shake her fringe out of her eyes, a restless soul. Had she not been living and working the peasant life outdoors, her skin would have been creamy white. It had freckled, rather than browned, in the little sunshine that graced this dreary climate.

Curious, Estela had asked Wyn about her and been told not to annoy 'that one'. Rumour said she'd killed Rhys' previous girl but 'an accident in the woods' was always possible, and Rhys had taken a fancy to her, so folk let it be.

What kind of people are these? Estela wondered, *where a murder is taken so lightly.* She stayed away from Mair but watched, as the girl flung herself onto Rhys or flirted her hips as she led his pony to water. Wyn had also said that nobody kept Rhys' attention for long. He liked a woman well enough but he liked a new one best of all.

As Dragonetz regained enough strength to walk, and then train, in the courtyard, he drew much feminine interest. Estela was aware of women glancing at her, wondering how hard she'd fight for her man. Very, was the answer, and she would stop work to go over to Dragonetz, rest her hand lightly on his arm. If he was sitting, she'd sit beside him, put her hand on his thigh, glare at any women within her line of sight. *Mine* her eyes told them, in the language she'd learned over the preceding days, one that needed no lessons in pronunciation.

She'd not thought of herself as innocent but she had never lived in a soldier's camp before. And none of these women were wives. Except herself, by Dragonetz' words. *Wife* carried status and along with the messages her eyes flashed, kept the women away from Dragonetz, who merely found the unspoken rivalries amusing. He would catch her possessive hand, take it to his lips, murmur what looked like sweet nothings to the envious onlookers. What he actually said could be anything from 'Chicken for dinner would be wonderful,' to 'They should have more men on the north wall. Approach by sea would be slow.' Or, of course, he might whisper sweet nothings, and make her blush.

They were indeed on the coast, but not upriver in Caerfyrddin as they had intended. Instead, they were not far from where they had crossed the mouth of the River Tywi, in Llansteffan Castle, well south of the stronghold where the Welshmen had left their wives and children as they struck out against their enemies. As to who those enemies might be, Estela was confused but, thanks to Halfpenny and Wyn, Dragonetz was able to explain.

The brothers wanted their land of Deheubarth back, and had made the most of the Franks fighting each other in the wars between Henri and Stephen. Neither King had time or troops to spare, to help their Marcher Lords hold the lands they'd stolen from the Welsh. Rhys and Maredudd were on a campaign to retake all of south Gwalia. They hoped to drive the Marcher Lords out of the southern and eastern tract of land where they'd settled, expanding from coastal bases. Caerfyrddin and Llansteffan were only two of the fortresses the brothers intended to claim for themselves.

First, they would deal with their old ally and old enemy, their uncle of Gwynedd. Uncle Owain had brought Gwynedd, the north of Gwalia, to their aid as they fought for their inheritance. But the treacherous northerners had then claimed Ceredigion to the east, for themselves. Ceredigion was part of Deheubarth and now was the time to remind Uncle Owain that his nephews were men grown, who would not leave him in peace.

'So,' Estela asked Dragonetz when they were alone. 'How will you make yourself indispensable?'

'Sing,' was the answer.

'Then so shall I!'

'And then Talharcant can sing too.' The sword named *Bladesong* in Occitan had been sheathed longer than its wont. 'Wyn tells me that the first steps to recovering Deheubarth lie to the west. Rhys wants to oust his uncle from Ceredigion first; Maredudd prefers to gain the coastal castles held by the Franks.'

Estela realised what was not being said. 'If Maredudd has his way, you'll be in the attacks against Henri's vassals, your peers.'

Dragonetz' face was grim. 'It will happen all the same even if we recover Ceredigion first.' *We* noted Estela.

He continued, 'That's why I needed to know more, to judge what was my duty before I ride out.'

'And you know now?'

He nodded.

'The Marcher Lords have no respect for Henri. They claim ever more land, war against each other, would wipe out the Welsh if they could. They've never met their Liege and he's been too busy claiming a future kingship to worry about Gwalia. Aliénor read it aright; Henri needs a balance here, not a victory. The Welsh can contain the overweening Marcher lords and those same lords can be forged into a weapon against the Welsh, should Henri choose, until all make oath to their Liege and keep it.'

Estela knew her knight. 'You seek balance, again, as in Les Baux.'

'It is the only way. Those who seek to kill all their enemies will waste their own lives in a task that only creates more enemies.'

'Then it doesn't matter whose choice you follow, Maredudd's or Rhys', you ride with the Welsh and help them win.'

He nodded. 'And whatever they decide, the brothers will ride together. That's why they win. I shall help them win more swiftly and, I hope, with honour.' *That* was why he looked grim. Not at the choice of enemy but at the probable manner of victory. He had never ridden with Welshmen before.

His next words, brutal, confirmed her guess. 'They do not take prisoners but they do take heads.'

'Because of their mother?' Estela remembered Rhys' bitterness.

'I think not,' Dragonetz replied. 'It is their way, of old. It might even be that the Princess was beheaded as a message, that Franks would treat the Welsh by their own customs. I witnessed such a response in the Holy Land. But there is no honour in cutting off the head of a brave lady who has led her men and lost a battle!'

'The man who did it – is he still alive? Will it be his castle that the Welsh attack if they choose the Franks next?'

'No, Kidwelly is too strong and Maurice de Londres is dead.' He hesitated. 'Estela, I wish you had not come with me.'

'Nonsense! If I hadn't, you might not still be alive. And I would not have heard the Welsh tales and songs.' *Or ways to pull a woman's hair and scratch at her eyes.* To lift his dark mood, Estela asked him what they should sing for the Lords of Deheubarth and she told him the style of song she'd heard from the women.

The prospect of something other than manual labour motivated Estela to work twice as hard and earned her an invitation to bake 'bara'. Baking bread was work she could enjoy and she sang as she explored the stores. The other women had no idea what she was singing but they smiled at the sound.

A girl with dimples and brown curls touched Estela on the arm, pointed to herself. 'Blodwen,' she said and she pointed to her mouth, said something that made the others nod in agreement. Then she started to sing and Estela understood. Blodwen was a singer too. Estela had no idea what the words were but the sound was sweet and rousing. A couple of women brushed tears from their eyes.

'Hiraeth,' one told Estela, her mouth twisting.

When Estela saw Wyn again, asked him what the word meant, and his mouth twisted too. 'It is a Welshness,' he told her. 'You do not feel it. The love and longing for your homeland. The pleasure of knowing such love and the grief of loss.'

'Hiraeth,' repeated Estela. Wyn was wrong; she knew that feeling well.

Rhys was delighted at Dragonetz' offer of entertainment but told him, 'We take song and verse seriously. A woman can play the harp or crwth nicely as you please but the voice is an instrument for men. I'd not waste my time listening to a woman. You'd not demean your wife by letting her make a fool of herself.' It was a statement, not a question.

However tactfully Dragonetz relayed the Lord' response, Estela understood all too well. Her confidence drained away. Even if she did sing, would these barbarians recognise her skills? When they didn't know the words, would they hear only her woman's voice that they had been taught to underestimate, to ignore? And if she sang, she would be thought immodest (a whore again!); if she did not sing, she was a goodwife, invisible – or worse, a mere table decoration, and in a place so barbaric there were no tables! Where they served themselves, and sat on their bedding rushes to eat from trenchers that were more like stone than bread. There was no risk of the trenchers crumbling into their beds! The hiraeth washed over her, for civilisation, for home, for Musca, Gilles and Nici. This place was so *other*.

She didn't know her head had drooped until she felt her chin lifted gently, Dragonetz eyes steady on hers. Those had been his very words, what felt like a lifetime ago. 'Do you want to be a table decoration?' he had asked her, when she was his student and felt a failure, missing notes and spoiling phrases. And she had worked so hard, learning everything he and Malik could teach her! She had come so far!

'What's a crwth?' she asked, summoning a weak smile.

'As far as I can work out, an instrument with strings, a bit like a rustic lute but held more like a viol. Lord Rhys has promised us the finest music of his court when he returns to his seat. Wyn says the women and children are in Dinefwr, in the north of the realm, so the softer artisans and musicians must be there too.'

He was not fooled by her smile for a second.

'No,' he said to her softly. 'My wife will not be demeaned by public performance. Because Estela de Matin will be the best singer in that Hall, whichever Welshmen the Lords call upon to strut their superiority.'

'Are you sure?'

'You've known worse audiences and we are together this time. This is what we'll do.'

CHAPTER SIXTEEN

The food was but a repetition of the usual fare, chunks of meat served on trenchers, each large enough for three people, and a small piece of bread to mop up the gravy. Though baked daily, bread was a luxury and one of the advantages of being a baker was that Estela could sneak an extra crust for herself and Dragonetz. And John Halfpenny, as he made up the third person sharing the trencher.

Estela chid herself for being so mean as to resent sharing. She had never known hunger before and realised that her charitable habits in the past were more comfortable from a full belly. For all their savage ways, Lords Rhys and Maredudd always said grace and put a symbolic portion of bread aside at table, for the poor. It was given to those who came to the castle gate after sun-up each day, along with a rather larger portion reserved from the daily bake. 'Cadell's tithe', the Welsh called it and when Estela enquired of Wyn, she learned that Cadell was a third brother, gone to Rome on pilgrimage that year.

'He took a beating. Then he put his brothers in charge and left to find healing of the soul.' Wyn was reluctant to discuss the matter.

The following day would be the Sabbath and Estela was again surprised to learn that no unholy activity was permitted. The men would not ride out and the laundry must wait a day to be taken to the stream, however brightly the sun might shine. The atmosphere was light with the prospect of a day's rest and instead of the usual ale, wine flowed freely.

When all had finished eating, the drinking continued and, with a nod of assent from Maredudd, Rhys called to one of his men, presumably to start the entertainment.

'Wyn!' Dragonetz caught the Welshman as he tried to slip past them and off to who-knows-where. As if that had always been his intention, he sat down beside them and resumed his role as interpreter.

He's paid well enough for it, thought Estela.

The older man called by Rhys struck a pose near the brothers, facing the audience, and declaimed in a resonant voice. Poetry perhaps?

'The lineage of our Lords,' whispered Wyn with pride. 'From Adam to Aeneas and down to the present day.'

'Aeneas!' Estela couldn't prevent her reaction but Wyn took it as ignorance rather than amusement and proceeded to enlighten her.

'Aeneas was the hero of the Trojans, who escaped and set sail, as recounted in Virgil's Aeneid, to found a line of heroes here in our mother country,' Wyn told her sotto voce. Unlike hunger, being patronised was something Estela had experienced before, and she held her tongue.

For what seemed an age, a whole Trojan war of names rolled out in sonorous Welsh. Informed that 'ap' meant 'son of', Estela could pick out the names but their descriptions were lost on her.

'Cadell ap Rhodri Mawr, Hywel ap Cadell, Owain ap Hywel Dda, Einon ab Owain, Cadell ab Einon, Tewdur ap Cadell, Rhys ap Tewdur, Gruffudd ap Rhys, Maredudd ap Gruffudd, Rhys ap Gruffudd,' the voice intoned and Estela could have cheered when she recognised the brothers' names. She was surprised by the order and guessed that Maredudd must be the elder brother. She had assumed Rhys to be because of his manner, not in the way he treated his brother but in his own bearing, a certain presence. Perhaps it was just because he'd stopped the badger-baiting. Or because he was the one with a reputation for poetry and song.

John Halfpenny was saying something to Dragonetz that she couldn't hear over the general noise as men called for more drink and the women stepped over each other to get the jugs and avoid the hands that reached up to stroke a passing leg. Women and men alike were bare-legged and mostly bare-footed. Many of the men even rode out on skirmishes unshod, their feet toughened as dog-pads.

'What are they doing?' Estela spoke into Dragonetz' ear, to be heard, and watched Halfpenny and Wyn stumbling towards the spot vacated by the genealogical bard.

'Wyn says he usually tells a few jokes, acts as a sort of jongleur I think, before the music. And Halfpenny insists he is funnier than Wyn so they have a wager on who gets the most laughter.'

'That's not an equal contest when Halfpenny has but a smattering of Welsh!'

'Ah but the only laughter to be measured is that of my Lords Rhys and Maredudd. I am to judge.'

Estela sighed. All she needed was endless tavern humour while her stomach churned, waiting for the moment she and Dragonetz took their turn. She checked for the umpteenth time that her oud was at her side, wrapped in its cloth.

'Would you like me to recite your ancestry unto the twentieth generation before you sing? She asked him. 'Dragonetz los Pros ap Dragon de Ruffec?'

'You will have quite enough to think about, Estela cydwedd Dragonetz.'

'Wife?' she guessed, hesitant.

'Yoke-mate,' he told her, his eyes dancing.

Then Rhys called for quiet and Wyn moved his arms a lot, spoke very fast and was appreciated by all in the audience but for her and Dragonetz, if she were to judge by the raucous laughter. She understood not one word.

When Halfpenny ended his tale of a cock and a rabbit with a punchline that relied on *susse* (know) sounding like *suce* (suck), she wished she hadn't understood a word of that either, but a few men in the Hall guffawed, and she could assume that those who didn't, couldn't understand the Frankish. Dragonetz' lack of response was no indicator as to the quality of the tale as he was completely absorbed in his study of the reactions from Maredudd and Rhys.

'One apiece,' he murmured. 'Even.'

Then it was Wyn's turn again and Estela could guess at the development of the story by the rhythm and volume, the pause and the open-armed gesture of hilarious climax. And it must have been because the Hall exploded in laughter.

Dragonetz shrugged. 'Two to one,' he said.

Halfpenny mopped the sweat from his brow and swore volubly and at length, which amused his audience more than his previous tale. He stood on his hands and waggled his legs, moving his feet so that they looked like two puppets talking to each other, as he provided the dialogue.

The left foot wiggled its complaint, simpering, 'This accursed language is only good for taxes and tolls. When a man tries to speak his mind in Frankish, the words sound like a girl's lawsuit, pretty and meaningless!'

'True, that is,' yelled one of the audience and there was a murmur of approval as the words were translated for all to understand.

'Who among you understand the language of gluttons and whoresons?' Nobody was keen to own up to this skill but the amusement made it clear how many in the Hall enjoyed the list of Frankish insults directed against the speakers of that language.

Then it was the right foot's turn to point toes at the audience and address them, in a gruff voice. This time, almost everybody in the Hall understood the words and there was uproar.

Almost everybody.

'That must have been funny,' Estela observed, as Halfpenny tumbled adroitly to his feet, took an agile bow and glanced with sideways challenge at his comic competition. 'It didn't even sound like Welsh.'

Dragonetz threw her a swift glance of sympathy, then returned to his study of the two Welsh lords. 'I think it was meant to be Frankish,' he told her.

Then he murmured, 'The decider, I think,' as Wyn cleared his throat and drew all eyes to him.

If there is anything less entertaining than men telling bawdy jokes in a tavern all night, it's men telling bawdy jokes in a foreign language, thought Estela as she watched the faces of the audience for clues as to what on earth Wyn was narrating.

Dragonetz drew breath sharply and there was a shocked pause, then Rhys laughed and everybody else joined in.

'What?' asked Estela, frustrated at being left out.

'All I heard was mention of Maurice de Londres, lord of Kidwelly,' Dragonetz told her. 'The man who beheaded the lords' mother.'

'That doesn't sound very funny!'

'Near the bone, whatever the story' agreed Dragonetz, 'but it shows the kind of men these are. Not ones to walk on tiptoes.'

'Tenso,' he told her, 'we'll sing a tenso.'

Estela could only nod understanding. He knew as well as she did the risks of singing a song that relied on insults aimed at, and bandied with, the highest-ranking members of the audience. There was no doubt that the audience enjoyed insults but just how close to the bone were they willing for foreign guests to cut? When Dragonetz improvised in a tenso there was no telling who he would insult, or how much, but that he would be clever and cutting was guaranteed. She sighed.

The tale drew to its inevitable climax, with loud applause and Halfpenny's riposte was an anti-climax; some quips and some jongling with boots he'd commandeered from members of the audience. He'd acquitted himself well, though, given the pressure, and he'd made friends.

Lord Rhys threw a purse to each man and thanked them, a level of courtesy Estela had not expected. The contradictions in the court continued to surprise her. Barbarians sometimes, and men of honour at others.

Flushed and beaming, the two raconteurs returned to their places. Dragonetz didn't have to give his verdict; John Halfpenny conceded cheerfully and paid up.

'Good health,' he said as he downed another cup of wine. He pulled a face. 'I prefer good ale to this Frankish stuff.'

Men were returning to their places and refilling their cups, after having relieved themselves outside. Some of the women were adjusting their skirts as they came back into the Hall, no doubt also having given the men relief, thought Estela cynically.

'Shall we?' Dragonetz asked her and for a confused heartbeat she though he was inviting her outside, until he reached for his lute.

She nodded, picked up her oud and held his hand tightly as he threaded a way through the lounging Welshmen to a place at the front where they could stand and perform. She would have liked a stool but no such luxury was available so she took her place behind Dragonetz, to accompany him as he sang.

He caught the audience's attention by speaking in Welsh, the words he'd memorised beforehand, thanking the lords of Deheubarth for their hospitality. He managed to include two generations of their lineage in naming them, to general approval around the Hall. Switching to Frankish, he told them that the Welsh were renowned throughout Christendom for the way they treated guests.

Perhaps they would be, once she'd completed *the Wise Traveller's Guide*, thought Estela, although she had not decided whether the renown would be positive or negative. Wyn *had* told them that no Welsh were beggars, and no man turned away travellers from his door, whether from hovel or castle, but Estela's own experience suggested some selectivity in defining 'traveller'.

Dragonetz' flattery had achieved its aim and, in the relaxed atmosphere created by food, drink and laughter, he introduced his song. 'As Wyn and Halfpenny competed in jest, so does my song allow one insult to cap another, in fun – and in verse. I know your people is even more renowned for song than for hospitality, so I invite any man who wishes to contribute to the song to do so when the chords await your voice.'

Invitation, my foot, thought Estela, as she tuned her oud, lightly strummed and repeated the chord that would allow a guest verse. Everyone in that Hall knew a challenge when they heard one and

Dragonetz had not misjudged the reaction of the lords of Deheubarth. Both Maredudd and Rhys had stiffened, like hounds scenting game on the wind, eyes glittering before the chase. Whether they would remain civilised throughout the tenso was less predictable.

A look from Dragonetz, a beat for rhythm and the quarry was off, singing of a young brown-haired man, who spent so much time drinking and wenching that his moustache was white from ale-froth and his knees shook from riding pretty ponies.

Nicely adapted, observed Estela, as her fingers plucked a humorous emphasis or left a pause. As was the tenso tradition, Dragonetz had not named Maredudd but all those in the Hall had made the connection and were sniggering. All that was needed to complete the satirical picture was a nickname. *Please God, let my lunatic man go gently* prayed Estela, as Dragonetz finished the verse with the term, 'Ass-ears', impeccably rhymed and scanned.

The audience sniggered and noted that Maredudd's ears were rather large and seemed more so thanks to the last rough shearing his straight brown hair had suffered. Dragonetz was not done though and launched straight into the second verse which was a traditional homily against greed, taking the 'Ass-ears' to be that Greek king, who was first punished for his golden touch, then for insulting a god.

Estela strummed the waiting chord, allowing time, in case one of the Welshmen should choose to sing a reply. Developing the allusion to Midas had removed the sting of the opening jibe and left the hearers free to question whether the insults were in their own mind. One more chord and then she'd let Dragonetz continue...

Maredudd stood. 'Long ears find out traitors,' he sang in Frankish, his voice thin but tuneful. Estela plucked softly, just to add atmosphere. The rest of his verse was in Welsh but there were repeated sounds, a music in the words themselves, as if there were some structure to the lines. If only she understood this language in which she was living! Although *she* didn't, others did, and the reaction was a murmur of appreciation, and something more.

Rhys stood too and bowed to his brother, in mock-appreciation that yet held real respect. He translated the reply to Frankish, apologising that he could not translate the poetic form of the Welsh.

> *'Long ears find out traitors*
> *and our mother earth reveals*
> *those who whisper against us,*
> *be it the whoreson hairdresser*
> *who left me thus shorn*
> *or the uninvited stag beetle*
> *whose carapace is all that's hard,*
> *hiding manhood soft and white as a grub.'*

Rhys bowed ironically to the stag beetle, and Dragonetz laughed, the happiest Estela had seen him since he'd been extricated from the sack. She had no need to play waiting chords; he was ready. Maredudd had shown he knew the Greek myth of Midas, so Dragonetz continued the story of 'Ass-ears', improvising twists to the old tale, for his current audience.

'What punishment could be hard enough
for such a hairdresser?' he sang cheerfully, while Estela plucked a dissonant note to add suspense.

'Surely the worst hairdresser in all Christendom.'

He paused for the laughter at the expense of Maredudd and an unfortunate Welshman Estela guessed to be responsible for the chopped locks.

> *'Whose tongue wagged like an ale-wife's,*
> *who told Ass-ears' secret to a hole in the ground*
> *and heard the words echoing round and around*
> *from every child's mouth, and every girl south*
> *of the mud-hole they lived in.'*

A murmur ran around the Hall as 'mud-hole they lived in' was translated for those who spoke no Frankish, and they recognised their home landscape. Dragonetz repeated the lines for their further enjoyment while Estela wondered at the pleasure men derived from insults, and continued playing.

> '... *every girl south*
> *of the mudhole they lived in*
> *would laugh at the king.*
> *When laughter's a crime then*
> *Criminal is the sanction...*'

Dragonetz paused for effect and then delivered the coup de grâce.

> '*devised by a brother whose ears*
> *were judged short; whose nature judged short.*
> *In short, he was Ass-ears' lesser brother and*
> *judged short in all, including the short sentence*
> *for treacherous haircutters*
> *that they be cut off.*'

There was an uneasy silence, some men uncertain as to how to take the insult to Rhys, others waiting for translation. Estela looked down, strumming the waiting chord, wondering if she could make an escape route by hitting somebody with her oud and running.

Then Rhys laughed, loud and long, repeated 'The lesser brother! Well called, my dangerous guest. Maredudd, he has us to rights!'

Estela risked a peep and saw that Maredudd too was relaxed and open, and she suddenly appreciated her lover's true genius. Had he called the brothers the other way around, the atmosphere would have been very different. Rhys the Lesser Brother was a title that lord would wear with the same pride and humour as a gigantic man nicknamed 'little.'

It was not over. Rhys signalled to Estela and sang his reply, in Frankish then in Welsh, in a tenor voice so rich it sent shivers along Estela's arms. She imagined their voices blending, her soprano, Dragonetz' deep baritone and this gift from God. What music they could make! Preferably with more dignified words.

'Close to the ground and close to each other
Ass-ears and Short-arse
have everything covered.
Greater and Lesser brothers,
like the sun and the moon,
rise and set and return,
make the tall stranger but a shadow
from the light they cast.
to be taller or shorter as they choose.
or gone, from too much light.'

In Welsh, Rhys was more fluent, the words again having that repetition of sounds Estela had heard in Maredudd's verse, but even in Frankish the thought was clever, and the delivery divine. Which of course had been Dragonetz' purpose all along. Estela played a closing chord as *The Shadow* bowed in acknowledgement that he'd been bettered in his own field.

The atmosphere could not have been better. The timing could not have been better. 'Now,' whispered Dragonetz and Estela left her oud with him so she could approach the brothers and ask her favour. She stumbled a little as she stepped around three women sitting on their pallet and excused herself without noticing who they were. Rhys and Maredudd's women, probably.

She had to reach the lords. She wanted so much to sing, to show what she could do, and Rhys' voice was still echoing in her head as she reached him and instinctively spoke to the Lesser Brother first.

'Sire,' she asked and curtseyed, the honorific coming naturally after she'd heard such skill in song. The noise around the Hall let her speak privately, for only Rhys to hear and she kept her voice low and modest. 'I would ask a boon. In my native land, I am known as a troubadour and I would offer one of my songs to your court, if it please you?'

The handsome face turned serious, kindly, like an uncle talking to a child. 'You play nicely,' he complimented her. Or, as she supposed, that was the intention. 'But song in public is a serious matter and not for women. You should be proud of your husband and his talent.' He paused, seeking words to soften her disappointment. 'You are a very pretty woman. If you were not married...'

Perhaps it was lucky for Dragonetz' mission that Estela's reply was cut off by a woman's scream. Before she could turn to see what was happening, Estela was knocked to the ground and flattened by somebody whose hands slipped round her neck, squeezing, digging in jagged nails, squeezing harder.

Through a wave of dizziness, Estela was aware of the uproar in the Hall. *Dragonetz* she thought, *trying to reach me.* The hands were not strong enough to keep up the pressure and a second's relaxation gave Estela all the time and rage it took to buck and roll. All the time it took to draw her dagger from the very practical belt in her underskirt, and prod the heaving mass of skirt beside her until a squeal said flesh had been reached.

Estela maintained the pressure, said 'Paid!' which she hoped was the Welsh for 'Don't!' Either her tone or the word worked because the woman lay still, sprawled on her stomach, with her skirt over her face and her naked rump bare to the world. Estela allowed herself the petty revenge of delaying a few seconds, amid coarse comments and laughter, then she pulled the skirt back into place to make decent her aggressor, jabbing a reminder with the dagger as she moved.

Mair spat out straw dislodged by the assault and let loose a string of words, of which Estela understood only 'Rhys', but that was enough, given the rumours about how Mair had dealt with her predecessor. Estela had seen enough hair-pulling, biting and punches during day-time work to know where jealousy led. How on earth could the woman have interpreted her approach to Rhys as a threat? Truly, she was in another country!

She stroked her sore neck with her free hand, saw blood on her fingers, wondered whether the stupid bitch had damaged vocal chords and kicked her in the rear, once, hard. Then Dragonetz reached her, wielding the oud against anybody who thought to approach them.

Estela smiled grimly as she rose to her feet, never taking her eyes off her opponent as she smoothed down her own skirt, one-handed. If there was to be another tenso with Greek allusions, what must they look like? She poised like Clytemnestra over the prone Welshwoman, and Dragonetz flailed an oud around, as men moved nearer to try and disarm them. *May Dame Fortune aid us!* she thought. Her escape plan might be needed after all.

Then Rhys' voice rang out, as calm as if murder attempts were the norm. *Which they might well be,* thought Estela, as her blood calmed and feeling returned to her sore throat. She was tempted to kick Mair again but she was a lady, after all, and Dragonetz deserved a turn. She didn't have to look at him to feel the heat of his anger. *So much for Welsh hospitality!*

Rhys' speech had stopped the men attempting to rush Dragonetz so the tableau was frozen: Dragonetz holding the oud as if it were a mace, and Estela wielding her knife over Mair, who dared not move.

The men parted before Rhys, who crossed the distance to Dragonetz, within reach of the oud. 'Please accept my apologies for this discourtesy to a guest. Women have no understanding of honour.'

Estela's boot twitched and if Rhys had been nearer, she might well have followed the instinct.

Dragonetz was cold steel. 'My Lady has every sense of honour and she has been insulted. What reparation do you offer?'

Rhys considered both the man and the matter. 'It seems to me that your Lady brought a weapon into my court and has drawn it, which is against all honourable behaviour as a guest. Were she a man, her life would be forfeit.'

'And she had not, her life would have been forfeit.' Dragonetz showed no compromise.

Estela wanted to speak for herself but she could not trust her voice. Croaking defiance would only draw laughter so she let Dragonetz champion her cause.

Before Rhys was driven to some judgement against Estela that nobody wanted, least of all Estela, Maredudd spoke. 'She *is* but a woman, Rhys. I doubt she knows how to use her little blade.'

Sore throat or not, Estela reacted. Yes, hoarse, but her words carried with the ease of professional practice. 'Not only can I use this dagger but I can throw it to kill or to miss, within three inches of a man's head!' Oh God, she'd meant to say six inches and give herself some leeway for the effects of alcohol and shock. Too late now.

'John Halfpenny!' she called. Her voice cracked and she called again but the word was already being passed from man to man, along with a translation of the sport promised. John Halfpenny was caught in the glare of attention.

Mair risked moving, rolling to one side, and Estela promptly stamped on her back to keep her down.

'Assume your position,' Estela ordered Halfpenny and pointed to the huge oak door. There was a sad lack of trees in the Hall but it would do. Though how in God's name she would pick the path and distance back from the door through this mob, she had no idea. Light-headed from surviving the attack, and seething at being belittled, Estela trusted in luck, or in justice, or both.

With slumped shoulders and a show of reluctance, Halfpenny took up the role they had practised so many times. Was it only a show? Never mind that, she had to concentrate.

'Let this be a trial by combat,' she declared. 'If God is on my side, then the dagger will fly true and John Halfpenny will be unharmed. All men will know that I bear this dagger for my own protection against such as... this–' It was only a small stamp. 'For women are not safe anywhere, not even in this court!'

'Estela,' murmured Dragonetz. 'If you kill him, you owe me an amusing English squire.'

Rhys had been sucking on his moustache and mutely consulted his brother. 'Very well,' he said. 'But it is no trial by combat when only one side is represented. God should indeed choose. You committed a crime against us and our court, but you also suffered a grievance and, for that, we owe you reparation.' He nodded to Dragonetz. 'Let the woman Mair be your target instead of the Englishman.

And she be untouched, she answers to your Lord's justice, and you are declared innocent. And she be harmed, so much as one nick, you shall be burned alive for treason, and your man gelded. Nobody carries weapons into my Hall, far less uses one!'

Mair's gasp of 'No!' was louder than Estela's indrawn breath but no doubt both women were closer in their feelings than at any previous moment, if for different reasons.

'I'm sorry,' Estela whispered, touching her lover's hand as she stepped back, allowed Mair to stand, walked her target to the door. The Welshwoman was shaking and Estela almost felt sorry for her. No doubt she expected certain mutilation or death, and the thought that she would take Estela with her would be little comfort.

If the woman kept shaking like that, there was every chance her expectations would be fulfilled! How Estela wished Halfpenny there instead, steady, trusting, greedy. She could hardly offer the woman a reward for staying still when this was a trial! Whatever she said, Mair wouldn't trust her, but if either of them were to come out of this unscathed, there was one essential piece of advice and only one person she could trust to give it.

'My lord Rhys,' Estela said. 'Please tell Lady Mair that all men flinch when a dagger comes at them and if she does so, she will surely move and die. This is not a matter for trial, it is inevitable. Tell her she must shut her eyes when I hold up my hand and keep them shut until I touch her and the trial is over.'

Although she did not understand the Frankish, the Welshwoman had reacted to her own name with the title 'Lady' in front. She was gazing wide-eyed at Estela. Maybe it was the first time anybody had so addressed her, this bedraggled woodland wench, lucky enough to bed a lord for a few months. *What if?* wondered Estela. *What if Dragonetz had bedded her and left her? Who and what would she be?*

The words came of their own accord, from deep within the source of her songs and her music. 'Tell the Lady Mair,' she emphasised the words as she spoke to Lord Rhys of Deheubarth, 'that we shall make a story here today of the courage of women, that shall be sung in Welsh halls for all time.'

Rhys spoke and Estela could only hope he translated her words true. Maybe it was hope that fooled her eyes but Estela thought Mair stood straighter and stiller against the door.

Then, there was just the mental preparation. Estela could not pace the distance. *Too bad!* she thought. Gilles would say she could not pace out the distance in battle. She tried not to think that killing would not matter too much in battle. She thought only of her grip, of the swing of her arm, imagining the movement and the moment to loose. She saw the arc in her mind's eye, the point in the door where she wanted the knife to stick, just above the parting in the short black curls. She felt the balance of her weight between front and back leg, the twist of her core that would follow through with the throw.

She raised her left arm and Mair shut her eyes.

The Hall was silent.

And then Estela threw.

CHAPTER SEVENTEEN

The whoosh of air, and thunk as the dagger hit its target, were the only sounds. Then Mair crumpled to the ground and mayhem broke out. The men nearest Estela grabbed her arms but she made no attempt to escape. She knew she didn't need to, and she turned to smile triumphantly at Dragonetz. She knew the sound of a point hitting wood, hard and true.

Rhys strode through the Hall to the door at the back, leaned over the woman's body to inspect the dagger lodged firmly in the solid oak. 'It is pointing slightly downwards,' he observed critically, reporting to the enthralled audience. 'There's a hair attached but I see no blood.'

Then he bent down to study the woman, who was stirring, struggling to sit up. Rhys grunted, muttered something to those nearest him, who passed him a full jug of water. He threw it in Mair's face and her shriek made it clear that she was recovering fast.

Wasting no more time on her, Rhys turned and gave judgement. 'I've never seen a finer throw.' General agreement was as enthusiastic about Estela's skills as it had been dismissive earlier.

Rhys continued, 'God has spoken. Estela de Matin –' he paused. *He* had *learned her name,* thought Estela. *More observant than he wished to appear.* '–has proved herself.' *Not exactly declared innocent then!* 'And in reparation for the assault upon her person while she was our guest, I make this provision for her and her alone, that she may bear her weapon, even in our court, so she promise to use it only in our defence and her own. Do you so swear?'

Estela shook off the restraining hands, went to Rhys and knelt. She made the required oath and waited, only too aware of the hatred burning in the living, breathing, Welshwoman so close beside her.

Without looking once at Mair, Rhys completed his judgement. 'The woman who broke our laws of hospitality is given to Lord Dragonetz, to punish as he sees fit.'

Estela sought Dragonetz' eyes across the Hall, pleaded mutely.

'I think my Lady has earned that right,' he said. 'Although the Usatges of Barcelone offer wise guidance in such matters and perhaps my Lords would be interested in this modern work...' He must have sensed the daggers in Estela's look for he finished quickly, '...at a more suitable time.' *Trust Dragonetz to bring up Ramon's precious Usatges whenever he could!*

Estela thought of women hauling ropes at the well, hefting sacks of corn from the carts to the kitchens, sweating over the cookfire, and still finding the energy to beautify as best they could before the men returned. She'd seen them rub sand over rough skin; clean their teeth as she did, with rosemary; shine their hair with cooking oil.

She was a woman and she would not give up. 'I ask a boon,' she said to Rhys, once again. 'The Lady Mair and I have made a story here today, of love and passion, of the courage of women and of the wise judgement of the lords of Deheubarth.'

It would be politic to include Maredudd. She continued, 'If I write this song, it will be sung in halls throughout my realm, where my name has worth. This song should be heard first in *your* halls, Lord Maredudd, and Lord Rhys. If you give your consent, it will be, for I shall sing it.'

She was *not* going to give the option of Dragonetz singing. Not after what she'd been through just to sing in front of these dung-pigs of barbarians! Partly to hide the anger she knew was sparking in her eyes, she reached down to Mair, to raise her to her feet. Bravely, the woman stood, waiting her fate.

Rhys laughed, said something to Maredudd in Welsh that made the other men laugh too.

Maredudd said, 'We must tell you more about our mother, for there has never been a woman like her. You,' he spoke to Estela, 'may carry your dagger and sing in our Hall when we return to Dinefwr, our home. Meanwhile you can write your song. She,' he indicated Mair, 'is your responsibility. My brother has more important matters to think about. If you wish her maimed or turned off, tell him and it shall be done.'

He then spoke curtly to Mair, who bowed her head, whether in acceptance or in simmering fury, Estela could not tell. What was certain was that Rhys would take another to his bed that night and he was already choosing as the jugs were cleared and the Hall made ready for play and for sleep.

Estela and Dragonetz chose sleep, which was slow to come. The music of the Welsh court in the dark filled Estela's imagination, as she sought the melody of her song-to-be. Heartbeats played tambour while muffled sobs of passion and of pain plucked strings. Breathing finally settled to the even rhythm of sleep, and Estela's last remembered thought was of Gwenllian, the warrior princess, mother to the princes of Deheubarth. Why couldn't Estela learn sword-fighting too? After all, she'd persuaded the brothers to let her sing at their court.

Sunday promised fair and Estela and Dragonetz found themselves at liberty in every sense of the word, for the first time since their capture. They gazed out from the battlements to the land that was misty but visible across the rippling sea.

'Normandie?' asked Estela, with a rush of hiraeth. So near and yet so far.

Dragonetz shook his head. 'Probably England,' he told her.

Down below them, the tide was out, but the sound of ebb and

flow carried on the breeze, along with seagulls mewing. Dry purplish seaweed outlined the pattern made by receding waves, and still glistened where it emerged from the white breakers.

'Let's go down,' Dragonetz suggested, taking her hand.

Apparently, they had earned some measure of trust and there was no objection to them walking out past the guards, through the gate as if they were two ordinary cottagers off to look for driftwood on the beach.

The September sun was a gift to treasure and although, from habit, Estela covered her head and neck with a cotton scarf, she thought it would not matter too much if she risked browning. Among all the dangers of travel and her current lifestyle, protecting her skin seemed unimportant. She had never been able to whiten her olive tones whatever she tried. If she must work like a peasant, she might as well have fun like one.

The short path down to the beach had been well-trodden and was easy underfoot, if a little muddy. Tufts of dune grasses marked the switch from earth to sand, and walking became more difficult, her boots sinking.

Dragonetz was already removing his footwear and he was barelegged like the Welshmen, his hose packed away for more formal times. Estela needed no encouragement to take off her boots and tie them round her neck, as she'd done when a child, playing by the river.

She looked back up the hill at the castle but was too far away to identify any of the human shapes on the battlements, and the stone walls with their blank-eyed arrow-slits made no judgement on her hoydenish behaviour. There was nobody else on the beach.

The breeze stirred her hair, the sand was warm and grainy between her toes, and she suddenly felt light, careless. On a holy day by the sea. She picked up her skirts and started running across the sand, following the curve of coast away from the river mouth, out to open sea.

Dragonetz caught her easily, tagging her as he ran past, as if they were children playing together. He stopped, just a little way ahead, teasing her. She darted towards him but he was too quick for her. Every time he stopped, just out of reach, she thought she could catch him and tag him back, but he ducked her touch and ran on again.

When she conceded defeat, calling, 'Enough!' they'd rounded the headland, the castle no longer in sight but above the rocks somewhere. She bent over, feigned a stitch and he came back to her, only to be tagged and left standing as she danced away. She hid behind a jagged pile of rocks so he could not get to her.

'You cheat,' he complained.

'I win,' she told him, cheeks red with exertion and sunshine.

'You win,' he told her, 'always.' And suddenly his voice wanted a more adult game. Behind the rocks was a cave. 'Come here,' he bade her and she obeyed, taking his hand, allowing herself to be led into the cave, into privacy such as they'd not known for weeks.

'I'll get sand on my gown,' she objected.

'No, you won't,' he replied, showing her with gentle hands exactly why not.

Then she stopped worrying about the sand and became one with the tide that ebbed and flowed, made its own rhythm, broke in waves and carried all life out to sea, the pounding heartbeat of life itself.

In the peace of a Welsh cove, time stopped for long enough to heal some of the damage caused by constant anxiety and sleepless nights. Estela allowed herself to relax. And then to pick up the burden of their mission, for it was no longer Dragonetz' mission. She was as deeply immersed in the Deheubarth court as he was.

Privacy allowed them to talk without fear of being overheard and they shared what knowledge they'd gleaned.

'Rhys gave me my sword, asked if I knew how to use it. He wants me to ride with them tomorrow,' Dragonetz told her. 'We go to take a castle: Tenby.'

Estela had known it would come but that didn't make it easier to bear. But, like the other women, she would bear it, and beautify for his home-coming. And hope he was among those who came home.

'And Maredudd?' she asked. 'Is he happy for you to ride with them?'

'I think so. They are uncommonly close. Wyn says there were six brothers and now there are only three. That Cadell was attacked and changed, so that he wished only to go on a pilgrimage and serve God, so he left for Rome in the spring, naming Rhys and Maredudd rulers in his stead.'

'Regents?'

'It seems not. According to Wyn, Cadell escaped with his life but lost all spirit. Nobody expects him to rule again, even if he returns.'

Estela frowned. 'There will be a falling-out at some time? Between Maredudd and Rhys, as to who rules? Maredudd is older but weaker. What is the custom for inheritance here?'

'From Wyn's stories, it seems that a realm is split between a man's sons, whoever their mothers, and, yes, there is usually maiming and murder until the strongest who are left hold their territory. There is usually no love between brothers, who grow up each in another lord's house, for apprenticeship. And where there is no love, and much competition, blinding and gelding are alternatives to murder.'

Estela winced. 'Do you really think Maredudd and Rhys are any different? Are you going to woo both for Henri or back the one who'll win?'

'Both.' Dragonetz thought. 'But it is easier to connect with Rhys, somehow.'

'Then I must win Maredudd.'

'Good God, and have another Welshwoman trying to kill you for stealing her man?'

Estela laughed. 'No, I have learned that lesson! But I have an idea that *won't* make other women jealous. I shall tell you if it works! And, speaking of other women, what shall we do with Mair?'

'Lady's maid? Translator? Or would you rather she were birched and put in the stocks?'

'I don't know...' began Estela, then corrected herself. 'No, of course I don't want her punished physically, but she needs employment, and she needs something to take her mind off losing Rhys. I'll think of something.'

Dragonetz had picked up a stick and was drawing an initial in the sand, while he listened to her. A curly letter E.

When he'd finished Estela held out her hand for the stick and enclosed the letter E in a letter D. She had to lean over to avoid smearing their work with her footprints but she was pleased with her work and reluctant to pass the stick back to her lover but he insisted. He added a tail to the D, a crude dragon head breathing flame.

'Txamusca,' he told her, 'part of us.'

Musca, the baby she'd named in defiance, to make his fatherhood plain to anybody who thought what Txamusca meant, a breath of fire.

'Will we see him again?' she asked.

'Surely,' he said, and she was reassured, despite knowing that *Inshallah* was the true reply.

'As long as we go back now!' Dragonetz pointed to the incoming waves, already lapping at their intertwined initials. Estela realised that not only had the tide turned but it would soon cut them off, trapping them in the cave. How quickly a sanctuary could become a death-trap!

There is only one answer to dangers, she thought, laughing and tagging Dragonetz lightly. *Run fast and dance among the waves, for as long as you can.* She grabbed her skirts and suited action to thought.

Back at the castle, Estela forced Wyn to stay with her and Mair long enough to explain to the Welshwoman that she was to help Estela with her work duties and her Welsh, so she would need to learn Frankish.

The woman nodded, expressionless. Then she picked a bit of seaweed off the bottom of Estela's gown.

She said what sounded like, 'Larver.'

Estela held the bit of seaweed. 'Larver,' she repeated.

'Bara lafwr,' Mair informed her.

Estela already knew that 'bara' meant bread so she guessed that somehow the seaweed could be turned into something edible. Wyn had slipped away the moment her attention was distracted so the conversation continued in sign language and pointing, with a visit to the kitchen for buckets.

Another visit to the beach resulted in two bucketfuls of the purplish lafwr, which Mair boiled down for hours to green pulp. While Dragonetz rode out on his first campaign with the Welshmen, Estela was rolling seaweed in oats and frying it.

'Bara lafwr,' she told the other women proudly and they smiled back at her.

'Bara lafwr,' they agreed.

Estela sang the words softly, felt the music in them, and then embroidered a lyric in her own Occitan around the Welsh phrase. She sang as she worked, incorporating the Welsh words she knew. Some of the women hummed as the repeating melody caught them.

When Estela paused, the woman who'd said she was a singer, Blodwen, made up a verse of her own, and then others joined in. Soon there was a kitchen-full of work-song. *Women's song*, thought Estela, listening to the ebb and flow of the voices, waves breaking, which she could hear but not understand.

When several of the women sang together, there was a moment Estela heard a way of singing she'd never heard before. Then it was gone and there were only women's voices singing in unison, each with her own sound. She shook her head to clear the fancies away.

Heavenly music indeed! And yet, if she should ever hear that sound again, she must speak to Dragonetz. If anybody knew of heavenly music, borne of dreams, he was the one. But she would not raise his hopes only to be dashed again. He had enough on his mind.

A hand on her arm distracted her and Mair claimed her attention. The women stopped singing. Estela sought her dagger-hilt, just in case. Holding her gaze, Mair sang and pointed. What Estela understood, was, 'Bara lafwr... you... me... all women... no men... no Rhys...'

Estela could do singing and pointing too. So she did, managing, 'Cofiwch,' the Welsh for 'remember' with some made-up word from 'ferch', 'daughter', that made them all laugh as she tried to sing 'Remember the women and forget the men!'

Stupid language that couldn't make a difference between 'daughters' and 'women'! Even when you tried to forget the men, you couldn't.

Pray God they came back safely.

CHAPTER EIGHTEEN

Dragonetz felt naked, and yet he was still wearing more protection than the Welshmen who rode with him. Most wore only peasant tunics and loose hose, bare-headed and often barefoot, quivers slung round their hips, bows and spears over their shoulders. A handful, including, Rhys and Maredudd, wore helms, hauberks and swords, like Dragonetz.

He'd been offered a bow and arrows but he was no archer. He accepted an axe instead. His pony was no Sadeek but reminded him of Damascan mares and battle tactics; steady-footed and fast on rough ground, built for 'rush and run' attacks, or for raining arrows from a distance, then disappearing into the landscape like mist.

They lacked the strength needed to carry a knight in full armour and would never have the fire that a destrier like Sadeek could bring to war, biting and stamping his own rage on a battlefield. There was, however, a good chance that this mount would take rabbit-holes and forest tracks in her stride, and get him back to Llansteffan safely. If the Franks of Tenby didn't kill him.

Dragonetz had asked the brothers for the names of their enemies but Maredudd's reply had been 'Franks and Flemings,' and a shrug.

'It's our land, our inheritance,' Rhys told Dragonetz. 'If you ride with us, that's all you need to know.'

'Do you ride *with* us?' Maredudd asked, at the same time as Rhys posed the question Dragonetz had been waiting for.

'*Why* do you ride with us?'

'I serve Aquitaine,' replied Dragonetz, 'and King Henri is my Lord, as he is yours.' He took the fact that he'd not been put in a sack as encouragement to continue. 'Marcher Lords who set themselves up as kings in Gwalia are no friend to King Henri. If you win back your lands, your inheritance, you could hold Deheubarth strong for the king, keep the Marcher Lords within bounds, make peace.'

It was the truth but whether the brothers would know the truth when they heard it, he doubted. Talharcant would need to win their trust first.

'Your way of oaths and allegiance, vassal and Liege, is not our way,' Maredudd told him curtly. 'The men of Deheubarth do not serve anybody.'

Rhys exchanged glances with his brother and nodded. 'You ride with us,' he said. Whether this was a judgement or permission was not clear. 'And you should not call our land Gwalia. This is the word used by outsiders, so we consider it an insult. Deheubarth is a realm of Cymru. You can tell us more about your politics when we go home to Dinefwr. Now is not the time for thinking. Now, we take Tenby!'

As far as Dragonetz could ascertain, 'taking Tenby' was to be achieved by riding hard and then hitting the Frankish stone keep there with their combined might. It did not seem like much of a plan and Dragonetz thought wistfully of engineers, siege weapons and soldiers who wore boots. How in God's name had the Welshmen taken back Caerfyrddin and Llansteffan? Sheer bloody-mindedness? Trickery?

Even though they rode through backwoods and byways, they could not avoid being seen by an occasional merchant. As they neared the coastal destination, the brothers' instructions were clear. Nobody lived to tell of the encounter; not the shepherd whose flock scattered in panic, turning as one to stare from a safe distance at the Deheubarth men; not the merchant whose bolts of fine wool unrolled from his pack, one on top of the other, as he fled on foot, brought down by an arrow in the back. Dragonetz noted the skill and speed of the aim, even as he queried the need to kill.

'Flemish,' Wyn told him and spat. 'Little England this is, since they brought their foreign ways here. You'll hear more English than Welsh when we sack the castle, and good riddance!'

They trampled heedless over the ells of wool, fit for a queen, but they took the merchant's pony onward with them.

A day's ride took them close enough to Tenby to see the castle on its promontory, like a mailed fist against the sky. It was smaller than Dragonetz had expected, barely the size of the old tower in the Aljaferia. Built in the old style, with a wooden stockade rather than walled citadel, the stronghold was little more than a fortified watchtower but its position made it difficult to approach. If only they could get inside the stronghold, it was unlikely that there were many men there for them to overcome. If they should succeed, it would be easy enough to hold the castle, once they'd taken it.

Like Llansteffan Castle, Tenby castle dominated a headland, protected by sea. But whereas Llansteffan had an easy approach landside, this one was on an isthmus, almost completely enclosed by cliffs, water and beach. The defenders would see them coming and retreat to the tower.

Deheubarth reinforcements were due from the north, so that Llansteffan would be strengthened while they were away, and some men would arrive here the following day, at the earliest. That would give them even greater strength in numbers but if they waited for reinforcements, there was more chance of them being discovered and reported to the Franks. Then they would face a castle prepared for attack.

In Dragonetz' experience that meant months of siege or failure, and high casualties. Even in a small tower like this, the occupants would have the defensive advantage. Unless, of course, they were not prepared; unless the Welshmen managed to find and kill every unfortunate who spotted them.

These woodlands were the best terrain for a halt that they'd found, after crossing moors and marshes. Each terrain had its hidden dangers, although Dragonetz was more concerned at the way the bogland sucked at the ponies' legs than at Wyn's tales of Yr Afanc. If the demon dwarf did appear, whether in his form as crocodile or giant beaver, he would take down one man and one horse. If the party stumbled onto sinking mud, they could all go down.

The woods offered shelter and a fast stream. Places that sheltered men also sheltered beasts but the party was large enough for safety. They were more likely to be pestered to death by midges enjoying a last blood-fest before winter came. Maredudd gave the order to break camp. The men saw to ponies, fetched water, stretched muscles weary from riding. The brothers drew apart, presumably to plan.

Dragonetz risked joining them, and listened. They knew he'd been a commander, they'd seen the quality of his sword and helm. They would ask his opinion if they wanted it. And if he knew their plans he might be able to intervene to prevent the bloodbath he predicted.

'We will wait here till the extra men arrive so we can storm the tower in one movement,' Maredudd told him.

'If they come tomorrow, they will be too late in the day to launch an attack,' Dragonetz thought aloud.

'Yes.'

Two days hiding a hundred and fifty men in the forest. The Welshmen would make their meagre rations last so that was no problem. One of their strengths as soldiers was their hardiness. They'd had no food all day and seemed not to notice. Dragonetz' stomach rumbled at the thought. *Their* survival would not be a problem for any length of time. They could always scavenge for food. Camping would even be pleasant, given the mild weather – and dry for a change! The full moon and cloudless sky the night before had made night like day.

'And then?' Dragonetz asked. 'When reinforcements arrive, what are we going to do.'

Rhys looked puzzled. 'Attack,' he replied.

'How will we approach the castle?' They looked down at the narrow approach, where a party with donkeys was moving through the huddle of dwellings to the fence and then past that to the gate of the keep. The guards on the tower could see anybody coming for miles.

'Fast,' said Rhys, grimly.

'Supposing we get our men near to the keep, is there a weak spot?' asked Dragonetz, patiently.

'I have no idea.'

'How do you breach the walls, usually?'

Rhys' eyes lit up with understanding. 'We fire arrows, rush in under cover and fire more, so that we kill the guards on the battlements and many inside. We retreat, give pause, then repeat the action. They're frightened, they run for cover, we destroy the gates and set fire to any wooden parts. If we catch anyone who matters to the Franks inside, we make an example of them until those inside the castle surrender.'

He shrugged. 'This is only a tenth of the size of the other castles we've taken back, no battlements and no outer walls, so one wave of attack should be enough.'

'How fast can the men fire arrows?' asked Dragonetz, curious and avoiding the question of how examples were made. He knew of many methods; they all shared the disadvantage of alienating the townspeople with whom the conquerors would have to co-habit after winning. That, and the unnecessary mutilation of fellow-humans. The Deheubarth brothers gave no impression they balked at such acts.

Aliénor and her king ought to know just how dangerous the Welsh were with their longbows. He must remember to put it in his report when he went home.

Rhys smiled. 'Fast enough. One every six heartbeats.'

Very dangerous was the answer. That fast was impressive and Rhys knew it.

'Do your methods always work?' Dragonetz asked,

'We need a bit of luck,' Maredudd said. They had the over-confidence of youths who'd known success in battle.

Dragonetz was not so young. He asked the question that every leader had to consider. 'How many men are you willing to lose?'

Rhys' smile faded. 'As many as it takes,' he said, and Maredudd nodded, eyes like slate.

It was the wrong answer. Even such a small stronghold would take Welsh lives, needlessly, if it was prepared for defence. What would Ramon Berenguer have done? Dragonetz felt a rush of regret and longing. Was this *hiraeth*, this wish for the Comte de Barcelone beside him as leader, with his unique combination of strength and restraint, his experience and his compassion? More even than siege weapons, he missed Ramon and Malik.

'What would you do?' asked Rhys, and the silence hung.

Dragonetz' chance of binding them to him had come. Ramon was not here but he was, and he'd learned many years ago that winning people was more important than winning battles. The brothers needed to think of this plan for themselves and it had to include all that was expected by the Welshmen. If they did not sack the castle, every man, woman and child in the surrounding area would pay.

'We have more cumbersome methods,' he began, 'with ladders, grappling hooks, wooden platforms. Once in, we rely on close fighting, in heavy armour.' He shook his head. 'None of that would work for you.' Then he chose his words very carefully. 'Like you, we wait for daybreak before attacking.' Then he waited. And waited.

Maybe he'd misjudged the level of intelligence? Maybe he needed to nudge more?

Then he saw light dawning in Rhys' eyes. Moonlight. 'What if we attacked at night?' Rhys asked, stuttering in excitement. 'Caught them by surprise? Nobody ever attacks at night!'

'How would we see to do so? We'd break our necks!' Maredudd objected.

Dragonetz feigned caution. '*If* the skies stay clear, the moon would light us. It was bright as day last night and not yet full.'

'So we reach the castle on foot. What then?' Rhys' enthusiasm wavered. 'The castle will be locked for the night, nobody going in or out. If we shot at the guards all we'd do is maybe kill a couple and wake the whole castle up. We'd be worse off than in day-time, with no hostages.'

Dragonetz silently counted to ten before having his idea. 'Maybe' he said, 'maybe we could break the door down? Then we could be inside while they're still in bed!' *Axes* he thought.

'Axes!' said Maredudd.

The details of the plan were quickly filled in. Then bemused men were informed that they needed to take what sleep they could for a few hours till the moon was high and the Franks asleep. Those who kept watch would remain with the ponies and provisions until word came back that the day – or rather the night – was won. Or until those left alive came back to make good their escape.

Dragonetz moved a couple of stones, stretched out on flattish ground, shut his eyes and obeyed the brothers' orders to the letter.

Their faces darkened with earth, the men of Deheubarth slung their weapons over their shoulders, or belted round their waists, and set out in the moonlight towards the castle.

A fanciful observer might have likened the black shape of Tenby on the promontory to a hunched Titan, forever rolling his punishment stone.

Long shadows turned trees to Tylwyth Teg, the fairy folk, their spindly limbs beckoning you in the breeze to a doom that appeared fair beyond your dreams. Whispered love words – *cariad, sweetheart* – stirred a man's senses and the dark perfumes of night made promises to be kept in the shadows.

Should a young man follow these will o' the wisps, leave the path and his fellows, he would taste pleasures unknown and a hundred years would pass in but a day. As he would find to his cost, if he returned, stooped and white-haired, to the land and people he thought he'd left behind. In truth, they'd have left him behind, after living their human lives of work, families and – if they were lucky – growing old, before finding eternal peace.

There was no peace for a man taken by the Tylwyth Teg. Whosoever has tasted of fairyland can never be satisfied with less. A man's dreams can be his undoing. Or so the stories warned.

A large party of warriors hell-bent on battle were immune to such fantasies but even they were quietened as much by the night transformation of the landscape as by the need to move with as much stealth as possible.

Night creatures made themselves known. A swoop of wings, a hoot of owl; rustling leaves and a scurrying through undergrowth or up a tree trunk; crashing of boar and sneaking of fox; and wolves howling.

'There will be fine hunting in wolf month,' observed Wyn. 'Enough tongues for tribute and skins for our backs.'

Such a large party risked little from even the largest predators at this time of year, when bellies were full, but no man sought privacy to relieve himself, just in case. Jests about the size of a man's private parts and squirrels were more predictable than meeting a bear would be. However slim the chance, this close to the settlement, nobody wanted to take a risk.

The moon was as bright as they'd hoped so they carried no torches. The way grew easier underfoot, flattened by carts and well-trodden, as they neared the huts that had sprung up outside the castle fences, a sign of confidence in their rulers. Over-confidence.

Although nobody spoke, the sounds made by the war party carried in the sleeping village, without the cover of trees and forest creatures. Metallic clinks from axes, belts, swords and the chainmail of those who wore hauberks; a sneeze, a cough, a stumble.

From one of the huts, a dog barked the alert. As one man, the Welshmen stood still, waiting.

The barking ended in a yelp, and a human curse. Then nothing.

Then a baby's hungry wail split the night, stopped, no doubt, by a full pap. Then nothing. Townspeople often knew when not to hear.

Rhys and Maredudd raised their arms and the signal passed down the line. The men waited.

Sword drawn, Dragonetz walked with the brothers, keeping to the shadows beside the rough dwellings, approaching the grassy mound across the ditch to the wicket-gate that gave access to the settlement inside the stockade, and the tower.

Over-confident indeed. Nobody manned the gate, which was hacked at the join, half-lifted, half-slid open, as quickly and quietly as three strong men could manage.

Once more a dog barked. This time it was Maredudd, giving the signal. Heedless of noise or light upon them, the Welshmen streamed up the hill across the bridge, past the huts and up again, to the oak door of the keep.

Dark round eyes in a small face watched them through a doorway, then disappeared as the child was pulled back by unseen hands.

Four of the Welshmen slipped into huts. Muffled sounds, followed; a groan. They returned with torches.

All subtlety was over and as many men with axes as could hack the door down at one time, did so. Dragonetz thought there might be a joke in this for John Halfpenny, later. If he were among those for whom there was a later. The little Englishman made no attempt to join those using brute strength on the door but was poised, eyes gleaming unnaturally in his mud-smeared face, waiting.

The last splintering crack as the door gave way was drowned in a roar.

'Cofiwch Gwenllian,' screamed Rhys and Maredudd, and the cry was taken up by their men. 'Remember Gwenllian'. *And remember a princess beheaded by these men now sleeping in their beds. Remember what mercy these Franks give and take revenge. Take back our kingdom. Take back our rightful inheritance.*

Dragonetz crossed himself and unleashed the inner wolf.

The battle cry set fire to the men and they streamed into the tower, sweeping through the stores on the ground floor, rushing the stairs to reach the men in their beds above.

In the stockade outside, carts and goods caught light. Fire calls to fire, and what was started by the stolen torches continued in spurts of flame that danced from wood to sack, from boxes to clothes, and from there to unwary flesh.

The Welshmen sacked the castle and its settlement, from the hillside where chickens zig-zagged in clucking terror to the upper level of the keep. The first men they reached were barely awake to know who killed them but some had been awoken by the noise and reached their weapons, fought back, protecting the man who must be their leader.

Where the Welshmen had the advantage of surprise, the Franks had swords and daggers, and were better prepared for close fighting with weapons. However, what the men of Deheubarth could do with axes, fists and feet, even bare feet, was a revelation to anyone trained as a knight.

Welsh leadership blazed red and white in the flames, 'Cofiwch Gwenllian' echoing from the stair. Maredudd was at once shouting orders from an arrow-slit and atop a burning pile of flour-sacks outside. Rhys' sword dispatched a route towards a small cadre defending their leader.

Dragonetz kept pace with Rhys, protecting his rear, swinging Talharcant in a circle that let nobody near the Welsh lord as he fought ever closer to the castle's lord. Until there were only Dragonetz and Rhys against the six Franks, sword against sword, tripping over bed palliasses.

One eruption of flame from below cast sudden light on the Franks huddled together, eyes wide and confused. Dragonetz picked up one of the straw mattresses, threw it at the men and Rhys moved in, knocking four down, reaching his target, hurling his war cry and delivering death. Naked or half-clothed, the Franks' vulnerability told against them and neither sword nor dagger could work fast enough against the fierce onslaught.

Again and again Rhys whirled his sword, until he and Dragonetz stood, panting. There was the sort of pause that allowed a leader to think, to plan for an end to hell while still surrounded by its flames. Then Rhys was off, shouting 'Maredudd!' running to find his brother and assess what remained to be done.

More experienced, Dragonetz could have told Rhys what remained to be done but that was not his place. The castle was theirs, so the problem was already turning from taking the keep to preserving some morsel of it, along with any of its people. Men from the huts had either run away or grabbed farm tools to defend themselves and their families.

The warriors' eyes burned with the need for more fire, more killing. Dragonetz watched as one, too battle-crazed to feel pain, picked up a brand and ran upstairs to torch the paillasses. His scream as he went up with the straw in a rush of flame went unheard in the general clamour.

Rhys found Maredudd but that only doubled the wildness as they finished off any bodies that moved, ducked under burning spars and encouraged their men to spread out back down the hillside, among the huts, where there were still people and plunder.

There was only one way to stop the madness. Dragonetz raced after the brothers, ignoring all around him. Or trying to. Sticking out of the doorway where a wide-eyed child had stood earlier, were two small bare feet, one closed like a fist, crippled at birth. Now lifeless. The pain of deformity and the joy of living ended.

Dragonetz caught up with Rhys and Maredudd as they linked arms and clashed two cups of beer, or even wine, against each other in loud toast. All that was needed now was to make the army drunk and there would be nothing left of Tenby by the morrow.

Maredudd grinned at Dragonetz. 'Drink to my brother! He comes of age today!'

Dragonetz was puzzled. This was not the first castle the brothers had taken and certainly not the first time Rhys had killed a man!

'I,' declared Rhys, tapping his own breast for emphasis and spilling alcohol down his already red-stained hauberk, 'I am twenty-one this day.'

Good, thought Dragonetz. *There might be a way out of this yet!* He took the cup offered, swigged a mouthful. 'Then you should *lead* the next attack,' he said.

Rhys' face showed the remark had hit home. He'd always been Maredudd's brother, the younger, in their previous victories.

As wild with enthusiasm as any man there, Dragonetz spoke to Maredudd. 'Now,' he said. 'Let's follow Lord Rhys to St Clears castle and make a birthday present nobody will ever forget. If we go now, collect our mounts, we can leave at dawn and be upon them before word reaches them of what happened here. You deserve two castles for your coming of age – and your first command. What say you, my Lord?'

Maredudd was in that stage of battle inebriation where Dragonetz could have proposed flying off the cliff and hacking a fleet of marauders to shreds; anything that involved fighting – and of course winning – was irresistibly attractive.

'My Lord says *yes!*" he yelled, planting a kiss on his brother's cheek. 'Go on then, call your men and lead us!' he told Rhys.

Cries of *To me, to me,* were rendered more effective by the addition of, *We go to sack St Clears!* When men saw Rhys and their comrades running away from the castle and towards the next adventure, they joined in and soon a tidal wave of Welshmen was sweeping through the town and back to their camp in the woods.

Night, bumps in the path and then the solidity of trees calmed some of the battle ardour but not enough to induce sense and sleep. Instead, Rhys allowed enough time for water and a sop of dry bread. Then he ordered them up and away.

St Clears Castle was also one of the old-fashioned kind but a tenth the size of Tenby. The attack was a success beyond the Welshmen's wildest dreams and their dreams were indeed wild after one sacked castle and a sleepless night. They swarmed the defences and laid about them with the confidence of victors.

Lord Rhys celebrated his twenty-first birthday hacking at the unfortunate victims of his first command. No man could have wished for a more auspicious day.

Until he realised that Maredudd had been wounded.

CHAPTER NINETEEN

The women were like over-tightened lute strings, so close to breaking that one thoughtless word led to blows. A wise traveller kept her mouth closed and worked, while her thoughts galloped alongside an army, ducked arrows and boiling oil. *Stay safe* she prayed.

The arrival of Deheubarth reinforcements from the north brought some distraction, especially for those women not attached to any one man, Mair among them. She had apparently accepted that her time as Rhys' woman was over, if her behaviour with the newcomers was any indication. Estela shrugged. She would not judge any woman's behaviour in a way of life she hoped never to experience.

The night was once more enlivened, and sleep spoiled, by the stifled sounds of coupling. Not that the women would have slept anyway for wondering what took place a day's ride away. Estela pulled her cloak over her ears and sought comfort in memories.

A kiss, a kindness, and the philosophy of Boethius; all part of the history she shared with Dragonetz. And one small boy. Silent tears trickled as she let herself miss home, as she worried about the future. She moved her hands down the cloak to find the Viking pathfinder brooch she kept pinned there, too precious to store in her saddlebags.

Tracing the runes she knew so well, their criss-crossed paths, she wondered whether she had gone astray, whether she would find herself alone in this alien land. Was it possible that one path continued without Dragonetz? That she would have to live like Mair?

A rough edge caught her finger, led her along a different bumpy line. *No,* she thought. *Never.* Dragonetz would always come back and he would always find her there to welcome him. In that she would be like the Welsh women, proud and patient, working by day, and beautiful for their men's return in the evening. And she would sing and write too!

Most of the reinforcements rode west the next day to join Rhys and the heaviness of waiting loomed over the castle. One day, a week, longer or not at all: nobody knew when the men would return.

Estela found herself seeking work and not needed, so she took to a quiet corner with paper and quill, and returned to her sadly neglected writing. Her readers would want to know all about Gwalia.

The song that was Gwalia raced through her mind: drumming as Dragonetz was beaten in a sack; a piercing whistle as Mair slumped to the ground beneath a dagger that still quivered in the oak door; light strings as a couple ran barefoot across the sands; full percussion for making lafwr bread.

She shook her head to clear the medley and concentrated on what her readers should know. *Start at the beginning,* with what Wyn had told her. She dipped her quill in the ink and started writing.

The Welcome given by the Welsh

In Gwalia, there is no need to ask for shelter. It is the custom of the Welsh people to host all peaceful travellers. They expect you to enter their home and they will offer water for washing feet. Should you thank them courteously but say you have no need of the water, this means you are continuing on your travels after such refreshments as they can offer. If you accept the water, this means you wish shelter for the night.

The wise traveller is a good guest, accepting what is offered as if it is palatial, whether it be straw in a barn or a royal bed in a castle. For in each case, the host is offering the same gift; he is sharing his home with you. Such a gift deserves appreciation but be wary of offering material goods in return, for hospitality cannot be bought and you cause offence if you imply that it can be.

She must ask the brothers where she could replenish her stock of ink. Perhaps an apothecary could be found in Caerfyrddin which sounded to be more civilised than Llansteffan? If so, there were sure to be Jews there, and they always had ink. A notary would be perfect. Lost in such practicalities, the sound of horses' hooves interrupted Estela's musing. The men were back.

Estela abandoned her book in the alcove and rushed down the stairway outdoors, to join all the other castle residents. Shoving, jostling, standing on tiptoes to peer over each other's shoulders, some women were counting aloud. Not counting numbers in the party surely? This behaviour was new but then, this was the biggest venture the men had attempted since Estela had been here.

With each number, a name. The first name was Maredudd.

Then Estela understood. She saw Rhys with a man slumped in front of him and a riderless pony being led behind them. For every riderless pony, there was a man dead or badly injured and these women knew which horse the men had ridden when they left. Maredudd was wounded.

The list of names continued and Estela's heart pounded, thinking she heard 'Dragonetz', knowing her imagination was playing tricks and that he wouldn't even merit a mention. If he did, it would be as *The Frank* or more affectionately as *Long Shadow*. But why couldn't she see him?

The wailing had begun as women realised who was missing. Estela felt the keening jar her very core as she raked the riders. He'd ridden out close to Rhys and Maredudd. Where was he? There was a gap. The last of the riders was inside the castle and no sign of Dragonetz. Men were dismounting, women greeting them – or sobbing.

Through the mêlée Estela still searched. He had to be there somewhere. She'd just missed him. But she knew she could not have missed him if he were there. However he was mounted, Dragonetz stood out for his height, his armour, his natural leadership.

Maybe that's what got him killed Estela's dark angel told her. She thought the whole world must hear her heartbeat. The men had almost closed the gate and were reaching for the bar when a voice rang out on the other side. Rhys yelled an order and this time it was not imagined. Estela heard the name *Dragonetz*. That was the moment she thought he'd died.

Then the gate swung open, and a weary pony stumbled through towards rest and water. Just as weary was the knight on her back, who held a swaying figure in front of him. Not Dragonetz but John Halfpenny was the man wounded. Estela rushed towards them and helped lift the Englishman down before he lost consciousness. Dragonetz looked little better but gave her his lopsided smile, said 'I think you'll be needed,' and went over to see how Maredudd fared.

The men argued. Rhys was hoarse with panic. He'd already ordered a cart to take his limp, bleeding brother a day's journey up-river to the nearest physician, in Caerfyrddin. He didn't mind John Halfpenny lying beside Maredudd in the cart. They were the only two Deheubarth men with more than grazes. Apart from those who were dead, of course, whose burial would be ensured by the new occupants of Tenby and St Clears. May the Lord forgive their sins, and lack of last rites, to those who'd died fighting for justice.

Rhys no longer minded anything. He shouted at everyone within earshot, blamed every man he could see and name for not watching over Maredudd. His fists smacked each other for want of a better target and he shook as he shifted from one foot to another like a caged bear.

Dragonetz had to shout to be heard. Again, he said, 'Estela is the best physician I know, trained by–' *What did these men know of Arabs or their medicine? How should he convey all that Malik was?* 'Trained by the King of Aragon's doctor.'

It was no use. Rhys was locked into his own anguish, desperate to take action, any action, not listening. If he had his way, there was every chance Maredudd would bleed to death on the journey, as if he hadn't been jolted enough by the ride back here.

Men looked down and stood still, not wanting to attract their Lord's attention but not wanting to leave him either. Dragonetz saw only one way to break the impasse and acted. He moved closer to Maredudd, who was lying on a mattress, ready to be lifted into the cart.

Dragonetz crouched beside him, took the limp hand and leaned over so his ear covered Maredudd's mouth. He was silent, listening, making sure Rhys was watching him. Dragonetz' quiet words rang out in the sudden silence. 'I'll tell him,' he said. 'It wasn't his fault.'

Tears streaked Rhys' face as he pushed Dragonetz aside to kneel by his brother. 'Maredudd!'

'He's gone again,' whispered Dragonetz. 'It was but a moment. But he will be back with us. Estela?'

She took the chance to look at Maredudd's leg. Something metal was sticking out amid a bloody mash.

'He will be back with us,' she echoed, 'but only if I'm allowed to do my work.'

The storm had broken and Rhys knelt there silent, holding his brother's hand.

Estela fetched Malik's surgical instruments as well as her medicine box. She thought about adapting the speech she'd made at Malik's bedside, to impress Rhys, but one look at his stricken face told her not to bother. The tableau was unchanged: Rhys kneeling by his brother, men as still as if at funeral rites.

The grave must wait. There would be no funeral rites. Not if she could help it!

She knelt beside Rhys and examined the wounded thigh. 'I will need to tie the leg to stop the blood, remove whatever that metal is, and stitch the wound before I let the blood flow again.'

'Don't bother,' Rhys said. 'You are right. There is no time to get him to Caerfyrddin. I've seen this type of injury before. It will kill him. One of my men will saw off the leg and give him a chance. Get a torch,' he ordered one of the men. 'We'll burn the stump.'

'No!' Estela wasn't just upset; she was fighting mad. She put down her medical instruments, open, to show the gleaming scalpel and needles. She drew her dagger, waving it as she spoke. 'It will indeed kill him because you are not doctors! Do I have to throw this again to show you what I can do? I might as well throw it at *him*,' she waved it at Maredudd, 'and give him a kind death as leave him in your hands!'

Dragonetz caught her flailing wrist and she let him take the dagger. She'd made her point.

Rhys looked up at her. 'You think you have the power?'

'It's not power, it's science!' She calmed a little, remembering the dignity of her calling. 'And yes, I know I can.' *Probably.*

'So be it.' Rhys crossed himself and stood up. His tone suggested he'd consigned his brother to the tomb but he rallied enough to glare at Estela. 'And if he dies–'

'I know, you'll burn me alive and geld Dragonetz. Save your threats for those who heed them! I have work to do.' She turned her back on Rhys, told two men, 'Carry Lord Maredudd to somewhere quiet, not up stairs, where I can tend him away from the others. Put the Englishman on a paillasse and take him there too.' She thought a minute and added 'Please,' in Welsh.

Rhys translated her needs, as she gave a list, and then the courtyard turned from the stillness of an altarpiece to purposeful bustle. There was barely time to let Dragonetz know she was glad to see him alive, before she swept off to tend to her patients, wishing she had not presented quite such an optimistic picture of their chances.

The two patients were on their bloodied mattresses in an alcove near enough to the kitchen that Estela could get freshly boiled water. If only she had some poppy tea but, for Dragonetz' sake she never carried any and there was no substitute in the castle. There wasn't even strong alcohol. The best painkiller available was wine. And nature's solution to pain. The men would lose consciousness when she hurt them beyond endurance, which would not take long.

When she stripped Maredudd's tattered clothing off his leg, bits of flesh came with the fabric and his involuntary groans made Halfpenny reach for the bucket, sickened by the prospect of what was in store.

Under the cynical gaze of Rhys, Estela used one of her precious bars of soap to wash the leg, which had started bleeding again but would not be fatal until the metal was pulled out – or left in to infect his whole body. There was time to attend to Halfpenny first.

The moneyer had a slash in his shoulder.

'Sword wound,' he confirmed.

Estela explained to Rhys that Maredudd would be no worse for waiting and that removing the metal would be the most dangerous work so she would ease Halfpenny first. She did not tell Rhys that it would also be better for Halfpenny if he did not listen to Maredudd's surgery before his own. She had to use simpler language so Rhys understood their wounds, as he had no understanding of anatomy or surgery.

Then she made Halfpenny sit and removed his jerkin. It too was stuck to the wound, which opened up again. She bathed it carefully, prodding to observe better whether there was any dirt. He reached for the wine while she was still washing the shoulder and he drank a flagon in one swing of his good arm.

Estela was satisfied this wound was clean and she told Halfpenny to drink all he could, then lie down and bite on a gag of cloth.

She laid Malik's instruments out on the wrapper of clean linen she kept for that purpose. She heard her mentor's words in her mind, as clearly as if he were beside her in the room, telling her what steps to take, reminding her of the dangers. She didn't need to be reminded of the danger of infection, not when she'd seen Malik himself brought so close to death by a rose thorn. The memory shot through her, a sudden anxiety. *He recovered* she reminded herself *and we'll discuss every detail of this surgery when we see each other again.*

As he'd always done, she shut her eyes and made silent prayer, entrusting her hands and work to a higher being. *Inshallah.*

Then she threaded a long sharp needle with linen filament. She swung the needle in a candle flame to disinfect it, rubbed goose grease along the thread for lubrication, and punctured the good skin at the side of the wound. She ignored the twitches her patient made and held the shoulder steady for the needle's exit on the other side of the wound.

'Eight and it will be over,' she told him. 'One,' she began, preparing him for each onslaught with a quiet count.

When she reached 'eight' she'd made four stitches in the wound, knotting each one and cutting the thread with her dagger.

When Estela had finished, she looked at her work. The ooze of blood between the stitches was browning already, with no pus, and the sides were cleanly matched. The stitches were evenly placed, not too far apart or the wound would gape, nor too close together or they might rip the good skin. Malik would be pleased with her. He would appreciate the finer details.

Maredudd blinked, showed enough wakefulness to be plied with wine, but most of it spilled. If he lost consciousness again, so much the better.

Her other patient would require more skill and more damage, and Estela gave Rhys the chance to leave the room. He wouldn't. He insisted on being one of the men she needed to hold Maredudd to the mattress, to hold him still while he struggled and bit on the gag, till the chamber filled with his stifled screams. Dragonetz knelt the other side of the wounded man, who lay pinioned on the mattress.

After Estela tied the leg at the top to stop the blood flowing, she chose a scalpel, and focused only on the science of each cut, to do the minimum damage around the metal that rose like a demon whale from a red sea.

She disciplined her unruly thoughts. The metal pointed upwards in the air from a broader base. Triangular? It would help to know, to visualise what she was cutting out and make sure she got all of it. Just one tiny sliver of metal left in the wound would kill.

She licked the sweat off her upper lip. 'Did anybody see the blow?' she asked. 'Know what this metal is?'

Orders were given, a man left the room, and Estela waited, observed the wound, till she knew each pore of torn skin, for what seemed hours.

Breathless, the man returned. 'No,' he said. 'All they saw was a man on the ground, stabbing upwards, hitting my Lord in the thigh.'

Upwards stroke. The gash below, the metal embedded above. But what shape was it below the surface?

'That my Lord be killed by such a weakling!' The Welshman's contempt rang clear. 'He broke his own sword against a wall, running from us!'

Estela frowned in concentration. *Broken sword. Metal pointed tip. What shape would break off?* She looked at the jagged shape, imagined a man on the ground holding the tip of a sword, looked at the part she could see.

'Triangle,' she said aloud, with the broken base dragged along, into the skin. She looked at the angle of the point and she set to work.

'Done,' Estela said, easing her back as she stood up. How she ached from working crouched or kneeling. If only they'd had a table! But no, her first surgery had to take place in a Welsh castle without the basics of civilisation. Which left the last question. What should she use as a poultice to keep infection at bay? She could mash herbs... or...

'Honey,' she told the ashen-faced Rhys. Bring me a jar of honey from the kitchen and clean linen from my saddle-bag.

John Halfpenny and Lord Maredudd were duly basted in honey and bandaged in linen strips. *Like two piglets for roasting*, thought Estela, regarding her work with satisfaction. Malik would be very proud of her.

CHAPTER TWENTY

Estela sat, invisible, on one of the two stools which had been brought to the makeshift sick-room. The other was empty as Lord Rhys was sitting on his brother's mattress, holding his hand.

Her patients were apparently asleep so Estela chewed the end of her quill, then bent over the traveller's guide.

'What are you writing?' Rhys asked quietly.

She'd been mistaken: she was not invisible.

'Advice for travellers,' she told him.

'Read it to me.'

Sleep

The capacity to sleep in any circumstances is a virtue when travelling. A paillasse is a luxury for the bones but can be a torment to the flesh as the straw is a haven for parasites of all kinds.

'Dragonetz is lucky to have such a wife.' Rhys looked at her in frank admiration. Maybe she had misjudged his attitude to women.

He continued, 'If I could find a woman as beautiful, who had such a good memory and could scribe my words to preserve them for the future, I would count myself fortunate.'

Estela's mouth had been open to thank him for the compliment. She closed it again.

'He's gifted, isn't he,' observed Rhys. 'He has a way with words. *A luxury for the bones and a torment to the flesh,*' he quoted. 'So true.'

'Yes,' said Estela, tight-lipped. 'He is, and he does.' She bent her head over her writing. It was either that or behave like a Welshwoman, rushing at him with teeth and nails. Which would not make for a peaceful sickroom and her patients' health, so she dipped her quill again and concentrated on ways to prevent and to soothe irritating stings and bites. *Like words,* she thought, *carrying small doses of poison.*

Maredudd stirred and Rhys was instantly attentive to his brother. The brothers spoke in Welsh but Estela understood the gist of their exchange and the love between them needed no translation. Rhys asked whether Maredudd needed anything, gave him water to sip, mopped his brow.

John Halfpenny lay with his eyes closed, as irrelevant as Estela, while Rhys blamed himself and the universe for what had happened to Maredudd.

'We should beget the next generation before we run out of brothers,' Maredudd attempted to deflect Rhys from his litany of 'might-have-beens'. He must have heard Rhys' compliments to Estela. Intended compliments.

'Marry?' Rhys was taken by surprise. Then he smiled. 'You're the elder. You first.'

Maredudd tried to shake his head and winced at the pain caused. He must still be suffering from the tension of the surgery, separate from the wound healing. 'I'm not brave enough! Only think what happened to the last brother who married!'

Rhys' face darkened but he followed the lighter path of the conversation, to entertain Maredudd. 'Who would you have me wed, then, brother?'

There followed a crude and lively discussion of suitable – and very unsuitable – candidates, which would have added useful Welsh to Estela's vocabulary had she been able to note and memorise it.

'Mair would have you back,' teased Maredudd.

Rhys said something that sounded like swearing. Then he looked up at Estela, 'You should have had her executed – she'll cause you trouble one day. You can't tame a fox.'

Maredudd suggested more brides, enjoying his brother's discomfort.

Then Rhys paused, silenced by something Maredudd had said.

'Maybe Powys,' he conceded. Estela knew that Powys was the Welsh realm in the middle of Gwalia, lesser than the great regions of the north and south, Gwynedd and Deheubarth.

'That would be Gwenllian ferch Madog, daughter of Powys,' mused Maredudd. 'Madog would be keen enough to wed Deheubarth, that's for sure. Best make an offer before Gwynedd gets the same idea! Why not send to Madog that you wish to try the girl? Have her sent to Dinefwr and if she falls with child, make the marriage?'

'And send her home if she's not fit?'

'Give her the choice of staying if she prefers. She'd find a man soon enough, even if she's barren. She's a pretty thing.'

Rhys thought about it. 'And Madog would appreciate the gesture, us being willing to keep her, even if she's not meet for marrying.'

Estela thought of Gwenllian, a pretty girl in Powys, who would be a princess if fertile and a puterelle if not. A girl with the same name as Rhys' legendary mother and the challenge of taking her place with a man who loved women in ways that barely remembered their names. Estela shivered though she was not cold, and drew her cloak tighter around her, refastening her pathfinder brooch, tracing the runes of the futures possible.

'What about Gwynedd?' asked Maredudd.

'It is time,' Rhys told him. 'We hold St Clears and Tenby, we are at the gates of Ceredigion and it is our land. It is time we took it back from those northern murderers. Make them pay for Anarawd.' No question now of keeping conversation light.

'But Owain Gwynedd had no part in that,' objected Maredudd.

'A man is responsible for his brother's actions.' Rhys was adamant. *And a woman* wondered Estela. *Must a woman pay for her brother's actions?*

'Ceredigion is ours by right. Gwynedd helped us take it back then kept it for themselves. Whichever brother matters not! They are all treacherous northerners, in bed with the English and the Franks, allied with whoever pays the most! I don't give a fart what Gwynedd thinks of us being allied to Powys because by then we'll hold Ceredigion too.'

'Give me two weeks and I'll be fit to ride with you,' said Maredudd, barely able to turn his head after such a tiring conversation. Estela would have intervened if she dared but she knew Rhys well enough to hold her tongue.

'No, let me do this for you, for us. I have proved myself in command and you must not ride before you're well or your fierce doctor will use one of her sharpest blades on parts I value.' A jerk of the head in Estela's direction. So, he was aware of her listening.

'It won't matter what I say,' murmured Maredudd, exhausted.

'No,' said Rhys and kissed him.

Within a day, most of the men left to wage war against the men of Gwynedd and take back their old realm of Ceredigion. If they won, Rhys and Maredudd could return home, celebrating the restoration of the kingdom their father and grandfather had lost. If they did not win, they would need their surgeon.

Estela knew she should say nothing more than Godspeed to a man leaving for war. *Say nothing that will haunt you if he doesn't come back,* was the code they lived by, women such as Layla and herself. But the words came, despite her.

'Will it end, Dragonetz? We are so deep in Welshness now, I find myself swearing like the coarsest of the camp followers, and in their own language! Will we ever go home?'

He tilted her chin, met her eyes with his own, deep, black, unreadable. If she didn't *know* he loved her, she would never tell from his eyes. But she knew.

'We will take Ceredigion,' he promised her. 'When Rhys and Maredudd go home, we will go with them to Dinefwr, tell them what they will gain from making peace and alliances with King Henri. Then we will go home.'

If you win. If you survive. If Rhys and Maredudd don't turn on us. Unlike his, her eyes played traitor and told him all the *ifs* in her mind.

'I know,' he told her and crushed her to him, so that afterwards she found bruises from his hauberk. 'I know.'

'Inshallah,' she murmured, summoning a smile as weak as any Maredudd had bestowed on his departing brother.

Knowing that the campaign against Ceredigion would take more than a week, perhaps more than a month, left a guilty peace lying over the castle. Fewer mouths to feed meant less work, and the tension over the home-coming could be postponed. Limbo was a quiet place, where Estela could tend to her patients, sit with them, and, as they recovered, converse with them.

'Why did you not leave us to go home?' she asked John Halfpenny.

'They don't appreciate my jokes,' he quipped.

She just waited until the serious answer came.

'I fled from Stephen's men and want to be sure King Henri holds the power before I risk returning.' He was quiet. 'Now I be so close, I be in no rush to find out how much has changed.' Estela understood. There was more than his profession to take up again from where he'd left off. To hope that he could do so. He'd been away for years. Was his wife still alive? Still waiting for him?

It was easier to think of the professional than the personal. 'Your skills will always find you work,' she told him. 'And King Henri is acknowledged. You heard what Rhys said.' *Keeping the mind strong heals the body faster.* As always, Malik's words guided Estela, however far away he might be in body.

Maredudd was listening with interest. He was weaker, and recovering more slowly, but that didn't prevent him groaning more at Halfpenny's jokes than at his bandage being changed.

When Estela told Dragonetz that she would draw Maredudd close, this was not what she had in mind but she would make the most of them passing their days together. Maybe she could still carry out her first plan, when he had recovered enough.

'Your brother, Anarawd. What happened?' she asked him, curious to know more about these brothers and their history.

Maredudd closed his eyes as he retold the story. 'It was over ten years ago. After our father's death, Anarawd was Lord of Deheubarth and he asked help from Owain, Lord of Gwynedd, to oust the Franks from our lands of Ceredigion. Fierce was the battle, but short-lived, with berserker Vikings on our side too, adding their crazed strength to our own. The Franks surrendered but Owain Gwynedd and his vile brother Cadwaladr kept Ceredigion for their own.

Anarawd and Cadell, the next in age, counselled diplomacy and Anarawd offered his hand for Owain's daughter, thinking to renew our blood ties and regain our lands through marriage.'

He opened his eyes, stony. 'He was murdered by Owain's brother Cadwaladr. Not by his hand directly – the coward! – but by his men. Not even Owain could bear the stench of such kin-killing and Cadwaladr fled like the white-livered rat he is, all the way to England. If they stop fighting each other and ride against Deheubarth, or even against Gwynedd, Cadwaladr will be at the head of Frankish troops.

My mother came from the north but she had none of their trickery. She fled her own people to marry my father and every time since, when we have formed an alliance, they have betrayed us. Owain is no more to be trusted than his brother.'

'I should not have asked,' murmured Estela, fascinated but worried over her patient's agitation.

'My brother grows angry when I say so but our family is cursed. To lose our mother in such a way!'

'I too lost my mother when I was very young.' Estela struggled to speak the words aloud. 'She is still with me, in all that I do.'

Maredudd gave no sign of hearing her as he followed his own thoughts, bitter as wormwood. 'With her my two brothers, barely sprouting hairs on their chin. Morgan, killed. Maelgwyn, captured, and we've never found him. Then my father, a year later, struck down by God.' He listed them on his fingers, a fierce gesture at each name. 'Then Anarawd murdered by his Gwynedd kin! And Cadell!'

He stopped.

'I thought he was on pilgrimage?' asked Estela.

'God struck him too. First with a murderous gang and stout sticks, then with piety. He survived the one but the other will not leave him. When he gave Rhys and me the governance of Deheubarth, he made it clear that his return would change nothing. If he returns.'

Five brothers, thought Estela. *And only one left.* She too had one brother. And none left.

'What you have, with Rhys...' she began.

'Is everything.'

She could not tell him he was lucky. But she could think it. She could think that it was *her* family that was cursed. And she could pray that its bad blood would not touch her son. *I will not let it!* She called on memories of her mother, her strength, her sweetness and her wisdom. All that was in her blood too, and in Musca.

'Your mother, Gwenllian, must have been very special,' she said, gently, testing, as if excising an infected place with Malik's sharpest scalpel.

'She was.' Maredudd's face softened and he talked about the woman others called the warrior princess, the woman whose name men cried in battle. To him she was Mam, and he missed her.

'She told us magical stories and invented some herself.'

'Tell me her stories,' she said, and the chamber filled with legends; the lady of the fountain, the cauldron of the underworld, King Arthur and the winning of Olwen, dreams and dragons.

Days passed in nursing and talk, until John Halfpenny had run out of jokes and Maredudd would no longer accept being confined to the sick-room.

The moment of truth came when the stitches were removed and

Estela heaved a sigh of relief at clean wounds, knitting together well. Maredudd's sigh of relief was less professional. He'd turned a whitish-green while Estela was snipping and pulling – *thank God for greased thread!*

'If this is how you treat a man kindly, remind me not to annoy you,' he told her faintly.

That seemed to be a good moment for Estela to ask her favour, to return to the plan she'd made to draw Maredudd close enough that he'd listen to her – and Dragonetz – on political matters.

He frowned. 'It is not seemly,' he said. 'If your husband will not do it for you then no other man should.'

'He is not here,' she said. 'And I want to surprise him.' She could see he was weakening, attracted by the novelty of the idea. 'Somebody taught your mother,' she pressed the point.

'And look what happened to her!' was the bitter retort but she could see him thinking, wanting to test what was possible, be his own man while Rhys – and Dragonetz – waged war elsewhere.

'Unless you're afraid you'll lose?' she challenged. The bargain was sealed.

Ramon Berenguer was holding council with his commander. He reread the letters on his table.

From El Rey Lobo: the Almohads were in their fifth year of siege against Granada, which could surely not hold out much longer, or so the Wolf King feared. When it fell, the south of Hispania would be in the hands of these extremists, who would stop at nothing to wipe out their fellow-Moors who'd settled here for generations. Who would also wage war against any Christians blocking their way to gaining territory.

Thanks to Dragonetz and Malik, the alliance between Ramon Berenguer and the Wolf King was solid and El Rey Lobo provided a strong buffer between these murderous newcomers and the kingdoms of Aragon and Barcelone. For now, Ramon's army was not needed to support his ally. Which was just as well, given the other news on the table.

The next papers brought a smile to his face. His long dance between alliance and enmity with the Republic of Genoa had left the merchant state – or pirate state, as many would say – in financial difficulties. Would the Comte de Barcelone like to purchase the Genoa shares in Tortosa? Ramon had dutifully shared Tortosa and its trading riches with his two partners when they had won that city back in the Reconquista, five years earlier. The Comte de Barcelone had been careful with his coffers and would very much like to help Genoa in their time of need. Now, he had the chance to buy the controlling shares. Let the bartering begin! He would finally gain control of Tortosa, a very useful trading post near the mouth of the River Ebro.

He skimmed news of the Holy Land. That Baldwin had taken control of the Kingdom of Jerusalem from his mother, Queen Mélisende, did not affect Hispania. In the last crusade, Ramon had waged holy war in Hispania and, given the news from Granada, he thought that there would be enough of God's work to do in his homeland. He would have loved to see Jerusalem but his duty dictated otherwise, and Ramon had never been Oltra mar. Not that the new Pope showed any sign of raising a new crusade. He too had enough unrest closer to home.

Not only was there a new Pope, but the catalyst to the last crusade, Bernard of Clairvaux, was dead. Surely this was a year of changes and Ramon could only act according to what was best for his own kingdom. What happened abroad was beyond his power to predict or influence. Which brought him, with a sigh, to the letter from Provence.

Petty acts of defiance by the family Les Baux made it clear that their oaths of allegiance had meant nothing. The truce had failed and the only question now was how long Ramon could tolerate the continual provocation by his arrogant vassals.

Knowing that he had lost the two best commanders he would ever lead, had let them go *knowing* how soon he would need them, did not help either. He was a man of his word. And by God, those who'd broken their word would pay for it! It would be *their* fault if Provence was torn in two!

'It might as well be a declaration of war from Les Baux.' His commander was young enough to show enthusiasm. 'We will miss Commander Malik.' What he meant was that he would have a chance to shine in the field.

Berenguer sighed. 'I do miss him. Among his many strengths, he could show restraint.'

De Montcada's jaw tightened at the emphasis on one of his missing qualities and Ramon relented. There was no point holding Malik over the young man's head as an example he could never live up to.

Ramon continued, 'But he is no longer young and I hear that his wife's death has hit him hard. He will not be returning to the guard, whatever we face.'

'I am sorry Sire.' The man had enough sense to maintain a respectful silence. Death always required a respectful silence. Gauging the length of that silence appropriate, the commander returned to business. 'Word is coming back from your allies and vassals?'

Berenguer sighed again. Young men were wearying but war even more so. 'Nothing from Toulouse,' he said. 'But that's no surprise. Montpelier and Narbonne are with us, of course. And Carcassonne.'

'*That* is good news!'

'Yes, it seems Trencavel of Carcassonne has finally come off the fence and is acting without regard for Toulouse, possibly even against him.'

'And he'll bring his vassals.'

Berenguer was following his own thoughts, of a commander he could never see again, the best, to whom he'd made a promise. *I cannot go to war against les Baux*, Dragonetz had said, kneeling, offering loyalty to Barcelone. *I will not make you*, Berenguer had replied. But nor would he let Dragonetz ride with les Baux, against him. The knight must be kept far away. Aliénor's summons had been for the best.

Damn you, Dragonetz! You, Malik and I, we were invincible.

'We'll be invincible!' the untried commander told his Lord.

'Yes, we will. But not yet. These petty insults might assuage Les Baux' pride and there will be no need of war. But we will be prepared. And yes, the Carcassonne vassals will add forces I had not expected. I think Dragonetz' lady came from that region?' He was glad Estela's family would be on his side.

Foolish to care, when Provence might be torn apart again. And for what? Wrong-headed pride on the part of a stubborn widow and her reckless sons. They had signed a truce; they had broken it. Dragonetz could not blame Ramon Berenguer for the war if it came. And yet he wished he could prevent it, for the sake of Provence, and for a man who was dear to him.

'Make a list of those who ride with us,' he instructed his commander. 'But we will wait as long as we can, be it one year or ten. If we can avoid war, we will.'

Alone, Ramon replied to the letters. Gratitude to El Rey Lobo. Terms to Genoa. And then a letter to Dragonetz, releasing him as promised. The knight would not be implicated if Ramon waged war on les Baux. He'd always said he would not take sides.

Ramon remembered heated debates over the Usatges, camaraderie on dusty plains and in halls. Most of all he remembered a hawk and friendship. Alone, he raised his cup to the men he would see no more. 'To Malik, whose ancestors shelter my descendants. And to Dragonetz, who will be his own ruler one day.'

Then he let the present fill his mind. Petronilla watched over their little boy like a farmer over a malformed calf and, so far, they had not conceived another heir. He had to reassure her daily that God was not punishing them and truly he could not think of any couple who deserved punishment less. But he did wonder, sometimes.

Still, in every day there was matter for rejoicing. He would gather his merchants and discuss new contracts, taxes and tariffs for Tortosa.

CHAPTER TWENTY-ONE

This time Dragonetz rode in at Rhys' side, at the head of men who'd glutted on victory and liked the taste. Tossing the reins to whoever stood near enough, Dragonetz dismounted in one fluid movement and pulled Estela into his arms, battle hunger turning to desire.

Rhys too was looking for one person, and found him just as quickly. 'Ceredigion is ours!' he told Maredudd, clasping him in a hug that nearly lifted them both off the ground.

The shadow of a darker expression crossed Maredudd's face, quickly replaced with an exaltation that mirrored his brother's. 'You've done it, then! They tried to pen us in Cantref Mawr but Deheubarth is ours again, all of it!'

'*We've* done it,' Rhys corrected quickly. 'And we'll celebrate tonight! I don't think anybody will be a threat for some time, so we can leave enough here to hold the castle and we can go home!' After the slightest pause, he added, 'What do you think?'

Maredudd smiled. 'How could I disagree?' He yelled for all the courtyard to hear. 'We celebrate my brother's victories, our victories, and then we go home! Open the casks, prepare some food – let's not waste our stores on the lazy lumps who'll stay here when we've gone!'

The uproar suggested that the night would be long and the morning longer, bedevilled with sore heads and bad tempers. But if that was the worst of it while they secured Llansteffan and prepared to leave, any leader would be well pleased.

'Celebrate and go home,' Dragonetz heard Estela whisper, her words muffled against the bare skin under his open jerkin.

The morning after, there were sore heads and bad tempers aplenty but the only unpleasant surprise for Dragonetz was the sight of Estela slipping out of castle with Maredudd. 'Sneaking off' was the term that came first to mind, shocking him with its implications.

He forced himself to think, not to rush after them, or Maredudd's head would be on the battlements. He counted heartbeats until they were out of sight and he couldn't see their animated conversation about God-knew-what.

Then it was worse. If he couldn't see them, he didn't know what they were doing and it could be worse than talking. What had she meant when she told him she'd win Maredudd over? Had she used the tactics she'd learned in the kitchen from these camp followers with whom she lived.

Crazy he told himself. *You're still battle-crazy.*

He was still unsettled by the emotions unleashed by a hard campaign. Not as bloody as the taking of Tenby, for the Gwynedd men saw defeat coming and had no motivation to hold Ceredigion against the passionate opponents. No man wanted to die for greed's sake but to regain the land his father had lost, when the prize dangled within reach, a man would always risk more. And Rhys inspired loyalty.

The rush of fighting anger that came as the battle cry *Cofiwch Gwenllian!* swept through the Deheubarth men, bonding them to the death: Dragonetz felt it too. He also felt a thousand other battles guiding his every move. A thousand times he'd allowed instinct to take over. It was not easy, afterwards, to put the inner wolf back in its cage, to behave with honour and courtesy, to remember that a sword did not solve all problems. Not even a sword like Talharcant.

Only other warriors could know how it felt, this duality, and few of them bothered to struggle. Dragonetz could count on his fingers the men who'd been true brothers at arms. Rhys was the wildest of them, courageous and ruthless. Estela would not joke about blinding and gelding if she knew how little Rhys would hesitate to give such an order, regardless of the man thus sentenced.

Malik had been the partner who completed him; scimitar with sword, experience with ingenuity, loyalty beyond question. *Dearest friend of my mind.*

Ramon Berenguer was the one leader who had claimed Dragonetz' service through respect, not just by a vassal's oath, and Barcelone's judgement and restraint were exemplary – El Sant indeed. Thinking about the best leader he'd ever known calmed Dragonetz, distracted him from the route to the beach his mind was taking, following Maredudd and Estela in his unruly imagination.

He stayed at his post watching the gate, waiting and reminiscing. There had been other comrades, once. Raoulf, who'd known him from boyhood, and who'd once been Dragonetz' right arm. Raoulf's son Arnaut, a friend for life, but for such a short life. Arnaut would have followed Rhys to hell and back, as he'd followed Dragonetz. Only he'd not come back.

And Geoffroi de Rançon. When Dragonetz and Geoffroi had fought back to back at Les Baux they had created something fine, a moment of pure chivalry, a true note in a song. Geoffroi, who'd kissed Estela. Dragonetz let the hatred rage red through his blood.

Geoffroi. Maredudd. These men who wanted his woman. Who touched her. Who did with her what he had done last night.

Then he unclenched his fists. *Enough* he told himself. *I am better than this.* Aliénor's court of love had decreed that there was no love without jealousy and maybe that was true but nothing said he had to let such a sin govern his behaviour. And he no longer doubted that it was a sin.

He did not like being ignorant of what Estela was doing with

Maredudd so, he must either ask her what it was, or suffer until she told him or he found out. As penance for his doubts, he decided on the latter course.

He'd almost turned to go when he caught the movement at the gate for which his heart had been waiting, wherever his thoughts wandered. Estela had returned, with Maredudd beside her, the two of them looking even more furtive than when they'd left about an hour earlier. Dragonetz was *not* imagining it.

He took his time going down the steps from the battlements but his hand rested on Talharcant and his gaze never left Estela.

He was watching as a woman suddenly screamed, launched herself at Estela from behind, gouging at her eyes, pulling her hair free of its net, into black waves. *Mair! Trying to finish what she'd started! But no, this one was light-haired.*

Dragonetz ran the remaining steps but before he could intervene, another woman, who *was* Mair, grabbed Estela's attacker and winded her with a well-placed knee, while Maredudd stood between Estela and the pair of Welshwomen.

As far as Dragonetz could understand the Welsh, Mair said something that started with a string of insults and finished, 'He was teaching her sword-fighting, you stupid bitch! Haven't you seen she has eyes only for Long Shadow, or I'd have killed her myself over Lord Rhys! Look you – Lord Maredudd is wearing two swords because she was using one of them to learn!'

Long Shadow observed that, sure enough, there were two swords belted round Maredudd's hips. *Thank God!* Dragonetz thought, understanding how stupid he'd been. The attacker, Maredudd's woman, was clearly acting from the same mistaken jealousy he'd been trying to fight.

'Estela, no!' he yelled, as she reached into her underskirt, red-faced and breathing heavily. He caught her wrist just in time to prevent her drawing a weapon close enough to the Lord of Deheubarth to alarm those around him.

However obvious the provocation to Estela, Dragonetz did *not* want to face another session of Deheubarth justice. He had spent hours during the campaign discussing Barcelone's Usatges with Rhys but he wouldn't want to test how fertile the ground had been by placing Estela (and himself) on trial again. The Deheubarth idea of mercy was still maiming, with or without incarceration.

'*Paid*,' he told her, the Welsh instinctive after riding so long with Rhys' band. 'Don't. Let my Lord Maredudd deal with it.'

She stilled under his restraint, although still flushed, her eyes flashing the daggers she dared not draw.

Dragonetz held his breath, knowing better than to plead leniency, knowing how Maredudd would react. If the Welsh lords chose to demonstrate their authority, they would do so, regardless of whether they thought any crime had been committed. Unlike Rhys, Maredudd had not been listening to extracts from the Usatges for the preceding weeks. He'd been confined to bed and then chafed by the knowledge that Rhys was fighting for Ceredigion – without him. And with Dragonetz. No, he was unlikely to be in the best of humours.

The courtyard was silent for a long moment as men watched to see how Maredudd would deal with his woman's attack on their guest. The second such attack. Mair had let go of the fair-haired woman, who stood, defiant, waiting for a reaction.

Then Maredudd threw back his head and roared with laughter, grabbed her, kissed her and slapped her behind in rough approval. His words made coarse reference to enjoying a woman with spirit and she slipped her gown off one shoulder in a flirtatious exchange, then the tenor changed. Maredudd took both her shoulders in his warrior's hands, held her away from him, spoke calmly but firmly. The woman turned and ran, sobbing. Mair went after her, shaking her head.

Incensed at this new insult to Estela, Dragonetz moved to speak his mind but it was Estela's turn to catch his arm and hold him back.

'*Paid*,' she echoed, 'Don't. He told her, Enid, that she's staying here when we leave tomorrow. When *he* leaves tomorrow. That the world holds many women and he has not finished trying them – but he has finished with her.'

'He showed disrespect to you,' murmured Dragonetz. 'There was no apology for your treatment.'

'I'm a woman.' Estela shrugged. She looked towards the two women, disappearing into the shelter of the kitchen. 'You see how women are treated.' Then her eyes gleamed with mischief. 'I caught him across the back of his shins this morning and he'll carry some bruises for underestimating me. And I've had the chance to prattle about politics, featherbrained female that I am.'

He couldn't help smiling. 'You'll stop now?' He tried not to plead. 'Not ask for sword practice with him again.'

'I'll stop,' she agreed. 'I've learned enough for it to be dangerous with a man of his temper. Especially after this morning. And we're moving north now. Everything will be different.' A thought struck her and she regarded him, eyes narrowed. 'You weren't jealous, were you?'

'Of course not,' he replied. 'In fact, I look forward to seeing what such a second-rate swordsman taught you. I hope I don't have to correct too many bad habits.'

Later, Estela spoke to Mair, thanked her.

'I didn't do it for you,' was the brusque response.

'Nevertheless,' persisted Estela. 'I understand.'

'Do you?' Mair looked at her. 'What do you think will happen to us now the men are going home?' She answered her own question. 'Some will stay here and carry on as we are, with the men who stay. But we can't all stay. The rest will go back to Caerfyrddin and to Dinefwr, where the wives and children wait. Some will have second-best children of their own, maybe supported if they're lucky, and they'll lead their second-best lives in their filthy huts, until they fall sick and die.'

Estela thought about Rhys, about his plans with Gwenllian. She did understand. 'You'll stay here,' she said.

'Yes,' said Mair. 'I'm one of the lucky ones.'

Enough provisions were left for the trimmed garrison and the rest packed into the wagons. The Welsh travelled light and by morning Rhys and Maredudd had their party on the road following the river north. By the end of the afternoon they were in Caerfyrddin, its grim hill fortress warning them against hopes of comfort.

Estela did not want to travel in a cart with the other women. Already, she could feel the difference between her status and theirs, of which Mair had reminded her. She had not thought of herself as a lady for months now but she must, if she were to greet women of noble Welsh blood. She could not even imagine how such women would dress or behave.

She rode with John Halfpenny, as Dragonetz was like a will o' the wisp, one moment with Rhys and Maredudd at the front and then checking the wagons and the men riding at the rear, alight with dangerous energy. She had not seen him like this since they came to Gwalia. Whereas she felt a growing need for caution and felt wary of the social requirements ahead, Dragonetz had come through battles unscathed and had let down his guard. He was dazzling in his armour and his confidence. She saw Maredudd glancing at him, watching the ease with which Rhys spoke to her knight. They had campaigned together. They had won Ceredigion. And Maredudd had not been there.

Her uneasy stomach warned her to be careful, reminded her of other times, other places, but however well she knew Dragonetz, he could always surprise her.

They were welcomed civilly enough, given food and watered wine, then allocated quarters and paillasses that smelled fresh. The night might even pass without being bitten by bugs. Dragonetz and Estela had the luxury of a curtained recess, with only a select handful of men sharing the chamber. Rubbing her weary legs, waiting for

Dragonetz to finish talking to Rhys and Maredudd, Estela thought she might even get a good night's sleep.

Then, Dragonetz told her what he had planned for the night. She had not seen that particular crazy light in his eyes since he accepted a Viking Prince's challenge to combat. And she had hoped to never see it again.

CHAPTER TWENTY-TWO

When Rhys had suggested the coracle race, inviting Dragonetz to be his partner, eyes dancing, Maredudd said, 'You will lose for the first time, my brother.'

'We always win, you and I!' Rhys replied, seemingly unaware of the hurt he'd caused. 'I need a new challenge! I think you underestimate Long Shadow!'

'You are the best of us,' acknowledged Maredudd, 'and with me you *will* always win! With this...' words failed him. 'I do not want to race against you, knowing I must win. There is no sport in that!'

'My Lords, if I can make a suggestion?' Dragonetz was all humility. 'Clearly, I am a beginner and a liability but there is a man even worse than I... if Lord Rhys is the best coracle fisherman, then he should pair with the worst, and I with Lord Maredudd.'

He gave a guileless smile at his proposed partner, who glared back.

'Who?' asked Rhys.

'John Halfpenny.'

They all stared at the moneyer, who turned white and stammered, 'My Lords, I... I...' He caught Dragonetz' eye. He gulped. 'It would be an honour,' he said.

They tossed a coin for which pair should start first downriver, established the rules, allowed time for wagers to be placed and a welcome committee to set off along the river to the point where the competitors would land. The pairs would then run home with their catch and coracles. Whichever pair reached Caerfyrddin Castle safely, with the bigger catch by weight, would be declared winner.

'You're going night fishing?'

Estela was looking at him wide-eyed as if he were talking in a foreign language.

Patiently, he repeated, 'It's a contest. We are going out in coracles – the Welsh use them for fishing. We'll be in pairs, to see who can catch the most fish – they say salmon or sewin will jump into the nets, and maybe eels too.'

'At night,' repeated Estela stupidly.

'It's a seven-stars night,' explained Dragonetz. 'The fishing is best after the first floods of autumn and when it's dark enough to only see seven stars.'

'It's night, it's November and you've never even seen a coracle, never mind rowed one. I take it that the two of you row the boat?'

'I *have* seen one!' Dragonetz was aggrieved. 'They keep them beside the stables. And it's a paddle, not an oar. And just one man to a boat. Though they say there are two-men boats in Ceredigion.' He deeply regretted not bringing one back. Two-men boats would have been fun. He could have invited Estela to be his partner.

'You and Rhys, partners?' she asked, disapproving.

That would have been the perfect partnership but he knew Estela had seen what he had. 'No,' he reassured her. 'Me and Maredudd.'

'Perfect,' she said. 'There's nothing like being out at night in the pitch-black on the sort of river men drown in by daylight, with a man so jealous of you he'd let a tree accidentally knock you unconscious.'

That was exactly what Dragonetz was looking forward to – a challenge that could win hearts without sacking a castle, where the only risk was to himself. That, and the sheer enjoyment of learning something new in the company of young men as desperate for action as he was.

'They're placing high bets on the outcome. We're the longest odds,' he told her with satisfaction. Trying to sound responsible, he added, 'The men need an outlet for their high spirits, after campaigning hard.'

She wasn't fooled. 'As do you,' she said. 'Well, if the odds are stacked against you, then you'd better win.'

He felt the rush of excitement coursing through him. 'I intend to,' he said.

Her lips tightened in a way that suggested the wise traveller's disapproval but she said nothing more.

'I'll take care,' he promised her and kissed her. 'Sleep well.'

Within the hour, Maredudd and Dragonetz were at work, trailing a net between the two coracles, with Rhys and Halfpenny somewhere behind them. *Going first should be an advantage* thought Dragonetz. *We'll have first pickings and if the fish are disturbed by us, they'll be wary. But then, perhaps disturbed fish would jump more readily into the net?* He had no idea whatsoever, and no intention of asking Maredudd, who would probably bite his head off for making a noise.

Pitch-black overestimated the light provided by the obligatory seven stars but Dragonetz' elation was only slightly dampened by the chill mist hanging over the water, which rolled endlessly before his fragile craft. His paddle dipped and rose, caught an awkward angle and made a scudding series of splashes. His partner hissed disapproval.

Although unseen, Maredudd was but a net's length away in his identical one-man boat. The coracle reminded Dragonetz of half a walnut shell, magicked to giant size for some children's tale of adventure. So light it bobbed and swung with each whim of the current, the coracle was more highly-strung than any horse Dragonetz had ever ridden. Through trial and error, he was learning to place and pace the paddle-stroke or the boat danced in a dizzy circle and tangled the net, earning more tsks through gritted teeth.

Dragonetz could see his end of the net but not where it reached the other coracle and his invisible partner. Maredudd's skilled paddle made barely a splash above the gush of rills entering the main flow, or splitting round drowned trees.

Boulders near the bank broke the verses and the water music sang its journey in Dragonetz' imagination until he could read the darkness. The east bank was more hazardous, whirls and stops, like a trumpet call then a flute, jarring; the west bank smoother, a consistent shake of tambour, an underlying rhythm. The coracles held to the middle and, now, Dragonetz could hear where the middle was, by listening to the banks either side. He could hear where Maredudd was by the noises the water made round the other coracle, the soft parting as men, boats and all creatures on and in the river, ran with the current.

All but the fish they sought. This was the season the salmon and sewin ran upriver, driven by an instinct stronger than any current, stronger even than waterfalls, the Welsh Lords had told Dragonetz. Hold your net until they come and they will rush into it like a man to a woman's arms, for the same urge drives them and they can't hold back or escape.

Could it really be so easy? Only if the fish came. An owl hooted and a small furry beast screamed. Night noises. And in the swirl of waters, Dragonetz heard something else, something he had only heard in his opium dreams. The river songs took different parts, played each its own melody and yet all harmonised in a beauty that brought tears.

Mists gathered, parted, streaked dragon's breath across the waters, whispered legends. Caerfyrddin, Myrddin's place, full of magic. On such a night, anything was possible. Dragonetz' paddle dipped and rose. He was more alone than he'd ever been in his life yet he felt no fear. The mists thickened, confused the music of the banks but the angle of the net told him he was still heading true, if Maredudd knew his way.

The mist breathed in and out, a living being, and in it shapes formed and murmured to him in the language of another world. Beyond the dragon's breath, he saw another vessel loom, a barque, one he'd seen before, the heart of the siren-song. He could even distinguish words, 'Dragon, Dragonetz...' then the vision wavered into white flames, shivered to wisps and disappeared, taking the ethereal music, leaving the slap of water.

'You know I could kill you here,' the voice whispered, disembodied. Dragonetz had been so lost in the night world, he took a minute to adjust, to realise the voice was all too human. 'Coracles tip so easily and the water is deep and cold. You would not get back into the boat without help.'

'I know,' Dragonetz whispered back, still unafraid. Even a whisper carried too far as if ancient demons might arise from the river-bed. The wise traveller could have told him the names of such demons and how many limbs and teeth they possessed. Maybe it was better not to know. There were demons enough abroad this night.

'What would *you* do if you fell in the water?' he asked Maredudd, as if they were discussing dinner. Which perhaps they were; fishes' dinner.

'Turn the coracle upside down, hold to it, bang on it like a drum and call for help. Hope that somebody heard.' Maredudd's words were visible to Dragonetz as wraiths of mist, dank and deadly, presaging his doom. 'Nobody will come for you, Long Shadow.'

The net shifted slightly and Dragonetz crossed himself, prepared for the jerk and capsize that would end his life but thinking of ways to live on.

The jerk when it came was a slippery, silver tidal wave accompanied by Welsh curses and then, impossibly, laughter. Instinctively, Dragonetz held the net for dear life, half-thinking he could cling to Maredudd's boat if he lost his own in a struggle. The net was nearly wrenched from his hands as fish after fish jumped into, over and around the net.

'Hold fast! They are running! Bring the net to me!' Maredudd hurled instructions as the net bulged, fighting like one trapped beast.

Dragonetz used his paddle to bring his coracle nearer the other. He reached across with his end of the net, helped Maredudd lift the catch, close and tie the net into a trap. This would have been the ideal moment to catch Dragonetz off-balance.

'It's too heavy,' Maredudd complained, shaking some fish out until he was happy the net would hold. The mist cleared enough for Dragonetz to see the glittering catch landed in Maredudd's boat, flipping tails.

'Would you like to beat your little brother?' Dragonetz asked.

'He might do just as well,' Maredudd pointed out.

'But not twice as well.' Dragonetz produced a second net from the bottom of his boat, and threw the end to Maredudd.

'We never use two nets!' Maredudd spoke, then thought, and grinned. 'But there's no rule against it.'

There was no time to waste while the shoal was running and as soon as the net was placed, the coracles parted to allow another shining mass to hit the mesh. This time Dragonetz was prepared for the body blow and the judgement of how big a haul they could keep and carry. With Maredudd's advice, he took the catch aboard, knotted the net safely and they paddled onwards, more slowly.

'That was fine sport, my Lord,' whispered Dragonetz.

'The best, Long Shadow. Save your strength to carry the catch back to the castle,' was the reply. They understood one another.

Behind the mists on the west bank was the red eye of fire. Dragon's breath and dragon flame changed to men's figures and beacons as they neared the landing stage, where the welcome party was waiting. Murmurs became shouts as the men named Maredudd, saw the catch that Dragonetz held up with pride.

When Maredudd held up the second haul, men dropped to their knees before him and talked of miracles, signs from God. With a more important goal in mind, Maredudd barely took time to enjoy the adulation. He threw Dragonetz' catch into a sack, tied it like a knapsack to the knight's back, strapped him into the coracle and told him to get going.

As he set off, Dragonetz was aware of Maredudd stealing a

man's cloak to enclose his own catch, for nobody had thought of a second net and Maredudd would not have Rhys cry foul for taking the other team's sack. Then, strapped into his own coracle, Maredudd caught up with Dragonetz and they jogged the path back to the castle. The supporters who accompanied them were already arguing about how much money they would make, as they lit the way with torches.

They must look ridiculous thought Dragonetz, like giant tortoises stumbling along in a race to beat the hare. Only the hare in this instance was another pair of tortoises. His heart pounding and his sense of smell deadened from brackish water and fishiness, Dragonetz followed in Maredudd's footsteps, at his pace, and knew they would win. He could feel that Maredudd knew it too. There were many ways to be brothers-in-arms.

Arrival at Caerfyrddin castle was an anti-climax but it was good to drop the weight of coracle and catch. The fish were weighed in the pan-balance installed specially for the occasion in the courtyard, and the noise suggested appropriate respect for their achievement.

Dragonetz barely noticed the weighing and comments. Sweat ran down his back, probably augmented by river-water and fishy fluids but he was oblivious to his appearance. He saw only the woman who had not gone to sleep but who was waiting there for his return, wearing blue ribbons, his colours. In a few strides, she was in his arms and he whirled her around, ignoring the instinctive recoil as she inhaled his perfume.

'We did it!' he told her.

'Of course you did.' She smiled. And somehow Maredudd was not included in either her words or her smile. *That* made Dragonetz feel even better.

There was even more cheering as Rhys and Halfpenny appeared, equally repellent in smell and appearance; equally exuberant. Rhys unloaded a catch bigger than Maredudd would have considered safe or portable. It should have been a winner. Maredudd and Dragonetz exchanged a glance of pure triumph as Rhys saw the two nets and his face fell. No weighing was needed to declare the winning team and matters quickly proceeded to the settlement of wagers accompanied by the necessary jugs of wine.

Even though he'd carried only his coracle, John Halfpenny was in the worst condition and he dropped to the ground, lying on his back, panting.

'Thank you,' Dragonetz told him quietly.

'I have spent so long with fishes I am quite floundering.' Halfpenny opened one eye. 'Battles,' he said. 'I prefer battles. And campaigns. Bloody ones.' He shut his eyes again. 'A bath. I be needing a bath.'

That was a sentiment with which all contestants could agree and despite the late hour, they found water. As much ducking and splashing as was possible for four men in a horse trough provided enough spectator sport to finish a match that was declared 'legendary' by all who were there.

CHAPTER TWENTY-THREE

Homecoming was a triumph. The Deheubarth men entered the stronghold in Dinefwr to impromptu fanfares and a growing crowd, as those who'd been left behind dropped what they'd been doing, to welcome their warriors.

Riding together at the rear of the party, Estela and Dragonetz benefited from the increased volume of roars as word of victory spread, and ever more people joined the throng.

'You must be proud,' Estela murmured.

'I am. That was the tastiest fish I have *ever* eaten! We should introduce sewin to the Ebro.'

'Parsley sauce,' observed Estela, 'and I don't think sewin would swim up to Zaragoza. You'd lose them at sea.'

'Wave,' he told her. 'They think we're heroes.'

Estela waved and smiled graciously. If Aliénor could only see how they'd carried out her commands. They were here in the heart of Deheubarth, honoured guests.

As the crowd parted, she saw the Welsh nobles, waiting at the foot of the main tower, across the courtyard. Although their clothes would seem rustic in Aliénor's court and the colours common, they were at least tailored and in blue, red and green rather than the dull browns to which Estela had become accustomed. Which she herself was wearing.

Although she had been schooling herself to return to society, Estela was shocked by how far she had grown used to living with camp followers and soldiers, living a spartan and communal existence. She flushed at how she must look and glanced at Dragonetz.

He had never looked finer, his hauberk and Damascene sword marking him out, long black locks escaping from the mail coif. He had flatly refused to let any man cut his hair, to the point where his comrades threatened to do so in his sleep, but he had conceded over facial hair. Estela thought his Welsh moustache rather attractive but maybe her judgement had been as corrupted as her behaviour by months in Llansteffan.

She glanced down at her grease-stained gown. If only women wore armour! 'Wave,' she told Dragonetz. 'They think we're heroes.'

The men they'd travelled with, lived with, and slept with, were dismounting, clasping loved ones. Every stone in the castle rang with love and laughter as old men welcomed their sons home; wives sent their children, giggling, to pull on their fathers' cloaks and fight for attention; grandmothers clucked and the warriors who'd been left behind demanded battle tales.

Estela watched a toddler trip as he reached cautiously for this strange man, his father, home from the wars. The man scooped him up, soothed him, called him *'bachgennyn'*, 'sweet little boy,' and Estela's heart broke into a million pieces. She kept the smile fixed on her face, dismounted, ignored Dragonetz calling to her and used the crowd to disappear, fight her way through to an arch and into darkness. Where she sobbed until she could control herself, pat her face dry, fix the smile back in place and then return to the mass of people.

When she had worked her way back to Dragonetz, she answered his anxious look. 'Just relieving myself before everyone here has the same need.'

He nodded acceptance of her excuse but the anxiety stayed in his eyes. He knew her too well.

'There is news,' he told her. 'While we reclaimed Deheubarth,

Henri has won England. He is Stephen's heir. The summer agreement is formal now, enshrined in a treaty and signed by all parties.'

'And Stephen's health?'

'Fading.'

So, time would bring Henri – and Aliénor – to the throne of England, God willing. Meanwhile, their loyal subjects must endeavor to win over their less-than-loyal subjects in Deheubarth.

In the familiar routine of castle life, horses were stabled, men billeted and guests allocated beds. Dragonetz and Estela were now guests. Treated as a lady, Estela remembered how a lady should behave, and her reward came in the form of two clean gowns, one red and one blue. Not all the finery of Aliénor's court seemed as beautiful to her as these simple garments. The addition of a pair of new boots was the cherry on the cake.

Peace and security were their new bedfellows, along with John Halfpenny and Wyn, who ensured a curtain was in place before Estela's head touched the pillow. When she woke in the night, she could take comfort in privacy; tracing the familiar outline of shoulder-blades, of the muscles in a man's sword-arm.

'When can we go home?' she whispered.

Dragonetz was not asleep either. He turned to hold her. 'Rhys says we must stay until Twelfth Night. It was not an invitation.'

'Another six weeks.' Her heart sank. 'And we spend Christmas here.'

'Then we go home,' he promised.

On Santa Barba's Day, Estela rose very early and went to the kitchen in search of soup bowls. The Welsh often made a soup they called cawl, and she had no problem finding suitable bowls. Three would not be missed among so many, and three was the number required by the seasonal tradition of her homeland.

Then she went outside and scooped enough earth from the kitchen garden to fill the bowls. She untied the little pouch she'd carried across land and sea, and shared the wheat seed between the bowls.

Musca and his little friend Primo should have been with her. They were old enough this year to put soil in the bowls with their stubby fingers, to press the seeds into the top, and to watch the magic of the next three weeks which would open those dry cases and let the green shoots grow.

She remembered her mother reminding her to water them each day; her own excitement as green shoots poked through the surface and sprang tall; her pride at table on Christmas Eve when she placed her three fine fields of wheat by the three candles. Had her father praised her or did her memories add love that never existed?

Her mother's warmth was no false imagining and she wished with all her soul that she could be to her son all that her mother had been to her. More than that: she wished she could be the heart of a domain as her mother had been to Montbrun. The heart of Dragonetz' domain.

Wiping her eyes with the back of her hand, Estela took the three bowls back into the kitchen, to the great fireplace, where yesterday's logs kept their heat without flames, ready to spark anew when today's wood joined them.

She placed the three bowls carefully at the back of the hearth, where they would be warm and get some light, but would not be scorched. She told a cook what she intended and the woman had taken pity on the foreign guest, assured her that the wheat for Santa Barba would come to no harm.

Satisfied with her work, Estela returned to her accommodation, slipped out of her gown and back into bed. Dragonetz half-woke, murmured, 'You've got mud on your nose,' and closed his eyes again.

Estela rubbed wet and soil around on her face, then went back to sleep.

Rhys and Maredudd had turned into the most considerate of hosts – or of gaolers. Estela was not sure which but she accepted all the invitations to ride out with them. Dragonetz must take every opportunity to plead for King Henri and she would do her part. In truth, discovering the Cantref Mawr, the land at the heart of Deheubarth, was no hardship to a curious mind. A wise traveller took every opportunity to learn all he – or she – could about a place and its people.

Before the brothers had regained their previous kingdom, Cantref Mawr had been all they were allowed to keep, a tiny portion of Deheubarth but a green land of woods, lakes, streams and legends.

'This is all part of the region where my mother and father lived in the woods, before he left for the north, and she for the last battle.' Maredudd told them, as they looked out across a vast lake, turquoise as kingfisher's wings. 'When we are at war, we retreat here, to the land around Caio. Our people can live in the woods, be harder to find than the Tylwyth Teg, build huts in a day and move as quickly.'

'On a day just like this, with the winter-fowl calling on the lake, my father passed by, returning from the English court, with some of the King's greatest lords for company. Earl Milo of Hereford mocked my father's claim to noble blood. He said there was a saying in Gwalia that should the land's rightful ruler order the birds on this lake to break into song, then they would obey.

'Then go you first,' said my father, 'as you believe in your right.'

First Milo, then Payn Fitzjohn, each in his turn, ordered the birds to sing but nothing happened.

Then my father prostrated himself as before a battle and prayed, saying to the Lord, 'If I am the true descendant of the five princes of Cymru, let these birds announce it in your name!' Then all the birds on the water, each in his manner, beat its wings and sang to acknowledge their rightful ruler.'

'It is a good tale,' Rhys pronounced, 'but I would not test it.'

'It is our tale, brother!'

They rode from the lake to the River Cothi, 'famed for its sewin'. Maredudd and Dragonetz exchanged a smile.

Did your people build something there?' Dragonetz was pointing into a ravine, towards what looked like a ruined tower.

'No, that's an illusion. It's just a stone,' Maredudd replied, 'but there are initials carved there and red bricks from old times, from the Romans who lived here centuries ago. They called it the Red Town for its red rock. There are old mineworks and a rock called Clochdy Gweno haunted by the ghost of a girl, Gweno.' He looked hard at Estela, 'She went exploring beyond the limits of the rock, into the caves and tunnels, and was taken by the forces of evil–'

Rhys cut in. 'Dragonetz has no interest in ancient history or ghost stories.' He turned his horse away from the ravine more smoothly than he turned the subject. 'When your King comes to his throne, will you ride beside him? Against Deheubarth?'

'He will have no need to ride against Deheubarth if you are his ally. And why would you not be?' countered Dragonetz. 'King Henri has done you no wrong and has no reason to love the lords you've defeated. He has regained his rightful kingdom, that his mother lost. You have regained your rightful lands, those your father lost. How could he not take your part? Especially when you keep the Marcher Lords from abusing their power.'

Rhys frowned. 'They will take their grievances to him, threaten to cause uprisings if he does not make good their claims to our land and help them get it back.'

'Yes, they will. And Henri will have to choose the force which offers his new kingdom more stability; the might of Deheubarth or a handful of Marcher Lords, who bicker among themselves at the drop of a gauntlet. He'll have to consider which poses the greater threat; Deheubarth slighted or that same handful of Marcher Lords. I know what choice I'd make, were I king! Or do you think so little of the might of Deheubarth?'

Rhys was no dullard and cut to the heart of what Dragonetz did not say. 'There is no question of our might. But if the king decides he cannot trust Deheubarth, he will choose the lesser force.'

'Can he?' asked Dragonetz. 'Can he trust Deheubarth?'

The question hung in the air. 'And if he doesn't. Will you ride with him against us?' Rhys answered question with question.

'I hope to be far from here, in my own domain, from which I have too long been absent.' Dragonetz also ducked the question. This was news to Estela. Did he mean Malik's villa in Zaragoza?

'But you are vassal to King Henri,' observed Rhys, pressing the point.

'As are you,' was Dragonetz' riposte.

'We do not acknowledge your system. No Welsh are vassals.' Rhys was adamant. *Which is why they can't be trusted* thought Estela. 'But you have taken an oath. One that matters to you.'

'Yes,' said Dragonetz.

'And you don't even know what the man looks like!' Rhys grunted his contempt and no more was said on the matter.

Later that evening, when they were alone, Estela broke off from describing her favourite parts in the day's ride when she saw that Dragonetz was not listening.

'What's wrong?' she quizzed him. 'You have sowed the seeds that should bloom into an alliance if the Welsh lords have any sense. They could not have been more amiable to us.'

'That's what worries me. They know I am Henri's man and yet they are showing me how attractive their lands are. They have hidden nothing from me of their military strength and tactics. In their place, I would hide every asset.'

'Maybe they trust you. And they wouldn't consider me important.'

'Maybe.'

CHAPTER TWENTY-FOUR

T*he vagaries of Winter weather in Cymru – Gwalia, as we call the land.*
When snow has fallen, the wise traveller should avoid boys, and men who behave like boys. Such people will look for every opportunity to compromise the dignity of others, whether by rendering paths slippery underfoot or by hurling compacted balls of snow.

Estela smiled as she sucked her bedraggled quill. Not since she'd been a girl bombarding her brother and Gilles from a perch in a tree had she so much enjoyed pelting a man with snowballs. Her face still glowed from the fresh cold and her back tingled, wet from a handful that had been thrust down the neck of her gown in very unchivalrous manner. Dragonetz was no doubt suffering from melting snow too. She smiled to herself again and hoped no prying eyes had followed their excursion into the glittering woods.

Perhaps they should have walked backwards so their footsteps hid an escape attempt, like that of King Henri's mother, Empress Matilda, when she left her castle prison. They too could have kept going, hired horses, fled to England and a sea-port, chartered a ship for home.

As if they would be able to hire horses! When she'd been told a million times, on every ride, that this was Deheubarth land, for days in every direction. The brothers would find them easily. And then there would be no leaving, ever. Her good humour vanished.

Patience. Tonight was Christmas Eve and there would be a celebration, with song. Maredudd and Rhys had promised them fine entertainment over the coming days and a chance for them to sing. Patience. Only thirteen days to wait.

The Christmas festivities were a mix of familiar and foreign traditions. Estela watched with approval as two men, chosen for their hulking strength, hobbled into the Great Hall with a Yule log that must have been half a well-aged tree. It would have been a fruit tree back home. Another familiar Christmas custom was the decoration of the Hall with boughs of holly, ivy and mistletoe, to keep evil spirits away.

Yes, that should burn through the twelve days, she thought, as the huge log was joined by its ceremonial partner. Rhys brought in the small, half-charred remnant of last year's Yule log, and lit it from kindling already burning in the great fireplace. The wood of the old year sparked the future and the flame lived on, witnessed by all the courtiers.

She could not sprinkle wine on the log, as should be done, but she reached for Dragonetz' hand and squeezed it, sharing the moment.

He murmured the appropriate blessing in Occitan, 'Alègre, Diou nous alègre Cacho fio ven, tout ben ven; Diou nous fagué la graci de veïre l'an que ven, Si sian pas mai que siguen pas men. Good is coming. May God bless us in the coming year; if we are not more, may we not be fewer.'

The fasting of Advent had given an appetite for Christmas fare but Dinefwr plans were all for the banquets from Christmas Day onward. Estela missed the supper that was a Christmas Eve tradition at home, where salt cod and cardoons were followed by fresh and dried fruit, nuts and nougat. The desserts would be left on the tables throughout the twelve days of Christmas.

Here in Deheubarth, the Christmas Eve supper was a simple but filling soup. Vegetables, as always, were added like herbs, for flavour not substance, but meat was plentiful, and there was much talk of the feast planned for the next day. Estela knew from her visits to the kitchen that roast boar was on the menu and a dessert that required six hundred eggs. Her stomach liked the idea that there would be dessert, whatever it might be.

As the boys commenced serving, Estela excused herself. She met six well-rehearsed page boys in the kitchen and gave each one his precious burden. Solemn, with well-scrubbed faces, they paraded the length of the Hall to the High Table. Under Estela's supervision, they carefully placed their three candles and three bowls of wheat shoots in front of Rhys and Maredudd, who looked to Dragonetz for an explanation.

'My wife will explain our custom to you,' he told them.

'This is *lo blat de la Santa Barba,* the wheat planted on Santa Barba's Day,' she told them. 'If the wheat grows well, so shall your harvests in the year to come. If you plant these shoots in offering to the land, she will be fruitful in return. This is what we say, in my country.'

Rhys was at his most gracious. 'It is a beautiful tradition, my Lady.' He looked to Maredudd and said, 'We thank you.'

'*Does* it grow well?' Maredudd asked, looking at the spindly shoots.

'*Very* well, my Lord,' Estela reassured him.

'You will see one of *our* traditions this night,' Rhys told her. 'We celebrate Mass during the darkest hours, in our ceremony of Plygain.'

Long past midnight, long past the hour when Estela thought of oxen and asses, their speech as miraculous as the birth they witnessed, she and Dragonetz joined a torchlight procession to Mass in the chapel.

The Latin service was familiar, with the priest and the monk each playing their part, from the thrice rung bell to the raising of the chalice. What followed, however, was uniquely Welsh.

Four men made their way to the altar, through the crowd standing there. They formed a line and faced the congregation, then they began to sing. Music fit for such a time and place resounded from the stone as if a whole choir of brethren gave voice.

The songs were tales of Christ's death and birth, but also of everyman's life. Estela could not understand all the words but she could hear the music in them. Some songs were twenty verses or more but nobody stirred in complaint at their length.

What made the music heavenly was the combination of voices, and Estela suddenly understood what she was hearing, what she had heard before among the women in Llansteffan kitchen but thought she must have dreamt it. She was hearing what Dragonetz *had* dreamt and what none of their countrymen believed possible. The men were singing in parts, each his own, different melody. It was nothing like the effect of different voices singing in unison. Each voice followed its own melody. When one voice soared, another fell, and the blend was beyond beautiful.

'B flat,' murmured Dragonetz as he moved towards the altar and the singers, like a child seeing the Christmas desserts on the table. 'They start and end on B flat.' Then he was out of her hearing, as close as he could get to the music that had been his quest for two years.

Estela watched him listening. He was lost to everything but the way each part contributed to the whole. In between songs, he turned to look at her, to share the Christmas miracle. His eyes brimmed with unshed tears.

For now, they let the music flow through them. The words they did understand were markers, like boulders in the stream of sound, giving shape to the current.

Later, they would analyse the techniques used, argue about how many voices could follow different paths. Dragonetz' vision had seven voices. Was this possible? For the Welsh, such music was their tradition, both in church and out of it, with no thought that it might be unfit for praising God.

'Bestial,' Dragonetz muttered bitterly. 'That's what the Abbot of San Pau told me such a variation from their chant would be.'

'Nobody could listen to such music and think that!' Estela was outraged. 'You must show them! Talk to the Welsh singers, find out all you can and we'll bring your dreamsong to life!'

Dragonetz shook his head at how impossible their discovery seemed. 'How can a race of such barbarism be so cultured? Like a pearl, made from common dew and growing in a coarse shell.'

Estela put that same question to herself many times during the period she still thought of as the Calendale, the festive season. Stuffed to bursting with all the foods missing during advent, Estela still found room each day for a little more roast boar, venison, bacon with mustard, partridge pie, hen stew or pottage with lashings of butter, cream and cheese. There was even the luxury of whole pieces of vegetable to aid digestion, cabbages and leeks, which grew well in these lands.

Rhys had not exaggerated. Interludes between feasts were filled with dancing, music and poetry. Estela found herself ringing handbells while Dragonetz hit the tambour, and the Lords of Deheubarth started a dance movement by making reverence to their partners. Within the span of one turn of the dance circle, Estela was the one gracefully accepting reverence from Rhys while Dragonetz bent his right knee to a giggling Welsh matron.

The diners were awash with spiced wine when cake was served. *Six hundred eggs,* thought Estela, as she found just enough room for a small piece – and then another one.

A sudden commotion at the far end of the Hall was followed by rowdy cheers. A man was lifted onto the table where he danced a little jig and sang an impromptu ditty whose sole lyrics were variations on, 'I found the bean.' He raised the item in question so everybody could see the cause of his celebration. Nobody could, so they all took his word for it. There was only one bean in the cake and closer inspection proved that this was indeed a bean, complete with cake crumbs.

'John Halfpenny,' groaned Dragonetz, his head in his hands.

Maredudd stood, calmed the gathering and confirmed John Halfpenny's authority as the Lord of Misrule. Somebody found a staff with a fool's head and John Halfpenny began reciting jokes in what was clearly poor Welsh and even poorer taste, to judge by the groans.

Estela whispered to Dragonetz, 'Don't they usually kill the Lord of Misrule after Twelfth Night and plant him in a cornfield?'

'I do hope so,' Dragonetz replied, earning a wave of the fool's staff in his direction, and a barbed comment which was some play on the words 'Long Shadow' that Estela preferred not to understand.

To give Halfpenny his due, he did not lack inventiveness, and if he occasionally drew blood with his satirical humour, he also drew laughter with the games he proposed. Exactly what was needed during the dark season.

Estela was drawing breath after a particularly vigorous game of blind man's buff, when Halfpenny shook the bells on his staff and made his announcement.

'This was your idea, wasn't it!' Estela accused Dragonetz, whose mischievous eyes appeared above the blindfold as he loosened the ties and removed the frayed band.

'Maybe,' he acknowledged. 'Just as well for you, too. I nearly had you.'

It was true. She'd been trapped in his blind-man's arms, condemned to be the next to wear the blindfold, when Halfpenny had called the game to a halt.

She was indignant. 'Only because you cheated! You said you'd hurt yourself and I believed you!'

'I was very convincing, wasn't I.' He grinned and limped a little, rubbing his poor thigh, then pulled her close, whispered, 'I should have let the sport continue. I swear these Welshwomen are well-practised in tormenting a blind man.'

Estela was well aware of the liberties taken by courtiers of both sexes in touching and prodding their blindfolded victim. Old scores could be settled and new amours proposed, all in the guise of Christmas fun. Dragonetz could well have been really hurt from some of the buffets given him by husbands who resented their wives' squeals at being nearly caught. It was all part of the game.

'Sh,' she told him, but she stayed in the circle of his arms.

Rhys was speaking, accepting the role he'd been given by Halfpenny. 'Let it be as the Lord of the Season wills! We'll all gather in the Great Hall this evening for a grand tournament, with prizes for the best musician, the best singer and the best bard!'

'So, this is when we are allowed to sing in public,' observed Estela with satisfaction.

'Yes,' he said, tightening his embrace. 'What shall we sing?'

So it was that Estela held Rhys to his promise and sang for the Lords of Deheubarth, despite being a woman. Wyn introduced each song with a summary in Welsh but music has its own language and the court of Dinefwr was well-versed.

Estela began with an aubade, the dawnsong written by Dragonetz, easy for the audience to understand and with a hook to the melody that lingered in the memory.

She sang for the composer, her lover, who accompanied her on his lute and hummed a soft background. *As if in preparation for partsinging,* she thought, as she drew out the moment of parting to the last mournful note.

'My sweet, my own, what shall we do?
Day is nigh and night is over.
We must be parted, my self missing
All the day away from you.'

She was experienced enough as a troubadour to know the moment her audience forgot their conversations and cares, the moment when they were carried away on the stream of music. The moment of silence when she finished the aubade told her they were with her, and she felt confident enough to let Wyn introduce her second song.

'A new song, written for a Welshwoman of exceptional passion and the fair Prince of Deheubarth who inspired her.

Estela inclined her head to acknowledge Rhys and waited till the murmuring subsided. No doubt all were now familiar with the tale behind the song. Maybe if she sang well enough, the echo would reach Mair one day, let her know that all women could be heroines, *were* the heroines of the songs that they lived each day.

She sang the closing verse, in tribute and in mourning.

'Red drops he spilled
For the land of his fathers
Red drops she spilled
For the man she would keep.'

Estela moved to the empty place at the High Table, laid out as a reminder of the poor, so that symbolic food could be placed there and show gratitude for the bounty enjoyed. The more visible poor massed in front of the castle gate each morning and were well-rewarded. If the courtiers ate well, their left-overs were rich pickings and Christmas-tide was a feast shared.

Estela picked up the goblet at the empty place, held it high, paused deliberately and sang the closing couplet.

Drain the red drops from the chalice of life
Without thought for those staining the blade of a knife.

She placed the cup upside down, for the absent friend. The Hall was still. Nobody was sure how to react. Rhys' face was grim. He stood up and Estela's heart beat fast. She could not have written or performed better but she did not know how the golden prince would respond.

He threw his arms wide. 'Wonderful,' he told the Hall. 'You brought the symbolism of our Lord's life to a story of one man and one woman, made it universal. No Welsh bard could have done better.'

For a moment, she waited for him to say more, thinking he might ask whether Dragonetz had written the lyrics but she chid herself for seeing insult when none was even contemplated.

For Mair, for the bara lafwr, for the work we shared, thought Estela as she took the applause and curtseyed. Was that *hiraeth* she felt? For Llansteffan and for Gwalia itself? A rush of affection for these people and their place. *Home,* she thought. *Soon we'll go home. Before we forget where home is.*

She returned to Dragonetz, took the stool beside him and picked up her oud.

'Bravo,' he said, 'Nicely done.' The praise that mattered most to her.

She looked to Dragonetz and he nodded. She took a stool beside him, picked up her oud and it was his turn to start the duet that had become their hallmark.

'Can vei la lauzeta mover
de joi sas alas contra.l rai.'

'When I see the lark beat its wings
With such joy against the sunbeam.'

The song was known, even here, and Estela saw some smiles of appreciation at the twist they gave to the well-known lines. Such a song could be interpreted differently each time.

Changing their usual allocation of lines, Estela claimed the ending, made an ironic bow to Rhys as she sang

'De chanter me gic e.m recre,
E de joi e d'amor m'escon.'

'From singing I will refrain
As I shun all joy, all love, all.'

There followed instrumentalists and singers, poets and declaimers. Estela bet on a fiddler to win, Dragonetz on a flautist until a harper thin as his strings placed the instrument to his left shoulder and plucked the strings. The faerie music rippled through the air and the small hairs on Estela's arm shivered to attention.

'The harper,' they agreed in unison as the last beautiful notes faded. Never had they heard a harp played with such a combination of technique and art. With an instrument so difficult too! Truly, this was the land of music.

Of the singers, they could be more critical, but there were two whose phrasing impressed them, a red-haired foxy-faced youth and a rotund baritone who drew on his deep voice with ease. The others struck them as melodramatic, especially a stocky, bearded tenor – who won.

For the Welsh, the most important performers were the bards. Not only were they melodramatic but their poetry was beyond the level of the troubadours' Welsh although they understood some phrases and could appreciate the music of the verses.

Some bards recited the old poets, Taliesin and Aneurin. Some recited their own compositions, spinning magic tales of ravens and thick-maned horses, sons who did not flee, fair Enid and lying mirrors. Truly, the reputation of Welsh bards was well-deserved.

'Don't get your hopes up,' Dragonetz whispered. 'The prizes will go to the Welshman with the deep voice, who told of *the king who does not cower and does not hoard*. He deserves them too.'

'And I was so looking forward to a longbow and arrows.' Estela remembered other tourneys, other prizes and she felt the runes on her Viking brooch.

John Halfpenny stood up, jangled the bells on his fool's staff and announced, 'Let the prize-giving begin! I award the special prize for music that nobody here understands to...' He gestured to the drummer and was given a drum roll for suspense.

'...to Dragonetz los Pros!'

Polite applause changed to laughter as people realized exactly what was being presented to the foreign guest by the Lord of Misrule.

'May your next haircut be truly Welsh!' declared Halfpenny,

presenting Dragonetz with a pudding basin. The knight had no option but to bow low and accept the honour.

Then Rhys took over the ceremony, presenting rather more valuable rewards. A Pembroke herding dog was presented to the bearded tenor.

'I'd have liked *his* prize,' murmured Estela wistfully, wondering how Nici would have liked a short-legged friend.

There was a jeweled belt for the harper; and a Book of Hours for the grey-cloaked bard. Then, Rhys asked the bard, Ivor, to sit in the carved oak chair he himself had just vacated. He placed a laurel wreath on the Bard's head, proclaimed Ivor victor of the games. Rhys gave the tournament winner food and drink, with his own hands and instated Ivor as a counterpart of the light to Halfpenny's dark misrule. There were four days left until Twelfth Night. Until Halfpenny's reign was ended and they would be allowed to go home.

'No,' said Dragonetz that night in bed.

'I never asked for anything,' replied Estela.

'You can't take a Pembroke puppy home with you. Their legs are too short.'

Estela made no reply. But she had indeed thought about it.

CHAPTER TWENTY-FIVE

Dragonetz had learned all he could from the Plygain singers and, with so little time left in this country, he thought of all he had discovered that would be useful to Aliénor. Had he missed anything important? Something nagged at him, made the frenzy of eating, drinking and games seem an irritation.

The snow had melted as quickly as it had come and the roads were all passable. Dragonetz had once asked the Lords what changes they made to their plans if rain fell.

They'd looked at him bemused. 'None,' they told him. 'Or we'd never do anything. If it rains, we get wet.'

He looked at the rain and decided he'd get wet. He needed to get away, ride out on his own. He suddenly felt cooped up, after months of being watched, fitting into strangers' ways. He needed to be alone.

He asked no permission as his place was assured now within the Welsh court, after so long riding with Rhys and Maredudd. He had a pony saddled, barely thinking of the difference between the sturdy mare and his own Sadeek, so accustomed had he become to what was normal here.

Instinct made him head towards the village of Caio and as he rode, letting his mind wander freely, enjoying the absence of chit-chat, he suddenly remembered what he wanted to discover. Why had Rhys been touchy when Maredudd talked of the mines? *That* was the mystery which had been nagging him.

Dragonetz had been curious, had asked Halfpenny what sort of mines they were. The thought of a silver mine had brightened Halfpenny's eyes but nobody thought it likely. Dragonetz even asked Wyn but the answer had been slippery as the man himself.

'There has been no mining there for hundreds of years,' Wyn told him. 'Nobody there but ghosts to say what happened. Best forget the place.'

And Dragonetz *had* forgotten the place. Until now. He had some idea of the location, which was not far, and he set a relaxed pace through the woods. Hoofbeats, heartbeats, and the rain a light percussion in the background. Creatures with any sense hid or sheltered in their winter dens. Some trees bowed as he passed, their branches sweeping low; others opened their leafy fists in the breeze and showered him. No wonder the Welsh stories were full of mysterious woods.

His long leather jerkin, boots and gloves kept the moisture out well and he was glad he'd acquired a Welsh-style leather hood too, that laced up at his throat and covered his shoulders like a small cape. Only when the wind lashed a wicked branch did the chill rain, flung aslant, slice his face.

Accustomed to the climate, his mare picked her route steadily, her ears flicking to show she noticed the sudden movements in the wind, but she neither skittered nor mis-stepped. Instead, it was Dragonetz who jumped when a five-headed giant loomed out of the mist, in the few seconds before he recognized the standing stone by the mine. What had Maredudd called it? The 'Pumpsaint', 'Five Saints.'

Dragonetz could see the four faces in the rock now, the four saints who'd found shelter while the fifth joined King Arthur, who was asleep in the cave, waiting on his country's need. Would the hero of legend take Henri's side? From all he'd heard, Dragonetz suspected that the future king of England would rather be a legendary hero himself than be helped by one.

The mist hung heavy over the River Cothi – *dragon's breath again,* thought Dragonetz, *protecting Arthur and his cave*. Dragonetz retraced the route they'd taken when he rode here with the brothers, until he found the red rock, the one that had looked man-made. In the silver shimmer of rain, it was man-like, shifting and restless like its surroundings. A place where rocks had names.

Silver, thought Dragonetz again. Maybe it was a silver mine after all, although surely John Halfpenny would have known if there were one in this region. The mere mention of the word 'silver' made the moneyer's eyes shine as if made of his favourite metal. If not silver, then what? And why would the brothers not want to discuss what the ancients had been doing here? Were they just afraid of the ghosts? The ones who roamed, like Gweno, coming out of her stone and driving men insane; or the ones who lay with King Arthur, biding their time.

Dragonetz tied his mount to a tree and set off upstream, studying the ground, where the rain had channeled rivulets, washing gravel aside and exposing the bedrock. He looked closely at the rock, shining wet. Shining in the smooth way that water does on a dull day, not glittering with silver. A foolish thought.

He walked across the hillside, drawn to a shape that looked odd in the tufted grass, and he found an old stone slab, like those covering antique drains in Zaragoza. The slope would certainly carry water away towards the river but a drain, here in the wilds?

Maybe there had been a settlement here in the past. But that did not sit easily with the fact there were mines, as Maredudd had let slip. The kind of people who had drains would not want to live by a smelly, noisy mine. Dragonetz looked over the rocks beside him, down into the river valley where the mist snaked thickly, and over to the other side where the hills rose from the mist like an island, floating. He walked down, towards the caves, the tunnels and the ghosts.

The patterns of the terrain, bumpy, with trenches, told of some form of quarrying. *Gemstones?* wondered Dragonetz, cursing his ignorance. The signs were all here, if only he could read them.

Maybe the river was important, as it had been to his papermaking, but there was no mill here, just water and, if the square coverstone was any sign, the movement of water. Dragonetz followed the workings in the land, towards the dark holes that led into the earth.

The rainwater lay in the trenches and trickled its way like a liquid tree in ever lengthening branches. While avoiding one such pool, Dragonetz was distracted by a small pile of gravel thrown up from the churning mud, held fast by something more solid. He crouched and saw something glinting through the gravel. *Not that foolish notion again* he chid himself, but he scraped the gravel aside all the same, to see what lodged beneath.

What he found took his breath away.

Estela wasn't worried. He'd been cooped up so long and a chance to get away on his own was just what Dragonetz needed, even in this incessant grey rain. She could escape into the kitchen, into tending the sick (when she was allowed), into writing her guide. Anything to distract her from the refrain shaking her whole being. *Tomorrow we go home.*

She still wasn't worried as the light faded and she moved nearer the torchlight to read back over her description of Welsh Christmas customs.

She refused to worry when men crowded into the alcove where she was writing; when Rhys and Maredudd pushed through to her side. Dragonetz always came back. She dipped the quill in the inkwell and tried to finish her sentence.

Rhys knelt in front of her and his mouth moved. Words came from it.

Sorry. Dragonetz dead. Bloody clothes. His horse, Dragonetz, wolves.

The quill hovered over the page, mid-sentence, trembling a little. Everyone was waiting. Estela was supposed to say something, ask questions.

'Which men found him?' she asked politely. She nodded, hearing nothing of the answer. *Bloody clothes, wolves. Just like the false trail she'd left when she'd run for her life. False trail.*

'Wolves are too scared to kill an armed man,' she told them. She thought of Nici. He would never let wolves harm any of them. He was bred to protect them from wolves. He would give his life to keep them safe.

Rhys' mouth was moving again. Then Wyn was beside him, kneeling too. *The translator. Dragonetz says he always knows what's going on. Watch his face as well as hear his words.* His face was twisted. Why? Her curiosity let the words in.

'Here, the wolves in winter are starving and will take any risk for food. There is no doubt, my Lady. We found...' he swallowed but continued, his face twisting again, 'the remains. Him and his horse, in the woods.'

Here. Nici was not here. Things were different here. Estela completed the sentence she had been writing and added a full stop. She put the quill in the stand.

'I will get my medicine box,' she said. 'Take me to him. He might need surgery.' She stood, testing the ground beneath her feet. It was still there but it rocked like a boat. Strange. She shifted her weight from one foot to the other, testing the ground. It steadied.

Still kneeling, Rhys took her hand. 'My men buried him in the woods. They had no choice. There is nothing to see.'

'Take me to him,' Estela persisted. 'He needs me.'

'My Lady,' Rhys still held her hand, 'Lord Dragonetz no longer needs anybody or anything. I feel honoured to have known him.' His face twisted too. 'He was peerless.'

Was. One word that changed everything. She knew why their faces twisted. She turned her back on the men in the room, stared at the wall to hide her own loss of control. Grief. That's what twisted faces.

She glanced down at her guide, at the last words she'd written.

Twelfth Night is a moment of joy, celebrated in Gwalia with song and wassail cup. To gain bounty from their lord, the wassailers sing carols that herald the bright year to come. They also carry the 'grey mare' on a stick, a horse's skull with bead eyes, felt ears and ribbons for reins

There was a blot and then the end of the sentence.

a horse's skull on a stick, a man's body buried in the woods.

Estela felt the howl growing inside her, blocking her ears to all but howls. Mair should be here, a woman who understood. They could howl together. Had the howl escaped into the room? Estela did not know but she saw that her hand had escaped Rhys' grip, that he stood up.

His mouth moved again. *Honour. Service. Chapel.* The men left.

Women came. They weren't Mair. Of course they weren't. Mair was in that other castle, the one they'd left to come here, so they could go home. They were going home tomorrow and everything would be all right.

Estela ignored the women she'd never bothered to spend time with, the women she didn't know. She stared at the signet ring Dragonetz had given her as a token, the one that would summon him from the ends of the earth to her side if she needed him. *Where are you?* she asked the ring.

Once, she had hung it around Musca's neck, the last time she had left her baby to follow Dragonetz into danger. They had come back home to Musca.

Home. Musca. She had to force herself but she must.

John Halfpenny came to see her. How different people looked when their faces twisted. How softly they spoke. She could hardly hear them.

'Nothing to keep us here.'

So, he was leaving too. They would leave together, he told her. She didn't care.

She went to the chapel when she was summoned.

A man who never knew Dragonetz said the deceased had served

Christendom and his Liege with loyalty and piety, that he'd been a Crusader, and purgatory would be short. That he'd surely died with God in his heart and would find the hereafter he deserved, even though he'd died unshriven. That man was born of woman and doomed to Adam's sin, and so on, and so on.

Estela, daughter of Eve, didn't care.

The leaving of Dinefwr was as anonymous as the entry had been triumphant. John Halfpenny had two horses saddled, ready, and a pack-horse for their goods. Estela would have preferred to take only what she'd come with but the brothers had insisted on giving presents. She barely looked at them but accepted that the clothes would be practical.

She almost forgot to pack her guide and her escritoire, but Musca was her future and she clung to his name as she rode away from Dinefwr, away from Gwalia, through the woods in which her lover's body lay moldering.

CHAPTER TWENTY-SIX

This time Dragonetz had not imagined metal glinting in the muddy shallows but it was gold, not silver. And not a nugget of the precious metal. He rinsed the object in the race of water, revealing an open-ended arm bracelet, each end a hissing snake, solid, crafted by a master. Perhaps there had been a settlement here, or at least a villa. Either the gold-worker or his customer had left this treasure buried. Perhaps there was more.

He turned the bracelet, admiring the scales engraved on the diamond snake-heads. He could not get his hand or wrist through the opening. A woman's bracelet. A gift that Estela would appreciate and a small way to show her some reward for all she'd borne in this barbaric, wet country. Tomorrow, at last, they would go home.

He hiked up his jerkin, tucked the bracelet into the scrip tied round his waist and quickly covered up again. The rain was not heavy but ceaseless, wearing. Now would be a good time to explore the tunnels and be sheltered.

Three dark mouths opened like screams in the mist. Dragonetz picked his way around the biggest puddles to the tunnel on the left, framed by old, rotting beams. He would just explore the entry, venturing only a little into the tunnel, until daylight grew too dim.

He had enough headroom to stand comfortably and it was a relief to be out of the rain. He had to watch his footing on the uneven ground, where crumbled rock shifted as he stepped on it. He stood still, looked at the walls, close enough either side to see the different strata. Once more he wished he knew more of mining, to confirm his theory.

Far enough into the tunnel to be sheltered from storms, Dragonetz spotted a stone lamp on a natural ledge, beside a tinder box. He didn't need a second invitation. He took the fire steel, flint and a piece of charcloth out of the box. On a damp day like this the tinder-dry cloth would catch more easily than the wick. He put the cloth on the fat touching the wick. Then he struck steel against flint until sparks came and the charcloth caught, then the wick. He took the lamp by its handle, the red stone smooth with who knows how many hands gripping it over the years. Now he could explore further. And further.

Daylight was long since gone and he could still walk without stooping, ever further downwards, but he discovered nothing new. The streaks in the rocks continued, shining in the soft lamplight but without glitter. Sometimes a rough edge caught his foot and he'd stumble, but the tunnel seemed safe enough, empty but for its ghosts, the workings long since abandoned. There were passages where old wooden beams supported the stone; diagonal struts and ceiling frames; evidence of walls being strengthened as they were chipped and quarried. A heap of chains told of the mine-workers' conditions. More ghosts.

He was ready to turn back when he heard water, so he continued. *Just a bit further* he told himself, seconds before he was forced to stop or fall down a shaft. Peering into the depths by what little light the lamp offered, Dragonetz saw wooden supports, in a pattern. Puzzled, he tried to make sense of what he saw. He recognized the pattern but not from this angle.

He turned the wood in his mind, saw it turning and then he knew – it was a wheel, like the wheel that had powered his paper mill. Far down below, he could hear water. So, the lower levels were filled with water and there was a wheel, maybe more than one wheel. He was not sure of their purpose but whatever it had been, he was sure that these wheels had not turned for years, hundreds of years to judge by the state of the workings on the surface.

He stood, looking down. Something many-legged and pale wriggled over his foot, fleeing the light. As it reached darkness, it glowed green, reminding Dragonetz of the ghosts who had suffered his presence without complaint, so far. He turned to head back to the surface, then, lost in his thoughts, stopped to run his hand along the rock face. He put down the lamp. What if?

He chose a streak, ochre-coloured with flecks in the myriad blue-greys of surrounding rock. He picked up a sharp stone and chipped at the wall. The *toc-toc* of his hammering rang out in the mine like an alarum to Arthur and his sleeping knights but Dragonetz thought of nothing but the repetition of hard rock hitting softer rock, chipping away. *Toc-toc* and some flakes on the floor. *Toc-toc* and he had a lump. He picked up the lamp, held it to the stone in his hand and saw the sparkle of gold.

He put down the lamp once more, leaned down awkwardly to get light as he slipped the precious sample into his scrip and heard the tell-tale slip of shale too late. The *toc-toc* had hidden the approach of whoever hit Dragonetz over the head, knocking him unconscious.

When he came to, he was back down the tunnel, sitting, his back against the wall, bound hand and foot and chained to a huge wooden strut. Holding the lamp and standing over him was Wyn. Lamplight drew demons over his face. Dragonetz closed his eyes and shook his head to clear his vision but when he opened them again, he still saw Wyn.

Perhaps the man thought him a thief? Dragonetz flushed at the thought. He *had* intended to keep what he'd found.

'Wyn?' His throat hurt. He'd been out for hours and not thought to sip water. All that rain and he was parched! 'I mean no harm. I was exploring. I found a bracelet. I followed the tunnel. I think–'

Wyn cut him off '–I don't wish to hear what you found. It makes no difference. And you can't bribe me. I won't touch anything from this accursed place.'

'Then, what? Why?' Dragonetz nodded towards his tied hands.

The Welshmen shrugged, his eyes dark pits in the shadows, unreadable.

'Your people would all be like you if they knew there was gold here. Like flies to a honeypot, not able to resist it. There would be no talk of allegiance and treaties or good King Henri's justice! Deheubarth is ours again after so many years and I'm not letting you destroy it with a word to your Henri about how rich this land is. So you're not going back.'

'I merit not this treatment!' Dragonetz used the formula Wyn had taught him but saw no weakening in the man's face.

'You are not one of us,' was all the answer.

'I give my oath I will say nothing of the gold.' *Nor of anything that would help Henri against the Welsh.* Dragonetz could not add. He would report to Aliénor if he could. If he lived.

'Would you hear a tale of oaths broken? That would outlast the winter! Oaths are worthless.'

'Take me to Lord Rhys and Lord Maredudd. Let me convince them. They know my oath is my bond.'

'Those are better bonds.' Wyn gestured at Dragonetz' tied body. 'Who do you think ordered me to follow and kill you?'

Rhys. Maredudd. All those months they'd ridden together meant nothing more than laughter and a catch of fish. Yet he was not dead, despite the orders. Hope remained.

'Then kill me,' he challenged Wyn. 'Or set me free. You will look foolish if I escape and stroll back into Dinefwr.'

'This is no place for a man to despatch another,' was the strange reply. 'It would show disrespect for those who dwell here. Why do you think we leave the gold where it is and keep it secret? It is our curse to know of it and now it is yours.

I offer you to the shades of Dolaucothi and it is up to them how they take you – fast, slow, mad or eaten to death. Your sacrifice today will please them and bring us the year we deserve. The men of Deheubarth will give you thanks throughout the year to come, at every harvest, in every castle you have helped regain. This is your last act to support Deheubarth and we thank you.' He swept a bow, real or in mockery Dragonetz could not say.

Wyn added, 'I return now to announce the sad news to the court that Lord Dragonetz was taken by wolves, his remains found in the forest, so bloodied they could only be buried there.'

Estela thought Dragonetz. *Estela packing to go home tomorrow.*

'The year ends as it must. May the gods accept our sacrifice for the year to come,' prayed Wyn as he gagged Dragonetz with a strip of damp cloth. Then he went. All light went with him.

All but blind men fear the dark, the shadow of death, whatever they pretend. Dragonetz had met fear and the shadow of death before, so he closed his eyes to keep the dark at a distance. He tested the binding but he'd been unconscious when tied, and it was tighter than when he'd been the badger in the Welsh bag. The gag stopped him using his teeth but the moisture was pleasant in his dry mouth.

He wriggled, turned towards the wall, reached it with his hands, rubbed against the wall, ignored the chafing as his skin was grazed. In time, he could scrape through the rope binding, free his mouth, free his feet. But the chain would remain.

Fretting at the ropes, fraying them strand by strand, Dragonetz tried to visualize where he was. Wyn had probably dragged him to the place he'd seen the chains.

What were the chains attached to? Stone? The wooden beams? If the latter, maybe he could bring down the beam itself to free the chain. There was little chance of freeing himself from the chain itself. Unless he cut off his lower leg, along with the anklet and chain.

He could hear what Estela would say, in her physician's voice, dispassionate, as if a leg was merely an object to be weighed in a balance. Which it was, with his life on the scales. He still had Talharcant and the cut could be clean. *You would gush blood and die before you could make fire and cauterize the stump. And you could not take the pain of doing this to yourself. No man could.*

It was a relief to accept this as truth. Hacking off his leg would be pointless. But it was a shock to realise that he had no better plan. That he should prepare for death. *Estela* he thought as he freed his hands. He ripped the gag from his mouth then stuffed it back in, to suck all the moisture from it.

He opened his eyes and Talharcant made swift work of loosing his feet from the rope. All that remained was the chain. One iron chain between him and his life. The dark mocked him as he stood there. *Fight me* it whispered. *I'm right here and you are a warrior. You have a fine sword. What are you waiting for? You can end this now or tomorrow, when your tongue cleaves to your palate and the waking dreams torment you. Or the day after, when you have lost yourself. But the day after that will be too late. You will be too weak to do anything other than die a slow death in your own dirt.*

Then Dragonetz understood that he would die and his only choice was how. The Romans called it courage for a man to throw himself on his own sword, those same Romans who made these tunnels, crafted the exquisite bracelet bumping against his hip.

Coward breathed their ghosts. *You dare not. You are not a man.* Words shook with laughter. *We will come for you anyway, one way or another. You know the ways we come. We have met before.*

A sudden poppy craving shook Dragonetz, made him sweat. Would he never be free? He remembered the dreams that had tortured him and he didn't know whether he could face their like, here in the dark, alone. But he had faced them and he had survived, and he had not been alone. Against the voices in the dark, he summoned his faith, that would not let him despair. And he summoned his loved ones, who had been with him in the worst of dreams, with him in the terrible time when they'd stopped him taking the poppy. Arnaut, Malik. Estela.

Join me invited another voice. *Sleep among my knights. Take your place here until we are called.*

Gladly murmured Dragonetz. *When my time comes.* And then he began to sing. If he brought the tunnel down and was crushed under stone, so be it. He would be himself for as long as he could be, and trust in God for what came next.

He sang of larks in springtime, lovers parting at dawn, capricious ladies and corrupt lords, the joys of passion and the patience of saints. For his ghostly audience, he sang every tale he knew of the Welsh seer Myrddin, of Arthur and his knights. His throat was dry again, but that wasn't why he stopped. He saw a light, the flicker of the lamp's flame coming back down the tunnel towards him. Wyn must have heard the noise and was coming back to complete his errand.

It was not Wyn.

'I'm sorry,' said John Halfpenny. 'I had to wait until I was sure the Welshmen had gone and they stayed talking for hours, sheltering where you left your horse. It was easier to find you than I thought it might be.'

Dragonetz couldn't speak. As the darkness receded, he understood how close he'd come to being swallowed up.

'Water,' he croaked, pointing at the skin Halfpenny carried on his belt. He wondered how he'd managed to sing so many songs. Where did such strength come from? He murmured a prayer of thanks and took several long swigs of precious water, leaning back against the wall.

Halfpenny was already investigating the pile of chains further along the tunnel. He grunted and came back with a key. He unlocked the leg fetter.

Dragonetz had been within feet of his salvation the whole time. Without light and with no mobility, he would never have known. He stood and gathered the little moneyer into an embrace that hid the grubby tears he could feel coursing down his cheeks. Then he sat again, abruptly, drained.

'Report,' he ordered.

'Wyn's been following you and I've been following Wyn. They all think me a fool with little Welsh so they speak as if I'm not there. You did not think they'd let you go home?'

'No,' Dragonetz sighed. 'But I did not foresee this. I thought Rhys and Maredudd would make a move, try me for some trumped-up crime – perhaps something Estela had done...' he smiled. 'So near to leaving, my guard was down. I even thought they might keep their word.'

'You are dead. They planned to announce your death when they returned to Dinefwr. That's why they waited, to make it more convincing that they'd searched and found you – not tracked you and killed you.'

'My pony?'

'They took it. Hid it in another settlement probably. Not that any Welshman would contradict Wyn's tale and I wouldn't know which horse you took! I don't think Estela would either.' A thought struck him. 'Was anything of importance with the horse?"

'Nothing.' Dragonetz said what must be said. 'I am dead. If I return to Dinefwr, they will make my death a reality and kill both you and Estela for being witnesses.'

'Yes. There is only one place they will not find you. Unless you sing all the time and they are passing.'

Dragonetz nodded. 'They won't look for me because they know I'm here. And they won't come here because I'm here to die – and they fear the place.' He did not add *with reason* but Halfpenny was far from a fool.

'I'm sorry,' the Englishman said. 'You must stay here and I daren't return. They'll notice.'

'Do you have any food?'

Halfpenny passed over the waterskin. 'You could fill this from the stream at night but don't risk lighting the lamp. This is all I have.' He pulled a hunk of stale bread from his belt, manna from heaven.

'I will live.' Dragonetz hesitated. 'Probably a week, with water. I'm not sure after that. I'll have to take risks, seek food in the forest.'

'We'll be back before that,' Halfpenny reassured him. 'Once the priest has played his part in this mummery, they will want rid of the fool and the widow. We will leave Dinefwr as soon as we can, to go home – and you will go with us!'

Dragonetz could think of no better plan. 'You'll tell Estela that I'm alive.' It was an order not a question but Halfpenny shook his head.

'I can't.'

Estela. The pain of it was searing. 'You must! Or she'll hate us both!'

'Then she must hate us. At least we'll all be alive.'

'I would trust her with my life!' Dragonetz said and he knew it was true.

'I can't.' Halfpenny was adamant. 'Godspeed,' he said gently. 'We'll be back as soon as we can be.'

Then, once more, the light wavered back up the tunnel until it was gone.

CHAPTER TWENTY-SEVEN

Anger coiled in Estela's gut, waiting to strike.
She dismounted, followed Halfpenny across the drying mud to the opening of a mine, where a man who looked like Dragonetz came to meet them. His eyes blinked in the light, flickered with crazy shadows, and he grabbed the bread Halfpenny held out to him, wolfed it down without manners, then controlled himself, paused, turned to her.

'I'm sorry,' he said, his words muffled by chewed bread. He couldn't even do her the courtesy of closing his mouth while he ate.

'That's what Rhys said when he told me you were dead,' she flung at him. Her voice broke. 'I believed you were dead!'

John Halfpenny cut in. 'He wanted me to tell you but I dared not, my Lady. If you had looked for one second as if you had hope, we'd all be dead.'

Estela ignored him, looked only at Dragonetz, waited for him to understand.

'I believed I was to die,' he told her.

Then it was she who understood, who imagined what he had suffered, what kind of death he faced and how hard it had been to wait days in the dark, starving, until Halfpenny returned.

'Oh, my dear,' she said and walked into his arms, felt the trembling of his body against hers. Of course he guessed what she had been through and felt her pain. As she did for him. As long as each thought for the other, they would come through this, together.

'I'm sorry,' he whispered, holding her too tightly.

'Do you want more to eat?'

'Yes.' His eyes showed the strain of hunger. 'But it's better if I wait, eat a little again later.'

He released her, rubbed his waist as if something had hurt him there. He reached into the pouch beneath his jerkin, clumsy, trying to find something, and the others waited. They said nothing, allowing him time to say and do what he needed, to return to the living from wherever he had been.

'Here,' he said, showing her a golden bracelet that glinted, even in the weak winter sunshine. 'This is for you. I found it here.' Open at either end, each finished with a snake's head, the bracelet was beautiful – and worth a fortune. Estela slipped her wrist into it, moved the bracelet up her arm, where it rested as if made specially for her. The diamond-shaped heads were cross-hatched in likeness of snakeskin and the small tongues had the hint of a fork, but not enough to weaken the gold.

'It's so beautiful.' Estela felt like a high priestess of some ancient cult with the double-headed snake coiled round her arm. Surely such a talisman would bring magic to its bearer. She brought her arm up close to study the snake heads more closely and caught the bracelet on her cloak brooch, pricking herself against the pin.

'Ouch!' She licked the tiny drop of blood from her arm, adjusted the brooch, automatically stroking the Pathfinder's runes as she did so. The crisscross of runes always reminded her of choices and crossroads. She looked again at the bracelet as a cloud hid the sun, dulling the snake-eyes to hooded threat.

Gold she thought, remembering. The bracelet no longer seemed a perfect fit but pinched, as if tightening. She suddenly panicked in case she couldn't get it off but she wriggled the band down towards her wrist and slipped out of it.

'What's wrong?' asked Dragonetz.

'This is.' She shrugged. 'I can't explain. I know it's beautiful but it's not ours.'

'I think these were gold mines. I'm right, aren't I?' Dragonetz asked Halfpenny.

'I thought there were no gold mines on the Isles of Albion or I would know of them,' Halfpenny replied, considering the matter. 'That's what I thought, anyways. But you be right, yes, these be old gold mines. And the Welsh Lords were – would be right to silence you. They would never be left in peace if word got out that there be gold here. That, and all you know about their strongholds, signed your death warrant.'

Estela was still holding the bracelet, reluctant to part with it, as she knew she must. A thought struck her. 'Why am I not worth killing?'

Both men looked at her.

'Oh.' The penny dropped. 'I'm just a woman.'

'If it be any consolation, I be just a fool,' said Halfpenny kindly. 'And we do have a long way to travel.'

Estela gave the bracelet back to Dragonetz. 'We must leave it here, where it was found. It's the right thing to do. No good can come of this gold. I would have to hide it anyway. Anyone who saw it would ask where it came from and I don't want to talk about this place.' She watched his face. 'Do you? Will you tell Aliénor when you report?' She turned to Halfpenny. 'Will you tell the English? The other moneyers?'

Halfpenny's response was instant. 'No. I hate gold. Terrible to work with and too valuable to be any use.'

'Dragonetz?' she prompted.

'I don't know,' he said. 'I need to think. But we will not take what isn't ours.' He reached once more into his pouch, pulled out a piece of rock and buried both the bracelet and the stone together in the mud.

Regret and relief warred but Estela took her lover's arm and they walked back to where the mounts were tethered.

'We'll take turns,' Halfpenny said. 'I'll walk first and we can pick up another horse at a settlement, when we be far enough away. They won't be looking for us anyways – glad to be rid of us, I think! But you can play the servant if you need to.'

Estela glanced at Dragonetz. He might well pass as a servant in his current state of exhaustion. 'Then you'd better let me have Talharcant,' she observed wryly.

He summoned a weak grin. 'Not till you show me what Maredudd taught you.'

Somewhere between the forests of Cantref Mawr and the port of Swansea, they bought an extra horse, and Dragonetz recovered enough to interrogate John Halfpenny about gold mines.

While working in Zaragoza, Halfpenny had heard all about the gold mines in a neighbouring kingdom, ancient in construction but still working. He spoke of channeling water into cascades to wash gold ore from the river and surface rock.

'The drains!' Dragonetz described the stone cover he'd found on the hillside.

Halfpenny nodded. 'There's likely water ducts below. They'll have exhausted all the gold they found on the surface and then made the deep mines.'

'What about the wheels I saw at the end of the tunnel, big as millwheels, down below?'

Halfpenny considered the matter. 'The tunnels would fill with water below and the wheels would bring it up, allow men to go deeper. 'How dangerous we have made the earth,' he quoted.

'An ancient?' guessed Dragonetz.

'Pliny. When I did my apprenticeship, my master read Pliny to me, how gold be mined, the *ruina montium*, the destruction of the mountain with tunnels and water forced through.'

It was hard to believe this was the same man who'd capered for the Welsh lords, but all skilled men could talk so about their passion. Dragonetz remembered a Damascene sword-maker, a rose-grower, a falconer.

'Did you see a large stone, bashed, strangely shaped?' asked Halfpenny. 'They'd need an anvil to hit the rock against, extract the ore.'

'Maybe,' said Dragonetz slowly. Maybe a rock with indentations like four saints' heads. 'Why don't the Welsh work the mines now?'

'Too difficult to reach the gold in the deeps. Or maybe they're afraid of the ghosts.' Halfpenny laughed. 'Did you see the ghost of Gweno?'

'Aye. She was your sort, blonde and buxom, with a penchant for little Englishmen and bags of silver,' replied Dragonetz lightly. He *had* seen ghosts but the worst were those he had taken in there with him. And he didn't want to talk about it.

Estela and he held each other, carefully, as if the other were silver filigree. Not gold. They didn't talk about the gold they'd left behind or whether Dragonetz would report it to Aliénor. They just held each other. Being alive and being together could not yet be taken for granted.

When they were hailed in Frankish, they moved another step nearer getting home safely and Halfpenny had been right. Nobody was looking for them and nobody was interested in three weary travellers among a nationful of weary travellers. Although he still sat on the throne, King Stephen's days were numbered and the king-to-be Henri was openly acclaimed. The English wars were over.

By cart or on horse, in company or by themselves, the threesome found the rhythm of travel that they'd known on their journey to these isles. Estela sometimes wrote in her guide and read pieces aloud but there were no games with knives. Nobody wished to test their luck.

When the ferry arrived at the far side of the Severn Sea, with Gwalia truly behind them and safe passage ahead, Dragonetz said, 'If you wish to travel back with us, your services will be rewarded.'

Halfpenny shook his head. 'It is time to go home.' Dragonetz felt the words in his own gut and surely Estela must do too. *Hiraeth*, the home-longing, was in all of them.

'But Stephen is still in power,' objected Estela. 'Are you safe?'

The moneyer gave a wry smile. 'Safer than I've been for many a year. I will find my way, and,' he crossed himself, 'God willing, my family.' He grinned. 'If you come across coins with my name as moneyer, you won't need to weigh them.'

'You've taught me much, Mintmaster, including the meaning of true coin and sterling. You are both and you have my thanks, and this.' Dragonetz drew one of his remaining diamonds from his scrip, saw Halfpenny hesitate. 'You don't have qualms about diamonds now too? These were earned, not stolen.'

'I did not do it for the reward,' Halfpenny said.

'I know,' said Dragonetz. 'Take it.'

Halfpenny drew their attention to his fidgety left hand and the diamond disappeared from his right, one of the jongling tricks he had done at the Welsh court, but not with diamonds. He bowed to Estela. 'My Lady. I doubt you will find another target so easily. I should have asked for bigger payment!'

'Yes, you should. We'll miss you.' How easily she spoke for both of them, and, to Dragonetz' surprise, he liked it.

With a bundle tied to a stick, Halfpenny quickly merged into the crowd, his walk a merry parody of those around him, hiding his feelings in comedy. Dragonetz remembered their first meeting, in a Les Baux prison where the moneyer was sentenced to worse than death for forgery.

'Paths and crossroads,' murmured Estela, fingering her Viking brooch, her eyes following and losing their companion.

Was it always to be like this, one thinking and the other speaking a thought aloud? He had not known two people could be so close. He should ask her now... but if she said no, they would have a long journey with no future that he could imagine. He would wait at least until they were across the sea. But he must ask her before they reached Aliénor.

As they travelled, they shared long silences with the same ease they talked. Their tongues tripped over Welsh words, speaking freely of Rhys and Maredudd, of Gwalia and its people. What had Estela said? *Too deep in Welshness*. Despite the doom planned for Dragonetz, some fondness for the Welsh was embedded in their core, like a splinter that hurt when pressed, but was now part of them. They even understood the doom planned for Dragonetz. Wouldn't King Henri have done the same? Or even Ramon Berenguer? For a ruler, the kingdom came first.

'What have we left behind?' Estela asked him.

So much, he thought. *We will never be the people we were.* 'I talked to Rhys of the Usatges. Maybe the Welsh laws will show that. And the castles he plans will be better built!'

'And I sang,' Estela declared with satisfaction.

'Such song.' Dragonetz carried with him the voices, each holding true to its own part. 'I will take the part song to our monks, show them how it's done.'

'We bring with us more than we left behind,' was Estela's judgement. 'I'm writing down the song, the one for Mair, the song of women working, loving, fighting.'

'Nobody will believe it,' said Dragonetz.

'They don't have to. It just has to be a wonderful song.'

'And it will be,' Dragonetz assured her.

Then there was the sea and a boat and Estela turned green. He was no longer tempted to ask her, not when she was struggling to hold the contents of her stomach, despite all her remedies.

At Barfleur, on Frankish soil at last, they took a room at an inn, and followed all the recommendations of the wise traveller for making the most of such luxury. Bathed, dressed in fresh clothes, over a private meal with a cup of good red wine – they were not sorry to leave behind the horrors of Welsh beverages – Dragonetz felt the moment had come.

Her hair rippled down her back below the waist, her eyes held his, the only gold he needed. And he did need her.

'Estela, my Lady,' he began. He could see in the anxious topaz of her eyes, in her stillness, that she knew what he was going to say.

'I called you wife in Gwalia. I want to continue to do so. I am yours as you are mine. Marry me.'

Her eyes clouded. 'Dear heart.' She stumbled over the words. 'I can't. I don't understand what you're asking. I'm married.' She paused, searching. 'I won't have you kill the man who was married to me.'

She saw that wasn't what he meant. 'Then I don't understand.' She pronounced the name of the man she'd married as if it were gravel in her mouth. 'And if Johans de Villeneuve were dead, naturally, and we married, it would make a bastard of Musca and he would always be inferior to any other child born to us. I could not allow that.' Her last words came out in a rush as if she was afraid of saying something different.

'Nor I,' said Dragonetz gently. 'But I have thought over what the notary said and there is a way we can be married, and Musca my legal son and heir. I will have to ask Aliénor but I will not ask her without having your consent.'

He asked again, 'Will you marry me?'

'Yes,' she said. 'If it is possible. But I fear you will find there are too many obstacles.'

'That's not very romantic!' he teased her.

'Marriage and romance are of a separate and opposite nature,' she quoted from Aliénor's playful court of love.

'Then let's enjoy romance while we still can.' Dragonetz scooped a handful of hair to one side so he could kiss her neck.

'The wise traveller makes no mention of such activities,' complained Estela, primly.

'The wise traveller should know when to stay silent,' murmured Dragonetz, ensuring that she did so.

CHAPTER TWENTY-EIGHT

For their private audience, Aliénor had dressed down and was merely resplendent in blue velvet and pearls. *Motherhood becomes her* thought Estela then, more cynically, *perhaps being Queen of England and mother of the heir to the English throne, becomes her.*

She listened to Dragonetz' report of the Welsh Lords' conquests, their independence, their willingness to hold their own lands without causing problems for King Henri, should he support them.

'Are they capable of holding those lands against the Marcher Lords,' Aliénor asked.

'Yes, as long as Rhys and Maredudd rule.' Dragonetz corrected himself. 'As long as one of them does.'

'There is tension between them?'

'None. But Rhys is the stronger.' Estela flicked him a glance but he had not forgotten. He would keep his word. 'The third brother is of no interest – he has turned monk. But there is a fourth. He was taken prisoner on a battlefield by the Lord of Kidwelly, Maurice de Londres. The missing brother is called Maelgwyn. The king will earn much gratitude from the Lords of Deheubarth if he finds their brother alive, or can tell them Maelgwyn's fate.'

'You are saying that to win them as allies, we should leave them the rights to the kingdom they've already taken, ignore the plaints of the Marcher Lords – do nothing, in effect and they will keep a balance for us, while we sympathise with those lords who've lost territory and power, make them work to win our favour.' Aliénor looked pleased with the strategy, as well she might. Rumour said the royal coffers were empty so any possibility of making allies without using bribery and gifts would be most welcome.

'You make them sound less barbaric than one supposed,' Aliénor observed.

Dragonetz weighed his words. 'They are both less, and more, barbaric than one supposed.'

'And are there assets we should know about?'

'Not in Deheubarth.' Dragonetz didn't pause. 'Pembrokeshire is richer, partly under Frankish rule and English is spoken there, not Welsh. The Belgian merchants there run a fine wool trade.' Aliénor's eyes lit up as he continued, 'Pembroke falcons are highly prized as are their herding dogs: a short-legged, brown race with foxlike face.'

Estela tried not to smile as he quoted *the Wise Traveller* word for word.

Almost girlish with excitement, Aliénor thought aloud. 'They would be the perfect gift for Henri!'

Dragonetz added, 'I was forgetting. There *is* one treasure beyond price in Deheubarth, in which the king would take great delight.' Estela held her breath. 'Their music-making is divine and a Welsh harper makes other instruments sound like a hen-coop. When you negotiate with Deheubarth, you could pay tribute to their fame and ask for a harper to grace your court.'

Aliénor nodded. 'What about the north of Gwalia?'

Dragonetz shrugged. 'It is a different country, often at war with the south. I know nothing of the northern rulers but what the southerners have told me. The men of Deheubarth won back a fortress from the northerners and there is little love between them.'

'This means that north or south Gwalia would ride with Henri against their countrymen?"

'Yes. They do not see each other as countrymen. If you have no option but to ride against Deheubarth, the northern Welshman

Cadwaladr will help you win. He is hated by his own people and by the southerners as a kin-killer, is loyal to nobody. He already rides with the English and if you pay him enough, he will serve your needs. None of the Welsh can be trusted but he is the worst of them.'

Aliénor nodded again.

'And if we fight them, what's the best way? What are their weaknesses?'

'Always remember that peace holds no attraction for them,' warned Dragonetz. 'They are fierce, proud, independent, living on plunder. Recruit them into your armies and they will thrive. Frankish military tactics do not suit the hilly terrain but you will always have the advantage of numbers, so can keep replacing men until the Welsh succumb. They are lightly-clad and fast. They shower arrows and flee. Heavily-armoured knights are good in close combat but are at a disadvantage against the Welsh style.'

Aliénor said it for him. 'As in the Holy Land.' She had been there, his Liege.

He just nodded. 'A people held in subjugation will always rebel and Deheubarth could be a danger to the king's rule. You cannot wipe out the Welsh so my advice is to win them instead. And keep your defences strong. Create an army to protect the castles on the western side of the great river facing Gwalia. Give special honours to the Border Lords – and to the Lords of Deheubarth, as allies. Try to conquer them and you will always regret it. They can be defeated in battle but you won't make slaves of them. It is not in their nature.'

'Then I was right? Gwalia is important?'

'You were right.'

'Now I have only to convince... others.' Aliénor's smile faded and Estela understood. The title of future Queen of England was as hollow a crown as that of Queen of France had been, as yet. 'Write down the strongholds and their rulers, the weapons, the geography – all you can.'

'It is done, my Lady.' Dragonetz passed her the precious report.

'It is well done, Dragonetz! And it shall be known throughout Aquitaine that you have served me well. I shall make sure your father knows that you deserve every honour.' Dragonetz' mouth tightened, no doubt remembering the insults sent in writing by Lord Dragon to his oath-breaker son.

'Furthermore,' continued Aliénor, 'I gift you the domain of Breyault, which is without heir, to add to your ancestral lands. It is well-managed but no doubt you will want to travel there as soon as possible, to consult with the steward.'

'My Lady is generous,' began Dragonetz and Aliénor's eyes narrowed.

'You ask more?'

'I ask my heart's desire,' Dragonetz told her. 'I ask that you annul my Lady's marriage to Johans de Villeneuve, for it was never a marriage, and that you acknowledge us to be man and wife, in the eyes of the law, on the grounds that we have lived in that state for four years.'

Aliénor glared at Estela. 'You wish to dissolve the marriage that the Viscomtesse of Narbonne so graciously offered you?' Estela curtseyed as deeply as she could manage, to avoid Aliénor's fierce gaze as much as to show modesty.

'I will always be grateful for the honour,' Estela murmured. 'but that was never a marriage. It was not consummated.' She flushed and swallowed. 'And I am as Lord Dragonetz' wife, keeping only to him. We have a son.' Her voice broke.

Aliénor dismissed Musca with an airy wave. 'He wouldn't be the first bastard to make a fine figure in the world. You disappoint me,' she told Estela, 'but it seems you have found a better catch.'

Estela bit her lip.

'And you,' Aliénor addressed Dragonetz, 'were fool enough to take her maidenhead and honourable enough to be trapped by a pretty girl with a nice voice.' She shook her head, disappointed.

'I was indeed there when she lost her maidenhead,' Dragonetz said carefully, telling no lies, 'and I want no other for wife.'

'Oh, very well. It is easy enough to annul a marriage that was never consummated.' She pondered. 'I shall write to my sister of Narbonne and smooth over your ingratitude.' She glared at Estela.

'And as you live together as man and wife, your marriage is but a formality. I will have the notary write up papers annulling the marriage and those too can be sent to Narbonne, in case the unfortunate husband should wish to marry someone more grateful.' Another glare. 'And I will put your names as Lord and Lady of Breyault on the title deeds to the estate, so that will be formal acknowledgement of your clandestine arrangement. And, of course, enable your issue to be declared legitimate.'

Estela felt stunned, too stunned to respond when Aliénor told Dragonetz, 'You deserve better! Leave me now.'

The moment he closed the door behind them, Dragonetz gathered Estela into his arms, whispered 'No, I don't,' and kissed her.

'Is it really as easy as that?' she asked. 'It seems like one of Halfpenny's jongling tricks.'

'Why should it not be easy? It is only the truth of our lives made public. The notary said that adultery was an insurmountable legal problem. Ergo, there was no adultery. If you were not married to de Villeneuve but married to me there was no adultery.' He looked sideways at her. 'Has there been any adultery?'

'Let me think... Maredudd was *very* attractive...'

Dragonetz laughed. 'If you'd said Rhys, I might have wondered. It's time to go home, my Lady Wife.'

'Yes, dear Husband. I can't believe we've done it! We've survived Gwalia, your reputation is as it should be. Life is good. Everything is good.' She took his arm and he too relaxed into pure happiness.

'As it should be. We'll return to Zaragoza tomorrow. I need to speak to Ramon but we can organize the household, you can take them to our new domain.'

'*We* can organize the household?' she challenged him. 'And I am *not* leaving without you.' It was wonderful to bicker over their plans for the future, each plan more pleasurable than the previous one.

They returned to the chamber allocated to them and there they found a page waiting, with two letters, one for Dragonetz and one for Estela. The seals were already broken. 'The Queen said these arrived for you while you were abroad, if you please.' Dragonetz dropped a coin into the outstretched hand and the boy disappeared before he could be asked any questions.

From Ramon Berenguer. Dragonetz scanned the lines, heavy-hearted, glanced at Estela. The letter trembled in her hand and her mouth contorted in a silent scream. No, everything was not good.

It was as well that Aliénor ordered the guards to let Dragonetz through or he would have killed them both. She was still alone in the ante-chamber where all had gone so well an hour earlier, a life-time earlier.

'You know what's in these letters and yet you kept them from us!'

Tall, stately, ice-cold, Aliénor chose to ignore his manner. 'Long enough to let you report fully, without distraction. A few hours will make no difference.'

Nothing will make any difference was what she meant. Dragonetz controlled his anger. Aliénor was not the real target.

'There is something you need? To deal with the situation?' Aliénor's face suggested she was stepping round dog turds.

'Twenty fighting men,' Dragonetz told her.

She nodded without questioning the number.

'You have pigeons from Ramon Berenguer? From Zaragoza?'

'Yes.'

'I would like to send three.'

'That's extravagant!'

He glared at her. 'I want to be sure one reaches my family, if they are still there. I think my family is worth three pigeons!'

She gave her assent, reluctantly, summoned her guards, sent her orders. Dragonetz took his leave with little courtesy.

He had already penned three identical messages. He rushed to the pigeon loft, re-read the note once more.

For Raoulf, Gilles and the household of Dragonetz los Pros. Bring the WHOLE household to Montbrun. Leave now and be there by May-day, not before. Estela and I will be there. Then we are moving north. Leave nothing. Leave nobody.

Dragonetz' seal was stamped at the bottom and Estela had written *with love*. Her signature was blotchy on one version. He rolled the messages up tiny and tight, fitted them into the leather cylinders that the falconer attached to three birds. Dragonetz noted that there were only four left in the crate. The Zaragoza pigeons were indeed precious and no other messenger could cross such a distance so quickly. He murmured a prayer for safe journey as he watched the handler loose each pigeon. May their recipients indeed be safe in Zaragoza!

Then, Dragonetz headed for the stables, to be met by Estela, ashen-faced and mounted. She was in her riding-gown, with little in her saddle-bags. They *were* going home, after all, thought Dragonetz, his mouth full of acid. They had no need to carry much.

A horse had been saddled for him too. Estela had been no laggard in following his instructions, though her face was still white and tear-streaked.

Twenty mounted men also awaited him. Dragonetz appraised them. Fighting men certainly so Aliénor had kept to the letter of her promise. But, if he were any judge, they were not Frankish fighting men. Apart from their foreign garb, with which he was very familiar, they carried bows and quivers. Was Aliénor mocking him? Fobbing him off with her husband's unwanted Englishmen?

Anger rose in him again as he looked at his 'army'.

'Sire,' said one man, in badly accented Frankish. 'We can wear armour, bring crossbows, if you prefer? We were told we were riding fast and light so we thought...'

Then Dragonetz remembered who he was, maybe thought for a few seconds of some other men, lightly clad, whooping as they laid waste to a castle on a wild headland. There were many ways to fight but only one thing mattered about those who fought alongside you.

He raised his voice, spoke to them in a mix of English and in Frankish, saw duty turn to respect in their eyes. 'I am Dragonetz los Pros. No man comes with me but of his own free will,' he told them.

'And you should bear the weapons you can use best. If they be longbows, then we shall fight with arrows. In truth, I'm not sure what awaits us but we have a month's ride to reach a stronghold near Carcassonne.'

'And then?' asked the man who seemed to be spokesman.

'Then we lay siege to my new brother-in-law and, with any luck, we kill him.'

Estela, tight-lipped, said nothing. They would argue again in private but as neither of them knew for sure what they would face, no decisions were final.

'If any man would rather stay with King Henri, let him leave now, with no shame.'

For answer, their leader walked his horse towards the gateway and nineteen archers followed him.

'Let's hope that what we most need is a cadre of English archers!' Dragonetz muttered, as much to himself as to Estela. At least Aliénor had not stinted on the horseflesh. He eased his mount past the men, to take his place at the front, made them wait until Estela was at his side and then they rode out, on as grim a mission as Dragonetz had ever known.

CHAPTER TWENTY-NINE

When they broke camp, Estela read the letters again, although she knew every word by heart.

Dearest Sister,
I was sent to Zaragoza by our Lord of Carcassonne to represent him in talks with the Comte de Barcelone regarding the uncertain situation in Provence.

I was so disappointed to find that you had gone to fulfil a duty to the Duchesse of Aquitaine but I paid a visit to your charming family in your absence. We all agreed that in these troubled times they would be safer in the family home at Montbrun and so here they are, hoping that you will join them as soon as your duties permit.

Your son is quite at home here and makes a touching picture with his baby cousin sitting beside him. They are of course too young to know that each represents a barrier to the other's inheritance.

I wish you safe journey and speedy return to Montbrun, which will give you the welcome you deserve.

Your devoted brother, Miquel

Her heart clenched again at the veiled threats, the image of Musca, so innocent, so unaware of the danger.

For the hundredth time, Dragonetz told her, 'It's a bluff, a crazy lie. Gilles and Raoulf would never have let Miquel anywhere near Musca. Neither would Nici. This is a way of getting you to come to Montbrun, an obvious trap from a twisted mind.'

'Probably,' Estela agreed. 'But what if it's true? What if he found some way... killed Gilles, kidnapped Musca. I don't know! It's dated October. That's over five months ago. Anything could have happened!'

'Which is why we go to Montbrun. We'll spring this trap, whatever Miquel means to happen. And we'll end this threat to your happiness – to our happiness – once and for all.'

'How long will the pigeons take to reach Zaragoza?'

'Perhaps as little as four days.'

'If they make it.' Bleak outcomes filled Estela's imagination. She had agreed with Dragonetz that they should cover both possibilities in their plan but it was difficult to believe any good would come of anything they did.

If Miquel was bluffing and their family was safe in Zaragoza, then the note carried by pigeon would send them to join Dragonetz and Estela in Montbrun, where Dragonetz would have ended Miquel's tyranny. The family could journey north to take up their happy future on the new estate gifted to them by Aliénor.

After the shocks she'd received, Estela had no faith in a happy future. How Dragonetz was going to deal with Miquel was something they did not talk about. Estela was afraid that she would speak aloud her darkest thoughts. *I want my brother dead.* She thought she was even capable of killing him herself. Perhaps she had been in Gwalia too long for the good of her soul.

If Miquel held Musca and any other members of their household in Montbrun, then Dragonetz intended to rescue them. How, Estela had no idea, and she dared not ask because she suspected Dragonetz had no idea either. But what he did have was experience she could only imagine. Experience in siege and warfare, in negotiation and truce. If anybody could outwit and outfight her mad brother, it was Dragonetz.

Estela couldn't help chewing over the what-ifs. 'Some of the letter is true,' she pointed out. 'We know from your letter that there has been new discussion of Provence. He probably *did* go to Zaragoza and he *would* try to reach Musca. He's tried to kill him before. What if he succeeded this time? What if he's already dead and Miquel is just tormenting us?'

'I'd know,' Dragonetz told her. 'I'd feel it, know that we'd lost him.'

His certitude ought to be comforting but Estela couldn't stop herself from lashing out. 'We didn't know Malik was dead!' There, she'd said it. Part of the news from the other letter.

Dragonetz,

You will have heard the sad news from Barcelone, and I send you and Estela my condolences. I know you and Estela spent many happy hours in Malik's household.

When we parted, I knew we might not ride together again, and for that too, I am sorry, but circumstances in Provence bode ill. I gave you my word that I would release you from my command if war broke out once more against Les Baux. If the current provocation escalates, then war is inevitable. I will hold off as long as is possible but the truce has been broken.

I know how hard you worked for peace and I am sorry to give you this news. You gave me to understand that you would withdraw from any part in such a war so I must, reluctantly, let you go. You have served me well. When I rode out with you and Malik, we made history. I miss you both.

I trust that you will take my Usatges with you, wheresoever you travel, and apply that justice we discussed so often together.

Please convey my respects to the Lady Estela and my gratitude for the times she has graced our court with her song and cheered my Lady with her entertainment.

God go with you both.
Ramon Berenguer
Comte de Barcelone and Prince of Aragon

Estela's anger erupted. 'I should have visited him. He was my patient as well as my friend and I should have gone to Barcelone, checked on his health. It's my fault he's dead and I didn't even say goodbye! I went off on a stupid mission with you! And I left Musca for you!'

'I didn't say goodbye to Malik either,' said Dragonetz quietly. 'I didn't spare two days to see the best friend of my life, one last time. Aliénor whistled and I obeyed. Don't you think I would do it all differently? If I'd known.'

'I'm sorry,' Estela said straight away. 'I need to take action, to hurt somebody and you bear the brunt.'

'I know,' he said. 'We cannot mourn Malik as he deserves while we worry about Musca – and about Prima, Gilles, Raoulf – all of them. Miquel would have to carve his way through a swathe of bodies to reach our son and he has not done it.' He tilted her chin, made her look at him. 'Estela, he has not done it!'

'I should never have left him,' she said, and she didn't mean Miquel. 'I'm no Aliénor, to put a kingdom before a little boy. I was stupid to think we could go away – for nearly a year now! – and find everything the same when we came back.'

'We will win through to the future. Trust me,' he said.

But she couldn't. And each day was another endless, numbing ride, while anything could be happening to Musca.

It was four days short of May Day and they were within two hours of Montbrun. Estela thought her mind would explode when Dragonetz insisted they spend the night in Carcassonne. He was right, of course. They did need to stock up on provisions, to be well fed and well rested before facing whatever waited them at Montbrun. *Well rested!* There was no chance of Estela sleeping a wink. She couldn't remember when she'd last slept well.

Dragonetz had accepted her plea to lie low, not seek out the Lord of Carcassonne, Raimon Trencavel. He would only invite them to be his guests and she could not pass the evening in social chit-chat, nor could she involve Trencavel in family matters when she didn't really know what was going on. She would stay in their room while Dragonetz and the men found a tavern and sought information.

Drinking together would consolidate the loyalty that Dragonetz had been working on for the weeks the men rode with him. Estela had watched him at work, learning names, assessing the strengths of each. When they broke camp, however tired he was he took the time to speak to someone so that they all had individual attention, in turn.

He asked them to show him their archery techniques and though they laughed at his awkwardness, they warmed to him for letting them show their skills. They asked him to demonstrate his swordsmanship. Nobody laughed at the ease with which he disarmed the three chosen to fight him. He taught them what he could but they would not be swordmasters, as he would never be an archer.

If they were anything like as good with bows as the men of Deheubarth, they could kill through a mail shirt at close range and pin a man to his horse from a distance.

By the time the party reached the inn, Estela sometimes felt she was just one member of Dragonetz' little army, the weakest of them. He gave her attention as even-handedly as he did the men. She was both reassured by his professional calm, and angry that he didn't fall to the ground screaming that his son was in danger.

Yet, in her own way, she did the same. There were two Estelas. Her insides fell to the floor, screamed, wanted to know why they were being punished like this. The other Estela fetched water, made food, tended the horses. She, too, learned the men's names and tried to get to know them.

She asked about their families but it was hard for her to ask about children. Maybe it was hard for them too, being asked. Perhaps those children were back in the Isles of Albion. Perhaps they were dead. Many children were dead, she told herself, seeing all those dead children, little ghosts. Maybe the little Prince of Zaragoza was one. She had to fight such trains of thought for they all led back to Musca.

Estela was lying on the bed staring at the ceiling when Dragonetz returned. 'Did you find out anything?'

'Nothing!'

'Why does that please you?'

'We asked about Miquel and travellers, whether a party with a child had passed through on their way to Montbrun, whether the Lord of Montbrun had escorted a party back to his estate. Whichever way the questions were posed, with whatever encouragement, we found only blank faces.'

Estela let the implications kindle hope. 'He's bluffing,' she said. 'He doesn't have Musca.'

'No. And we shall have him!'

'He'll know you're coming. Somebody you asked will hope for a reward by warning him of strangers asking his business.'

'Yes. But it was worth it.'

'Then it's me he wants. Why?'

That was a question neither of them could answer.

They left Carcassonne at sun-up, the moment the guards opened the great gates, and they were at the bottom of the hill, hidden in a copse, looking up at Montbrun's walls, within two hours.

The last time Estela had seen her childhood home, she had been running away, running for her life, afraid. Montbrun seemed smaller now and she was not afraid, even though the gates to the castle were closed. Miquel knew they were coming.

Not once had Dragonetz asked her to stay behind, to stay safe, and in return she put her trust in his leadership. She would do what he thought best. She asked him simply, 'What now?'

He answered her loudly enough for all the men to hear. There were to be no secrets. 'I want two men to approach the gate, close enough to be heard but not to be reached by arrows. Ask entry. If the gates are opened, we'll all join you. If entry is refused, report back here on what you find. If they open fire, run back here.'

These were men who could judge to a flight's length how far an arrow would reach in the hands of an expert archer so they would risk nothing. Their leader, who had become Dragonetz' lieutenant at the start of their journey, chose two men and Estela watched them walk up the hill to the gatehouse.

'It's bigger than Tenby,' observed Dragonetz, at her side. She knew he was matching the reality to the picture in his head, created from all the details she'd given him. She had tried to turn a girl's memories into military facts, but curtain walls and sentry posts turned into the place you could see the full moon on a dark night, and the steps she skipped up and down before her world fell apart.

The archers looked like beetles as they slogged uphill. Then they stopped, presumably exchanging words with invisible guards. The wait was long, longer than was needed to say, 'We'll open the gate,' or, 'No, you can't come in.' Then the two men turned, broke into a jog and looked human-size again as they rejoined their comrades.

Catching his breath, one told Dragonetz, 'They had orders not to allow entry.'

'The Lord of Montbrun came to speak in person. He said he wants to speak to his sister, not to anybody else. He knows she's here. She should go up alone.'

'No,' said Dragonetz.

'He won't kill me.' Estela sounded more confident than she felt and yet, even though she did not trust him, she did not fear him.

Something in her had changed during her stay in Gwalia. She had lived Dragonetz' death and no longer feared her own. She would face whatever came. But Dragonetz would never allow such a risk.

'My Lord,' said the man, hesitating. 'In case you should wish my Lady to do so, I placed my waterskin on the ground, where we stood to talk, at a distance that is safe.'

'Dragonetz?' Estela did not plead. He must make the decision.

'All right,' he agreed reluctantly. 'But talk and return. Even if they open the gates, I don't want you going through without us. I don't trust him.'

'If I talk him into letting you join me, I could signal you?'

Dragonetz nodded. 'Wave this.' He fetched a blue horse blanket.

'Your colour,' she smiled at him.

'Our colour,' he reminded her.

Then she picked up her skirts and trekked up the hill, five years older and aeons wiser than when she'd left the castle gates.

There was a path worn by many feet, directly to the gate and Estela spotted the waterskin easily enough. Her safety line. She stopped and looked up at the window in the gatehouse, saw the outline of a man.

'Miquel,' she yelled up. 'I'm here. What do you want.'

'You have to come in, so we can talk, so you can see your son.' His voice made her flinch instinctively. So many memories. Underneath the recent ones, of insults, blows, murder threatened and committed. Underneath all that they were still two children, huddling together while talk of 'the Lady... dead' told them they had lost their mother.

'I know you're lying,' she shouted. 'My son is home, safe. Say what you want to say and be done with it. Either you surrender and we talk terms or Dragonetz will lay waste to Montbrun.' Had she really said that? The little girl she'd once been stood a little taller, shook off the last constraints forged within these walls. She could be the woman she chose to be.

'You don't understand,' Miquel's voice held a whine, a plea. 'I had to make you come.'

They were right. Musca *wasn't* there. Relief flooded Estela.

'I found out what your scarf means, the initials, everything. There's a metal box. It was hidden in the cellars. I found it when... never mind that now. You'll understand when you see it. The box explains everything, everything that's wrong. Estela, we have no choice. We have to do the right thing and kill them both so it ends here. You always did the right thing and I want you with me, so we can do it together because it will hurt. You'll understand...' his voice tailed off.

His words made no sense to her. If he had found out something, then it had only pushed him over the edge. He was possessed, beyond her reach.

There was movement at the window then an object was dangled out of the small aperture. An object that wailed, objecting to the rude treatment.

'No!' shouted Estela as Miquel dangled the baby out the window, over the lethal drop.

'We need to kill them, Estela,' repeated Miquel. 'Your nephew and your son, both of them. End it here. Make it right. But you need to bring your issue here. It has to be both of them or my work is wasted.'

Realisation hit Estela like an arrow in the chest. The baby was pulled back from the void, out of sight. Her heart raced. How did you reason with insanity? He'd admitted the baby was his, or that he thought it was. Who knew what was true. And he thought he had to kill it. But he was waiting for her to fetch Musca, to join him in infanticide.

She wanted to be sick. *Musca is safe*, she told herself. *Put him out of mind. What would Dragonetz do? What would he want me to do?*

'I want to see the box, to understand,' she told her brother, 'but Dragonetz is very protective. I can only come in if he is with me.' She had the blue blanket ready to wave, hoping.

The answer was uncompromising. 'No. Dragonetz will have to take Montbrun to enter and that he'll never do. Just you. Come in, alone, and you'll understand everything. You need to know what we've done. Brought monsters into the world! We have to put it right! Not let it carry on.'

Estela hesitated, stroking her pathfinder brooch as had become her habit when she had to make a difficult decision. He was her brother, however troubled. Couldn't she take what was offered? Go into Montbrun?

If they opened the gates, maybe Dragonetz and his men could storm the hill and come in with her? She dismissed the thought instantly. Montbrun had been built on such a hill to ensure nobody had time to approach unseen. There was always time to close the gate and then she would be alone with Miquel, having lost any trust he might feel.

What would Dragonetz think if she went into Montbrun, defied his orders? *Trust,* she thought. *Trust matters.*

'I promised my husband I would not go in alone.' The truth could be so simple. 'Won't you let us come in together?'

'No!'

'Then Dragonetz will lay siege.'

'Let him! Let him batter himself against Montbrun. You will come in eventually.'

His words rang in her head as she walked back down the hill, listening all the time for a baby crying. What if he held the baby out the window again but dropped him this time? *Then he'd have no hostage* she told herself, assuming mad logic when all she was sure of was the madness.

She fell into Dragonetz' arms, told him Miquel was insane, wanted her alone to talk with about some family matter that made no sense, that the only way in was by fighting. She told him Miquel was mad enough to kill his own baby and that they had to think of the child in any attack they planned. But she didn't tell him what Miquel had said about Musca. She couldn't. What if she saw what was inside the metal box and the horror stuck her too?

They had made as much speed as could be expected, given the possessions that Prima and the cook considered to be essential. When Dragonetz' wrote *all the household* he had not meant every single cooking pot and vase. It's a pity that bit of the note hadn't been smudged and illegible like the other parts. The women explained how fine the Zaragoza pottery was – irreplaceable – and he lost the argument. He just hoped the damned collection wasn't shattered after the weeks bumping along in the wagons.

Gilles saw to the human accommodation while Raoulf paid a groom to look after the horses. Malik wanted to personally stay with Sadeek and the wagons, and would sleep there, as would the domestic staff and guards they'd hired for the journey.

Many times on the road, Gilles and Raoulf had been glad of Malik's strength and experience but his presence was a strain. He had aged since his wife's death, retreated even further into the reserve that had always formed a barrier between him and most men. He spent more time with Sadeek than with his human companions and only with the destrier did the sadness sometimes leave his eyes.

Gilles had sent a messenger to Barcelone, to let Malik know they were leaving his Zaragoza home and the reply had been Malik himself, asking questions about Dragonetz. When he talked about Dragonetz and Estela some of the light came back into his eyes. Gilles thought Malik would stay in Zaragoza where there must be so many memories but, instead, he volunteered his services for the journey, said he would see them safely to Montbrun.

Gilles accepted without question, knowing that Dragonetz would approve, would be happy to see Malik again. But it was a relief when the Moor was elsewhere, so Gilles could talk comfortably with Raoulf, watch the children playing 'bump down the step on bottoms', without feeling guilty for Malik's loss. He carried his wife's death like a black cloud that blocked the sun from anyone near to him. Gilles did not want to imagine what he felt. Was his own affection for Prima as deep as that? What would either of them feel if the other died. *There.* He shook himself. That was exactly the kind of thought he didn't want and that Malik elicited by his silent presence.

It was strange for Gilles to be back home, where he'd done his best by two motherless children. He skirted the darker memories and thought of bringing Estela's child to her in Montbrun. How her mother would have welcomed this sunny grandchild, who played with his foster-brother as if they were true kin.

He remembered Estela's brother as a little boy, wondered what she and Dragonetz were doing in Montbrun, but their orders had been clear. He would find out soon enough and Dragonetz would be pleased that they were early. They had worked hard to make out the words on the note but they had agreed on *May-day or before*. And they had made it! They were in Carcassonne with three days to May-day and would be in Montbrun the very next day.

A wet nose rubbed against Gilles' hand and he caressed Nici absent-mindedly. 'Soon, boy, soon. You can run around tomorrow. We're going home.'

Dragonetz' summary had been succinct and blunt. He had even included Estela's wish that the inhabitants of Montbrun should be spared if possible, even her mad brother. Their aim was to get into the castle; disarm, disable or kill (if necessary) any defenders; find Miquel and take him prisoner – a glance at Estela; and rescue the baby. Whether there were any other children, or any women, still in Montbrun, they had no idea.

'How do you think we should proceed?' he asked his men. He'd already told Estela that four months and a mangonel would make things easier.

'Two destroy the gate with hand-axes while the others fire arrows for cover,' was one suggestion.

Dragonetz waited, let the objection come from within their ranks. 'We don't have the numbers to take losses and they could pour scalding water or oil from the gatehouse onto the men with axes. They'd risk nothing and we'd lose men.'

There was a silence while they thought.

'We used night as cover, in Gwalia, and took the gate down, caught them unawares,' Dragonetz told them.

'They know we're here. The guards won't let twenty men climbing a hill go unnoticed, even at night.' The lieutenant considered the matter. 'What about fire? We can shoot flaming arrows over the walls, shoot enough that wood or produce will catch fire, cause chaos.'

'We could shoot fire arrows into the gate too, finish it with axes if the guard's distracted. I doubt there are that many defenders. They'll all need to work to put fires out.'

'Can you make fire arrows?' Dragonetz asked.

'Aye. We have oil and tows.'

'Tows?'

'Cloths to dip in oil and tie below the arrow-head. We'll need to make fires, up near the castle so we can light the arrows quickly, fire volleys together.'

'Then they'll know our numbers and there will be no surprise.'

Estela's voice sounded loud to her own ears as she spoke into the silence. 'I think Miquel is afraid of fire.'

The men looked at her and she swallowed, licked her dry lips, betrayed her brother. 'He was badly burned. That's why he wears a mask over half his face.'

Dragonetz nodded grimly. 'I'd forgotten. Then fire it is.' He turned to Estela. 'Fire hits where it will so there might be casualties but fewer than if we aimed to kill. And the baby is more likely to be safe. If Miquel is panicking over fire, somebody else will keep the baby safe.'

More likely. Estela nodded. 'I'll carry a torch, help light the arrows.'

They did all the preparation they could, then climbed the hill. Quiverfuls of arrows fluttered their tows gaily in the breeze, like dancers round a maypole. Each tow was dipped in oil, waiting only for the spark. Dragonetz and the men carried wood, and Estela carried a tinder-box.

They stopped when the leading archer said, 'Here.'

'I thought you had to be close to the walls to shoot over?' Dragonetz queried.

'The difference between good archers and mediocre is enough to get these arrows into that castle without us being killed,' the archer replied.

Then they set to their fire-lighting, watched by the figures in the gate-house. Twelve archers were to shoot, eight plus Dragonetz and Estela to light the tows.

The fire was soon crackling. A few feeble attempts were made to fire water bombs from the gate-house at the fire but the English archers mocked their enemy as the weighted arrows dropped well short.

'What will they be doing?' asked Estela as she held her brand in the fire, her hand wrapped in water-soaked cloth to protect it.

'If they have any sense, they're throwing water and vinegar over any cloth they find and putting it against the gate.'

Then the brand caught and Estela rushed to her designated archer, as did the other fire-lighters, each with his brand, and the sky filled with fire and screaming. Again and again and again.

When the brand was burning too much Estela rushed back to the fire, threw it in, grabbed another thick stick from the pile, waited till it caught and rushed back to her archer. Her face streamed with sweat and grime. She was coughing with the fumes from unseasoned wood. She barely saw the gate catch fire, the men rush it with axes, hack away the blazing fragments.

The gate burned like the entry to hell as the men ran through into the mayhem inside. Estela dropped her burning stick, then worried that the hillside would catch fire. Why did nobody tell you all the practical decisions required in storming a castle? She took off her pathfinder brooch, pinned it to her gown and threw her cloak over the stick to smother the flames.

Then she raced after them through a blaze of wood that would need more than a lady's cloak to put it out. She didn't stop. She had only two thoughts: Miquel; baby. Her instinct told her she would find them both as far from the flames as possible; in the cellars.

She didn't look back, just rushed across the courtyard, ignoring the confusion around her. She had to stoop to get through the door, be careful on the stone steps but she knew every treacherous dimple and barely paused as she went down below daylight.

There was always fire. Even Miquel could not avoid flames. In the torchlight, the leather part of the mask was black demon. His half face flickered with their father's features, then, even more terribly, with their mother's. Then his face was half a boy's again. A boy holding a sword, pointing it at an old iron box. Crooked in his other arm was a baby, sleeping.

'I knew you'd come,' he said, quietly, not waking the baby. 'This is it, the box I told you about. Let me show you.'

'Yes, show me,' she said, moving carefully, slowly now, so as not to startle him into sudden action. 'Shall I hold the baby while you open the box?' She reached out her arms.

Miquel was holding the baby out towards her when somebody moaned in the darkness and he snatched the baby back, his expression darkening. 'Ignore her,' he said. 'She always came between us.'

Estela moved towards the candle-holder, in a niche in the wall. She lifted it, saw Miquel flinch from the flame. 'I'm just looking around,' she reassured him. She moved around him with the candle, keeping a distance but heading towards the wall from where the groan had come.

The candle briefly lit up some rags that raised skeletal hands over deadened eyes, reminding Estela of somebody she'd once known. Then she jumped backwards as Miquel moved between her and the captive – for so she assumed this person to be.

'You believed she was dead, didn't you!' He was triumphant, more like the malicious creature who'd tried to murder her son. And yet he crowed like he had at seven when he'd tricked her out of climbing higher in the apple tree than he could.

'I believed everything you said, Miquel. I trusted you.'

'No, it wasn't because you trusted me. You *wanted* her dead, so you believed me when I said she was. It would have been so *nice* for you if she was dead. So *easy*. She taught me that.' He kicked, the bundle of rags. Another groan.

'Costansa,' he sang out, like a child playing hide and seek, 'guess who's here to see you? It's Estela! Say hello to Estela. Nicely.'

'Hello Estela,' said a voice without colour, beyond pain.

Estela's insides twisted. She had not wished this on her stepmother. She had not!

'Look after my baby.' The voice was barely a whisper, gasping for each breath.

Costansa's words made Miquel snarl.

'We'll both look after your baby,' he told her, sneering. 'But this is what Estela wants for *you*!'

As Estela screamed 'No!' Miquel thrust his sword into what was left of the woman.

Estela took the chance to grab the squalling baby from his precarious position in Miquel's left arm. But within seconds her brother had control of his sword again, was pointing it at her, or rather at the baby she clutched against her bosom. The nursling sought his usual comfort, making soft popping noises with his mouth as he nudged her bodice and found only the hard edges of Estela's brooch. Frustrated, he began to wail again.

She jostled the baby, saying foolishly, 'There, there,' as if she could sing a lullaby and put the world right. She folded the baby into her arms, covering his head and as much of his body as she could, so that Miquel's sword would hit her first if he lunged.

Miquel's pupils were enlarged, his eyes crazed as he waved the sword at her breast, edging his way to stand between her and the steps, between her and any chance of escape. She shut her eyes, not sure what he would do next. She didn't dare move in case he reacted with the sword and she knew she would flinch. *All men flinch when a dagger comes at them. Or a sword,* she added. She didn't want to die a coward. Screaming like a baby.

The box was behind her. She'd have to wait, talk to him, hope that Miquel would make a move that didn't kill her.

'You need to see,' Miquel complained, 'see what's in the box, so we don't leave these monsters in the world.'

Her eyes flicked open only to realise that she must truly be dead and that heaven – or hell – was more complicated than she could ever have dreamed.

Malik was running down the steps, his scimitar unsheathed, shouting words in Arabic that Estela had only read in medical textbooks.

Miquel turned and ran his sword through the Moor, efficiently, dropping him to the floor.

Somebody's voice was screaming. Estela thought it might be hers, if dead people screamed. If she weren't dead, she should be terrified but the shock wouldn't allow any other feelings. She didn't have time to wonder if Miquel was going to kill her next before a white fury stormed down the steps.

With the rage he'd been bred for, Nici hurled himself onto Miquel, raked him with his claws, rolled him, buried his teeth in the throat of the predator who threatened his mistress and shook him till his lifeless corpse thumped against the floor.

'Nici, stop!' she ordered him but he couldn't. He finished the work he'd started when this enemy threatened his little Musca. Estela shut her eyes but she could still hear.

Then she felt him rub against her, soft fur, his tongue licking the baby, worried at the crying. She shifted the baby to one arm so she could stroke Nici, trying not to see the blood. 'Good boy,' she told him, through shaking teeth.

People were coming down the steps; Dragonetz, Gilles, Raoulf. Not Musca, thank God. Somebody took the baby from her. The wailing went out of the cellar, fainter until it stopped.

She crawled over to Malik, not trusting her knees to stand. She cradled Malik's head in her lap, not knowing why he was alive, but knowing that he was dying, knowing he'd given his life to save her.

'Inshallah,' he murmured but he struggled to say something more. She bent her lips close. 'Te'borny,' he whispered, and he was not talking to her.

Dragonetz crouched down.

'I don't understand,' she said.

Dragonetz gently closed Malik's eyes. 'Come,' he said, his voice breaking. 'Musca wants to see his Mama.'

Later, when everyone thought she was resting, Estela returned to the cellar with a candle. The flickering shadows replayed Costansa, huddled against a wall, her death. *Estela wants this* Miquel had said, then he'd killed her stepmother. Was she responsible?

Miquel fought her again, pleaded with her again, died again. Would he have killed her if Malik had not arrived? Would she have killed him? When he whirled to face Malik, she had the chance to stab her brother in the back. She'd been too slow, hesitated and Malik had died.

She knew her brother to be a good swordsman but he'd had the light playing to his advantage too. When she walked down the steps again, she'd blinked, waited till her eyes were accustomed to the light, as Malik must have done. He'd hid his weakness behind his flashing blade and oaths but in that moment, the younger man had killed him.

She remembered her lessons with Maredudd. What a fool she'd been, playing with a sword. Miquel had taught her the purpose of a weapon. Then he'd died at the teeth of her true weapon, one beyond her control, too dangerous now to be allowed to live. The sounds of Miquel's death worried at her again but the hardest truth was that she could not wish it otherwise.

The metal locks to the iron box were open and she set the candle-holder on the dusty floor beside it, then she sat down. Dirt was the least of the day's worries.

She pulled out a scarf, different colours but the same weave as the one she'd left in the Cathedral of Our Lady of the Pillar, with the same initials intertwined. And there was a scroll. What words could possibly do so much damage? She hesitated, then she unscrolled the missive. A love letter, in Arabic, was the answer.

Dear heart,
When our people settled in your islands, I thought all Christians were enemies, light of skin and fickle in faith. When I came upon you, hiding in the cave, you touched something in me that had not yet learned to live. When my people left, I did not go with them.

For you, I took on a new name, and I saw that our faiths were not so different, so I took your words for my beliefs. Our initials intertwine like our faiths, like us. I want to leave these words with my oud, to be passed on to our children, and to their children, so they know they were born from great love.

They should know that their ancestor was not without honour in his African homeland, nor in Zaragoza, before he found his woman and stayed in Provence.

The name in Arabic was also written in an Occitan form and she knew it. Her mother's family name.

She pieced the story together in her mind. A Moor had come from Africa, worked in Zaragoza, maybe as an architect of the palace itself, had maybe carved the work she had seen on the wall. Or one of his relatives had. He'd travelled with the armies that occupied the islands off the shores of Provence. He'd invaded the region round Les Baux, found a girl in a cave, perhaps the very cave where Estela had found the scarf with the initials.

How had the scarf found itself back there? Had the couple left treasure in the cave that was their special place? She could only guess at what had happened generations ago. Her mother had ended up here, with an iron box and an oud, and with her father.

Estela had inherited the oud and what Miquel was trying to tell her was that they had bad blood, Moorish blood, which they'd passed on to the next generation.

She sat very still, thinking, so still that she heard her companion breathing.

'Dragonetz,' she said. He was sitting on a step, watching her, waiting.

'I washed Nici,' he told her. 'And he's gone off, chasing something white and female, I think.'

'There will be puppies,' she stated, 'and he's a dangerous dog. He killed a man.' Her voice wobbled. 'He's not safe any more. He might kill again. We should... make sure he can't.' There. She'd said it aloud, tried to be responsible, but it hurt beyond bearing, even after all the other hurts of the day.

Then Dragonetz came down to her, sat on the floor beside her, took her hands in his. 'I've killed a man,' he said. 'And I will kill again, if I have to.'

She nodded, swallowed. 'So we'll keep him? And the puppies?' she asked.

'I think Montbrun needs dogs like Nici that can protect their own.'

'Then let's hope the bitch is better with sheep than Nici is!'

He waited.

'You looked in the box,' she said.

Of course he had.

'You can annul our marriage,' she said. 'You didn't know about my,' she swallowed, 'my background.' *Musca,* she thought.

He was still holding her hands. He told her, 'All it means is that somebody, maybe your great great grandfather, was of Malik's race and religion. I wish we could tell our friend the good news. We thought we had lost him and we had no time to mourn. Now we must make time. He was the best of us.'

Then she started to cry.

Dragonetz said, 'The Welsh say it's a disgrace to die in bed and an honour to die in battle. Maybe Malik-al-Judhami of the Banu Hud died as he would have wished. He was not meant to end his life in chair days.'

'Without Layla.' She told him then, about Malik's last words.

'We were lucky to have known such a man, to be loved by such a friend.' He put one arm around her, picked up the letter, looked at the beautiful arabesques, and spoke of another couple. 'This man was of noble birth, he converted to our faith and he loved your great great grandmother very much. He left you a beautiful oud and the rest is none of anybody else's business.'

She scrubbed at the wet patch she was making on his shoulder then settled her head there again.

'What do you think we should do with Montbrun?' he asked, as if making casual conversation.

'It belongs to the baby,' she realized.

'What Ramon Berenguer would do would be to appoint a guardian, somebody trustworthy, and a good nurse to look after the baby.'

'Gilles and Prima. I approve.' She wanted the baby safe, looked after, but she balked at the idea of bringing up the baby born of her brother and his stepmother. 'The baby deserves his chance of a good life, of his rights,' she said, fingering her brooch, wondering about a baby with such a father.

She gave a bitter laugh. 'Miquel was tormented by the thought of Moorish blood and it's his I'm worried about! Where did his madness come from?'

'Who knows what Costansa did to his mind.'

'She paid for it.' Estela shuddered. Payment will be taken. *The Gyptian's words echoed. Payment for Estela's knowledge of her ancestry. Only it had not been Estela who'd paid. Miquel. Costansa. And Malik. Now Montbrun would belong to a baby.*

Then she thought of the consequences for their own little family if Gilles and Prima stayed at Montbrun, bringing up the young heir. 'Musca will miss Primo terribly.'

'Yes.' Dragonetz shrugged his shoulders. 'He will no doubt throw tantrums all the way from here to Ruffec. That will afford you some distraction but I think you will have the upper hand by journey's end. You can read to him from *The Wise Traveller*.'

It was too soon to smile but she appreciated his intention. She would be queen of her own domain, like Layla, like her mother. Her life would be a tribute to the women she'd loved. And Dragonetz would rule in *his* domain, outshine Ramon Berenguer, among his own people.

It was time to leave this cellar, with its darkness and bloodstains. She must ask for it to be cleaned. There was a frightened household to organize. Miquel's guards and servants all needed to know they were safe, to be given work to do. They all needed food and drink. She would see what was in the kitchen.

Dragonetz raised her to her feet, held her close, whispered, 'I remember the first time I saw you, standing beside a ditch with a big white dog beside you, and your oud wrapped in a bundle. We started with a song at dawn, and we will have song hereafter, I promise.'

EPILOGUE

In Aquitaine, the Lady of Ruffec held her son tight for a long, wordless moment. When she released him, she turned a level gaze, black-eyed like her son, on the woman who was apparently her daughter-in-law. Who met her gaze.

Finally, she nodded. 'You are a brave woman,' was the verdict.

Then she crouched down, spoke to the little boy hiding behind his mother's skirt. 'You owe me a cuddle, and I owe you a swordbelt that your father wore when he was as big as you.' The word 'swordbelt' dealt with any hesitation and her grandson ran into her open arms.

On 19th December 1154 Henri and Aliénor were crowned King and Queen of England. Aliénor started a new phase of her life as Eleanor, but her hereditary title stayed with her: Eleanor of Aquitaine.

Cadell returned from pilgrimage with no desire to take up governance of Deheubarth and he retired to a monastery, giving the realm wholly to Lords Maredudd and Rhys.

While King Henri postponed dealing with the thorn in his side that was Gwalia, the brothers ap Gruffudd continued to reclaim parts of their ancient kingdom. Henri never knew there was a goldmine in his realm and his bare coffers remained even more of a problem than were the Welsh.

Mental Preparation for a Journey

The wise traveller leaves a pair of stout boots always beside the door because he never knows when he might be called upon to travel or how quickly he must leave.

There are always reasons not to leave home but the most propitious time for a journey is when you are asked to go on one. Without adventures, what stories will you have when you are old, to tell around the fire?

May your spirit of adventure be found with your boots, in readiness.

Finis

HISTORICAL NOTE
WARNING - CONTAINS SPOILERS

My ten year journey with Dragonetz and Estela will never be over because each time a reader reviews my books or contacts me to discuss the 12th century, my stories live again. I could blog about the history behind the books forever and never run out of wonderful material. I promise you that the history most queried in my books as 'unbelievable' is that based most solidly on primary sources and academic historians' research, so here is a little background, to be continued on my blog at www.jeangill.blogspot.com

Estela's *Wise Traveller* was inspired by the guide written by an 11th century French lady for her son, that he might read it in the future when he returned home safe after being hostage for his father's good behaviour. Noble parents and children were often separated by politics and by the custom of fostering other nobles' children as part of their education, so when Estela leaves Musca to accompany Dragonetz, this was not as hard to understand as nowadays. Aliénor left her toddler to go on the Second Crusade. Some of the practical detail in *The Wise Traveller,* and elsewhere in my novel, came from *Le Mesnagier de Paris,* a guide to being a good wife written by an older husband for the young lady he married. Thanks to this book I discovered tests for wives' obedience, cameline sauce and red nigellas' use in wine coloration. I also discovered the complexity of medieval gender politics. 'Above all, enchant him,' was *not* a piece of advice I expected amidst all the piety.

I visited Zaragoza on one of what I call my R & R trips – research and romance. I'm not sure what my husband calls them but he is willing to provide the romance. Wearing my photographer hat, I staked out the blue hour so I could shoot the basilica from the bridge. Although the cathedral of 1154 was a different building, its towers would still have presented the magical appearance that Estela sees from the same bridge. The Aljaferia has later layers of building and décor but it, too, has magic.

'Malik's ancestral home' (as I think of it) does have the birds, fruit and even the script by a cheeky architect dating from before 1154: 'Should you find any mistake in my work, I shall be surprised!' The Muslim prohibition against representing living beings did not apply in secular buildings. Neither were 12th century Muslim women suppressed in the ways that are often presented in historical fiction. They took a full part in religious and intellectual community life, both in eastern cities such as Damascus and in northern Hispania/Spain.

12th century Gwalia/Wales was not multi-faith or multi-cultural in the way Occitania was. The culture clash was largely between the Franks and the indigenous Welsh, whose nobles adopted the Frankish language and some habits, such as wearing armour. Gerald of Wales is a key source as he is writing in 1170, and is half Welsh and half Norman. I've used some of his details, such as haircuts, fighting habits and national characteristics, without trusting them all as facts. As I lived in Deheubarth for over twenty years, the geography is from first-hand knowledge and I have visited the gold-mine at Dolaucothi. I have seen the dragon's breath on the Tywi and I know the meaning of *hiraeth*. When Aliénor says she worries that Henri underestimates the importance of Wales, I want to cheer. Underestimating Wales is an English national pastime.

I did find several references to polyphony in medieval Wales, not just in Gerald's work, at a time when it was at best an early experiment elsewhere in Europe. Gerald provided me with the detail of part song beginning and ending on B flat and of course for Dragonetz to hear his dream in reality is wonderful. Lord Rhys is a character who deserves more recognition and who is credited with holding the first Eisteddfod, so it seemed obvious that Dragonetz sparked the idea, as well as ensuring the success of the brothers ap Gruffudd in regaining their ancestral land in 1153. Lord Rhys' relationship with King Henri deserves a book in itself, but the fate of Maelgwyn, the missing brother, remains a mystery, as does the death of Maredudd.

While spending time with Estela and Dragonetz, I became

obsessed with marriage and bastardy, and was surprised to discover how little codified was the status of either in 1154. Towards the end of the 12th century many loose cultural norms were hardened into laws but the notion of the 'medieval period' as covering 400 years leads to popular misconceptions about a time period as narrow as my books. *The Troubadours Quartet* takes place between 1150 and 1154, which was a period of change, fluidity and far more sophistication than is usually credited.

I wanted to keep the flavour of the medieval period and the many languages my characters speak so I play with place names, trying to be consistent within The Troubadours books and to let readers recognise the modern places. Gwalia is a name still used in Wales despite it being considered insulting in 12th century Cymru.

I have also invented words like 'jongling' from the French 'jongleur', the origin of juggler. I hope the meanings are clear in context and I know many of my readers enjoy setting off on a treasure hunt after reading the books, tracking down some of the stranger vocabulary and even stranger historical facts.

I can now tell you the secret of WHY I had to keep to such a narrow time period. It is less than a dog's life span. I didn't know when I started writing whether Nici would live or die during the story. Most writers kill off the dog to get an easy emotional jerk reaction from the reader. In a longer time span Nici could not have lived. I wanted him to have the same chance as the human characters of reaching a happy ending. No more: no less.

Dragonetz and Estela are fictional characters living in real historical events and I have tried to bring them and their world to life. I hope you enjoyed your visit to the 12th century and that it felt real to you.

I contacted several historians as part of my research and had some wonderful replies. This one is printed on my desk, to motivate me. We all love history. Thank you for sharing *The Troubadours* with me, and may we find new books and new adventures together.

'Historical fiction is a GREAT way to educate! Make (your readers) care enough to come looking for me or send their children to me, or even better, have some perspective, that's really all I ask.'

Do stop by the Troubadours page on facebook and have fun with the TVTrope page

SOME HISTORICAL SOURCES:

Henry II – W.L. Warren
The Lord Rhys – Roger Turvey
A Journey through Wales – Gerald of Wales (translated by Lewis Thorpe) Penguin Classics
Medieval Iberia (Readings from Christian, Muslim and Jewish Sources) – edited by Olivia Remie Constable
Royal Bastards 800-1230 – Sara McDougall
The Usatges of Barcelona (the fundamental law of Catalonia) – translated by Donald J. Kagay
The Sultan's Sex Potions (Arab Aphrodisiacs in the Middle Ages) – Nasīr al-Dīn al-Tūsī (translated by Daniel L. Newman)
Le Mesnagier de Paris – Collection dirigée par Michael Zink (livre de poche)
L'amor de Lonh: Medieval Songs of Love and Loss (musical CD) – Ensemble Gilles Binchois. The first track is the haunting Sephardic love song Estela hears in Chapter 3
Poems of Arab Andalusia – translated by Cola Franza (City Lights Publishers)
Too many online sources to mention, including the medieval Welsh dictionary
Geiriadur Prifysgol Cymru http://welsh-dictionary.ac.uk/gpc/gpc.html

HISTORICAL CHARACTERS APPEARING IN THE TROUBADOURS SERIES

Occitania/Provence

- *Aaron ben Asher* – Jewish sage, who annotated the sacred Torah later known as the Keter Aram Sola/ the Aleppo Codex
- *Abd-al-Malik* – the last King of Zaragoza, grandfather of my invented character Malik
- *Aliénor of Aquitaine/ Eleanor of Aquitaine* – Duchess of Aquitaine and Queen of France
- *Abraham ben Isaac/ Raavad II* – Jewish leader in Narbonne
- *Alphonse*, nicknamed 'Jourdain' / 'Jordan'– Comte de Toulouse, father of Raymond, killed by poison in Caesarea in 1148
- *Alphonso,* King of Castile, Emperor of Hispania – died in 1144 leaving his estate to the Templars
- *Bèatriz* – the future Comtesssa de Dia/ Comtesse de Die and famous troubairitz
- *Bernard de Clairvaux* – advisor to Louis, abbot leading and reforming the Cistercian order
- *Bernard d'Anduze* – Ermengarda's titular husband, brother of the Archbishop of Narbonne
- *Bernard de Tremelay* – Templar Grand Master 1151
- *Constance* – widow of the Prince of Antioch, Mélisende's niece
- *Dolca* – Etiennette's sister, heir to Provence, grandmother to the young Comte, Ramon Berenguer II
- *Archbishop of Narbonne*, Pierre d'Anduze – brother of Ermengarda's husband
- *El Rey Lobo, the Wolf King, Abu 'Abd Allāh Muhammad ibn Mardanīš* – King of Murcia

- *Ermengarda/Ermengarde* – Viscomtesse of Narbonne
- *Etiennette/Stéphania* – widowed Lady of Les Baux-de-Provence
- *Geoffroi de Rançon* (the father) – Commander of Aliénor's Guard in 1148
- *Geoffroi de Rançon* (the son) – possibly more than one
- *Guilhelm de Poitiers* – married Bèatriz
- *Hugues des Baux* – Lord of Les-Baux-de-Provence, son of Etiennette
- *Isoard*, Comte de Dia/Die – Bèatriz' father (very little known about Bèatriz)
- *Montcada* family – powerful Barcelone nobles, advisors to the Prince
- *Pedro of Aragon* – 1152-1157 heir to Aragon, son of Petronilla and Ramon Berenguer IV
- *Petronilla* – Queen of Aragon, married to Ramon Berenguer IV
- *Pons* family – the rulers of Les-Baux-de-Provence
- *Porcelet* family – (First names are my invention)
- *Ramon Trencavel* – brother to Roger and Comte de Carcassonne on his brother's death in 1150
- *Ramon Berenguer IV* – 'El Sant', Comte de Barcelone, Prince of Aragon and Regent of Provence
- *Ramon Berenguer II* – Comte de Provence, nephew to 'El Sant'
- *Raymond V* – Comte de Toulouse
- *Raymond and Stéphania (Etiennette) of Les Baux* – rulers in Provence
- *Roger Trencavel*, Comte de Carcassonne – died in 1150
- *Sicard de Llautrec* – ally of Toulouse

- **The troubadours** – Jaufre Rudel, Marcabru, Cercamon, Peire Rogier from the Auvergne, Raimbaut d'Aurenja/Raymon of Aurenja, Guiraut de Bornelh, Bernart de Ventadorn

- *In charge of the Templar Commandery at Douzens* – Peter Radels, Master; Isarn of Molaria and Bernard of Roquefort, joint Commanders

Frankish Lands, the Kingdom of France

- *Archbishop Suger* – royal prelate in Paris, adviser to King Louis
- *Eustace IV* – Count of Boulogne, King Stephen's son and heir. Died 1153, suspected food poisoning
- *Henri d'Anjou, King of England* – married Aliénor (2nd husband)
- *Louis VII* – King of France, married to Aliénor
- *de Maurienne, Comte* – uncle and adviser to Louis VII
- *Matilda, Empress Matilda* – briefly Queen of England, Stephen's cousin, mother to Henri d'Anjou
- *Stephen de Blois* – King of England from 1135-1154
- *William I* – Comte de Boulogne (after brother's death 1153) King Stephen's son, gave up claim to throne

Wales/Gwalia

- *Cadell ap Gruffudd* – Rhys' brother, ruler of Deheubarth from 1143-1151 (his attack and renunciation)
- *Cadwaladr ap Gruffudd* – Owain of Gwynnedd's brother, accused of murdering Rhys' brother Anarawd
- *Gruffudd ap Cynan* – King of Gwynedd (1055-1137)
- *Gruffudd ap Rhys* – Lord of Deheubarth, father of Rhys, Maredudd, Cadell 1081-1137
- *Gwenllian the Warrior Princess* – wife of Gruffudd ap Rhys d 1136 beheaded on battlefield
- *Maredudd ap Gruffudd* – Rhys' brother. Joint ruler of Deheubarth from 1151-1155 (his death)
- *Maurice de Londres* – Frankish Lord of Kidwelly who defeated Gwenllian in 1136

- *Owain ap Gruffudd* – ruler of Gwynedd from 1137-1170, Gwenllian's brother
- *Rhys ap Gruffudd* – Lord of Deheubarth 1155-1197

- **Welsh bards** – Taliesin, Aneurin

Oltra mar/ The Holy Land

- *Amaury* – younger son of Mélisende
- *Baudouin*, King of Jerusalem – Mélisende's son
- *Chirkhouh* – Nur ad-Din's general, killed Prince Raymond of Antioch
- *Everard des Barres* – Grand Master of the Templars during the Second Crusade
- *Foulques* – King of Jerusalem by marriage to Mélisende. Died 1146
- *Hodierne*, Comtesse de Tripoli – sister of Mélisende, Queen of Jerusalem
- *Ismat ad-Dhin* – Nur ad-Din's wife, Unur's daughter
- *Joscelyn*, Comte d'Edessa – deserted and lost the city to Muslim forces, starting the Second Crusade
- *Maimonides* – Jewish philosopher
- *Manassés* – Constable of Jerusalem
- *Mélisende* – Queen of Jerusalem
- *Mujir ad-Din* – ruler of Damascus, 1151
- *Nur ad-Din* – Muslim Atabeg (ruler and general), uncle of Saladin
- *Raymond*, Comte de Tripoli – Hodierne's husband and relation of Toulouse, killed by Assassins in 1152
- *Raymon/Ramon/Raymond*, Prince of Antioch – Aliénor's uncle and rumoured lover, killed by Saracen troops in 1148
- *Raymond de Puy* – Hospitalers' Grand Master 1151
- *Saint Paul/ Saul of Tarsus* – famously converted on the road to Damascus

- *Salah ad-Din/Saladin* – Muslim leader during the Third Crusade
- *Unur* – Muslim general, defended Damascus in the Second Crusade
- *Zengi/Imad ad-Din Zengi* – father of Nur ad-Din, murdered in 1146

- **Persian poets** – Omar Khayyam, Sanai

- *The Hashashins/Assassins* – the Isma'ili Muslim sect

Elsewhere in Christendom

- *Conrad* – Holy Roman Emperor, ruler of the Germanic peoples
- *Jarl Rognvaldr Kali Kolsson* – Prince of Orkney
- *Manuel Komnenos/Comnenus* – Emperor of Byzantium
- *Pope Eugene III*

- **Medical authorities** – Aristotle, Ahmad ibn Abi al-Ash'ath, Al-Razi, Hildegard von Bingen, Galen, Hippocrates, Inb al-Haytham, Nicolaus of Salerno, Trota, Plato, Pythagoras, Yahja Ibn Adi.

MAIN FICTIONAL CHARACTERS

The Troubadours

- *Estela de Matin* – troubadour name of Roxeane de Montbrun (a domain near Carcassonne)
- *Dragonetz, nicknamed los Pros, 'the Brave'* – ex-crusader, troubadour and son of Lord Dragon of Ruffec in Aquitaine. Dragonetz means 'little Dragon' in Occitan
- *Txamusca, nicknamed Musca* – the troubadours' son. His name means 'Fire' in Occitan
- *Nici* – a Great Pyrenees dog, useless with sheep, who ran away with Estela. His name means 'Useless' in Occitan
- *Prima* – the wet-nurse, first Raoulf's mistress, then Gilles' lover
- *Primo* – Prima's son and Musca's foster-brother

Estela's family and entourage

- *Savaric Tibau de Montbrun* – Estela's father, castellan of Montbrun, vassal to Carcassonne and his Liege of Toulouse
- *Costansa de Montbrun* – Estela's stepmother, responsible for Estela's exile from the family home
- *Miquel de Montbrun* – Estela's brother, corrupted from childhood by Costansa

- *Johans de Villeneuve* – Estela's husband in a marriage arranged for her as a favour by Ermengarda of Narbonne and Aliénor of Aquitaine
- *Peire de Quadra, 'Peire the Stable'* – with whom Estela had her first sexual encounter, murdered by her brother

- *Gilles Lackhand* – Estela's man, her protector from childhood after her mother died. He helped her escape from Ruffec and was punished by having a hand removed

Dragonetz' family and entourage

- *Lord Dragon de Ruffec* – Dragonetz' father, Lord of Ruffec in Aquitaine, vassal and sometime Commander to Aliénor of Aquitaine
- *Sadeek* – Dragonetz' prized black Arab destrier, gift from Malik. His name means 'friend' in Arabic
- *Vertat* – Dragonetz' female goshawk, chosen from the falconry at les Baux. Her name means 'Truth'
- *Talharcant* – Dragonetz' Damascene sword, named 'Bladesong' in Occitan

Dragonetz' men

- *Raoulf* – with Dragonetz on the 2nd Crusade, knew him from babyhood
- *Arnaut* – Raoulf's son, Dragonetz' friend

Friends, Enemies and Cyphers

- *Malik-al-Judhami of the Banu Hud / al-Hisba al-Andalus*, 'the man from al-Andalus', disinherited Emir to the taifa of Zaragosa; physician, warrior and musician; best friend and mentor to Dragonetz and Estela
- *Dame Fairnette Babtista, the Gyptian* – a Romany fortune-teller, whose obscure prophecies can be interpreted as having come true
- *Sancha de Provence* – a transexual who lost her husband in the Crusades, is in love with Dragonetz, spies for him at one time, and becomes Estela's friend

- *Muganni* – a Hashashin boy with the voice of an angel, mentored by Dragonetz and Estela, murdered in the Holy Land by Geoffroi de Rançon
- *Geoffroi de Rançon* – Dragonetz' crusade companion and would-be nemesis, Estela's friend through trickery
- *Bar Philipos* – Damascus Christian, who played a double game in the 2nd Crusade and later held Dragonetz prisoner
- *Yalda* – Bar Philipos' daughter, used in Damascus by her father to entrap a drug-addled Dragonetz

MAPS

A 1903 map showing the kingdoms and key cities of Hispania/Spain in 1210, by which time the Almohads have gained much of the south, including El Rey Lobo's kingdom of Murcia. As this is a 'modern' map, it shows lines of latitude and longitude, curved in the awareness that the earth is round.

THE SPANISH KINGDOMS 1210

FRANCE IN 1154

SHOWING THE ANGEVIN EMPIRE

WALES IN 1153

The Welsh Lords Rhys and Maredudd expanded their realm of Deheubarth into the territories held by the Frankish Marcher Lords, and they took back Ceredigion from Owain, Lord of Gwynedd.

ACKNOWLEDGMENTS

Many thanks to:
my editor and friend, Lesley Geekie, who stayed calm through the second crusade and mis-spellings in five different languages.

Claire, Karen, Kristin and Jane for their historical and literary input. I couldn't do this without you.

Professor Sara McDougall, medieval history specialist, John Jay College of Criminal Justice, NY, for her expert input and enthusiastic discussion of bastardy and marriage in the 12th century, and of Petronilla's status in particular.

Regia Anglorum Re-enactment Group for permission to use a photo on the front cover https://regia.org/

John N. Green, University of Bradford, for his help with the lyrics and translation of Ventadorn's *The Lark*. All wilful interpretations and (mis)translations are mine, not his.

Quotations from Ventadorn's poetry are from Martin de Riquer's version
Riquer, Martín de (ed.) (1940) Bernatz de Ventadorn. Poesía. Selección, traducción y prólogo de Martín de Riquer (Poetas Catalano - Provenzales, 1). Barcelona: Editorial Yunque, 119 pp. [Introduction by MdeR (7-13), biography of BdeV by Uc de Saint Circ (14-21, bilingual Occitan and Spanish in parallel text), 13 poems with Spanish translation, notes.

Excerpts from *The Trotula*, translated by Monica H.Green. reprinted by kind permission of *University of Pennsylvania Press.*

Excerpts from *Hildegard von Bingen's Physica*, translated by Priscilla Throop, reprinted by kind permission of *Healing Arts Press.*

Map of the Spanish Kingdoms, courtesy of the University of Texas Libraries, The University of Texas at Austin.

Map of France 1154 is in the Public Domain.

Map of Wales 986-99 (Maredudd ab Owain), courtesy of AlexD under the Creative Commons license.

ABOUT THE AUTHOR

I'm a Welsh writer and photographer living in the south of France with two scruffy dogs, a beehive named 'Endeavour', a Nikon D750 and a man. I taught English in Wales for many years and my claim to fame is that I was the first woman to be a secondary headteacher in Carmarthenshire. I'm mother or stepmother to five children so life has been pretty hectic.

I've published all kinds of books, both with traditional publishers and self-published. You'll find everything under my name from prize-winning poetry and novels, military history, translated books on dog training, to a cookery book on goat cheese. My work with top dog-trainer Michel Hasbrouck has taken me deep into the world of dogs with problems, and inspired one of my novels. With Scottish parents, an English birthplace and French residence, I can usually support the winning team on most sporting occasions.

www.jeangill.com

facebook.com/writerjeangill
twitter.com/writerjeangill
instagram.com/writerjeangill
goodreads.com/JeanGill

Join Jean Gill's Special Readers' Group

for private news, views and offers, with an exclusive ebook copy of

How White is My Valley

as a welcome gift.

Sign up at *jeangill.com*

The follow-up to her memoir *How Blue is My Valley* about moving to France from rainy Wales, tells the true story of how Jean

- nearly became a certified dog trainer.
- should have been certified and became a beekeeper.
- developed from keen photographer to hold her first exhibition.
- held 12th century Damascene steel.
- looks for adventure in whatever comes her way.

THE RING BREAKER

1139 ORKNEYJAR

If you enjoyed *The Troubadours Quartet,*
you can return to the 12th century
- this time in Viking Orkney.

Publication Date October 2022

Loyalty has a price the children pay.
In the twilight of the old gods, when the last Vikings rule the seas,
two cursed orphans meet on an Orkney beach
and their fates collide.

CHAPTER 1 SAMPLE

He was a sickly baby so his father took him to the beach and left him on the wrack-strewn pebbles for time and tide to claim a life not meant to be.

A kind man, his father had set out twice to do his duty, returning each time with the baby still in his arms. On the third occasion, his arms were empty. The mother flew through the door like a Valkyrie, her obedience tested beyond limits. As she later told the tale, she searched every cove and crevice for days, without food, drink or sleep, until she came across the cormorant.

It stuttered at her and opened its wings in warning, shielding its treasure on rocks velvety-green with moss. The treasure began to cry, the wail of a hungry baby, and the mother scrambled onto the rock, defied the bird's anger, to snatch her baby from the nest and latch him onto her breast.

The cormorant stabbed her once with its beak, drawing blood from her cheek but she ignored it, feeling only the unexpected warmth of the baby in her arms. Warm, like the two other nestlings still huddling under the broody bird, which fixed her in a glassy-eyed stare, demanding what was owed.

What was due for the life of a baby? How could she free him from a debt to the otherworld?

His mother held him up to show the bird.

'Skarfr,' she named the baby. 'Cormorant.'

The bird shook its wings, shaking sea-drops over them both in a salty baptism.

Without words, the cormorant told Skarfr's mother that he would make sagas. She accepted this fate on his behalf along with a bone shard that the bird pushed towards her to seal their compact. Then she climbed down carefully, clutching him in her arms, watched by beady eyes as green as the moss. The cormorant stayed by its chicks and let her leave.

His mother, Kristin, bore the scar until the day she died. She said she deserved it. She told his father that the gods had returned their son to make sagas and had named him Skarfr but that he could follow whatever Christian naming rites he wished. And he could beat her for disobedience. But the baby was staying.

His father told her to hush. Whether he had no stomach for a fourth trudge to the beach or whether he accepted the gods' intervention, he kept both the baby and the bone, saying nothing was ever so bad that something good couldn't come of it.

The family lurched from one meagre meal to the next until Skarfr was seven years old. No further babies were born, or if they were, no cormorant intervened in their fate.

Desperate for plunder to trade for livestock, the father accompanied his lordship the Jarl on a raiding trip and was axed in the head as blood payment for some grievance against that same lord. The father's name became a byword for loyalty. The longships returned and the father's promise of riches was kept despite the inconvenience of his death. The Jarl paid generous compensation and the mother was now a wealthy widow. The family was allocated a longhouse, a cow, some sheep, chickens, and even a pony.

'The price of a man's murder,' his mother said, as she inspected the cold hearth at the centre of cosy living quarters. Stone walls were caulked with peat and only one weakness in the patchwork roof allowed Orkney's bitter wind to knife through, cutting smoke into choking backdraughts.

When the hearth was aglow and the fish smoking above it, the shades of a man, his wife and his son formed in the grey wisps and vanished into the sky. Or so it seemed.

'Your father would have been happy here,' she said, watching the smoke, her face so lined with poverty that grief left no trace.

She died of an ague within a year of his father's death. Her last words were, 'Always remember how your father was rewarded for his loyalty to the Jarl of Orkneyjar.' Presumably she meant the long-house. Skarfr was left rich and alone, too young to be either.

As was the custom, foster-parents were sought and their suitability debated at the Thing, their local council. Usually, an orphan would have many foster-homes, with perhaps a year in each to spread the burden, but in his case volunteers were torn between greed and fear. Skarfr's wealth meant he would need one foster-father until he came of age but the rumours of how he got his name made good Christians cross themselves and many men fingered the hammer amulets beneath their jerkins.

'Unnatural, touched by the gods,' they whispered when they thought he couldn't hear.

As always, the ruling jarl spoke for peace and found a solution that nobody could find fault with. Except Skarfr. And what did an eight-year-old know? A lot, as it turned out.

Botolf Begla, a skald newly arrived from the Old Country, was lodging with a family who needed more space and – so Botolf said – who dried up his inspiration with their ceaseless tattle. A skald as famous as Botolf for his poetry and sagas merited better.

Killing two birds with one stone, the Thing chose Botolf as foster-father so he formally adopted a boy now called Skarfr Botolffson. In silence, the boy refused the name. He was Skarfr Kristinsson, for the two mothers who'd nurtured him.

Botolf moved into the longhouse that would not be Skarfr's for eight years, if his foster-father judged him ready, or for up to thirteen years, should such a judgement be withheld. Botolf began training him as a skald. And beating him when he forgot to feed the chickens or milk the cow, or when he let the fire go out. Or when he could only think of *eagle-feeder* as a poetic term for warrior and forgot all the others he'd been taught. His master was a peerless skald but a poor teacher. Even so, despite lashings from tongue and whip, Skarfr learned.

When Botolf acquired a male thrall to do the heavy work, and a female one to tend to the house and cook, Skarfr's duties lessened and his training as skald intensified. At first, the thralls made overtures of kindness to him but when he opened his mouth to reply to their soft-spoken questions, he saw Botolf's body freeze, from face through clenched fists to his boots that seemed part of the tamped earth floor. That rigidity was prequel to the whip so Skarfr wiped the smile off his face, turned away, pretended he didn't know their names. The ones Botolf never used. Fergus and Brigid.

The sea taught him to swim, cradling him afloat in cold salt, tempting him to dive for shells on the rare occasions the waves unveiled the seabed. Water called to him, cormorant that he was, and he soon discovered that lochs reflected fluffy clouds but hid depths and eddies more dangerous than those of the sea. Such risks meant nothing to him in the joy of weightless twists and turns, less alone among the otters and bobbing eider ducks than in that longhouse where smoked walls made dreary what was once his home.

Botolf was afraid of the sea, which made Skarfr love it even more. The skald never set foot in their faering, a two-man rowboat, but he sent Fergus out fishing and the boy slunk out with him. Limiting their words to *net, line* and *kreel,* they let the current flow around them and knew smiles over a silvery catch. The boat was offshore, outside Botolf's law.

In the house, Skarfr behaved as if Fergus and Brigid were invisible, and Botolf relaxed, not realising he'd taught his ward to hold in the precious words a skald needs to say aloud, to play with. So it was that Skarfr learned the craft of poetry but not the art. If he had any, it was buried with his grief for his mother and his bitterness over his father's death. Not even his cormorant could gift him golden speech. Botolf had beaten a fatal flaw into his masterwork and was doomed to as much disappointment as Skarfr's parents would have felt.

He was not to make sagas after all, neither to be the story nor tell it. He believed what men said of him, reported with glee by Botolf. Skarfr was 'unnatural, touched by the gods,' and a disappointment, condemned to live with a cold genius of a man.

Until Skarfr was fourteen, when he met Hlif on a beach and they fled the storm of swords that came from the whale's way.

Printed in Great Britain
by Amazon